SUNNIVA DEE

Copyright © 2015 by Sunniva Dee

Cover design by Monika MacFarlane
Editing by Kim Grenfell
Interior book design by John Gibson

Without limiting the rights under copyright reserved above, no part of this publication may be reproduced, stored in, or introduced into a retrieval system, or transmitted, in any form, or by any means (electronic, mechanical, photocopying, recording, or otherwise) without the prior written permission from the above author of this book.

This is a work of fiction. Names, characters, places, brands, media, and incidents are either the product of the author's imagination or are used fictitiously. The author acknowledges the trademarked status and trademark owners of the various products referenced in this work of fiction. The publication/use of these trademarks is not authorized, associated with, or sponsored by the trademark owners.

Synopsis

"Bo Lindgren: musical genius and heartless heartbreaker."
—Star Gossip, January Edition.

My bestie, Zoe, talked me into going to the concert.
It was just one show.
Neither of us could have foreseen the rest.

"Meet Bo Lindgren, the most coveted bad boy of Indie Rock."
—Fan Chicks, February Edition.

Rock god. Legend. Prodigy.
Pale winter eyes that seared you to the bone.
First, he zeroed in on me from the stage.
Next, he shook the hell out of my lonesome world.

"Bo Lindgren leaves own concert with dark-haired beauty."
—Tabloid Minute, Thursday Edition

One night with a rock star would have been fine.
But Bo felt my darkness, my secrets, my guilt,
and his heart wasn't as empty as people thought.
Fast, I became his muse.
Too soon, he craved more than I could give.
There was nothing I wanted more than his love, but if I surrendered, I'd be giving up my normal, my reality, my…
Jude.

"Did waitress Nadia Vidal inspire Bo Lindgren's viral smash hit, 'F*ck You?"
—Star Gossip, April Edition"

*Christian S.
This book is for you.*

Please don't judge me.
*I **am** not what you see.*
I am the opposite.

—Nadia's lipstick note on Bo's mirror.

PART 1
Refusal

Living without reality
Because though pain is inevitable
Suffering is optional

CHAPTER One

MORNING

NADIA

"Baby," I croak before I open my eyes. I stretch beneath our sheets, writhing at the sound of the alarm clock. Awakened from dreams colored by our past, my first thought goes to my husband. "Turn it off, babe? Please," I say.

The alarm keeps beeping, *beep-beep-beeping*. It's annoying and chased by my customary just-awake confusion. "Jude, you know how much I hate that sound."

I'm at home in our apartment in St. Aimo, Los Angeles. Slowly, it registers that the alarm is for me, not him. I turn to face him, whine softly, but he doesn't give me the response I crave: a chuckle and a kiss while he playfully commiserates with me.

"Oh sweetie," he usually murmurs. "I'm sorry you have to leave for school. Maybe you should play hooky and stay in bed for a rubdown? I'll rub… all the way down."

I always crack a smirk then, reading between the lines. He would leave us mumbling heated words and gasping for air if I surrendered.

Deep in my belly, something contracts. Something bittersweet and beautiful that hurts, because today, again, he doesn't react.

I slide from the covers and sit on the edge of the bed. My head feels heavy. It needs support, and for a second, I'm struck by how alive my hand is when I cup my cheek with it.

Soon, I find the courage to rise.

The bathroom door is closed, but I go to it anyway. "Do you remember when you first came to our church?" My words stutter, sleep-exhausted. I exhale and lean my forehead against the door. "Your eyes were bright with fear as you entered the Heavenly Harbor between your parents. You were lanky, a gangly fourteen-year-old, a little boy big enough to have gotten yourself into trouble."

My throat produces hard lumps so easily these days. This one I muscle down. I control the sadness accompanying it and let a small smile filter out instead. "Oh Jude baby. We didn't know then, of all the adventures to come.

"I remember sitting in the pews between Mother and Father, head twisted at the creak of the door. You entered on a lull between psalms.

"I didn't know. We didn't know."

I sniff, an attempt at stanching the tears.

The wood of the doorframe cools my cheek. Presses into it as my memories brighten. "Your skin," I mumble. He's quiet behind the panel. The shower has stopped—in our bathroom or in the one above us, I'm not sure. If he's moving, he's not making a sound. Perhaps he's listening to me.

"Fine veins shone blue at your temple beneath your too-long hair." I snort out a wet laugh. "And the sun reached you through the stained-glass window, spilling the rainbow over your face."

I roll my forehead to the side against the door. "Funny how your parents picked our church because 'Heavenly Harbor' sounded like the right kind of place. They wanted the best haven for you."

Not long ago, my Jude would have grinned at this. He'd pull me in, golden bangs falling over me and tickling me while he ran his nose up mine. He'd croon, "Oh and weren't they right. I found my haven—in you."

I'd push him good-naturedly, not allowing fear of the future to ruin our love. "But you'd be safe at home with your parents if they hadn't crushed on the name of our church."

He'd kiss my nose, groan, and say, "Right, and I wouldn't have a beautiful wife."

"A child bride," I teased once.

"Nineteen is a fine age. Get them early." He winked, knowing well he only held two months on me.

We were young. Married. And so on the run.

I WAS BORN TO MODEST PARENTS in Buenos Aires. Until I was seven, life tore along like a flawless football game. Love abounded, and unlike some of my classmates, I never went hungry.

On weeknights, friends knocked, asking me out to play, and on the weekends, my big, close-knit family on Mom's side worshipped my cousins and me. I remember laughter. Heartfelt, lingering hugs. Daylong meals and sleepovers with hose-downs in my grandparents' backyard when we became rowdy from the summer heat. I remember wet smooches from aunts and uncles, my *tías* and *tíos*. Secrets shared with cousins, fights when Diego, Mariana, and I disagreed, and smacks from our mothers when the disputes escalated.

We played in tree houses we built and rebuilt in the city park while the public grill simmered, the aroma from our family *parrilla* the only thing able to draw us away.

My parents struggled to make ends meet but didn't involve me in their adult concerns. With dedication and modesty, my father paid rent on our home, month after painstaking month. My friends and I all grew up in studio apartments within rundown, wooden buildings on the water, but even the colors of our houses—bright blues, reds, yellows, and greens—hinted at nothing but abundance.

Never did I identify the Vidal family's poverty. Such a concept, such gloom, exists only when compared to outlandish cornucopias I didn't encounter in La Boca.

I was an only child for longer than most in my neighborhood and rejoiced when Mom's belly began growing. To touch it, to see my brother swell into an eight-month piece of art made my child heart inflate with bliss. He ballooned my mother's shape and caused happy grins on my father's face. Yes, life was good in La Boca. Life was good.

My parents did not drive a car recklessly to get themselves killed. They took a chance on a quarter-mile crosswalk on an *avenida* in Barrio Norte, en route for the zoo. The Lord knows why I was not with them. Onlookers said a Coca-Cola truck sped up at the sight of them braving such a busy road. The driver's plan had been to scare them, but instead it hit... hit—

Grief roars as loudly in seven-year-olds as in adults. I cried for my parents. For Ariel, the baby brother I'd never meet. I sobbed over dress-up games I'd never force him to play, and my tears became the Sin Flood as my grandparents on my father's side moved me into their house.

Life comes with expenses, the cost sometimes steeper than the reward. I lost my parents and my brother. Then my neighborhood, the contact with Mom's family—cousins, aunts, uncles, and my grandparents.

Soon, I'd lose my country.

I JUMP WHEN KNUCKLES RAP on the front door.

"I'll get it," I breathe to Jude. Silence walls me from the bathroom as I walk into our tiny den. There's still seventies-style, deep red carpet under my toes. We own our creep-in; Jude bought it outright before his parents cut him off and popped the savings they'd set up for him in a trust fund. "Misuse," they called it. "Hasty teenagers.

"As much as we love Nadia," they added.

The carpet stays for now—we can't afford to replace it. Instead, I've painted the walls a matching, faded red and the window frames a warm mahogany. Jude accepted it because "it's Nadia."

"I love everything *you*," he said back then.

I hear Zoe like she's inside already. Paper-thin walls and ceilings strip privacy away, leaving only the most laid-back tenants to renew their contracts in the leased apartments.

"Come on, Nadia!" she shouts.

Out of habit, I let my gaze scan our place before I go to open: the bathroom, teetering between the sleeping alcove and the den; the nonexistent hallway; the front door swinging straight into our tiny living room. It's tidy. Presentable. Just that one sock of Jude's collecting dust on the bathroom floor. The distance is short between where I stand and the entrance. It takes me seconds to crook my fingers around the chain link. I unhook it and allow her to enter.

Blue eyes dim at the sight of me. "Get dressed," she says.

My eyes go to the wristwatch I rarely pay attention to. "It's four thirty in the afternoon—it's not the morning, and I'm not supposed to go to work."

"Yeah, sweetie," she whispers, like she feels bad for me, causing a lump to ferment in my throat.

"Don't do the pity thing," I say.

Zoe. When I started working at Scott's Diner, she quickly became my friend. In the beginning, I was her awkward, inexperienced acquaintance, but we grew close, and she has since picked up the pieces of my sanity in more ways than I could have imagined.

Zoe. She's always here for me. Sometimes, I wonder about her patience. She's not a saint, and yet her patience is saintly. Sometimes, I want her to just go away. Like now.

"I'm not coming wherever it is," I tell her, but she brushes my bed-hair away from my face and nods.

"Yeah, you are. Concert, remember? We're going to see Luminessence tonight, and even better, the hot Swedish guys in their opening band, Clown Irruption."

I feel my head move from side to side, rejecting our former agreement. Zoe stops it with both hands, holding my face still, and I close my eyes.

"No, you're not backing out of this. The tickets are already paid for."

"We've seen both bands before."

"Precisely."

I'm not following her logic. Been there, done that is my take on this.

"Plus, you promised," she says. "It's in the freaking *arena,* and they'll be selling beer and wine."

"We sell beer and wine at Scott's."

"—*and* work there. And it's not a concert. Nadia, Nadia," she *tsks*.

The sigh sieving out of my lungs depletes me of energy. I want to go back to bed. I shoot a longing gaze behind me to crumpled sheets and indentations in pillows. See the sweet depression in Jude's where his head should be next to mine right now.

"No, don't even think about it. Let's. Get. Dressed."

"Who says that?" I mutter, trotting back to the bedroom. "Preschool teacher much? No need to include yourself in the 'getting dressed' part."

I shoot her a onceover that reveals studiously straightened, shiny, blonde lengths surrounding her doll face. Nose pointy but small, still powdered to perfection in the blazing L.A. afternoon heat. Pink miniskirt, silk top with ruffles accentuates her boobs in the front, and her stilettos are so tall only Zoe can pull them off. Today, they're a bright, Melrose Place gold.

"Yay, she's being testy. Now, we're talkin'," Zoe says. We rifle through the small closet I share with Jude. My clothes outweigh his, but neither of us has a lot. I don't want to think about how beautifully folded his are. My heart drops, recalling how they've become fewer, month by month. I make a mental note to keep that from happening.

Jude.

In the end, Zoe and I settle on an outfit she thinks is too dark and I think has a too-deep neckline. My husband bought it for me. I've worn it a couple of times, but it's not me.

"Shut up," Zoe says. "Your waist is crazy narrow, and this dress really shows off your curves." Her critical eye scours my backside before she scales to my head. "Okay, so those long, chocolate locks of yours will need a twirling. Hmm."

I don't like the look on her face. Zoe pinches her mouth with two fingers and blows air into her hand, getting ready to shoot me The Truth.

"I'm done watching you get thinner. And thinner and thinner. Something has to be done. You don't have a butt anymore either, and guys love a good butt."

"Guys? I'm married," I say.

Zoe's head snaps up from the shoes she's holding, and

blue eyes ten shades lighter than Jude's ignite with fury. "But he's not doing it for you now, is he?"

"I'M SORRY—I'M SORRY—I'M SORRY." Zoe's pitch slinks low and repentant from next to me in the cab. It took her long enough.

"You're mean. I should have stayed at home," I say, but her hand goes out and pets my cheek, fingers feminine-smooth, silky soft and different from Jude's.

"What good would it do though, sweetie? You need to live a little." She means well, and I love her. She needs to stop talking.

"*You* fucking live." My outburst is unintentional and leaves Zoe momentarily speechless. The taxi driver turns up the radio, some country song melding with the smell of *Wunderbaum*. Who decided car fresheners were worthy of an invention anyway? I feel sick.

"I am living." Zoe's voice lowers through the words. "We're going to a concert. We'll have drinks. Dance, Nadia. Remember dancing?"

"I don't want to dance."

"Bull. Once we're there, the crowd will be fantastic. Everyone will be on their feet, probably rushing the front of the stage and mosh-pitting."

"Oh no," I mutter as her short, black nails go to her mouth for a quick nibble of happy-jittery energy.

I stare out the window. Let my eyes first fix then give up on each palm tree passing us. Zoe is the life of the party, a quirky, charming blast to be around in this mood.

Just—*you* have to be in the mood too. I hope she calms down.

I should go home.

"Emil…" Zoe hums. "He's so freaking hot. Kisses like a pro too."

"Emil who?" I ask because it will make her talk about something besides mosh pits.

Her jaw drops in exaggerated surprise. "Don't tell me you've forgotten the lead singer of Clown Irruption? He squirms up there on stage, all smarmy and slinking around his microphone. All sweaty, and then—"

"Ew," I say.

"Oh come on, 'sweaty' is like sex. Or, like, sex *is* sweaty."

I groan. "I'm not comfortable talking about this, Zoe."

"Which you need to get over and I'm helping. Did you see when he was singing that one song, the super-sad, really beautiful song, how he massaged his bulge on the mic stand? I swear he's got a full-on joystick. Maybe I'll volunteer to help him with it." She yells the last part, because the driver has notched the radio up to concert level, despite the tune being slower than a psalm.

Zoe bounces closer to me. Leans her chin on my shoulder so she's sure I can hear her when she says, "You notice that? The driver"—she wheeze-shouts now—"is a fellow prude of yours!"

CHAPTER Two

CONCERT

NADIA

"No, we're on the guest list," Zoe says, mouth against the round window of one of the ticket booths. People shift patiently behind us, clearing their throats and leaning on each other or hugging.

Nightfall dropped over us like a blanket midway up the line. Bottles came out of purses and backpacks, and now the guy right behind me takes an unsteady step into my body while apologizing.

I miss my little apartment. I want to *not* be here. I'm about to leave Zoe alone.

"Whose list?" the crusty old man asks. Thick glasses hang low, creating painful-looking dents over the bridge of his nose.

She snickers, pleased. "Clown Irruption's. You thought I meant Luminessence's list?"

Zoe swings to me and lifts one of the curling iron

coils she created on my head before we left. She speaks directly into my ear like I'm deaf. "I told you how I got the backstage passes, right?"

I shake her off. "Yeah, you—"

"I totes messaged their tour manager on Facebook and told him Emil wanted me there. Sent him a pic too to jog his memory of our make-out session the last time Clown Irruption came through."

She's all grins. It makes me smile too. "Let me guess. He didn't remember you?" I joke, because who wouldn't remember Zoe?

"Right, uh-huh!" The giggle she emits comes from deep within her. It's the kind of profoundly happy sound I used to make playing in the ocean with Jude. Or when he tickled me. When he teased me. When we ran off to Vegas to get married by the Beauty and the Beast in a tiny church.

"Emil friended me on Facebook, you know." If Zoe's grin gets any bigger, I'm afraid her head might split horizontally and drop to the ground like a heel of bread.

"And your status? 'It's complicated?'"

"Ah you think you're so funny. Wait…" She turns to the employee again. Accepts two tickets and holds them up victoriously next to a couple of black all-access stickers. "Score!"

She's contagious.

"He loves you." I'm smiling big too. Perhaps it wasn't so bad to come along.

"And I lust him!"

A STOCKY GUARD with a blue button-up and *Security* sprawled over a breast—yes, breast—lifts his chin at my insistent friend. "I'm sorry, ma'am, the concert is about to start, and there's no backstage access until after the show."

"No, listen to me. Just *ask* their manager. Emil wants me there. He needs me like air to prepare. I'm, like, his *Prozac*. Do you want this to be a lousy show for him because I'm not with him? Because you stopped his love from being at his side?"

My cheeks heat with embarrassment at the scene Zoe's making, complete with frantic hand gestures and puckered lips. Ninety percent of the time, she gets her way with her mixture of sex appeal and unwavering dedication. Tonight, she's convincing as hell. So convincing, in fact, that I'm surprised when the guard doesn't relent.

We're creating a line. People are huffing behind us, wanting to get to their seats inside. "Call Troll," she insists.

The man cups her elbow to usher her forward. "As I said, the concert is on in fifty minutes. If you're not ready to enter, please step out of the line."

"'Troll?'" I ask.

She yanks free and grumbles as she moves forward. "Idiot. He could've gotten him on the phone. Yeah, they call the tour manager 'Troll' because apparently he's Norwegian. Where trolls are from or something? And they turn into stone in the sun—which isn't a good thing—because then they crack open and fall apart."

"Which... is relevant how?"

"He doesn't like the sun either. Troll doesn't. The guy. Stupid-ass security guard. Watch though. We'll get in."

Five minutes later, I slouch in a bright orange plastic seat that's lined up between four hundred million others in a half circle. Zoe must have made an impact on cute-boy Emil because even I realize that, despite their generic appearance, we have particularly good seats. We're first row, slightly to the left, and so close to the stage that I can see the sweat at the temple of one of the stagehands.

Zoe deserts me. I groan as she hops the barricade to the ground floor of the arena and unceremoniously wedges herself in behind the sound desk. The youngest of the two men fiddling with buttons greets her with a polite nod.

Annnd: let the Zoe-style persuasion ensue.

I can't watch her do this. Me, I tip toward introverted, and to witness my fearless, extremely extroverted friend go all out gesticulating, pointing to the stage, clutching her own heart, even mimicking Emil singing, is just... ah.

The sound guy's brows arch until they disappear under his bangs. Then he nods once and picks up his phone.

There's movement in my peripheral vision. Security. He passes me, descends the remaining few steps, and—great. It's the guy from the door. Now he's on floor duty? He grabs Zoe's arm. She jerks herself free while the sound guy speaks on the phone. Security Nazi doesn't give up. With calm assertiveness—of the kind that makes Zoe very mad—he guides her away and tucks her behind the barricades. To be sure, he leans his stocky, middle-aged behind against the bar dividing them.

Zoe's cheeks flame with anger as she stomps toward

me. "Can you believe it? Old dude's a complete moron. He needs to get a *life*!"

"Indeed," I say—she's not paying attention anyway. She plops her butt on the chair next to me and chews off another layer of nail polish while she waits for the sound person to get off the phone. Once he does, he meets her gaze and breaks into a reassuring smile. Comes over, leans on the railing right in front of us, and says, "Troll's coming for you."

"My Zoay!" Emil rasps out in a road-worn rock-singer pitch. "She's the coolest chick!" he assures bandmates and a few others wearing black rock 'n roll T-shirts. One looks up from a guitar, mutters, "Hey, Zoay," and digs back into his work, tightening strings and adding one that's missing.

"Where've you been since last year?" Emil asks.

"*Emeel*." Zoe draws his name out, long and intimate, the way she does when she puts effort into snagging a guy. "Working and stuff, you know. Saving for college."

"College? Bah. College is for pussies."

"You're full of it, handsome," my friend purrs. "Last time, your buddy told me you did the college dance already."

The singer's eyes narrow with flirty intensity. He bites his lip then lets it go as he scans her body. "Oh really? I'm full of it? Come here." He crooks a finger, beckoning her closer, and it's like watching a cheesy, romantic comedy when Zoe saunters forward.

A few minutes later, I'm even more uncomfortable. I remind myself that Zoe did introduce me (briefly) at one point. It could have been worse.

In thirty minutes, we need to take our seats, and time seriously just snails by. Everyone else pops in and out of the dressing room as they get ready, while I'm stuck in Zoe-and-love-interest-land.

Unfortunately, the boy-band-blond singer never covers up. The shirt I suspect is his remains draped over his chair. And Zoe has planted herself on his lap. They're not kissing yet, but there's a heck of a lot of nose-touching and murmuring into each other's ear. Emil's green eyes twinkle with humor at whatever Zoe says, and when he admonishes, "Oh Zoay, Zoay, Zoay," and rocks her flush on top of his—

Anyway, that's when I take action.

Zoe is remarkably observant. My hand barely curves around the door handle before she calls out, "Nadia, what're you doing?"

Sweat dews at the base of my neck. I can't stay in this room. "Nothing," I say. One of the waves she coiled down my chest won't leave my eye. With two fingers, I push it over my shoulder with the rest of my hair, hoping it stays put.

A hairband. Once I get to a restroom somewhere in this enormous basement, I'll wring my purse inside out and find one. "I'll grab our seats, okay? You come when you're ready."

That does it. Zoe rockets off Emil's lap and stretches a hand out for me like we're in some Shakespearean play. "Nadia, no, wait up. I'll go with you. Sorry, I promise—"

She doesn't get far because King Emil of Clown Irruption stands, hovering above her, and draws her back in against his chest. Suddenly two sets of eyes, round with childlike need for control, stare back at me.

"Dude!" Emil exclaims, losing his Swedish accent on the one word. "I want you two to watch from the side. I'll talk to Troll."

"Where, pumpkin?" Zoe swivels to meet his eyes. I can tell he has no idea what *pumpkin* means in this context but decides it's not important.

"On stage, Zee," he says like it's self-explanatory, and Zoe claps her hands.

"See, Nadia? Emil's gonna get us the best seats. Behind you guys, right?"

These two don't know each other at all, and yet they're eerily synced. They act as if life is simple, like they're boyfriend and girlfriend—this is playground love at a slightly more mature level. Ha, the universe must be on an Emil-and-Zoe wavelength tonight, because what could be better than playground love?

He nods against the top of her head. "Ja, to the side. Only the best for you."

I roll my eyes.

"Hey, I saw that," my BFF says.

"Zoe, I can't stay here."

"Oh come on, Nadia, we'll get to see everyone's ass while they play. Don't be a buzzkill."

"Oh wine." Emil's puppy-pretty features smoothen with his solution. "Duh, your friend wants to get sloshed. Wait, I'll show you where the booze is."

He lets go of Zoe and aims at a side door.

"No, Pump, she doesn't. See Nadia, she's just…"

I hold my breath, afraid of what she'll say. I breathe out, relieved when she finishes: "really hungry." If only she'd stopped there. "Just look at her," she adds. "She wasn't always this skinny. It's her husband's fault."

"She's married? How old are you?" he asks, eyes straight on me. I all but bash the door open at his next comment: "A little young to be married, don't you think?"

"It's complicated, Emil. Do you have any food?" Zoe reaches me before I can exit, links my arm with her own, and pulls me back in. "Wait up… pretty please? For me?"

"Ja! We totally have food. There're pre-show deli trays in the other room with Bo. Next to the wine, by the way. You want wine, Zoay?" The last sentence he says low in the voice he probably uses on all his girls.

"'Ja?'" Zoe giggles. "What's that supposed to mean?"

"Oh yeah, it means 'yes' in my language."

"Swedish," Zoe croons equally low, and I'm done. Out of here. Sadly, Emil is strong. He hooks an arm around my waist and snatches me back in.

"Can you guys stop freaking *handling* me?" I burst out.

Emil flings the side door open, grabs "Zoay" with his other hand, and all but pushes me in. "'Kay, so here're the deli trays. Go crazy, Nadia. And the wine's in there too, Zee, or do you want champagne? I'll hunt down Troll. He'll get us champagne if you want."

"Naw, wine's good," she says. I hear a loud smack then some suckling noises behind me. My urge to flee roars to an unprecedented level. I wish I'd been faster—I could have been in my arena seat by now.

Twenty minutes until they get on stage.

The room is even crummier than the former one. Dark, with peeling paint, it doesn't embody the beautiful arena meeting you upstairs. A small table tilts on three legs against a wall, and two chairs balance, one on top of the other, at the end of it.

On the opposite side... sits a man with a guitar.

"Play nice, Bo, okay?" Emil warns him. "These are my guests. Zee-sweets, and Nadia, her friend. We're grabbing the Jameson," he adds about the only bottle of hard liquor. Then he tugs Zoe with him back out. The last I hear is my friend's soft chuckling before my access to her slams shut.

I don't do strangers. Unless it's work, I don't talk with them, I don't mingle, and I don't interact. This isn't work, and the stranger in front of me is intimidating. I feel his gaze slide over me, but the dark room makes it difficult to read his expression.

Bo's focus sinks to the guitar in his lap. His fingers begin to move, caressing metal strings gently. Short and measured, the notes breed until they form a fractured melody. It's passionate, rich. Slowly, it fills the room.

Black bangs fall in chunky tips over his forehead, obscuring his eyes. From the shadows, the angles of his face protrude in a firm chin and the peak of a bone above a sunken cheek.

He plays love and solitude. Longing and sadness of the kind I don't want to feel anymore. He strums the complexity of life on his guitar. I lean back, my hands falling open in my lap as I absorb the tapestry his notes weave.

Strong fingers dominate the rhythm and level off the

tempo. The volume fades with the slowing speed. His yearning wanes with it too, the shift in him jarring me. When the last raps on the strings reverberate out to the room, they're objective, concert-quality professional but not pulsating with the ragged intensity he communicated before.

Bo shuts off his music abruptly and mid-beat. It's bereaving. Instinctively, I know he has a finished song in his head, that he's not playing the rest. I want him to continue; he needs to fill the silence, because I can't be a regular, polite person right now.

I'm in a crummy room with three-legged tables, stacked chairs, booze, and premade deli trays. And there's this man sitting here with me. He's hiding, wanting to be left alone… and yet he played his heart out to me.

"Hi," he interrupts softly. The darkness concealing him eases as he sits up, revealing delicate features and pale skin. His cheekbones emerge from beneath hair that still droops low along his face like an anime character's.

I can't form words. The fingertips on my left hand rise automatically, waving my acknowledgment.

"It's strange," he murmurs, not taking my hand, not repeating our names. He does a subtle, fast shake of his head, getting rid of the spike hanging over his eyes. When they come into view, I blink against mid-winter frost irises, the grey so deep it sparks an ache at the center of my chest.

"Music is everything." His knuckles hit the wooden carcass of his guitar. A brief, hollow rhythm, sure beneath his fingertips, cuts the air. "Not notoriety, not being discovered by legends like Luminessence and invited on the road with them. Fans, fame—"

He hums out his amusement, a tune, the choked, musical version of *what-was-I-thinking*. "Nothing is truer than a guitar. You know why it's hollow?" he asks me, his stare glinting in the gloom around us.

"No…"

"It needs room to house the musician's soul."

I swallow, and he laughs quietly. Fingers drum against the wood, move up and down, pulling muted calls of love back from the instrument.

"You hear it?" he whispers but doesn't wait for a response. Curving in over the guitar neck, he adjusts a knob and gives me a taste of his voice. I don't recall how Emil sings, but Bo's voice is smooth, a silky, rich and husky sort of sound that makes me swallow again. Halfway into the second bar, he interrupts himself with a chortle, and—*God*, I think, *I hope he sings on stage too*.

"I hear *you*," I respond, and a nugget of something forms close to my heart, because for me it's rare to feel kinship. To understand.

Suddenly the minutes breeze by fast. The darkness creeps away as Bo becomes more and more visible. Him—*he* does. Eyes arced with a need to share, he doesn't tell me his stories. He sings them, knocks them out in rhythms against the guitar's body, folding in soft laughs. Songs I've never heard, tunes he invents while he speaks. It's breathtakingly beautiful, and it makes me forget. I listen—just listen—and I nod. His presence sucks me in, his beauty musician-strong and fragile at once, androgynous, urban yet primeval—I'm overcome with an urge to film him.

Instinctively, I know he is what legends are made of.

For the genius I sense in his music and for the charisma elevating him above regular people. Eternal personalities clip through my mind like in a kaleidoscope. Presidents, actors, rock stars. People who, simply by being in the room, claim your attention. Jimi Hendrix, Marilyn Monroe, Jim Morrison, James Dean. I'm no expert, but Bo is Kurt-Cobain material.

I sense tragedy in Bo, and I hope it's in the past. Not—not—in the now. I fumble with my camera app, trying to be subtle. It's for me, not anyone else. I want to brand the imprint of this moment to a photo, make it last long after it has left me because I know about past moments. They don't ever return.

"What are you doing?" he asks gently.

My heart skips. "Oh just looking up your songs." My finger trembles. Shoots a single picture of him while my cheeks flush warm.

"I'll give you my songs," he says. Bo sets his guitar on the floor, rises slowly, and zips a backpack open on the table. It's the first time I see him without a guitar. Sharp shoulders with no padding rock as he retrieves a stack of CDs. His eyes aren't on me, so I study him freely.

He's young, a few years older than me maybe, but the contour of a wrinkle already sits firm between his brows. He draws them together now while he searches for the right CD. Blows air out through his nose in a short, unconscious breath.

The door flies open. Bo looks up, expression alert and grey eyes expectant. "Now?"

Troll stands in the doorway, the silhouette of him against the fluorescent hallway light doesn't reveal his face. "Yep, grab your shit. We're on in five. Emil's ready. And—hey." He bobs his head at me.

"Hey," I reply.

"Your girl—Emil says they'll watch from the stage?" he says to Bo.

"Ah right," Bo improvises.

"'Kay, it'll be to the left, next to monitors. No seats though. You good with that?" he asks me.

I nod quickly. A small rush of excitement hits me, like I'm the one going on stage. The tour manager ducks his head into the hallway to shout out orders and questions. I don't hear the answers.

"Here." Bo slips me two CDs. Our eyes lock as our fingers meet, but then Troll returns, all attention on Bo.

"Ready, man?"

Bo holds a guitar up high. It's not the wooden acoustic guitar he's been playing. This one is black and electric. "Sure, boss."

In the hallway, Emil, Zoe, and two other guys wait for us. Zoe is under Emil's arm, their mouths colliding between smiles and giggles. I guess once they started kissing in the dressing room, they never stopped. Zoe breaks free to call out, "Nadia, there you are."

"Go. Go," Troll orders, and together we walk down one long, white concrete hallway, then another. Bo checks for me over his shoulder. When I'm slow around a corner, he stops and waits for me. Shifts his guitar over to his left hand so he can grab mine with the other.

I let him.

I'M NOT A ROCKER GIRL, but this alt-rock—indie-rock—whatever they call it, is different. I don't remember much of the last time Zoe and I went to see Clown Irruption. It was at a small club on Sunset. That's about all I recall because it coincided with a bad period of my life.

Now that Emil is up front, Zoe clings to me instead. With an arm draped over my shoulder, she screams, "Check out his ass. Isn't he just so yummy?"

My eyes go to Bo. The way he cradles his guitar, strumming the first notes of a new song out into the audience. It's sensual, a deep belief in what he's doing second nature to every shift he does.

"Not him, silly. Emil! Emil's butt," Zoe says.

As if feeling my eyes on him, Bo turns his head enough to locate me. A small smile crooks his lip on one side.

"You know, this is one good-looking band," Zoe interrupts my stare fest. "Every one of them is, like, drop-dead delish. I mean, are all Swedish guys this sexy? None of their asses have a thing on Emil's though, and guess what? It's as thick and firm as it looks, girl. Hell yeah, and I know because I've grabbed that ass. Imma gonna grab it again too," she brags, aware that the last thing I want is for her to launch into specifics.

"Bo, why don't *you* run with this one," Emil rumbles out, making some girls at the front of the crowd launch into discordant squeals.

Bo snorts into his microphone and peers at his bandmate. "You always pull this shit on me, Emil. One of these days it'll work and you'll be out of a job," he murmurs. A smattering of laughter trickles through the audience.

"I looooove youuuuu, Bo!" a single female voice shrieks. "Siiiiiing it! Siiiiing *Never Ever*!"

"Oh that sad-as-shit song?" Emil asks. Beside me Zoe giggles. Come to think of it, she's been giggling a lot since we got to the arena.

"Nah, he'll never sing that one. Will you, sugar-pop?" Securing the mic stand with one hand, Emil rushes Bo's space, stomping like he's trying to squish a roach. Bo withdraws his foot last second, looking unperturbed by the mini-attack. These two have played games before, probably since before they became band buddies.

Bo laughs softly. "Hey, you're good at singing my pain. Go ahead, wallow. I mean, enjoy."

THIS IS A MINI-VACATION FROM MY LIFE. I have a sunshine-bright kernel growing in my chest, right at the solar plexus, a feeling I haven't experienced in eighteen months. Back then, the color of my existence switched from glistening gold to black. At present, my days are grey, but tonight, this kernel of something else gives me hope, and—it makes me feel guilty.

Jude.

I trail behind Zoe and the band off stage, down the stairs to the dressing rooms. She tries to remain behind with me at first, but Emil scoops her into the air, whooping with an endorphin burst I recognize because I used to experience it too.

"Eww, you're all nasty!" Zoe squeaks.

"If sweat is nasty to you, how do you feel about sex?"

Soul mates. No. Seriously.

"Jesus," their tour manager mutters to himself. "All right, guys. After-show pizzas coming in ten. Refill of beers and wine on the way."

"Troll, can you get us a bottle of champagne?" Emil asks sweetly. He sets puppy-eyes on the tour manager, which makes me guess he doesn't always get his way with him.

Troll stops and turns fully. "Emil. Did you mark *champagne* anywhere, I mean *anywhere at all* on the hospitality writer for this gig?"

"No." Emil tries to hold back an embarrassed snicker. "But in my defense, I didn't know I'd have a sexy-ass girl visiting either."

"Don't you always," Troll mumbles too low for Zoe to hear. "Sure, not a problem." I get the distinct feeling it *is* a problem when he continues louder, "This'll come out of your per diem, all right?"

Emil doesn't take the hint though. "Awesome! Sure, put it on my tab. Champagne, babe," he croons against Zoe's ear.

"Yum!"

"Just don't pull anything stupid on me." Troll lumbers past the lead group and blocks the entrance to the biggest dressing room. "Meet-n-greet. Right here in the hallway since we've got no additional space without bothering Luminessence. Got it?"

The guys chat among themselves.

"I said, 'Got it.'"

There's a murmur of weak agreement around us, which makes me smile. High school boys being bossed around by the gym teacher is my first thought. They pay him to boss them around?

The drummer spews out beer, laughing at something the guitar-fixer-person says.

"And Troy? Clean up after yourself. Your mom doesn't work here. Crazy fan-girls will be here in…" Troll checks his watch. "Forty minutes. Should give you more than enough time to eat and—get drunk." The last part he sighs out.

"Bo. And you too, Emil. The chicks are here for you. Give them some TLC."

Emil wiggles his ass and forms boobs with his hands over his chest, while Bo remains serious.

"Dork," Zoe says. "They don't come for your boobs."

"Oh great. Another opinionated addition," Troll mutters. "Pow." He holds an imaginary gun to his head before he moves on. When he disappears to berate someone who's in the wrong dressing room, Zoe whispers, "Troll, huh?"

The drummer chuckles. "Yeah, because he *is* one."

"Dude, it's early," Zoe says, but I need to go home. She's so happy though, glued to Emil's side even as he charms the fans coming in for autographs. I sink back a little, out of the crowd, but not far enough to make Zoe search for me.

People act like Clown Irruption is huge. If it weren't for Zoe, I'd have never heard of them. Last year the club they played on Sunset was tiny—which according to Zoe means nothing. Apparently even famous bands like to scale down at times and play stripped versions of their shows for an intimate audience.

When I look at Bo, I see a different man than on stage. A much different person than the one who wrung his soul open in the dressing room before the concert.

This man is private and guarded. Stance studiously relaxed, his hands nestle deep in his pockets as if trying to hide what he can. He tips his head back, laughing softly at a silly comment from a fan gushing over his talents. Mostly they gush over his looks. Straight to his face. Do they have no pride?

A girl touches him. Another fumbles for his arms to pull him into a hug. For one uneasy second, I think he'll snub her, but then he relents, drops his hand from his pocket, and accepts a one-armed embrace.

The backstage-pass VIP group isn't large. Twenty minutes in, Emil is roaring with laughter, while Bo's eyes turn darker by the second. My watch says ten thirty, not at all late. How long is this "party" going to last? Intuitively, I know Bo won't break. He seems too controlled to storm off—or snap at the girl pressing herself against him right now.

I'm quietly outraged. Shouldn't someone step in? At least get them to quit touching him when he so clearly doesn't want it? I flick a glance at Troll, who's entertaining a few fans or friends. They're older, maybe from the music business, nothing like the three teenaged girls corralling Bo like he's a puppy in a pet store.

I check out Emil's situation again. Yes, the girls are there too, but Emil's personality seems to feed off the situation. In addition, Zoe acts as an unintentional buffer.

From my seat on top of a table, I slide off and step toward Bo. His peripheral vision finds me, his gaze descending on me before returning to the girl who we now know almost fainted watching him greet the audience at the last concert.

I'm not sure what my plan is. Oh right, Zoe's behind him with Emil; I'll go tell her I'm leaving. I'll just cab it home alone.

"All good?" I ask as I pass Bo.

He turns to me, breaking the circle he's trapped in. "Yeah. You want a beer?"

And against myself, I say, "Yes."

CHAPTER Three

HELP

NADIA

Zoe joins me when I leave. It surprises me because it's not even midnight. The tour manager has just ushered the last fan out of the venue, and the band is being politely chucked out by staff. Apparently, they've overstayed their welcome, and judging by the grumbled curses from Troll, it's a band habit.

"Guess what? Emil and Bo live in town," Zoe says, flaking black polish off a nail. Within a day and a half, it'll all be gone. Sometimes I wonder why she paints them at all. I point at her left front tooth, which now looks like it's got cartoon-style cavities. She rubs with a fingertip, but ends up whipping a mirror out of her purse and gets rid of it that way. "And they're off tour for a week. We're meeting them tomorrow."

She sniffs and stares out the cab window like it's her job to rule my schedule.

"You—? Nuh-uh. Don't include me in these things, Zoe."

"What? Like you have anything better to do. How long has your life been on standstill, Nadia? Is it going to get any better unless you—*you*—take action?"

"Zoe!"

We have the same damn cab driver. What are the odds? He's turning up the music again, and this time it's reggae.

I don't want to have this conversation. I do *not*.

"You never look at anyone the way you looked at Bo tonight, Nadia. Admit it: you're fascinated. You didn't take your eyes off him through the entire after-party."

"Really? You've never seen me look at someone like that? Try Jude," I yell. "My. Husband."

"Exactly—not since your husband was *good* for you!"

I breathe hard. This is a lot even from Zoe. The damn reggae roars from the speakers in the front. It distorts, adding to the showdown Zoe wants to keep me in.

"Just leave it alone," I sigh.

"No. Because I love you. We're best friends, Nadia—we've been through a shit-ton together, and you're stuck with my crazy ass for life, all right?"

I cover my mouth to stop my chin from quivering. "Just don't push me."

Her arms go around me and pull me close. She cradles my head against her like I'm little. Today had been good, but here I go, unable to stop the tears from leaking out again. Every day. Every, every day.

"You had fun. I saw it. Will you lower the damn music!" she shouts at the driver. He turns it down infinitesimally. "More! Asshole." She mutters the last part, knowing he'd probably toss us out right here, in downtown L.A., if he heard.

"Girl, I'm not sure what made you glow tonight, but something did, and I think it had to do with Bo. I don't care if it was something he said, or if you're being shallow and getting off on how eerily beautiful he is."

"Zoe—"

"No, listen: I just want you to forget a little bit. Lose the gloom, baby, like you did in there. Tomorrow won't be a date, okay? We'll just hang out."

I'm quiet as we pull onto my street, contemplate her suggestion. I could come with and be her chaperone. Yeah right. There's no chaperoning Zoe.

"We're going to the park in plain daylight, Nadia. No candlelit dinner on a rooftop. You and Bo can watch us dry-hump on a blanket. No, kidding!" she adds when I groan and wiggle free of her embrace. "Imma gonna kiss him tho. Kisses are fine, right?"

I hold back a smile at her silly monologue.

"You and I. And two pretty boys in the park. Feeding ducklings. And flying kites. We'll buy breadcrumbs for the crazy geese. They're so dangerous!" she adds to bring my smile out all the way.

"Oh stop," I say, pursing my lips to hold back; I don't think I can stomach an over-the-top victory gloat from my friend tonight if I give in.

At my doorstep, she offers to sleep over. I'm not sure why. For me this is late, and I need my husband—alone. I want the past with him, the memories. I want to block out our future because I'd rather not deal.

His parents come by once a month for dinner at some

fancy place to make me feel better. I love them, but what can they do besides dole out money? Now they dole out money. Now, now they do. I wish they did before.

I leave the light off when I let myself in. The neon sign across the street bathes the living room in an alien glow. The neighbors must be asleep, because it's silent in here. So silent. Too silent.

I swallow as I sit down and pull my feet in under me on the seat meant for lovers like us. I cross my legs and push two fingers against my eyes. I wish he were here instead of across from me. Wives are supposed to be in their husbands' arms.

"Do you know how much I love you?" I ask, not expecting a reply and not getting one. Heck, he knows.

My forever, my baby.

Under his gaze, I grab matches and light the three fresh tea lights, a citrusy scent instantly infusing the air.

"You'd traveled so far that day. From San Francisco and *aaaall* the way down to sweet little Payne Point, leaving everything behind because of your bad choices." I smile at the story he told me years ago. He'd been part groaning adolescent, part thankful that his dad had been so insistent:

"I have an addictive personality, Nadia," he'd said, grinning as his fingers traced my belly button. Half-heartedly, I'd pushed them away.

"You do?"

"Yes. Drugs, you know. Just marijuana, but then they found me with something harder in my pocket."

"Crack. Before you'd even tried it."

"Yeah. The old man. Damn, he was on me." He chuckled, and I sat up in my bed, tall enough to kiss him. We had our ways, Jude and I, even with my grandparents around, to claim the intimacy we both craved. "Yep, Dad locked me up, called his secretary, who pinged a moving company and rented us a house. Whoosh, three days later, we were out of there. Mom and I—that look you say we had on our faces when we came into the church? Let's just say it's not every day you get thrown into a car and hauled off forever."

"And now?" I asked. "Are you a total drug addict?" I bit my lip in anticipation because over the last six months, his answer had been exhilarating variations of the same response.

"Yeah, even Payne Point has drugs. My drug of choice is called 'Nadia.' It's in ready supply—"

I swatted him. "Shut up!"

"—and I'm the only one who gets any. Mm-hmm, your village is okay."

Since I was thirteen, I've loved this man. Now, I look over the candles and deep into those sweet, blue, dear eyes I've stared into for eight years. "There's no one like you."

THE LOSS OF MY FAMILY still paralyzed me when my paternal grandparents took me from my country. At seven years of age, a new world met me, wide, affluent, and incomprehensible. I saw cornucopias in Payne Point, an abundance I did not know existed, and the world spoke a language I did not understand.

My grandfather chose Payne Point, Southern California, for his elder brother, the erector, owner, almighty ruler of the Heavenly Harbor, an old bachelor who spent his energy on literal interpretations of the Bible.

I suddenly had a new uncle in *Tío* Rafael, one I had not known about. As the months passed, "*Tío* Rafael" disappeared in favor of "Elder Rafael," and "Grandmother" and "Grandfather" gave way to "Mother" and "Father," because they were there, while Mom and Dad were not.

The first year in Payne Point was drenched with tears, but Elder Rafael preached of accepting the will of the Lord. Small sins came with big punishments. Good Christians repented, he said, while my child heart clearly did not. And so I learned. Stopped confessing my grief. And I tinned my sadness until it transformed into guilt.

During the first summer, neighbor girls my age afforded me temporary reprieve. My grandparents were wary but allowed me to play. In the ways of children, my new friends chattered, assuming I understood their curly words, asking questions and answering themselves when I couldn't reply.

In those sixty days of summer heat, I learned English. In another month, I found sanctuary from my guilt at the public elementary school.

Mother would walk me to class from Elder Rafael's house where we lived. I'd subdue my excited-yet-anxious smile, while Mother's frown fixed me until the school gates slammed her out. Every day she returned before the bell rang, and she squeezed my hand the whole way back home.

The first years, Mother allowed me to play with the neighbor kids several times a week. Then playtime was limited to Saturdays. By the time I was ten, the congregation of the Heavenly Harbor had grown enough for Elder Rafael to open a school, and I was among the first enrolled.

I didn't mind going in the beginning. I had not been provided the luxury of nurturing friendships at the public school, and at the church, I knew the children.

At the age of ten, I spoke Spanish and English. I kept my sins to myself. And, like in Buenos Aires, I played with other children—during the breaks between classes. For a while, life was okay.

I LOVE THESE MOMENTS before I'm fully awake. Sleep-soaked and confused, I'm happy.

"I had the best dream," I murmur. I extend an arm and gather Jude beneath me. "You were in it. We were— Remember our first time?" His side of the comforter sinks under my fingers. I pat it. He's not there.

I roll back, heaving a leaden eight-o-clock sigh. I remember now; it's Saturday, and Zoe and I are both off from work. We're going to the park. Nothing crazy. Just bringing kites and spending time with friends, with—

Bo.

I don't like how I felt with him last night. His grey eyes smattered with small silver speckles, they kept my mind busy. A too-familiar sensation of guilt seeps in at the thought.

People change when they love and lose. They gain soul, they gain depth, and their colors glow richer without being louder. Bo harbors a sadness I know well, only he doesn't wear it like me. For him, his sadness is a means and a remedy, the stories he told me already lyrics in the making. Bo, I realize, is a lover who has lost.

Hours later, my hands press against our closed bathroom door. It's not locked, but I can't open and expose what's inside. It's better this way. I'll just say goodbye with the door closed. I hate goodbyes, but not getting to say them is worse.

Our shower isn't running. The sound of shuffling might come from our bathroom cabinets, but it could also come from upstairs because our neighbors take their time on Saturdays.

My voice doesn't crack when I shout, "Baby, I'll be back later. I'm going out with Zoe and her friends. We'll soak up some sun in the park."

Instinct urges me to ask him along. He'd have come along before. My rational side stops me, stops me, because I have yet to lose my mind.

CHAPTER four

WHY?

NADIA

"Never?" I ask.

Bo lifts his shoulders, tendons and hard muscle outlined against the cotton of his shirt. "Never thought about it, really. We do have kites in Sweden, but I guess I never prioritized learning how to fly one."

"That's sort of funny," I say, freeing a smile that feels crooked on my face while he works to assemble the world's cheapest kite from a souvenir store. "It's not exactly rocket science."

His swift side-glance acknowledges my amusement. He straightens in his crisscross position on the grass and squints playfully at me. Bo seems at ease sitting here, doing what he's doing. With slow, deliberate moves, nimble fingers fiddle with the rope. They tie it and check the strength before he traps my gaze again.

Bo testing ropes is oddly erotic. And I don't know how

my thoughts took me there when it's been ages since I was in that mindset. Zoe would have said that's exactly why I'm thinking such things. My cheeks warm with guilt.

I break eye contact, but his features still linger with me. Inked black hair when everyone else's is streaked blond by the sun. Pale skin in the vibrating L.A. heat, such a wintry contrast to the golden, beach-sandy tourists. Those eyes. I've never been farther north than L.A., and yet my mind strays to glaciers when I allow myself to watch them. The man is a little bit electrifying.

I swallow and turn my focus to Emil and Zoe, who are laughing and fighting over their limp kite at the cliff's edge. There's no wind—there usually isn't down here in St. Aimo. Zoe tends to get her will though, and we're all here humoring her.

"What happened?" Bo asks, studying my hot face. "Did I do something?"

I let out a huff that's supposed to be a laugh. At best, I sound helpless. "Ha, no. What makes you say that?"

Ugh. Please don't answer.

"You look uncomfortable. Beautiful but uncomfortable." His eyes skim my face, travel down my left arm, and stop on my hand. My two-year-old wedding band gleams in the sunshine.

"You mean uncomfortable like you last night at the afterparty?" I quip, because, *God yes, let's talk about him instead.*

He drops the kite and breathes out quietly, taking my bait. With idle hands resting in his lap, he blows air out through his nose. "Yeah, I'm not much for crowds."

"But you're so relaxed on stage in front of thousands of people."

"Well, that's different. On stage, I just enjoy playing my music."

"You hide behind your music, huh?" I smile and play with a chunk of dry grass between us. "One of *those* guys?" I say as if I know a slew of people with the same habit.

He lets out a chuckle. It's intimate-sounding, like he could emit it to a girl lying on his arm. My lower abdomen clenches, and I wish it didn't. This attraction. It's so desperately futile.

"I'm not hiding. It's sort of the opposite. As you saw at the party last night, I'm not the people-person in the band. I tend to keep stuff to myself. *Feelings* and shit." He rolls his eyes.

"Everyone has feelings," I defend everyone. "So you just pop them into songs instead of talking about them?"

"Yep, same difference, right?" he says. The kite rests obediently on the ground, a plastic alien waiting for our attention. Not a single gust of air tickles my skin, and over at the precipice, Zoe half howls, half giggles in Emil's arms while he angles her out over the edge.

"Of course. I get it," I tease. "The misunderstood, reclusive artist who only ever expresses his feelings through his lyrics."

His eyes twinkle when he's amused, and God have mercy, I like him amused. Now, he lets out the silkiest little laugh, reminding me of how open he was in that dim dressing room yesterday.

"You're funny," he says. "But yeah, I might just be that reclusive person. And if people think I love it when they touch me and gush in my face, then you're right: I'm misunderstood too."

"You don't like to be touched?"

Whoa, shut up, Nadia.

Suddenly, I'm more aware than ever of how close we sit. When he leans forward over crisscrossed legs, our knees touch, and hope, illicit hope, tethers in my chest.

"No, Nadia. I do like to be touched. By the right person in the right place, I like it a lot. And I like to touch too."

My entire body responds to his words, a delicious heat spreading under my skin. I could blame the sun, the stifling day, but like his lyrics, the simple way he says it reaches me deep inside. Unlike his songs though, these words aren't love, yearning, and loss. They're nearness and want. Sexy and… a lot to take in when you're starving.

Bo's little finger extends from atop his knee. Touches my elbow. We're so close he fills my space entirely. He doesn't say anything. Just studies my expression, and I burn hotter by the second.

I don't pull my arm away, because…

Because?

Bo's voice is for me only. "I remember you from a concert a while ago. I saw you out there in the sea of people. Your eyes were big. Full of secrets. Your mind was somewhere else entirely, and you stuck with me after, in my mind." He exhales quietly, letting his gaze detour over my face. "Last night—I'm not sure what happened."

My breath stutters as he weaves our fingers together. I let him do it even though my brain shouts no.

"You came into the dressing room while I was in my pre-show ritual mode."

"And you were different." At first I think he doesn't

understand what I mean. But then he nods with chunks of black hair falling softly over his eyes.

"I've tried to figure out how it happened. How I could ramble on so freely when I didn't even know you. I don't pull that shit on people." Bo raises our hands between us. Twists and studies my simple ring, then lifts my hand high enough to brush his nose over the back of it. "Has anyone told you you're easy to talk to?" He inhales slowly, like he's pulling in my scent, and I gasp.

"No, I... People don't say that."

"Pure luck yesterday then?" The hook of his mouth curls up.

In all I do, I'm measured, but to this man, in a rush of candor, I say, "No, that was you letting me into your mind, and I am so honored. I'm no expert, Bo—I don't even listen to music much—but you scream genius. I hope you know that."

God. I just revealed my awe. How could I be so blunt? Bo cracked his soul open last night, and this is how I pay him back? Fans probably shower him in this crap nightly.

I only just met him, but his opinion of me means something. I'd hate it if he thought less of me over my cheap outburst. I might as well have yelped out, "I'm your biggest faaan!"

I force myself to look up and find him unperturbed, gaze still open, a new curiosity flickering in them.

"You're married?" he asks. My heart does a heavy skip.

"Yeah."

"Why?"

Because Jude and I don't go anywhere together, people sometimes wonder about my ring. Some ask straight out about my husband, but no one ever asks why I'm married.

"You're uncomfortable again. Does that mean you regret it?" He lowers our hands between us but doesn't let go. I'm hyperaware of his thumb gliding slowly over my knuckle.

"No, I love Jude and don't regret our eloping for a minute. It's just complicated. Long story."

"I have time."

I'm not sure I can deal with this man. He's so intense. Works to penetrate my shield. That ever-present glob in my chest swells, a leaden magnet for emotions I should resist, while he waits for me to continue. Too soon, it obstructs my breathing, and all I want to do is cry.

"Nadia? I've made you sad. I'm sorry." He gets to his feet at the same time I do. Tries to put a hand on my shoulder to soothe me, but I spin and take the first steps toward Zoe. My vision blurs, so I blink the tears away as I walk.

"It's okay. I need to go home anyway," I say.

Then I do.

Though it's daytime, my candles burn in our living room. It's my thing; as soon as I'm home, I light them. Whenever I'm drawn in by my baby, they soften the angles of his face, highlight a subtly crooked nose and the golden stubble on his chin. I love it so much.

"Disaster," I tell Jude. "Total disaster. I hate it when people ask about you. I become all weird." It felt like a date with Bo, which I'm not telling my husband. "I should keep to myself," I say instead. "Hang at home and stuff."

Jude wants me to get serious about my education though. His plan was always for me to finish my veterinarian studies. Ladies first, right? It's some gentlemanly thing of his. I'd suggested both of us at once, but he just crossed his arms at me. Stubborn. Always so stubborn, my Jude.

No, he wants to start his own education *after* me. A mechanic, he'd hummed once, eyes dreamy. "How cool, Nadia, if I ended up working for Tesla. Can you imagine, digging around inside the motors of a bunch of Teslas for a living?"

I couldn't, but I nodded, dreaming with him. All I wanted was to see him happy—as happy as he made me. He grinned big, grasped my hips, and scooted me into a nearby chair.

"Look at me, wifey."

I did, biting my lip.

"Screw Mom and Dad for cutting off my funds. They won't be hampering us. I'm going to pay our bills with my gas station job, okay? I swear to you: we'll never take out high-interest loans to get us through shit."

"No, Jude." I shook my head, for once adamant. "We're in this together. You're not going to slave away while I have fun studying."

"Shhh, sweetie." Soft with love, Jude's gaze stilled on me, waiting until I relaxed enough to listen. "Once you're a vet, once you earn destructive amounts of money, I'll quit my job at the gas station and become a full-time student. You'll support your deadbeat, good-for-nothing husband, and no one in your office'll get what the hell you see in me."

Bubbles of bliss surge in my throat as I think back to that day. "You were irresistible, Jude, when you said that." My smile wobbles, but when I look up at him, my husband is giving me his knowing, quiet smile. "Bah, you're always irresistible," I say.

"Afterward, we'll have babies," he'd told me. "We'll be this little family. One boy—because it'd be stupid to think we could handle more than one rebellious replica of me—and two girls with long, brown hair and carob eyes like you. We'll raise them with tons of love and freedom. And move to a deserted island if any of them act up on us."

Post-Argentina, the two years in the Heavenly Harbor elementary school were the highlight of my childhood. Elder Rafael entrusted an old schoolmistress of the congregation with the minds of us children. Our group was small, varying between five and eight students, all quiet and well trained by devout parents.

We didn't laugh and horse around like in Buenos Aires, but we had each other, and for a few hours a day I was out of Mother's scope.

Life deteriorated when our teacher was excommunicated for remaining in contact with her grown daughter after she left our sect. We children were spared the details even as adults gossiped in pre-sermon groups.

Mother was instated as our new teacher, which coincided with my twelfth birthday. Our curriculum was updated. Extended Bible Studies suddenly replaced World History, but for me, losing my daily breaks from Mother was the biggest change.

My period arrived. I had no idea what was happening to me and hid it for months in the belief that I was dying. One hundred and eleven days in, a congregation member in the next-door restroom stall caught me cleaning up my mess. She explained the female miracle, how the monthly cycle is natural. After that, all I recall is shame. Until the day I met Jude.

"BECAUSE DINNER IS JUST DINNER and it'll be fun," Zoe explains. She pulls a handful of pins from her hair and busies herself in my hallway mirror, arranging her sloppy bun back up into a disheveled princess 'do. "You like Bo, and—"

"Stop saying that."

"What? Tell me I'm wrong then."

"You are. Sort of. Just—ah. I don't want to talk."

"Always the same thing. Always, always," she mutters around the remaining pins in her mouth. "Okay, how 'bout this: no talking. Only eating and laughing and having fun. You know, Bo asked a hell of a lot of questions after you left."

"Did he? You didn't…?"

"I'm *your* friend. Not his." She narrows perfectly lined eyes at me. "I'd be stupid to try and rush a confession out of you by squealing on your behalf. We're doing hibachi, by the way."

I sigh, shaking my head. After the way I stormed off a few hours ago, Bo must be crazy for wanting to hang out. Then again, Emil is his buddy. Bo is coming along to support him. Or maybe he adores Japanese steakhouses. Either way, it's definitely not because of me.

Zoe and I arrive first. The steakhouse smells stale from years of grease steaming from enormous burners in a room with bad circulation. As we get seated, I hear, "Four Sapporos!" from behind us. "Oh and get us sake too. A few bottles."

"Carafes," Bo specifies. "And ice water, please, if the ladies haven't ordered drinks yet?"

"Yeah, carafes, whatever-you-call-it." Emil jerks his head in the direction of our table, continuing, "And what *he* said, and to that table."

Zoe's latest infatuation is a rush of fresh air, I think to myself. Now, he lifts a hand, waving like we're far away and he hasn't seen Zoe in days.

Bo's eyes linger on me. To break the contact, I pull a lipstick out of my purse. "I'm not going to drink," I mumble to Zoe.

"Just loosen up for freaking once," she hisses. "I want to have fun with my best friend and some cool guys, and I don't want to worry about you running off again. Some alcohol will do you good."

"Zoe." I always feel guilty. There isn't a moment of the day that I don't. And she's a saint—a nutty saint—for dragging me along everywhere. Nadia, the party pooper. When did I last drink more than a few sips? Probably on Jude's twentieth birthday.

"Just go with it," she says. "Go with the flow. Let's have

a good time."

The hibachi grill is wide with room for a chef in the middle and a bar counter in a squared U-shape around it. I sense Bo's presence even before I look up. It's psychological, I know, but he feels warm at my side. I instantly blush. I hate my cheeks.

"How are you?" he asks, voice quiet from the chair next to me. I guess I assumed I'd be safe with Emil and Zoe seated between us.

"Emil! You have to use the *tip* of your tongue first. *Then* you swirl," Zoe exclaims.

"You're teaching me how to kiss now? I kissed you just fine earlier, I believe," Emil hums while kissing more.

"'Tis just a suggestion. Check this out," Zoe says. Irregular breathing ensues.

"Jesus," Bo mumbles into his hand, and I feel my own face tug into a smile. "You two—simmer down on the affection, will you?"

"Really, it's too much for you, Bo?" Emil manages between smacks and suckling noises. "This isn't exactly R-rated."

"True, which is surprising. We've been in this place for, what, two minutes?" Bo leans in against my ear and whispers loud enough for our friends to hear, "If they start to remove clothing, I'll get you out of here before they claim more casualties."

The first sip of ice-cold beer tastes amazing. The second one does too. Our ninja chef chops meat and fries veggies, and because we wait so long for our table to fill up with guests, we're on our second round of hot sake before the food arrives.

Emil's hands are on Zoe most of the time, only letting go to grab his glass. The banter flicks back and forth between the guys, while Zoe shoots off the perfect witticism, adding her quirky flavor to Emil's whims.

It's probably the alcohol, but I feel myself relaxing, a sensation so rare that it's odd. I can't decide if I should fight it. I'd benefit from drinking more often, I think for a moment. Until I rethink and decide I would not.

The seating arrangement leaves us so close to each other that Bo's arm brushes my shoulder with every shift in our chairs. I don't tense up over it like I commonly would. I'd never drink enough to lose my inhibitions though.

"So you're not a chopstick guy?" I ask Bo the obvious. He hasn't even opened his packet. Instead he has opted for the cheap, bendable fork that's part of our place setting—and he asked for a knife!

He crooks a beautiful smirk around the fried shrimp and mussels in his mouth, and flushes the mouthful down with beer. "Naw, never really got into it."

"Like with the kites?" I find myself leaning in playfully, and it's a whole lot like flirting. Bo relaxes against the back of his chair, inviting me closer with a squinted smile.

"Yeah. Like with the kites."

"I can teach you," I say, the thought tumbling out on its own. I comb my brain for objections or remorse, but neither appears… because my offer is innocent. It can't be wrong to teach someone how to use chopsticks, right?

Minutes later, a strange chuckle escapes me. Bo, who dominates his guitar with strong, agile fingers, should be predestined to master whatever requires nimble handling, yet he cannot get a grip on chopsticks.

"No!" I laugh out loud. "You don't understand, do you?" His "never really got into it" is a definite understatement.

Bo's cheek connects with my shoulder while he groans out his impatience, and his shampoo tickles me with an elusive drift of pine and musk. Soft hairs trail up his lower arm, his skin bare and warm at my touch.

I force myself to focus on our hands, on how I'm forming his fingers around the chopsticks in an attempt to nestle them in the perfect spot: one on top of his middle finger and the other between his thumb and index. As I let go, they fall from his grip for the fourth time.

"See? Unlike you, I wasn't Asian in a former life," he tells me.

"Ha, but you're not trying," I laugh.

"Wow, Nadia's having fun," Zoe informs Emil. I ignore her because I can't deny that I am. Between Bo's inept approach to the chopsticks and my own buzz, I feel lighthearted. Thankfully I don't have to own up, comment, deal. Bo is too busy defending himself to pay attention to Zoe.

I leave my brain on "idle." Slide my fingers down Bo's, and hold the chopsticks tight with his hand between my own. Then the two of us lift a shrivel of chicken to his mouth. It makes it high enough to smear his lips with grease. I watch the tip of his tongue come out, moist and poised to whip the food inside, but at the last second, the chicken slips from our grasp and rolls down his shirt.

"Dammit, so close!" he exclaims, making me laugh—

again—and I quickly reach down and locate the stray piece of food on his formerly white shirt. Bo doesn't seem worried.

"You're gonna have to soak the shirt overnight to get rid of the skid marks," I say.

"Mm-hmm," he murmurs, looking at me, not the food or his shirt.

I fuss, suddenly shy. I wrap the piece of chicken in a napkin, a useless act because—where would it go except for in the trash? When I glance up, a few droplets of sauce gleam golden against his pale throat. Without thinking, I bring a finger to them. Who wouldn't want to help? It's the right thing to do, to help, just—I'm cleaning him up with my *finger*.

At first, it's natural and instinctive. Then it's hot when his Adam's apple bobs at my touch, and I can't find the strength to withdraw.

"You're even prettier when you smile," he whispers. There's sauce at the corner of his mouth too, right where his lip plumps into succulent, living art made to—

I should clean him up with his napkin or show him so he could do it himself. But captivated, I lift my hand and approach his mouth. Bo's eyelids flutter as I touch him, the response so sensual, I bite down on my lip.

Pull away. Sit up straight, Nadia.

I'm not sure how much I've had to drink, but this is the alcohol acting. Not me. It's been a happy night—I'm, I'm… touching a man's mouth.

I stroke his lips with the digit I used to remove the sauce. Soft, giving, alive, fleshy. Everything I imagined they would be. When you're intoxicated, the importance of time fades, and sometimes it speeds by. Like now.

I'm not sure how long I sit there, touching him and seeing us from the outside: a strange girl enthralled by the mouth of an utterly charismatic man.

Gifs of his lips form in my mind, cycling on loops before retracting for others. In miniature film clips, I remember them shifting, smiling, parting in barely acknowledged disbelief. They round with a riff he pulled from his guitar and let cry out over the audience last night.

Then this mouth I'm touching puckers. Kisses my finger, and my heart races like I'm scared. Because I am, or I would be, if hot sake hadn't numbed my responses.

Carefully, he steadies my hand with both of his and breathes against my palm.

"Very lucky husband," he murmurs.

I pull my hand free, stand up, and run to the bathroom.

CHAPTER Five

LOVE MUSCLE

BO

"We'll be back any minute!" Zoe shouts as she takes off with Emil. Nadia doesn't object. An eye-roll is all she commits, and I lean on the kitchen counter, studying her.

Emil's and my place is walking distance from the Kagawa Hibachi House. He lured the girls back with us after dinner, tempting them with green tea ice cream and acting really fucking surprised when we didn't have it. I mean, of course we didn't. We never buy ice cream.

Now, Nadia and I are alone in the apartment.

Or *she's* alone with *me*.

I remember her well from a concert we played a year ago. Remember her friend too. Zoe came with Emil to Troy's after-party that time, where the two of them engaged in some heavy petting in a corner. Nadia though, had disappeared, and I didn't see her again until last night.

To me, music is everything. Not that it wasn't while I was with my ex, Ingela, but since our final breakup, it's been truer than ever. I'm a been-there-done-that sort of dude with relationships. At twenty-five, I've lived in the US for two years, and whether it's in Sweden or here, *going steady* works neither for me nor for the poor chick involved.

Back when I made an effort at it, what I accomplished was a whole lot of tears from my ex, who loves with so much heart it's painful to watch. She used to say I don't have a love muscle, a good expression, really. Doesn't mean I don't appreciate a hot girl.

My ex was perfect. Sweet and funny. The sex kicked ass too. She was made for me, but after five years of giving her nothing but unintentional agony, I understood what I should have ages ago; I don't possess the whatever-it-is that makes a person love beyond how you love family.

It's not a big deal. In my business, people exchange partners like they do underwear, and that's what the ladies expect. They feel lucky if they get a night with the guitar player, the bandleader, whatever, while for me good sex relieves stress. Hell, even bad sex does. Sometimes, I miss the closeness Ingela and I had, but I have my bandmates. I'm good.

Tonight, I'm here with Nadia. She's stunning, for sure, but beauties flock to this neck of the woods for work, so that's not what makes her stand out. No, the girl hides secrets. They simmer under her skin, at the back of her gaze, and they make her damn near irresistible to me.

With her gaze glistening dark beneath long lashes, she's relaxed from the booze and tempting as hell. I want to excavate her like an archeological site. If it weren't for that wedding band, I'd want her in my bed, I'd do things to her—find out how to pluck her strings and make her sing.

She looks Hispanic. Half the population of L.A. is from somewhere in Latin America, I've learned, and I'm not good at discerning accents. "Where are you from originally?" I ask. "Born in California?"

She smiles. "Buenos Aires, Argentina. I moved here, or to Payne Point down by San Diego, when I was seven."

"Ah. What made you guys move from your country?"

She shrugs. The lightness of the shrug is telling; she's sad. I consider pulling her in and holding her until the tension eases. I'm a pro at that.

"Family." Her thoughts spill across her expression. She's deciding how much to say and ends up giving me more than I expected. "My parents died."

"Shit. I'm so sorry," I say.

"No, it's fine. I was little. I miss them but… Anyway. My grandparents and I moved here to be with family."

"That's cool. Family rocks," I reply, missing my own back home in Sweden. "Are you close?"

Her eyes widen gorgeously at my question. "Ha, not at all." There's sorrow and humor in them at the same time. "My great uncle runs a very… extreme church, and I got excommunicated for not following the rules. There were some severe punishments for having— Crap. Sorry. This is a lot."

"I don't mind. Keep going," I say.

"Ah that's okay. I don't usually talk about these things." Nadia ran off like a startled bunny over too many questions earlier today, so when she continues, "Do you have anything to drink?" I allow the change in subject and lead her to the kitchen.

"Tea? Coffee? We deff have alcohol. Loads of it."

"I bet you do." She smiles up at me. "Black tea?"

"Yep, got it. It's, how you say, 'Oooooolong.'" Nadia doesn't strike me as the belly-laughing kind of girl, but I drag out the type of tea for a fleeting chuckle.

Emil and Zoe are taking forever—which I don't mind. While we wait for the water to boil, Nadia sits on my kitchen counter, busying herself with the mugs and pouring spoonfuls of sugar into them.

She's shy again, and I'm thinking her buzz is waning. I hope she doesn't clam up. Of the little I've seen, Nadia open and accessible is awesome, like on our hours-long hibachi house visit and the detour through the park we took kites to earlier.

But I'm making her nervous. Her fingers are unsteady around the handle of the mug once she's done depositing the teabag inside of it. I support my elbows on the counter. I still her hand with mine and narrow my eyes while I try to read her.

It's two in the morning. Because I'm curious and I don't get it, my question cuts from me without premeditation.

"Isn't your husband expecting you home?"

Her sweet face immediately crumbles.

NADIA

When Jude came to Payne Point, I was young, confused, and unhappy. Once we found each other, he wouldn't leave me alone long enough to simmer in my family's dark convictions.

Jude's love was shiny, new, and ever-seeming. The times we were in the same room in public—in church—I couldn't stop looking at him.

Soon, he became my mood stabilizer and my reason for sanity, and early on, I knew that my life would not be worth living if he let our sinful love go.

"Shhh, don't worry. They've got it wrong, Nadia. They don't know. They don't know," he whispered while I dug my face into the pillow on my bed, my head heavy with tears and fear and guilt.

"How do you *know* that, Jude? Have you been in Heaven? No. So how *could* you know? My uncle says sinners who don't repent aren't invited in. What if we're sent to Hell?"

Jude's fists barged into the comforter on both sides of my head. My heart skipped, but I didn't cower because Father, not Jude, was the one who hurt me.

"*BECAUSE*, Nadia. There is no way how we feel for each other is sinful. Innocent as children: isn't that what we're supposed to be in your uncle's religion? We're innocent as hell! You need to believe in us. If you don't, how are we going to pull this off?

"You want to end up married to some old guy you don't love in a few years? Someone rich enough to suit the Heavenly Harbor and shed out tithes on the level of my parents' monthly contribution when we attended?

"Even if I wanted to, I wouldn't be able to pull off tithes like that. So then you'll have to have babies with that old, rich guy, lots and lots of babies—do your duty as a woman to spread Elder Rafael's crazy story to the masses!"

I sobbed, my face burning with red-hot anxiety.

"I don't believe in any of your uncle's tales, the bullshit he concocts with his literal interpretation of two-thousand-year-old crap that means nothing anymore. And why are there no women disciples in the Bible? What about Mary Magdalene? Was she not present too? Did Jesus not love her? Love, Nadia. LOVE! Does *Elder Rafael* ever take a minute to think about what he's doing to people's brains with his crazy doctrine? It is *not fair*!"

"Jude, please," I cried, loving him so much. His thoughts were far out, so much more radical than my brain could comprehend, but in the soft darkness of our nights, I agreed with him in this: the feelings we had for each other could not be sinful.

Life wasn't easy in Payne Point, but it was safe. It was predictable. For a few years, I even controlled the demand for extreme penance.

Because of Jude's appearance in our lives and my obvious attraction to him, Mother quit her job as a teacher at the Heavenly Harbor to homeschool me. My days were supposed to be: Mother, sermons, Mother, Mother, then Father's belt if my penance didn't cut it. I was rarely allowed outdoors now.

"Baby. Baby, baby, baby. Look at us. We've done this for years. Your grandparents are asleep, and I'm here at two in the morning because we have to sneak around. We're seventeen years old. How much longer are you going to accept living in guilt and shame and denial when what we feel for each other is real and forever? At my high school, heck, everywhere else, people feel like fucking *sunshine* when they're in love. Why don't we? Why *can't* we?"

"We do, Jude."

"Yes, for the stolen hours we have together. I can't take you to the movies. Go bowling. I can't join you when you walk the dog because someone could see us. Hell, I'd love to take you out for ice cream, have you over to my house more than twice in four years. Every night I come to see you, you've relapsed. You're inside that grey *muddy* world of the Harbor, full of illogical shit and rules. Tell me you disagree."

I drew in a shuddering breath. I wanted his hands on me, those gentle, demanding hands that extracted pleasures I should not allow from deep, deep inside of me. Jude's fierce tenderness was how I survived now that I had learned the beauty of unselfish love between a man and a woman.

To my church, what Jude and I had should not exist. It was dark, immoral, unchristian. But with Jude, I hovered closer to Paradise than I ever did at the Heavenly Harbor.

At sunrise, once his murmurs of love and his promises of saving me dissipated, another day with Mother awaited.

Oblivious to his nightly visits, Mother hauled me to Earth in the mornings. When I wasn't in Heaven with my Jude, Mother stirred the dirt up high down here. She anchored me in the desert of pitch-black religion. Spooned out shame over my small but noticeable breasts, the curve of my hips, and the sudden slenderness of my waist.

But then the night would return with Jude's love-struck gaze and reverent touches. He healed me, made me see my transformation the way he did, as something natural, something beautiful and pure.

"I shouldn't have to tell you this. You should *know* how beautiful you are. Never be embarrassed. And mothers are supposed to be there for you, to make you understand and believe in yourself."

I'd turn the lamp off then, and thus the conversation. Leaving us in the charcoal night, nestled in ourselves. Because besides his words, Mother's were the only ones I knew. And I had no reply.

BO

"Isn't your husband expecting you home?" I dislike making her sad as much as I like making her smile, but at least she doesn't scamper off at my question.

"Not really," she says.

She's sad and trying to hide it even with her eyes glistening like this. I dry moisture off the tip of an eyelash and remove a stray hair from her face.

"I didn't mean to upset you. *Again*. Damn me," I mutter while I pull her in for a hug. Still on the kitchen counter, she allows me to hold her, and I rest my nose on top of her head. It feels good to keep her like this. She's warm and soft in my arms. I notice now how skinny she is. She's supple lines broken up by sharp hipbones and bony shoulders. Despite the makeup and the glossy hair, she doesn't seem to take very good care of herself.

"Tell me what you do. You're a student, right?" I rock her back and forth, soothing her. I've got practice in this, five years with my ex, only with her I'd been the reason for her sadness, not just a catalyst.

"Yeah, besides working with Zoe at the café, I finally finished my GED."

"Which is?" I stroke her hair while I ask.

She pulls back enough to study me. "You don't know? It's a high school equivalency test. It's something you do when you never completed high school. You get your diploma afterward and can go on to college."

I'm puzzled. Slant my head so I can look into her stunners. "Do they allow people to not finish high school in the US?" Nadia blinks back at me, embarrassed, until she understands that I'm curious, not disapproving.

"Umm, not really. My parents homeschooled me because of their religion, and they didn't do a very good job."

"Oh come on. It was you all along. You were a terrible student—be honest," I tease, risking that she breaks into sobs. Instead, she chuckles, getting my humor.

"Try being educated by born-again extremists," she murmurs, her amusement fading.

"Are you serious? Like on TV?"

"I wouldn't know."

"Because you can't watch TV?"

"Or more because I'd rather not see what others have been through. Zoe tells me I should go to support groups with people who've been through what I have—which would have worked for her. Me, I don't need more reminders than the ones in my head."

I let my fingers brush over her cheek. "Your friend would rule that group."

"Yep, and hold them captive in all senses of the word," she says, smiling at her own addition. I love it.

Layers upon layers breathe below her surface; she's a secret keeper. All the stuff I keep bottled up, the shit I only litter out through my music, stems from a focused, obsessive nature, and right now, that nature is focused on her.

"I'm going to ask you another question, and I don't want you to freak out on me," I say. She doesn't object, but her lithe little body tenses as she braces herself.

"Tea?" she deflects, and I let go to pour the overly boiled water.

"Living room?"

She nods, and I balance our cups as we leave the kitchen. Our couch is a deep two-seater boasting wide, too-soft cushions. With a single lamp lit on a coffee table, it's pretty intimate-looking, I'd say.

"Okay. My question." I watch her lift her gaze from the tea. When she fixes it on me, I dive in.

"So you moved here from Argentina. To become part of a religious cult?" In lieu of a "yes," Nadia pulls her knees up in the corner of my couch, steeling herself. I pick my guitar up by the neck, rest it in my lap, and start plucking out some notes.

"Does that sect decide who their women marry?"

She doesn't answer at first. I let my hair fall over my face to give her a moment. Through my bangs, I observe her while I fiddle out a new string of chords.

She remains quiet, so I tip my head up to meet her eyes. They shimmer in the semi-dark, but her voice is steady when she eventually replies. "Yes. We were to marry good men selected by the church leaders."

She must see my next question coming. "Was your husband one of those good men? Selected by your leaders?"

She laughs out loud. It surprises me, and I commit a D minor, drawing an accidental cacophony from the guitar. I stop. Give her my undivided attention.

"Ha, no. Jude was anything but. The church hated him and his parents after the first few months. It didn't take the Bancroft family long to realize what they'd gotten themselves into at the Heavenly Harbor. With no apology, even withholding most of their tithe, they migrated to a mainstream Lutheran church. Elder Rafael was furious."

"But the two of you got to hang out?"

"God, no." She grins big, displaying a wicked streak she hasn't shown before. "Jude and I, we noticed each other the minute he entered the Harbor during their first sermon with us. We kept stealing glances and small smiles throughout.

"Afterward, we had church coffee with the members and their children, and with Mother and Father being outstanding, long-lasting members of the congregation, they had a job to do, inviting the new family in. Harsh penances and such came later. See, in the beginning it was always about love and inclusion and securing the tithe."

"And tithe is…?"

"It means that people pay ten percent of their earnings to the church."

"Jesus. People do that?"

"Depending on the church, they do. Ours was pretty notorious about guilting people into it. Anyway, after that, Jude and I would be in sermon together, and he'd sit as close to me as he could. He'd always have a million questions for me during church coffee, and during class, he'd be the only student who chitchatted."

"You were in the same class?"

"Yeah, for a little while. Mother taught at our church's school, and I attended it, so Jude told his parents he wanted to go too."

"Ah. Small school?"

"Very, and Jude stood out." She squeezes her eyes shut, embarrassed. "After his third day in class, Mother bought me wide sweaters in muddy colors and skirts that reached my calves. She threw away my regular skirts, and when I protested, begging to have my old clothes back, Father…" She swallows, cutting herself off.

"What," I say. "Physical punishment?"

"A little bit. 'Children, obey your parents in the Lord, for this is right,' as Father used to quote." She shrugs and adds, "'Whoever spares the rod hates his son, but he who loves him is diligent to discipline him.' Let's just say,

Father was fond of his belt. I had a rough few weeks, but they were tolerable because of Jude."

Jesus H. Did she commit to this Jude at thirteen? I guess if you're raised in Hell and you meet someone who can save you, you're all for it.

"How old was Jude?" I ask.

"A few months older than me."

I drop the guitar and haul her into me. Nadia's story is the saddest thing. I've been through shit too, but it's just regular crap that doesn't shape your life forever. Nadia slinks into me, almost like a cat, and she seems so fragile, I mold my arm around her to protect her from… what? Her past?

"I don't know why I tell you these things, Bo."

I kiss her temple—just to comfort her. Then I think about her husband, how she said he's not waiting up for her.

If they started dating at thirteen and she's a few years younger than me, they've been together for a decade. As far as I know, she hasn't texted or called anyone during this whole time, and the husband hasn't been trying to get a hold of *her*. If I were him, I would; it's really late. I mean, what douchebag isn't worried about his wife at this hour?

To me, it seems that Nadia isn't simply annoyed with her life and her husband. She appears plain unhappy about it. And that's how dares are born for me. Now I want to glean contentment from this girl.

I hum softly, a melody I've been working on, and she doesn't push away from me when I nuzzle her temple. It's kind of addictive.

I have no intentions of taking advantage of the situation, so my hardening cock isn't what I concentrate on. I don't usually pause to think about a girl's scent either, but Nadia's? It's this mouthwatering mix of skin and flowers.

She turns into me, a small hand going up to cup my face, and because my mouth is already on her, our lips connect without my doing. Hers are salty from tears and tasting mildly of black tea. When she opens, letting her tongue find mine, a new sugary flavor draws an awed grunt from me.

"Shit. Nadia?"

She emits the quietest little whimper, and it's so hot my brain implodes with caveman needs. I want to throw her on her back and tear her clothes off starting at the center of her body. I want to peel her open like a birthday present, inhale the sight of her. Nuzzle. Suck—

My imagination is already going amok. What kind of nipples does she have? Are they light pink, bright red, or dark brown? Are they of the blooming, swollen sort or the small, delicate type? Somewhere in between?

I need to watch them stiffen.

Whoa, I'm ready to debauch a married woman. What kind of depraved person am I? Fuck. Whatever. I'll just kiss her and dream. Then I'll have my way with myself once she's out of my house. I'll definitely be picturing in detail everything I'd do to her.

For a moment, I press her close. Her thigh has migrated over mine, giving more access, the friction of my cock against denim already maddening.

I'm just making her think about something besides her sad life.

Her breath stutters, assuring me that she likes this. She

moves slowly over me, her body shifting so she's partly on top. Nadia's hands travel into my hair, grasping, tugging a little while we kiss.

She makes me harder.

She makes it harder to stop.

I don't want to stop.

"Ah you're so hot," I pant. It's a complaint, and she knows. I grab her hips. Roll her over me, back and forth, back and forth. With each roll, I'm more demanding, and her breathing grows heavier and heavier. God, that is a beautiful sound. I catch her sighs with my mouth. We sort of gasp against each other, and like the teenager I've become, I'm so horny I'm about to erupt in my pants.

This is platonic, I remind myself, and I'd laugh if I weren't so horny. Sure, it's platonic, and yet so, so, so not. Before I can summon my good intentions, they rush out of sight.

My hand trails down the fleshy part of her where spine meets ass, and wedges into her crevice. Nadia whines softly and bucks up, craving my touch. I think my heart actually pauses.

The situation turns me on so hard I see red—a soft, velvety, moist red I'd love to sink my teeth into.

How can she be like this with me?

I can't figure her out. From my experience, the extremes in this country are so very extreme. In general, Sweden is sexually more lax, but there are minorities in the US, to which some of my groupies pertain, who are mind-bogglingly liberated. Other minorities, like the cult Nadia has broken out of, seem so repressed I can't understand how they conduct physical relationships at all.

In neither camp is there consent to cheat.

What makes a woman as reserved as Nadia, one who has only good things to say about her husband, rub against a man she doesn't know? Her body's on fire for me, and there's no mistaking that she wants more than grinding.

I squeeze my eyes shut, searching for my morale. Fight to care if a guy I've never met finds out that I've slept with his wife. With the palm of my hand, I lock over her breast, enjoying its firmness as she arches into my touch. I move upward, massaging slowly, and that nipple—whichever gorgeous type it is—does what I wanted. It hardens, and it makes me moan.

"I… Can we?" she asks sweetly, like I'd ever say no to her. "Do you want…?" she continues, too shy or too wanton to finish.

"Fuck yeah, I do." I suck her lip into my mouth, breathing out harshly as I rock her closer. I squeeze her tight and inhale a long, calming breath, trying to refrain from combusting. I won't talk about that ring. Hell, she knows. I'll just make this night worthwhile.

I'm an expert in this field. I sense subtle signals from the female body. I touch, press, and build heat until they can no longer take it. I glide moisture through hidden crevices, intensifying the pressure in the exact spot and the precise moment when I know they'll soar. Oh I'll take care of Nadia. If she has regrets tomorrow, it won't be on me.

Just like that, my wish to console this girl, to make her forget her lousy life, turns selfish. I stand abruptly, bringing her with me. She yelps, legs clamping tight around my waist. Our mouths are slick with lust and saliva, and I don't stop kissing her as I move us. Her breathing is shallow. The girl is fucking starving for intimacy. Doesn't her husband make love to her?

The front door slams open, and Emil and Zoe tumble in, laughing in each other's arms. "Damn, they have hot magazines at the Twenty-Four Mart—Who knew?" Emil snickers.

"Shhh," Zoe slurs, way more sloshed than when we last saw them. Besides X-rated magazines, they must have located alcohol too.

"Guys, you here?" Zoe yells. I'm frozen, my back against the wall and Nadia's butt nestled over my raging hard-on.

"Ooh, they're—Look at that," Emil exclaims, arm heavy over Zoe's shoulders. "They're kissy-sweet with each other."

Zoe bursts out laughing. "Oh pumpy! You say the strangest things!" Then she narrows her eyes against the darkness—who does that—and as I walk us down the hallway, Zoe's slow, drunken applause erupts behind us.

"Yay, Nadia's finally getting laid. Treat her right, 'kay, sweetie? Make it count. Cuz that happens, like, never."

Whoa.

Neither of us replies to their cheers. I don't waver as I take her to my room and shut the door behind us. I do sober up a bit. Good thing too, because I was seconds from slamming her into the mattress and just—yeah.

I look at her now, sitting awkwardly at the end of my bed with her enormous, brown eyes twinkling up at me. She's shy, so damn gorgeous and shy. Is this the same girl who clung to me seconds ago, all but begging me to take her?

Christ, I don't remember the last time I've reacted this way to a chick. There's something going on between us—chemistry, electricity—whatever people call it. All I know is everything she does turns me on and makes me hornier than hell: the swirl of a lock of hair around a finger; teeth sinking into her lower lip.

I caught it back when I saw her at the Sunset show. It was our first concert warming up for Luminessence. Back then, she just gazed at me with those deep, secret-keeper eyes of hers, and I don't even think she remembers. The room took a thousand people. Among the thousand, I saw her and didn't forget.

"Are you okay?" I murmur, sinking to my knees in front of her. She worries her lip between her teeth. "I'm sorry about Emil. He's always like that."

Nadia shakes her head, and in the dim shine from the streetlamp outside, I catch the twist of her mouth when she answers. "No, don't be sorry. Your friend, he's sort of perfect for *my* friend." She lets out a sound that could be a laugh.

"She's pretty hardcore too, huh?" I laugh softly, not wanting to scare her off.

In this glow, I see her differently. Her face is a perfect oval with small, protruding cheekbones and skin that's unnaturally smooth in the dim light. Her lips seem redder than before. I want… Shit, I might *need* that color to be from my kisses.

"Zoe is crazy, and she puts up with me and my different kind of crazy, and I love her like crazy." The awkwardness recedes when she talks about her friend, and the nearness we had before leaks back in.

"So crazy loves crazy?" I help, which makes her snicker.

"Yeah, I think so."

My hands slide along the sides of her thighs, up the comforter until I circle her hips. Mirth sits in my throat at our easy banter. The gleam in her eye remains playful.

But then we connect; this sweet girl's knees peak around my body, and I'm welcomed by her. She's warm against me, her breathing changing. If destiny interrupted us with our friends' return, then now is when we're back on track. I'm going to please her.

"Are you where you want to be right now?" I ask quietly.

She nods, chocolate hair flowing over her shoulders. "I think I need this." The answer shoots straight to my crotch.

"In that case, I'm going to undress you."

On the couch in the den, she'd been writhing against me, all sensation and needing me bad. Now, I don't know why, but she continues on sheer willpower. Just—

If we do this? It's going to be because she craves me.

CHAPTER Six

DEEDS

NADIA

I keep telling him I want this. Keep telling him I'm ready. On his couch, I'd erased everything except his nearness, the sensation new and offbeat after such a long time.

He's in my space and insistent, beautiful in his desire for me. It's crazy to have someone want me like this again, stare at me as if they want to devour me, like they can't thwart what their body wants to do to me.

Bo nods once, another question from his position on the floor between my knees. I nod back, and my heart skips in anticipation. I exhale. Begin unbuttoning my shirt. The top one always gets stuck with its too-narrow eyelet.

Bo's hand comes up between us. Gently, he takes over where my fingers trembled, and he kisses me, kisses me the way he did when I forgot everything in the den. Bo's touch saturates me while strong fingers glide from one button to the next, revealing more of me with each move. My breath stutters because I'm not used to the heat pooling in my abdomen.

"You sure?" he whispers again.

"I'm sure…" My skin puckers in goose bumps at the quiet slide of fabric to the mattress. I hunch my shoulders protectively before warm hands cup them and skate the straps of my bra down my arms.

My awareness shifts to my breasts. The skin there is so sensitive right now, the cotton scrapes against my nipples as he pulls the cups down. Bo unhooks the bra with a sure hand, and I'm bare, so insanely bare in front of him.

A small, guttural noise vibrates in his throat, and my nipples tighten from it, giving me away. For a second, he sits back on his haunches, gazing at me. A part of me wants to keep my eyes open, but shame wins and makes me close them.

"Don't be embarrassed. You are so beautiful," he whispers, and I think of someone else saying the same thing. Guilt and freedom amalgamate in my chest. It's a strange, strange blend.

I suck in the deepest breath, waiting for his next move.

"I've wanted to see these babies," he whispers. "I've fantasized, imagining them. And they're—ah. I'm going to need my hands on them. I'll make you feel good, Nadia."

Before I can reply, he rises above me, hikes me up onto the bed, and lies down beside me, a leg over mine, so close he's firm against my thigh. Then his mouth comes down on mine. His fingers rake into my hair, tugging me flush against him, and with his other hand, he finally caresses my breasts.

I'm tight and warm inside. Instinctively, I clench my stomach. Bo shifts downward, and I stop breathing for a second as he latches on to a nipple and sucks me in with an insistence that makes my spine bow off the mattress.

I want more—need more—I'm not thinking clearly. So I shut my eyes. Block out memories, the past, and my grey future. I let myself experience this moment only, knowing deep down I deserve it. And it is—

Good!

I don't see him undress the rest of me. I don't see him peel off his own clothes. All I know is that not for a moment does he deprive me of his touch. A strong knee widening my posture on the mattress. His nose tickling hot air against me. Fingers caress and stroke, and when he needs both hands, his mouth is there, making me sigh.

"Hot damn," he husks as he blankets me, warm, scented with man and cologne, and I'd forgotten how soft skin is when it slides over mine. I curl my arms around his neck. Dip into the heat at his nape and inhale him.

I shouldn't feel this good.

I push the thought away, knowing we're here to savor. Bo presses a palm down past my hipbone, toward the center of my stomach and holds still, pushing in gently. I feel his eyes burning on me while he soaks in the whimper he extracts from me.

I'm already climbing. It's so hot between my legs, it's difficult to think straight.

That's when he begins to lap at me. First, he tastes my boobs, then he trails down my stomach until he finds me—*me*—and makes out with my—

I yelp. Stars prick behind my eyelids. I'm swollen there, ready, so made for this with him. He suckles on me, murmuring out his hunger.

"You are so delicious," he tells me, and when two fingers slide inside me and he twists my warmest nub between his teeth, I hold my breath so I don't squeal out my release.

My legs start shaking.

I fly. I fly so high.

After, I see the way Bo looks at me. His eyes are awed. How can his eyes be awed? We're not married. Bo doesn't love me. We don't even know each other.

"That was gorgeous," he whispers. Gaze still fixed on me, he sits up on his knee and fumbles with something. It's a condom.

I bite my lip, anxious. Wriggle uncomfortably beneath him. I want to get up and run off, but…

I also need him really deep.

He obeys my last wish, sinking quietly over me and spreading my knees with his. Panic rises in me because—

What about Jude?

"Are you okay?" Bo breathes against my ear. Hard at the apex of my thighs, he glides in my sudden slickness. It feels so amazing, I can't stop my hips from helping him. The perfection of the moment flashes through my brain. What I do might not be right, but it is good.

"I am," I say on a small pant, the word coinciding with a new sting of lust at the bottom of my belly. The anticipation, the dread and desire, they're slowly destroying me. He needs to do this, or I'll morph into something else. Yes, right now I am orange and flammable, but I can shrivel into grey remorse in seconds.

Bo understands.

Bo stops moving.

Bo presses against me with pleasure-soothing hardness, and when he insists, my body cleaves open, accepting his entry.

He's wide, unyielding even when the impulse to flee tenses my body. I make a noise that sounds like a croak, but it doesn't scare him off. He continues, pressing slowly into me, and then his breath hitches.

"You're tight," he sighs out. "Please, I don't want to hurt you. Tell me if I do." He fills me completely, my walls stretching to accommodate him. I can't really speak, because I'm bursting with the moment.

Sinking closer, he envelops me in his arms, his breath uneven against my neck while he waits for me to be comfortable. Only I am comfortable. So very, very comfortable. Timidly, I tilt my pelvis, a quiet encouragement.

My fingers dig into his shoulders, begging, and again he understands. We move. We both do, a synchronized, quiet dance, a wave of two bodies joined.

He feels better than anything has in so long. Every inch of my skin reacts to him as he claims me—carries me with him to this place where the good outshines the bad. Where guilt doesn't exist and misery has no place.

Bo doesn't stop until it's too much, and I subdue a scream below him, swelling and tightening around our contact. "Is it sweet?" he asks just when I can't think anymore, and that too adds to my pleasure.

My muscles quiver, lasting, lasting, but in the end, they relax, landing from the flight he took me on. His movements over me turn jerky, and his breath shudders hot at my ear.

I open my eyes, wanting to absorb how I make him feel, and in the dim light I see his bottomless ones, blind with desire, and the beauty of having caused such bliss rushes a shiver through me.

"Ah Nadia," he pleads, like he wants me to do something. My response is instinctive. I cup his face with my hands and make him moan out his climax against my mouth.

I REMEMBER BO RETURNING TO THE BED with a warm washcloth and cleaning my body. I remember being patted down with a dry towel afterward, making me feel cared for in my sated state. But I don't recall falling asleep.

It's light outside when I wake up. I'm in Bo's arms, and his chin is nestled over my head. I fit in against him, and with his arm loosely around my waist, we're in this sleep-embrace that's so natural it stings. I swallow, letting the morning flood me with the sins of yesterday.

"Yeah, that's how you jack someone off," Emil's voice mutters through the wall.

"Really?" Zoe asks, sounding surprised.

"No! If you had one yourself, you'd destroy it in three seconds flat."

Low snickers from Zoe.

I hear them so clearly, a flush of shame creeps up my throat and into my face. I don't want to consider what they might have heard of Bo and me last night. He'd been quiet though. *I'd* been quiet.

I'm always quiet.

"Hey, beautiful." Bo's voice is morning-raspy. I tilt my head back to see his face.

"Good morning." There's a smile in my voice. I hear it myself, and it's strange.

"Are they at it in there?" he asks, and I titter, uneasy.

"I don't know. It's hard to tell what they're doing."

"'Jack off?' Nah, it's pretty clear. As far as I know, it means—"

"Shhh," I cut him off instinctively, and he raises an eyebrow at me. "Dirty word?"

He retracts to better study me, but I hide quickly against his neck.

"Hmm. Nadia's blushing," he explains to himself. "You're even prettier when you blush, like last night when you—"

"Please!" I never raise my voice, but he can't say that word.

"Came?" His voice is silky and teasing and a bit merciless.

"You're mean," I mumble, my cheeks so hot I'm dying.

Lean arms cage me in and tighten around me. "You were perfect."

I don't reply because I'm embarrassed. Why would he mention something that personal? I don't *know* this man. And… I don't do this stuff.

Shame is a friend, a family member. She has returned full force, and now I fight her sister too: guilt. Guilt is never far behind.

Hard raps on the door interrupt us. "Nadia? You there?"

"Yeah," I start, then rinse my voice with a small cough and repeat it louder. I expect Zoe to open, not giving me privacy to get into my clothes. I even expect a few clever comments. I don't get either.

"We're heading out for breakfast. You coming?" she asks.

No. I need to go home.

"Sure, give us five," Bo replies.

"'Kay!" my friend sings out.

"I can't," I tell Bo.

"Aren't you hungry?" He brushes hair from my face the way he did last night when he comforted me. He pulls on a lock and tucks it between my shoulder and the pillow. Silly.

"Yeah, but…"

"He's waiting for you?"

I shut my eyes and taste the metallic flavor of guilt in my mouth. "Not waiting—"

"He's there though, right? Or is he deployed or something?"

Bo should be repulsed by my actions—he knows I'm married. My hands go up on their own, and the goal is to cover my face and black out his expression. Just… he doesn't look repulsed. He looks concerned.

Last night, the booze talked for me. This morning, I'm not an open book anymore.

"Ah no. I'm not an army wife," I say. I force myself to relax, and I say the only thing I can think of that will stop his questions.

"Okay, I'll do breakfast."

Chapter Seven

PAST

NADIA

I'M NOT IN OUR BEDROOM. I can't take it right now. My intestines rebel—they're rebelling and cracking open from the inside out. It's my heart and my stomach fracturing and bleeding out pain and sorrow and guilt, and I barely hold back the scream trapped at the back of my throat.

I'm face down on the sectional Jude and I bought at a yard sale nineteen months ago. We were so excited. I kept shushing him, mortified as he lipped off under his breath about all we could do on such a beauty in the right place. On the way home, he'd whispered details against my ear even though I'd told him it was too much. To commit these deeds was one thing, but to talk about them? He laughed. He was sweet, funny, and adorable. My beautiful husband that I'd do anything to make happy.

But now I'm face down. Just.

Face down.

Jude isn't here. I need him to hold me and forgive me over last night. I bawl into the pillow.

Zoe's at the door, banging, but I'm not opening. How can I? I'm a mess. I hate myself. I hate what I did. *Me.* All I want is Jude's embrace so tight around me I can't move a muscle.

I can smell him even when he's not here. It's a crazy, symbiotic thing where I need him so much, I—

Zoe says it's not healthy. My parents would agree if they'd remained around after the excommunication. After I disobeyed them. After we eloped.

Work. Do I have work today?

"Nadia. Open the damn door. I hear you in there."

I don't care— I don't care— Let her… whatever she's doing.

My Jude.

"I'm demolishing your front door, babe." Zoe's voice flutters through, china-doll squealy and hyper-feminine. I'm lost in a misery I don't want to hold back because it's what I need and what I deserve.

"How can you understand?" I yell, replying to a question no one asked, but she hears and pleads and croons and lures.

I autopilot to her. Open. I'm back on our big couch. I want to suffocate in the depths of fabric-covered stuffing.

"Sweetie, Nadia-baby. It's okay." The compassion in her tone verges on pity, but I can't ponder the difference.

"It's not," I manage. "Who does what I did?"

"No-no. Baby girl. You were happy. Bo made you happy. I saw you." She wedges herself into the cushion, sinks down far enough to have my body slide into her lap. Light elbows nudge my thighs before she makes herself comfortable.

"You're so scared, Nadia. Don't be that, you know?" she murmurs. "Sometimes I wish I could pull you out of yourself and make you watch someone *like* you—but not really you—on a film or something. It'd all be so clear to you."

I don't say anything. I'm too busy controlling the blood splattering in a nonexistent carnage of my entrails. God, it hurts so much. I wouldn't wish this upon anybody.

There's a tremble in Zoe's voice too. "You deserve happiness. Can I ask you a question? Not if it makes you more upset though."

I can't think straight. The destruction beneath my ribcage roars. All I want is to fall to my side and heave my knees up beneath my chin. Curve my body into a ball.

Later, she makes me tea. My gaze keeps going to the door, looking, waiting, and when I do, Zoe's eyes blink quickly, forcing back moisture. "You're killing me, bitch, all right?" she says.

She doesn't ask her question until I've accepted cream and sugar in my tea. Until she has stirred it in. Until I take sips bigger than the initial, symbolic one to make her stop insisting. But when I've held the cup, drinking for a few minutes without coiling in over myself in pain, she stabs me with it.

"Have you thought about moving?"

"Moving? From *where*, our *apartment*?"

"Yeah. Don't you think it would be better to sell this place and get something new, a fresh start without the reminder of—"

"Of *what*, Zoe?" My question is a shriek, clumsy and harsh.

"Nadia, please." Zoe whizzes out a breath before she continues. "These last days have been difficult for you. I see that, and I— Whatever. I'm just gonna say it again: I need you to remember that you're my best friend. I love you so much, and there's nothing in the world I want more than for you to be truly happy.

"My grandma, a very smart lady, used to say that happiness is a fleeting thing. It's not a constant you achieve once and for all and then you're set. Well, I saw you happy for a long time yesterday. You even seemed happy for a sec at breakfast this morning."

"No, because I felt guilty. And there's no moving anywhere. Our apartment is perfect for us, with everything I've done to it. Perfect."

Zoe's chin quivers. It's the weirdest thing because she's usually unhampered by others' crazies. She's the kind of person who thrusts her head up and takes life on with a tilted smirk. If she were me, she'd *own* the pain instead of burying herself in it.

"Time," she whispers. "I wish you didn't need so much of it."

Zoe leaves a few hours later. She wants me to come along; Emil and she are going to a movie. Bo has tried to call me, she says, but my phone is off. That's the way it'll remain. Tomorrow, work will keep me busy. I have the early shift, and if Scott needs me, I might do a double.

I go to bed early. Wake up a couple of times throughout the night, soaking in my husband next to me. No words of reproach reach me like they should have from my vehement, fierce man. There's no grabbing my wrists and staring into my eyes, demanding to know, *"What the fuck?"*

I need his forgiveness or his anger hard. I drift off, and what I dream, I don't deserve. It's too good, the exact rerun of Jude's and my first time together.

"Are you afraid?" Jude whispers, blue eyes wide with concern for me. He cups my face with both of his slim, young, unfinished fourteen-year-old hands and kisses me before I can answer.

He wants me to be ready. His body trembles because it's not easy for a teenaged boy who visits his girlfriend nightly to stop at holding her close.

Jude's hair is too long. It tickles. He's less clumsy than a year ago when he first kissed me behind the church. I'm oversensitive and trembling like he is when his mouth finds my throat.

We've thought about this for months. It's serious, the ultimate rebellion against Mother, against Elder Rafael's dogmas. Yes, our union tonight is premeditated, and I probably wouldn't have done it if my boyfriend weren't Jude.

I need Jude closer than Mother. I need him under my skin. Once we consummate our love, the sensation of him will last through the day when he's not with me. I'll carry his memory within me stronger. For longer.

I wish he'd remained at the Heavenly Harbor School. It's closer to our house than his public school. I'd see him from my window, and his family would still be a part of our lives. Thank God no one stops outsiders from attending our sermons. My Jude is clockwork, showing up every Sunday. He seats himself in the pew behind me, infuriating Mother, and during the sermon his eyes keep my back and my heart warm.

Sometimes, I sneak off to the bathroom afterward, and if I'm lucky, I get a moment with him in the hallway. Last Sunday we lucked out. He caught my arms and hiked me up against the wall and kissed me deep with the fervor of someone drowning.

"You don't understand how much I love you, Nadia," he rasped.

But I do know. Because it's as much as I love him.

Now, his breath stumbles over the urge to groan out loud, and I let him remove my nightgown. "I brought protection," he whispers, fumbling down my stomach until he finds my mound. I shut my eyes when his fingers trace lower and locate my secret place.

The shame sits in my throat, wanting to stop me. My body tells me it's all sin, but my heart remains on Jude's side and it's stubborn.

My knee falls to the side, making things easier. We're not good at this though. "I think I need some light," he apologizes and turns it on. It's so much brighter than I can take. I cover my face with my hands.

"I'm sorry I'm not a pro yet," Jude chuckles, and despite it all, he makes me smile. This is Jude—*my* Jude—and he's pieces of funny, of wicked, of fierce, of sweet, the reason why I don't get up and scamper off.

The crinkling of a bag startles me. I close my legs, making them teepee between us and shutting me off from his actions. Intent on his work, he doesn't object. "Damn condom. I bet it's defective. They can't all be this difficult, right? Geez, big rubber factories, how 'bout you make something that works?" he mutters.

I roll to my side, knees up under my chin. Try to cover my butt with a part of the sheet.

"It broke. Hold on—I bought plenty. I figured I'd leave them here on your nightstand after," he jokes.

But then he's over me, all heavy boy, nuzzling my cheek and kissing my neck. "It's on. We can do it! You want me to make love to you, baby?" he asks.

"Dunno," I muffle into my pillow.

Jude turns me so I'm flat on my back and peeking at him from between my lashes. His eyes are so full of love my heart is about to explode. His body, naked like God put him on Earth. His member, latex-wrapped and pointing at me.

"You can always say no. I love you so much, Nadia. If you want to sleep instead, we will."

I hesitate. Seeing Jude like this, so gentle and soft and wanting me, makes me want to give myself to him. In my mind, the black smog of Elder Rafael's creed wavers, receding slowly with all its negativity. "I love you too. Come," I sigh out.

When he slumps down over me, he's eager and clumsy, and kisses I thought we'd perfected revert to ungainly. Teeth clack between our lips, and I giggle without a sound while he searches for me with a hand.

"Remember it will hurt at first," he says breathlessly. "I have to rupture something in you. The hymen."

"Okay…" My pulse quickens. What if I can't hold back? What if I cry out from the pain? Oh Lord please don't let my parents hear me. No, God—please don't watch us do this.

I hope He is far away, busy with someone else's wrongdoings while Jude and I love and sin. Or maybe Jude is right and God isn't revengeful. Maybe he's not the implacable god my family believes in.

Jude's mouth has turned hot against mine, hips grinding hard where I suddenly need him so much. Love is bright and shiny, sweet like my lover. He pushes me open between us with awkward tenderness.

"I'm going in now," he warns me, pitch breaking.

"Okay," I whisper because I can't take the suspense any longer.

"Okay… Putting it in," he pants, and from the sound, he almost doesn't need to be inside of me.

I'm anxious. I want the pain to be over. I want to be beyond the fear of waking my parents up. *Please, get it over with.*

"Stop if I start screaming," I say, and he freezes on top of me.

"You won't hurt that bad?" He wants to reassure me, but his words are a question. Jude's the one who told me how I'd feel. He researched it on the Internet, while I rarely have access to Father's computer. All I could do was believe him.

The pressure of him increases against me, and suddenly I don't feel like he should be down there. I already own all of his love; this—joining us—can't possibly make it grow bigger. The buildup against one small area of my body with him harder than bone doesn't feel natural.

I erase the thought. Breathe through the initial pain until he ruptures the first, soft barrier and exhales in a shallow pant as he pushes deeper.

"This… it?" I ask, because I hope it is. It's already a lot.

"No… there's more," he answers, his voice shaking.

"Hush," I whisper, reminding him to be quiet, but then a searing pain stabs me in hot, red places I'll never reach and it's my unplanned penance for the sin we're committing—

Oh God! Oh God!

Jerkily, erratically, he moves over me. I moan from the friction. Jude is merciless, hurting me… and rousing a little bit of wonderful at the same time. Unsure, I shape my hands over his behind. My heart skips at the tautness when his butt flexes.

The searing pain dulls, leaving moisture and warmth in its wake. He thrusts, working to make us both soar, but then he collapses so very quickly, wheezing a small groan out with his apology.

Skin pearled with sweat against my own, he whispers, "Ah. I'm sorry, Nadia. I had no idea it would feel this good. It's like you're squeezing around me— I… Shit. I couldn't control it at all." He chortles, embarrassed. "It'll be better the next time."

I emerge from the dream slowly, a smile in my heart at my silly Jude. Enveloped by love, by awkward sincerity, by unselfishness that couldn't outdo desire, I can't imagine a more beautiful way to lose my virginity.

"Jude," I sigh out. "Do you remember?"

PART 2
Wrath

Slamming the door shut on pain
Because turning it to rage is refuge

CHAPTER Eight

SMUT

BO

"Storage key?" I snap my fingers at Emil who doesn't react. That just-blow-dried, meticulously shaggy head of his dives into his backpack instead, in search of tweezers. Dude's the poster child for a lead singer, two hundred percent narcissistic, and now there's supposedly a stray hair between his brows. God forbid he rehearses with anything off-kilter on his face.

"In my pocket," he mumbles, rearranging the inside of his bag.

"Dude, I warn you. If you don't fish the key out ASAP, I'll be reaching in there for it myself," I tell him.

"Pff, hold on."

"You might never get to make mini-Emils," I add for fun.

"Shithead."

We're at the Marzania Rehearsal Studios where we rent

storage for our gear and rehearsal space while we're off tour. Los Angeles is full of bands, and rehearsal space doesn't just plop into your lap. When we got word of an opening a few months back, we immediately grabbed the chance. Marzania is expensive, but we're also with the big bands here. We rub elbows with Luminessence—who put in a good word for us to the owner—and other legends like Tom Rocks and Witch Cockers.

We finally stride down the hallway to our assigned room for the day, Emil with a bright pinprick on his forehead, a reminder that he ended up finding the tweezers. A text from Troy comes in, saying he'll be here in a few. He's just picking up bagels for us. Right. I have yet to eat today.

Coffee too? I text back.

Shit yeah. You owe me 20. Like 4th bagel run now.

3rd, I reply because I'm pretty sure.

No. 4th. Got receipts.

And Troy's the typical drummer: organized and on the ball to a fault. The only times he'll be late is if he's doing something for the band. Like now. He's the only American in Clown Irruption too. Our original Swedish drummer couldn't stand leaving his girlfriend and chose hos over bros back in the motherland. Yep, you got it: he too was assembly-line-worthy drummer material.

All rooms at Marzania are the same. Small and utilitarian, with matte black walls scuffed up by boots and instrument travel cases. Our room has a small podium where Troy assembles his shit once he arrives—drums always take the longest to set up—while the rest of us tune guitars and fiddle with the soundboard until Elias, the bass player, arrives.

"Dude, I forgot," he says, blowing white hair out of his hyper-light blue eyes.

"Did it have anything to do with a groupie?" Troy asks, eyes on the cymbal he's mounting.

"Oh hell yeah. Freaking Ebele from Nigeria. Damn, she's beautiful. She's like a New Year's Eve firework! Her boobs, man, and her ass—and her skin is so black it's, like, almost blue." Elias' eyes turn all beamy.

Emil starts humming *Ebony and Ivory*, and I can't help snorting out a laugh. Because seriously, it's hard to get any less colorful than Elias. He'd give hospital sheets a run for their money.

Troy, who's African American, a taller version of Lenny Kravitz, and a total babe magnet with his safari green eyes, smirks. "Opposites attract—again, Elias."

"All right," I say. "Enough talk about chicks or Emil will be demanding a shower break before we even start, here."

Troy points at me and moves his hand seamlessly into the universal sign for rubbing dollar bills between his fingers. "True, time's money. It's ten already."

"Exactly." Elias flings his arms out. "Why does Bo get to decide this shit? We're a *rock* band. Party until dawn, roll out of bed in the late afternoon, then rehearse all night."

"Elias is shouting," Emil mutters into the microphone in lieu of the regular "*Testing, testing*."

"Okay, quick reminder everyone." I grab Emil's mic unnecessarily. My own is wired and ready to go, but he's mounted his on the stand already. "Nights in this joint are always—*always*—booked solid. We good?"

Thankfully, once Clown Irruption starts, we don't stop. We don't take breaks until someone's bodily functions crave it, and with that I don't mean Emil's sex drive. Not usually.

At one fifteen, we all pee like racehorses. We have the room for another four hours—a good day—and we're not wasting it on a lunch break.

At three, Elias' skinny-ass stomach is growling. He sets the mic against it and turns the volume up, which coincides with Zoe calling Emil to let him know she's outside.

"You're all pussies," I tell them.

"Bo's being a butt," Emil says into the phone and angles me a look. "He's in a mood, all obsessive and shit. He won't let me out to play."

"Dude," I mumble. "We're on a roll." This is an uncalled-for break, so I might as well spend it wisely and exchange my guitar cable. The old one has been causing random static all day.

"He's *inspired*," Emil mock-specifies. "Hold on, I'm gonna take my chances and let you in, Zee."

I'm pretty sure those words are the death sentence for today's rehearsal; once Emil's got a girl over, all he wants is to swoon out lounge lizard versions of our ballads with the purpose of drenching the girl's panties. Then he whisks them off to the bathroom to perform damage control slash first aid on his victim. Always the romantic.

The two of them are all over each other by the time they trip in the door. The rest of us greet Zoe with a chin pump or a wave. She's cute, for sure, and has that playful blonde thing going for her that Emil likes. They've hung out for days now, ever since we got off the road Sunday. I'm impressed. Might be her mouth, in more ways than one.

"Hey guys," she greets us back. "Emil says you've got a new song."

And that'd be an understatement. We've been working on five, but I know which one Emil means—the X-rated one. Elias enjoys playing the bass line on it, the main reason why we've been concentrating on it for so long today. Not to brag, but it's sexy as hell, with a slow, deep, lingering thud that vibrates through your balls. Emil grates out the melody and the lyrics, his voice still road-worn, which suits the song.

I wrote it after Nadia left that morning. I was hard the rest of the day and needed an outlet. All I could think about was the agonized, heated look in her eyes, the timid way she'd raised her hips to meet me, guilt and denial and lust warring in every shift of her body.

At one point I'd pushed her wrists into the mattress. Stared into her eyes and *owned* her. I told her sweet things I meant, about how beautiful she was and how she shouldn't be ashamed. If you do it, mean it, they say, and for me, that girl was gasoline. I fucking did it, and I meant it hard.

Is it biological that we react to people in different ways? Why did one night with Nadia flood me with a level of creative juices I haven't experienced since my string of breakups with Ingela? To this day, the only song of mine that has set college radio stations on fire is *Never Ever*, which I wrote while I was dying over a love my ex deserved and I didn't have in me to give her.

Nadia. Christ, she gave herself to me, and yet she's not going to be easy. I should lay off—the girl's baggage is *boulders*. Just, she jacks my pulse up with how she slinks off and doles out fragments of herself.

I'm in trouble. There's so much there, behind that chocolate brown curtain of hair and those well-deep eyes. I want to own her secrets.

Nadia, I begin in my mind, *maybe I just need to—*

"*Fuck You*," Emil says, "is the name of the song."

"What? That's a crazy title. You know you'll have to come up with an alternative, right, because it's going to be censored the crap out of on the radio," Zoe tells us.

"See?" Elias says as if we haven't already discussed this.

"Yes, and we don't give a damn, Bo says," Emil nods out.

"Or maybe what he actually said was 'let's wait until we cross that bridge. It's not even finished yet,'" Troy supplies, and I feel special because they're treating me like the bandleader I am for once.

"Soo… are you going to play it for me?" Zoe asks.

"Oh babe, yeah, yeah, because it was written for you," Emil smarms out, thrusting his cock against her hip. Dog.

"Reaaallyyy? Omigod, you're so sweet."

We all turn, fiddle with monitors or scratch our foreheads while Emil sticks his tongue so far down Zoe's throat he might as well have gone for a blow job.

Damn, I think Zoe gets Emil. I mean, when has a girl ever found a song named *Fuck You* romantic? The minor issue about me writing it over another girl doesn't faze him. I did get a quick "Sounds like Bo's stoked on a lady?" from Troy when I first played it, but apart from that, the guys have stuck to music-related comments.

"Sugar Cookie," Zoe hums between smacking noises. "You don't have to lick my teeth. People don't have nerves in their teeth."

"No, I think they do," Sugar Cookie says, squeezing her butt. I'm seeing a bathroom visit in their near future, maybe even before we play the song.

"Oh yeah," she agrees. "Like for instance, it hurts at the dentist's sometimes."

Emil *mm-hmms* and presses her into the wall.

"Okay. 'Nuff public display of all-but-nudity," I say, and Emil lets out a disgruntled huff.

"Dude's so bossy."

"You realize minutes and rehearsal dollars are ticking away from us while you grope each other, right?"

"Your drummer makes us sound dirty, Cooks," Zoe murmurs, all sexy-sounding.

"See? Now you've hurt her feelings, Troy."

I clap my hands. "Okay, eyes on me? Ready to roll?"

Wide-legged, Emil trots back to his stand, grabs the microphone, and does another *mm-hmm* into it for the sake of the girl. She giggles… and freaking puts a finger in her mouth. Jesus. If she sucks on it, that's it: I'm tossing them both out. We're not made of icicles.

Troy counts us off without waiting for me, probably catching on to how I'm about to lose it. Elias cuts in with the slow, sexy bass line, nailing you right in the cock. Emil's little *uh-huhs* and *yeahs* begin to slink out. He's a pro at sounding like he's under the same sheets as the woman he stares at in the audience, and this song is perfect for it.

The little groans of contentment the tune calls for are exactly what Emil emits through the wall between our bedrooms most nights. My cunning plan is to get us a new apartment with the sleeping quarters on opposite sides of the digs. It probably won't muffle the lighter pitch of his girls, whose sounds I can absolutely live with, but it should keep Emil's grunts from haunting my dreams.

I compose most of our songs, and I'm also Clown Irruption's lyric writer. This particular tune though is all music. The words are banal and repetitive, but they're only there as another instrument to add to the mood. And the mood I wanted to create was—

Horny as hell, sexy as shit, go-all-out hotness, and plain old dirty, all-consuming lust. Oh yeah. Exactly the way I felt buried deep inside Nadia, staring into her eyes and wanting to possess her and convert her too into pure pleasure.

Holy shit, when she came.

"Fuck you. Fuck you. I want to fuck you again," Emil husks out. Sex is so thick in his voice, he's sobbing the words out. Hell, I'm growing behind my guitar.

"Oh I'll take you 'til you come, come, come."

Who needs porn when you can sing songs, right?

The initial sluggish, lingering rhythm is the first slow strokes inside a woman, sensing her warmth, her moisture, the tight embrace, the ultimate welcome.

Troy's drums, man. He's in it, his body moving seamlessly, a slow wave behind the skins as he bangs out the most perfect lay, speeding us up steadily until we're frantic, banging, banging, my back-up vocals gravel-gritty, supporting Emil's roar of mercy.

Troy's hands blur as he punishes the drums, rocking,

shaking in his seat, death-metal hard and so fast he could have doubled with a clone. I barely catch a glimpse of Elias from within my own haze. His fingers fly across the bass, ripping, faster, faster, simulating the last sprint of my last fuck if I hadn't held back.

We've rehearsed this: we're completely in tune, freezing the song just when everything becomes a maelstrom of sensation, pleasure, insanity—hysteria! It's the ultimate orgasm, and the last echo lingering for just the barest nanosecond is Emil's *"Gimme more!"*

I'm not the only one slumping my shoulders once it's over. Like *Never Ever*, this little thing won't be our opening song. It's a workout, and you either want to take a nap, like after an actual lay, or just… barge out in search of the real thing. Yeah. I can see it as one of the last songs of the night.

Besides everyone's harsh breathing, the room has gone quiet. I don't care enough to check out our one-female audience's response to *Fuck You*. I wrote it to relieve some pent-up horniness over a woman I'll probably never have in the way I describe in this song, and the guys happened to like it, so—done deal.

The skin on my index finger, so calloused from the constant contact with metal strings, has ruptured. There's the faintest hint of pink shining through, and under the right circumstances it could be taken for blood. I'm surprised. Because from years of abuse by guitars, my fingertips could probably rebuff gunshots.

I guess hammering this song out in front of my muse's friend did inspire me; Emil might not be the only one giving his all—which is how it works between the four of us: one band member's inspiration gets the others rocking. If two of us, like in this case, go ape, insanity ensues, and it's out-of-body. I wish we'd caught it on film.

Finally, I focus on our audience. In my limited experience with Zoe, she's not one to be rendered speechless. Turns out she is now, and in her expression, there's a naked vulnerability, an openness you don't see unless you're in bed with someone who loves you and trusts you like crazy. Someone this unguarded can make the most jaded bystander uncomfortable. But we're bare too, after giving it all in this song.

"Zoe," Emil croaks out. "Let's…"

I hear the others shift around us. Start unplugging gear and crinkling with bags. We're giving them privacy.

Yeah, this was too much. Zoe wasn't prepared for her own reaction to the song and neither were we.

Emil, he's utterly extroverted and everyone's best friend, including mine. When he embraces her, it's like he wants to shield her from our unintentional voyeurism by making her disappear in his arms.

He mumbles something against her ear, and Zoe's short replies erupt with a breathing pattern that speaks of a heat no one but Emil should be privy to. It makes me clear my throat in an attempt to block her out.

"Guys, we're off," Emil says after a minute, and I'm impressed. No rambunctious laughter or silly behavior from my best friend and no bathroom visit for his chick. Emil's hooked. It makes me wonder if it's the real deal.

"All righty then," Elias quips, head in the song and thoughts probably in the Nigerian girl.

All of these feelings. I guess I just wrote us some smut.

CHAPTER Nine

THANKS

NADIA

"How could you do this to me?" I sob out. "You suck, Jude! I'd never pull this on you." I'm flinging cups and plates in our kitchen, all china Jude took me to buy with his first paycheck. "You're the worst husband ever, and I hate the day I fell in love with you!"

My phone rings, and it's making me mad too. I can't deal with this much crap at once. All of this. Every single problem in my life. Is due to my beautiful, wild, sweet, kind husband who's a traitor.

I slump to the kitchen tiles, raking shards between my fingers, not budging when they pierce the flesh of my left ring finger—because it's perfect, right, true to who I am right now.

"See?" I hold up my hand, do a small circle on my knees in the kitchen, showing him, showing him. "Okay,

I can do better," I yell. "Here."

I was raised to become a silent, subservient wife to a godly husband. Twice now in as many days, I've lost my temper, and it makes me sadder than I was before. On TV, people say it's good for you to "let it out," but me, I feel worse.

I just screamed my heart out at the love of my life, and I hurt so bad. I'm furious, my cracked-open heart destroying me, and though I'll regret it later, I shoot the simple, gold band through the room and watch it ricochet off the wall and bounce in short, metallic clangs against the ceramic.

"Your. Fault! Help me, baby. Help me."

Jude doesn't come in.

The phone. The goddamn phone. That's work buzzing me, and I'm supposed to be there. As I get ready, putting makeup on in the mirror, hyperventilating, drinking cold, thick coffee from the machine, I calm down enough to seem coherent.

"Remember? Everyone came. Full-on party, it was. Flowers everywhere, no surface spared. Your parents, all of your best friends from San Francisco from before you moved to Payne Point—people I hadn't even heard of came. Your high school buds from Payne Point, hey, even the cheerleader that liked you so much. My family didn't come, of course, but everyone else wore their most expensive, most beautiful clothes as they entered 'The Garden.'

"I did too. I wore the red, silk-like dress. Remember how I surprised you with it when we got engaged on our way to Vegas before the wedding? Thanks to Mother's rules, you hadn't seen me in anything like it before. We'd escaped my family's claws. Love won!"

I pull open the bottom drawer. Haul the blow dryer out and stare at my reflection. I wet my hair down and blow from the top, smoothing it down so it's as flat as it can go despite its natural texture with the waves trying to break through.

"The outfit you wore, amidst the beautiful decorations in 'The Garden,' was the most gorgeous suit I've ever seen you in. Better than what we hastily rented in Vegas before Beauty hauled you inside the church and the Beast grabbed my hand for you and plopped it in yours for holy matrimony."

I shove my feet into my work shoes. Take steps that are too long to be comfortable toward the door. I need to get out, away, be done with this. As I turn, a faded flicker of light at the far end of our hallway catches my attention, but it disappears before I can register what it is.

"I gotta go. *Someone's* got to work, Jude. Just, you need to know how much you suck. Everyone was there, dressed to a T, loving you. And you?

"I don't want to remember your face, because it was just a salt-stone non-expression. Never, never, never had you done this to me. Okay, I'm not dumb. I get why, but… How could that expression accompany the best suit of your life? We were all there for you, and you—

"The lack of emotion in every limb of your body… damn you, Jude!"

I lock the door behind me and start down the narrow driveway. Then I turn and scream back at our windows. "Thanks for screwing me over!"

NADIA

It's easy to forget my outburst in the stacks of cups, tourists, dirty plates, spoons, and the napkins stuck to the restaurant floor. I can do this. Two hours into work, I'm having one of my better days. The owner, Scott, nudges my side and winks conspiratorially at me, wanting me to know he's got my back. He's a sweetie. Around fifty, not yet obese but getting there, his bluish nose a reminder of steady alcohol abuse.

"Good job, Nadia. The customers like you," he reminds me. Since I started here, he's been my cheerleader. Zoe's original impression was that he liked me too much, but in the years I've worked at the diner, he has never eyed me in an uncomfortable way. I think he just wants the best for me.

"They love your food is all," I reply, making him chuckle happily. Scott's Diner is not only his livelihood. It's his life. Scott's regulars become his friends, and he's as much in the kitchen whipping up food as the cooks.

The bell jangles over the door. It's four thirty, late for the lunch crowd, but the group entering takes my breath away. I don't need to see perky Zoe in the front troupe to recognize them. No, these boys are their own sort of recognizable.

Somehow they stand side by side inside the narrow entrance. Four guys, the same height, broad shoulders and slender build. They're different shades of color, from Troy's gorgeous chocolate, via Emil's sun-kissed Scandinavian and Bo's indoor artist pale, to Elias' ghostly white. Every one of them with model-worthy features and different degrees of smoldering. What the heck are they doing here? Emil's eyes burn against Zoe's bottom. Elias' milky blues scan the locale and briefly settle on a booth with four girls in their early twenties, whose skin color chessboard-matches Elias'. Troy, the drummer, seems to be the only one intent on food. Because Bo—

Is staring at me.

Oh Lord.

With Zoe being off and Victoria on break, I'm the only waitress on the floor. Victoria will be back in fifteen, I tell myself for no reason because no restaurant would wait to seat a party of five when there are ten booths open.

Zoe leaps in to hug me. Over her shoulder, Bo's eyes remain fixed on me. It's odd, so odd to see him at my job. We know each other in a different way.

I've had Bo's arms around me. His body against mine. He moved inside me, I—I've heard him sigh out in pleasure, and now he's just standing there. Customers pass him like it's no big deal that he's in here.

My cheeks flame.

Bo folds his arms over his chest, the angles of broad, bony shoulders making him look impervious to American food and oversized portions. The man is startlingly gorgeous, and my stare is glued to him.

My heart shoots into a crazy flight. I try to breathe inside Zoe's embrace while she chatters about super sexy songs, about intercourse, wild boys, Emil, even something about Bo and me.

I finally break free of her. Striding toward the restroom, I call out for Scott to seat them. He nods and gives me a thumbs-up, but I know he expects me to take their orders once I'm back. *At least take care of their beverages,* I plead inwardly.

I'm not a big drinker, but now I wish I had a flask of something strong hidden in the bathroom. I lock the door behind me and hang over the sink, palms pushing down against the porcelain. What did I think would happen? That I'd never see him again? Zoe has a crush on Emil, and they live five minutes from my job! It's a miracle I haven't seen them in here before. I lift my gaze and find myself in the mirror.

"Nadia. You okay?" Zoe calls from outside.

"Yeah, be right there."

Half an hour ago, I gathered my hair in a loose ponytail. Now I pull the hairband out and shake my head carefully so it doesn't poof up. Brown kohl still lines my eyes. I'm not wearing lipstick, so I bite my lips to force some color back into them. Then I blush, realizing that I'm primping for Bo.

Crap. Crap. Crap.

I'm so confused right now.

I draw in a deep breath before I leave the restroom. Zoe has seated them herself. I can tell because she chose her favorite, ten-person booth with the great view of the street.

The guys are chatting quietly among themselves, Troy writing something out on a napkin with Elias nodding his approval. Bo isn't paying attention. He's leaned back against the faux-leather upholstery at the center of the booth, his eyes twinkling from beneath his bangs as he follows my progress toward them. I swallow, sensing the blush creep up my throat.

"Hi, guys," I say, clicking my pen open over my order pad. If I can slide back into my waitressing mode, I'll be fine. "Good to see you. What're you having today?"

"Nadia!" Emil calls out like we're best friends. He nudges Zoe in against his side, and she grins, charmed. "How've you been? Why didn't you come to the movies with us the other night? T'was a good movie. Something about a, um..."

"A boxer who needed to win a championship to get the girl," Zoe helps. "It was romantic. Nadia knows. I've told her about it."

"No." Emil shakes his head. "T'was more of a cool movie. That was some bad-ass boxing." He juts his chin at Bo. "Remember all the blood in that last scene? Whoosh! And sex. Geez, but it took the poor guy forever to get laid."

The good thing about Emil and Zoe together is that I don't have to say much; Emil put me on the spot for exactly two seconds before they went out on a tangent about a completely different subject. Sometimes I wish I could do that. Switch gears on a whim and just... snap out of things.

"How are you?" Bo's voice is much lower than the others', but I still hear him better and it spreads instant heat in my abdomen.

"Good," I manage. "Working. Busy, you know."

"Right," he says. "When are you off?"

I'm too stunned to lie. "Eight."

"Plans after?"

"Well, no but—"

"Is he waiting for you?" His eyes gleam as they glide down to my left hand. On impulse, I hide it behind my back.

"Sort of," I reply at the same time Zoe murmurs, "He never does."

Bo sits forward in the seat, elbows on the tabletop, and it feels like we're inches apart instead of on opposite sides. His intensity eats up the space around us, and I'm not the only one feeling it. Besides Zoe's input, our exchange has been so quiet it's almost a whisper, and yet the conversation dies out among the others. That includes a few regulars at the bar.

"Can I pick you up?"

"I'm eating here," I blurt out clumsily.

Calmly, he negotiates with me. "Then we won't eat. I'll take you somewhere else. The boardwalk?"

"I. Um. I mean… no."

Even Emil turns his head to look at Bo. "Bowling?" he cuts in, and that breaks the silence around the table.

"Hell yeah," Troy laughs. "Bo sucks at bowling. Let's do it!"

"Fuck," Bo mutters and sinks his forehead into a hand. The smirk lifting his mouth isn't lost on me—it makes my heart skip; I'm affected by every little thing he does, it seems, and it's both delightful and painful.

"Are we talking similar to his kite-flying skills?" I can't help asking, which sets Emil and Elias off into guffaws.

"Yes! He's one for the books. Ah you've got to see this, Nadia. Sorry to say, you might not like him anymore after," Emil says, drying an eye, and then I blush again because—really, that's how obvious I am? Anyone, even egocentric Emil notices.

Thankfully, no one comments on my general state of flustered. Bo keeps an eye on me though while I take their orders. Thank you God they're straightforward: burgers and fries all around.

"Eight o'clock," Bo reminds me as I walk away with their orders.

"Eight," he whispers playfully every time I come by to refill their drinks. When they get up to leave, with Zoe wrapped around Emil's throat and half-carried out onto the sidewalk, Bo turns in the doorway to give me one last mouthed *Eight*, and I smile.

I smile!

CHAPTER Ten

TRUTH OR DARE

BO

GIRLS JUMP MY COCK WHENEVER I ALLOW IT—I'm used to giving and taking what I want. They hunt me down before shows, after shows, even in bars and in back alleys. They're creative too, good at making me curious. It's the rocker thing: chicks dig it. All I need is to lean back and watch. But here I am now, in this situation where I'm chasing a married woman—even though I've already had her. It's absurd.

I know who I am and what I'm capable of. Those bedroom eyes from the audience? They get to my wang, but they don't get to *me*.

Nadia showing up at our last show made me ponder my relationship with my ex again. Year after year, Ingela looked at me with adoration in her eyes, while I, no matter how deep I searched, found nothing in my black, selfish soul. Over and over I hurt her because I couldn't fake what I didn't have—a goddamn heart. It's why I stare out over the masses in arenas without the awe Emil's face sometimes reveals.

I told Nadia that night; people don't do it for me—music does. Just another way of being emotionally stumped, I guess. I haven't looked into it closely enough to diagnose my condition, but I know I'm not a sociopath. Not a psychopath. Definitely not asexual—hell, sex is the only way I make a woman happy.

At the last thought, my mind returns to Nadia, and my dick twitches. Sex with her was insane. Not since I last slept with my ex over a year ago have I had sex that good. I was so turned on I couldn't think straight.

It's weird, because she wasn't trying to blow my mind. There've been acrobatics involved throughout our tours—overflow Luminessence groupies with a limberness beyond anyone's fantasies and swallowing techniques that can blow a guy's mind. None of that came close to the simple, real, understated sex with Nadia.

The scent of her hair, the flower perfume or soap or whatever she'd used. Then the secret aroma of her pussy. It called to me, I swear. Great, and now I'm rock hard again.

Because I like her, the situation with her husband is starting to piss me off. Nadia is young. She's wasting her life on some asshole who doesn't appreciate her. She's miserable, and you don't need to be a rocket scientist to get that it's his fault.

I've been that guy. In my case, at least I never married the girl, and I made love to her as often as she needed it. In my defense, I tried. I really tried to make it work.

From Nadia's reaction to my slightest touch, I'd say she hadn't been fucked in a while, and that's just wrong. If she doesn't turn him on, then *her husband* must be stumped.

And seriously: what kind of douchebag doesn't care enough to call his wife when she hasn't returned from a concert at nine—the morning after?

Yeah, me chasing this particular married woman might not be so absurd. If she's game, I'll brighten her day again. Make her understand how beautiful she is, how easy it is for her to make a guy feel horny as shit.

Hell, this is me paying back karma over Ingela. Right—good. That's why I'm picking Nadia up from the restaurant right now.

"Hey," she murmurs timidly. She's still wearing her apron and tugs to get it off.

"Hey," I reply, the grin growing on my face. She's tired, but she must have done something to her face and hair, because the redness in her eyes is the only thing giving her away.

"I like your lips," I say, because I do. I shrug inwardly. I'm not a blurt-out kind of dude, but I guess that one escaped. She flushes immediately, which doesn't help my already aroused state, and I hear myself say, "Screw bowling. Want to go to my place?"

She gasps like I'm being indecent. Which, to be fair, I am.

"No, I mean, we can pick up a movie."

Smooth, Bo.

"What movie?" she asks, and I feel like she's buying time. Then she hurries on, not waiting for my reply, "No,

I'd like to watch you bowl."

And so we go. I take her to the bowling hall and struggle through a few hours of Emil's inane chuckling and Elias' chicken dance whenever he gets a good score. Troy discretely kicks everyone's ass, whooshing his ball down the lane like a pro.

Turns out Troy *was* a pro for a year, and his father owns a bowling hall. Sadly for us, he collects his winnings before he reveals this. How did I not know that about him? Nadia was the one asking—I never even thought of it. We all put too much money into the bets too, so here we go, shoveling out green to Troy yet again. I'm amazed at his financial astuteness. It almost rivals his drummer talent.

"Just for five minutes?" Zoe bats her lashes to her friend, who looks uncomfortable.

"I need to go home to Jude," Nadia mumbles.

Zoe's reaction is interesting. Her eyes flare with anger, her hands actually fisting at her sides, and when she opens her mouth, it's like she's trying out words first, censoring herself before she selects the few clipped ones she uses. "No, you do not."

Nadia has responded to my charm before, so I turn it on. With my arms folded, I nudge her with my elbow and go, "Nadia, the ice cream Emil and Zoe bought the other night? Is still in the freezer. Shh," I add, tip my head in against hers, and glance around us surreptitiously. "It's calling your name."

"Yeah, dude!" Emil exclaims, pointing at Nadia, probably worried that Zoe will leave with her if she doesn't come along. Everything Emil does is for Emil.

"Do you work tomorrow?"

"I have a full-time job, yes," Nadia says.

"Early?" I insist.

"No, late shift."

"So that decides it. Let's get going before the ice cream melts."

Nadia's lips are a plump, succulent red, and now she can't stop them from stretching. Shit, she's sweet when she smiles. "Melting in the freezer, huh?"

"Probably. Thinking of you."

Out in the parking lot, I glimpse her face. She's bright red. Maybe at my last flirty comment? Damn, I feel young—puberty-raging-hormones young. I'm thinking it could be uncomfortable to spend a lot of time with her if the night doesn't go the way I want.

Once we pull up to our place, Emil and Zoe spill out of the backseat and head upstairs without waiting. From inside, Zoe's halfhearted call, "Nadia, let me know if you need me, just—um, knock on Emil's door," reaches us.

I look at Nadia, really look, under the porch light. She doesn't meet my gaze. I brush hair away from her face and tilt her chin so I can study her. She doesn't object, but her lashes flutter low enough to conceal her eyes.

I curl my hand, using the backside of it to touch her cheek. Move it down slowly until I reach her throat. "Do you want to come upstairs?" I ask quietly. "I'd like you to. Very much."

I'm not making up stories now. Her throat lifts and sinks as she swallows, struggling with herself. She understands that what I'm implying is not ice cream on separate chairs in front of the TV.

She doesn't reply, so I grab her hand and take the first steps. She hesitates, but then comes along, her grip in mine tightening. And damn if that doesn't make my bloodstream come alive. It rushes through me, pumping fast in anticipation.

"You're special," I whisper as I kiss her backwards in through the apartment door. "I've never met anyone like you, Nadia. Jesus, you're so…"

I'm not a bedroom talker. I'm your quiet guy, the one who prefers to make the girl babble and moan and scream. I observe, enjoy what I do to her. My own voice? I hear it enough as it is. And yet here I am, rambling to Nadia between kisses.

Her mouth puckers through our kiss, tongue meeting mine and sucking. My bedroom door is behind her. I push it open and bring her with me, an arm under hers, lifting her off the floor. I'm impatient. Damn, I'm—

Bo, she's skittish. Calm the fuck down.

I need to rein myself in.

With a palm at the back of her neck, I angle her upward for better access to her mouth. I lick, and ah, the top button of her shirt has come undone. I slide a hand inside, flat against her sternum, and stroke downward until I cup a breast inside her bra.

"Uh." The sound puffs out of her, and it's natural and genuine. Such a small sound. She's not trying to impress with fake pleasure—I'm losing my shit!

"I love your tits, all of you. You're so damn delicious."

Her breathing speeds into short, shallow pants at my words, and I haven't even removed her clothes yet.

"I was afraid you wouldn't come with me tonight. So

glad you did," I pant out, grinding her against the leg I've wedged in between hers. She clamps around me, not riding, but holding on like a good girl.

"I… wanted to," she says.

"You like me?" I sound like a five-year-old.

"Who doesn't?" is her answer.

I lift her and press her against the wall—the same wall Emil is already banging Zoe against on the other side. I smooth my palms against her skin, pulling upward, crumpling her shirt up and helping her raise her arms so I can tug it off. Boob, lots of boob quivering on such a skinny little body. I stroke the indentations between each rib and wrestle her bra up over taut nipples.

"I don't know all of your secrets, baby," I groan, pressing myself into her, crowding her. "But I'm going to extract every damn detail. I want to know everything about you. Nadia, you're a mystery, a fucking million songs waiting to be written."

She likes what I'm saying. She lets out a small, guttural sound, her body alive and squirming against me.

"Since the other night, you've been all I can think of," I whisper, setting her down to work on her skirt. "The way you felt under me, and…" I cover her mound with my hand, pressing my middle finger inward right at the center. "…*around* me."

Shock and pleasure intermingles in her eyes, and I let go of her panty-clad pussy to grab her face and hold it steady against the wall. I suckle on her mouth, lubricating it with my tongue the way I will her honeypot in a minute. She's going weak in my arms, but she's holding on, fingers clutching around my shoulders.

"Did you like it too?" I ask, daring her to peek outside her sheltered, demure world. A small whimper is her answer. I thrust myself hard against her center and repeat, "Did. You. Like. It?"

Her whimper is louder, and it turns me on so hard I'd come on the spot. I don't though. Hell no, I'm not ruining this.

"That a 'yes,' baby?"

"Yeah…"

Because she made me wait, because I didn't speed up and pound her the way I wanted to the last time, because I dreamed of her while writing *Fuck You*—I grab her panties on both sides where only a string holds them together, and rip them off.

Nadia lets out a shocked little squeal, and I'm hardly recognizing the way I make love nowadays. It's her. All her. So modest, reserved, unpretentious, worried… secretive. I want to own her, and I'm impatient. I want her free—as free as in that small moment when she came the other night, spasming around me.

"Turn, sweetie," I manage, my voice thick.

She does, and she's all naked, the slope of her behind arching for me to feast on. I push myself against her first. Then I lower my shorts so I can rub my dick through her crack. Nice, warm cheeks just here for my pleasure, ready to do with what I want.

My hands go around her waist, fingers digging in so I can hold her tight. "Have you had sex against a wall before?" I ask, thrusting without entering. I shift to reach her boobs and knead while I work against her, gliding in her juices.

"No…"

I'm relieved and pissed for her at once.

Fucking husband.

"Raise your butt in the air," Emil grunts.

"I am!" Zoe replies.

"I know, but higher. You want me all the way in, right? This is, like, half the length—you're squeezing me out!"

"Hold on," she mumbles. "There?"

"Yeah, spread those bunny-buns, baby," he smarms, and I rip Nadia away from the wall and carry her to the bed.

"Shit, so sorry. It's ridiculous in this apartment."

"In ours too… the neighbors… all the time," she manages.

Emil has a full-on headboard. It's heavy hardwood, and I've told him time and again that he needs to move the bed farther out into the room. The guy never does. Now, it rattles hard against the wall as the two of them agree on a breakneck speed.

Nadia's eyes glimmer beneath me, desire and shame warring in them. She's withdrawing from me, becoming unreachable, and for her sake—for mine—I can't allow it.

I form the comforter around her, a makeshift cocoon, revealing enough skin for me to caress. In sweeps much lighter than I crave, I tease her with my nails first, then add the length of my fingers as I draw a nipple out in a gentler version of a kiss.

I keep my gaze hidden beneath my hair; she's not the type who gets a kick out of me studying her. I might get her there at some point, but tonight she's too conflicted, maybe too hampered by her upbringing as well. I need her to feel safe, safe enough to fall apart despite the insanity in the next room.

I'm over her, leaning on one elbow, thighs pleated with hers, my dick resting along her hip. I don't push against her anymore. No, I want Nadia to climb so slowly she's unaware of what's happening. I want her to surrender to pleasure in a way that would disregard a jumbo jet crashing into our room.

I make out with this girl slowly. We're already naked, and I'm dying to rush things so I can feel her around me, but we're better off with me putting no pressure, no time constraint on this.

The slightest massage of one breast as we kiss changes the rhythm of her breathing, and I don't move down her belly, don't explore other parts of her until she's arching into my caress with each hard inhale. When she does, I shift my hand to the delicate skin beneath her arm, touching her lightly, adding pressure with my fingertips. It's not what she wants—she's eager, goose bumps mixing with hot dampness.

Oh Nadia. She's impatient. We're getting there. I subdue my own need to groan. I wonder if I can make her beg? It might be too much too soon. Subtly, I rub myself along her hip in one stroke. She whimpers, a strong response to such a small move, and I pucker my mouth into our kiss to hide my pleased smile.

Finally, I lower myself. Slide my hand down her waist and find her hip. Just once, I grasp it firmly, showing her the control I could exert over her if I wanted to, and she lets out the smallest sob that goes straight to my cock.

"You're destroying me," I whisper.

"Why aren't you…?" She doesn't continue.

"Because I'm not sure you want it."

"But…" her voice is a whimper.

"But what?"

"I—do." Two small words that take effort for her to push out.

The headboard has stopped rocking in Emil's room. Thank you, Lord. Just quiet murmurs and small giggles reach us now and then.

"Can I unwrap you from the sheets?" I ask, nuzzling her ear.

"Yes."

I pull the blankets to the side one by one like I'm opening a gift. It's how I thought of her the first time too: a fucking present. If she were a guitar, she'd be a custom Fender in comparison to the crappy Epiphones offering themselves up after every show.

I want to play this Fender the way it's supposed to be played. I roll down her body, licking my way to that succulent flower of hers. Its light aroma causes that groan to finally vibrate from me, and she lifts her ass from the mattress, wanting my tongue deeper.

I'll give you deeper.

"Oh goodness," she sighs, surprised, a slight tremble in the muscles at the back of her thigh. I squeeze them and lap at her. "Bo…"

"Yes, darling?" The endearment just escapes, and I don't regret it.

Oh darling.

"I think I need…"

Ah she's about to beg. My hard-on rages. I want her to continue.

"Tell me what you need." I suckle, waiting, burying my tongue in her, tasting, loving her heat, and hoping she'll do it.

Nadia undulates against my face, working with me, helping. She whimpers again, and I adore the understated sounds she can't hold back. They mean so much more than any screams of pleasure.

"You don't want to say it?" I whisper hot against her clit. "Ask me, darling, and I'll give you whatever you want."

She inhales sharply and holds her breath for an instant. There's an internal fight going on, that much I catch. Then she exhales, and with the air she lets out comes what I've prayed for. "Bo, please… can we be… together?"

"All the way together? Joined?" I lash out a long stroke across her cleft again, making her jolt.

Her impatience with me is growing. Good. "Yes!"

"As in you want to feel me inside of you?"

"Oh God," she says, squirming beneath me. She doesn't answer, so I act like I'm going to lie back down again. "No, no! I mean—yes, please come inside of me."

"Come. Inside of me." Oh fuck me.

And so I do. I wrap myself in latex and press inside of her. I flip us around and stretch her out on top of me. She's timid, barely moves, flat and tense against me—until I start rocking into her, pressing her hips down so there is no space left between us.

"Oh darling," I mumble, "darling, darling," and her body reacts to my pleasure and starts a rhythm, rubbing her sweetest spot against me. When we come, we do it together. I'm deep inside her, swelling, twitching, and she clings to me, arms around my body and thighs clamped around mine as her orgasm shivers free.

I don't withdraw right after. The intimacy of the moment is too great, and I'm not going to lose it right now. Nadia's face is buried deep against my neck, and I feel her heart skittering as she comes down from the heights I sent her to.

I stroke her back like I'm her boyfriend. Soothe her until I realize she's crying. I drape a sheet over us because I don't want her to get cold.

"Are you all right?" I ask, because you never know with girls. Ingela cried a few times after a good orgasm. I hope that's Nadia's issue right now.

"Yeah." She sniffles. Rubs her face against the pillow beneath us before she turns back in against my neck. "I liked it a lot."

"So you're crying because I was a good lay?" I want her to giggle.

"Many reasons. That. My husband. My life. You know, good and bad mixed together," she says.

I roll her to her back. It's time I look her in the eyes again. I've never run away from hardcore emotions, and I'm not about to start now that this girl might be cracking a door open.

"Uh," she protests while I pick a strand of hair from her face and pull it out of the way. "You… slipped out."

"Feeling empty?" I ask, and she looks up at me.

"How did you know?"

"I've had girlfriends." I don't commonly speak about

my past. I sing about it.

"Do you have a girlfriend now?" she wonders, blinking. I can't tell what she'd think if my answer had been yes.

"No, we broke up a year ago."

"Do you miss her?" The question surprises me. Sure, this is pillow talk, but usually girls prod to make me say the sex was bad, that they're better, etc. etc. I never bite.

"Yeah, I do," I say.

"She broke up with you?" she asks too, and it's such a high-school question it makes me chuckle. What does it matter who breaks up with who?

"Yes, she finally found someone better. Someone who had it in him to love."

"To love *her*, you mean," Nadia says.

"Yeah. That too. I don't actually love though. I'm not made that way."

A small frown appears between her eyebrows, and maybe it's good we talk about this. I might as well lay it out in the open in case she, against all odds, ends up attached to me. What a shitty situation, right, to be married to a guy who doesn't appreciate her, and then taking a lover on the side who's unable to love her either. I laugh softly to myself.

"What?"

"No, I mean, really. I had the best girlfriend in the world. I meant everything to her, and she meant more than most things to me. But that was it. I'm a walking heartbreak."

She smiles at me instead of being outraged. Tips her chin up as if she's above me and looking down at me. "Nah. Hey, I believe the last part, that you're a walking heartbreak to the girls at your concerts, but of course you can love someone. You'll see.

"One of these days you'll meet the right girl, and you'll love her like crazy. I might not have much experience, but the way you listen to my needs without me even speaking tells me what an exceptional human being you are. Once you find that girl, the one you'll love the way your ex loved you, she'll be the luckiest woman in the world."

I'm stunned silent. It's the most I've heard this beautiful girl say in one sitting.

"Huh," I muster in the end. I knew she had depths she wasn't showing, that the mystery surrounding her is a big part of my attraction to her, but—wow.

"Sorry." She hides against my neck again, and I have no idea what she's apologizing for. "It wasn't my place to go in and psycho-babble you," she clarifies. "That just slipped out." She pulls away enough to meet my eyes again for a split second and says, "I meant every word though. You're a little bit... amazing."

Oh no, and then there's a sob in her throat again. She swallows it quickly, but she's still in my arms so I feel it quaver before it disappears. "Nadia," I say, sounding sterner than I am. "Just... ah. We need to talk. Can we talk?"

"I'd rather not."

I wish I knew what triggers her sadness. Is it just her husband? The whole getting hitched too early and being stuck in a cold marriage? She's too young and too special to deal with that. I can't even imagine.

"Nadia." I sit up against the wall and hoist her with me. She lets me, a small sigh of reluctance surging from her.

"Listen," I murmur. "There's this huge elephant in the room. I'll be nice—I won't pressure you into talking about it. I'll just tell you what I've gathered, and I want you to nod if I'm right and shake your head if I'm wrong. Can you do that for me?"

It takes her forever to respond. She's mulling it over. Her body rests on me, the weight of her head nice against my chest. I wonder if she hears the slow, steady thumps my heart makes, so different to the rhythm it jackhammered out while we made love.

"Darling," I whisper against her head. "That okay?"

This time she nods uncertainly.

I rake my hand into her hair and pull her back. Nadia's face is innocent, open, and anxious. The mixture does it for me, my dick engorging lazily beneath her thigh. It's been a long time since everything about a woman turned me on like this.

"So," I begin. "Your husband might have made you happy at some point, but he doesn't anymore." Really, what does it matter today if he made her happy back when? "Am I right?"

I wait. Slowly, she nods against my chest.

"You wouldn't have had sex outside your marriage if you got it at home." Every silent inch of her screams that I'm right. I still hold my breath, steeling myself for her answer, because what if she does this often? She could patent that look, that gorgeous display of innocence and restrained carnal need. Who the hell wouldn't want to please her right the fuck now with those eyes?

Yeah. I don't want that to be the case.

"No. Never," she says, and it's fierce and open and so

true my chest tightens with relief.

"Okay, down to the tiny issues. I'm curious. Bear with me."

She groans, worried, but she doesn't object. She snuggles tighter into me beneath the covers, a bare, warm embrace I haven't indulged in for months.

"Your husband's name is Jude."

She nods.

"He was born... the same year as you?"

She nods.

"You don't spend time together lately."

She doesn't nod. She doesn't shake her head at me either. Is there an intermediate level to this? You either spend or don't spend time with your significant other, right? Like when Ingela and I lived oceans apart. No time together. When we both lived in Gothenburg: tons of time together. Duh.

"No answer?"

She nods to that.

"Because it's complicated?"

She nods.

"Okay. Here's a new addition to your answers," I improvise. "If the answer isn't 'yes' or 'no,' just kiss my chest."

Through the mist of sadness my questions bring, her eyes narrow in a smile. "I can do that," she murmurs, and I kiss her lips, sucking a little on the lower one because I need to.

"Your husband is an asshole."

She kisses my chest. *It's complicated.*

"He's not currently appreciating you the way he should."

She nods.

"It's been like this for months."

"More," she responds without nodding or shaking her head.

"A year."

"More."

"Damn, Nadia. A year and a half?"

She nods.

"He hits you."

She shakes her head, adding, "Never. And that's it. I'm done talking about Jude."

"Ah come on. We just started!" I exclaim, surprising myself. I get focused as hell—it's why I'm a songwriter—but unless it's my siblings, I lose interest in people's dramas lightning fast. Not so with Nadia.

"Never mind. Sorry. You owe me no explanations. All we've done together is *not* play kites, suck at bowling, and… totally pull off slumber parties."

She hides her smile against my chest, and it makes me smile too.

I should let this go while she's okay, but instead I fire off another question. And while I utter it, I think, *What if someone had asked* me *that while Ingela and I were struggling?* I know what I would have done: I would have dodged the question like a cheap-stringed guitar.

"Have you considered leaving him?"

Her reply isn't a nod. It's not a shake of her head or a kiss on my chest. No. It's enunciated clearly, her eyes right on mine. "There *is* no leaving him behind."

CHAPTER Eleven
CONFUSION

BO

OPPORTUNITIES FLOAT THROUGH YOUR SPHERE, and it's up to you to seize them. Sometimes they stream back around, giving you another chance if you miss out, but that once-in-a-lifetime chance, you'll never see again.

Troll calls me while Nadia is still asleep. I don't release her from my arms when I grab the phone from the nightstand and answer.

"Bo. Radio One needs a fill-in. Tom Rocks was supposed to head up Luminessence on the night show, but they backed out last minute, and Luminessence's artist manager called yours. Clown Irruption is in."

Adrenaline rushes through my body. "Are you *kidding* me? Radio One?"

"Hell yeah, man. Radio Fucking One."

I start laughing. My stomach rocks, stirring Nadia

from her sleep. She *uh-huhms?* and I pull her close, kissing her temple way loudly for someone who's still in dreamland.

"Better make it, son," Troll grumbles, grouchy-sounding as usual.

"Of course, Captain. We'll be there. Are you emailing us directions and times?" It's a redundant question. He's always on top of the details, and he's snippy as hell about being second-guessed.

"Yeah, unless you've got *Internet*," he counters. "Ooh it's so hard to locate Radio One in L.A."

I bite my lip, suppressing my amusement. "What time?"

"Dude, I am going to email you, okay? God forbid you girls get lost."

"Thank you, Troll. I appreciate it," I say, and he muffle-growls something indistinguishable before hanging up.

The girl in my bed looks up, big, beautiful eyes bright with anticipation for me. "You're excited. What's going on?"

She smiles when I tell her. Rolls slowly over my body and on top of me the way she lied last night, nudges her nose against my throat like a sleepy kitten. I get to see this other Nadia before she veils herself in sadness again. This early morning version of her is addictive.

I kiss her before she rethinks shit. Slide my fingers in between her butt cheeks and caress her rosebud. Then I move down, finding a warmth I already crave, slickness from yesterday, and I whisper my plea in her ear.

"Again?"

Still sleepy, she relents, her body awake enough to

tremble through a climax with me, but as her mind clears fully, I watch her retract again, her eyes dimming as she gets dressed. Nadia sits through breakfast with us, that small wrinkle between her brows reappearing.

When she stands, getting ready to leave, I don't give a damn that I look pathetic when I say, "Hey," catch her hand in passing, and entwine our fingers. I don't get up from my seat, but I pull her close enough to latch around her waist. "Can you make it to the show? I'd like to have you there."

"I want to go so bad!" Zoe sings. "Emil invited me, right you did, Cupcake? Nadia, we'll talk to Scott—figure something out. This is the awesomest reason ever to bail in the middle of our shifts."

Nadia tenses in my hold. She doesn't withdraw, but it's clear that she wants to. Instinctively, I kiss her stomach the way I used to back when I had a girlfriend. Our small kitchen goes dead silent at my move, and it dawns on me how intimate that was. Much more intimate than casual sex.

"Tell me you'll try," I say. My voice is raspy. "We'll kick ass if you come." That releases the tension around the table, and with a half-hearted nod, Nadia leaves my house.

BO

WE'VE BEEN AT THE RADIO STATION for a few hours. They've provided us with a rehearsal room, we've been briefed on the two questions they'll ask, and how we'll be introduced before Luminessence. We get one song only. Troll is pissed, because he wants us to do our almost-hit, *Never Ever*, but I'm pretty sure we're doing *Fuck You.*

"They'll censor the crap out of your damn song," he says.

"It's live, isn't it? How can they?" I retort. "Plus, it's college radio, not FCC-governed commercial radio."

Troll's great, but tonight he's not helping. I'd much rather get in my pre-show groove than deal with his BS. I end up making a run for beer to get away from him. On the way back, I make an executive decision: we'll play *Fuck You* if Nadia comes. If she doesn't, we'll appease Troll and go with what Emil refers to as our "sad-as-shit" song.

"Dudes," I call as soon as I'm back. Pop a few bottles open while I toe the door to the rehearsal room shut. "Get ready for extremes: it's *Never Ever* or *Fuck You,* depending."

"On what, man?" Troy is juggling drumsticks, his only tell of being anxious.

"We'll be in the mood for *Fuck You* if we get a female audience," I say, take a swig of beer, and start fiddling with my guitar. Yeah, fiddle. Because I need the attention off myself.

"Perfect!" Emil exclaims, insisting on a high five. "If the chicks come, I'll be good to go. You're right—if I don't have a set of killer jugs to eye-fuck, I'm better off playing safe with an oldie-but-goodie." And thus Emil's narcissism saves me from making a lovesick fool out of myself.

NADIA

Zoe watches me, eyes soft with compassion as I sling clothes around in my closet. "I don't know what to wear!" I yell.

"Sweetie, it's not a big deal. Bo—"

"Don't! Mention him here," I shout. One of my candles has extinguished in the den. I rush out to light a new one.

I press air out through pursed lips, trying to gather my wits. Waking up with Bo this morning, hard-bodied and smooth-skinned, warm and enveloping me. It rattled me more than the sex did. Because it's how things used to be with Jude and me.

Jude and I had issues—serious issues that disappeared with our flight from Payne Point. He saved me from the rest of my life, from old husbands and ten children. From religious extremism and painful submission. I can never pay him back for what he did, for the new, compassionate, generous world he brought me into.

But here I am, searching for an outfit for a radio show Clown Irruption has been invited to.

"How 'bout you wear one of your ankle-length skirts from your Payne Point days?" Zoe asks. I snort while rubbing my eye dry of liquid and old mascara.

"Yeah, right. I don't have any of those left. Jude helped me burn them in the backyard as soon as we'd moved into this place."

"I beg to differ." She holds up a burgundy flannel skirt. *Flannel.* Do you have any idea of how much flannel sucks in a place as warm as Payne Point?

And suddenly, I'm giggling. Zoe joins me too, making pole-dancer moves with the living-room-drapes-worthy chunk of fabric she's carrying.

"Mother would have had a heart attack," I manage, pointing at her dancing.

"She'd deserve it," Zoe quips, and that makes me laugh harder. Crap, I might be having a panic attack. Jude isn't here, and I'm about to head off to Bo's gig. Radio One is the biggest college station in Southern California, serving eight campuses at once, and the honor of playing live is beyond belief for the guys.

"Sexy, sweets. You can do it. Come on. Blow Bo's mind, will you? He's so freaking into you I'm jealous."

"What, of me?"

She rolls her eyes. "Bah, I'm into the *Scandinavian* rocker thing, not the whatever metro-sexy, worldly, mysterious musician thingy. Though, hey, judging by the itty-bitty squeals you couldn't hold back last night, sounds like he'd be worth a trial ride."

"No! Oh Lord, Zoe. Please." I slump on my bed. I'll never put myself in that situation again. Never will Zoe and I have a single, thin wall between us when we… when we're with…

She giggles merrily. Tosses out a small, red skirt she bought me a few months ago. "You've never worn this one. You've got ahmazing legs, all curvy and stupid, so wear it."

"Too short."

"Said Nadia's grandmother."

"Okay, fine!"

She keeps rummaging in our closet, and I'm worried. *I don't have any daring tops*, I have time to think before she finds one and chucks it at my face.

"White. Super-pretty with the red skirt, and look at the cuuuut!" She drags out the last word like bubblegum.

I recognize the only item shipped to me from my family in Argentina over the last few years. My favorite aunt, *Tía* Rosa, sent me this sexy, half-transparent, pearly white top with a neckline so plungy it commits suicide between my breasts. I never put it on for Jude.

"No way," I say. "I didn't buy that thing."

"Yep, I figured. Now, put it on. It'll be gorgeous."

Because Zoe doesn't give up easily, I try it on, hating the way her eyes grow into saucers in front of me. "Dayumm," she says. "What a rack, girl."

"No, it's just the top."

"Yeah, whatevs, and done deal. It's what you're wearing, although Bo might be in trouble. Here's to hoping they play their newest song."

"Which song?"

"The crazy sexy one. The porn song? Emil says it's about me, but Bo wrote it, and I'm purrty, purrty sure it isn't about me," she says, grinning.

And when I leave my house, with Jude nowhere to hug goodbye, I'm somehow wearing the short, red silk skirt, *Tía* Rosa's stripper top—with a pin at the center keeping it from kamikaze-diving—and Zoe's mile-high red Loboutins.

I don't know *me* anymore.

CHAPTER Twelve

SUPPORT

BO

WE'RE ON IN TEN MINUTES, the girls haven't arrived yet, and I have a very grumpy tour manager stomping around and yapping at staff about the potential entrances they might be waiting at. Troll is opinionated, but once we make our choices, he puts one hundred and ten percent effort into them whether he agrees or not.

"And no phone numbers for any of them?" he asks me again.

"No. Well, Emil might have Zoe's."

The lead singer in question isn't available. He has shut himself into the bathroom where he belts out song after song, making them bounce against the walls. He entered shirtless, so when he's quiet it's because he's doing his shadowboxing thing, pumping himself up.

"Prep for *Never Ever*, guys," I tell Troy and Elias.

"It's on," Troy nods, grabs his drumsticks, and gets up. Besides the guitars and Troy's favorite snare drum, we're using Luminessence's gear in the studio, so we travel light when we stride down the hallway. Emil's there already and sweaty as hell. With glowing eyes, he's ready to give it all.

"Shirt?" I ask, holding it out to him, and he grabs it absentmindedly only to fling it over a shoulder. "Dude. We're going to rock the house!"

"Hell yeah." We run through the usual backslaps and headlocks—and straighten at the apparition at the end of the hallway. Because there, with Troll proudly in front of them, are Nadia and Zoe.

"Chicks," Elias says. "I guess *Fuck You* is on?"

"Woo-hooh! And after, I'm tapping that," Emil eloquently chimes in. He bounces to his feet and makes a run for Zoe.

But *Nadia*. Is with her. And she's a goddamn vision. What the hell happened to her? She's got the shortest little skirt on. It's bright red, skulking over her hips, and—shit, her legs! They're crazy—in those shoes—and, Jesus.

Boobs.

I set my longneck on the floor and cross my arms while watching her approach. She's got red flecks of embarrassment on her cheeks, and when my eyes travel south, down her never-ending cleavage, she covers herself by mirroring my crossed arms.

"Troll," I say. "We're ready, and it'll be the new song." Then I swallow the distance to Nadia, grind her against my body, and kiss her like she's mine.

NADIA

Bo's kiss leaves me gasping for oxygen. His eyes burn, and he presses me so close it's like he wants to brand me.

"You came," he husks out. "This'll be good." Then he grabs my hand, swings, and marches us inside the studio. There's a woman with headphones on, speaking into a microphone. A guy my age with his headphones half-cocked on his head nods at us. He reaches over the desk and shakes everyone's hands.

"Bo?" he asks Bo last. Bo nods and listens to the guy's full name. "All right. Sharon'll introduce you in..." Radio Guy glances at a wall clock. "Thirty sec."

The rest of the band seat themselves. Troy behind his drums and Elias on a stool with his bass guitar. Emil, still with Zoe tucked at his side, pulls the microphone up high on the stand.

Bo stares at him. "Dude." He juts his chin at Zoe, and Emil rolls his eyes.

"Yeah, dude. She'll be sitting over there"—he points at three chairs along the wall—"before you're done talking."

"Listeners!" Sharon sings into her microphone. "I have a treat for you! With us tonight is a brand new band that was discovered by none other than our beloved Luminessence. Well, I guess they've been around for a little while, but mostly in their home country, Sweden. Now, here I am, chitchatting with bandleader Bo Lindgren. Bo, what made you guys drift over to America?"

"Hey, Sharon, thanks for having us," Bo murmurs. His voice has changed. It's the melodic, deeper one he uses when he does backup vocals for Clown Irruption. He hasn't let go of my hand and nods toward the only seat available by their desk. I shake my head and drop back toward the three chairs by the wall.

"Well, we figured we'd take on this village and see if anyone liked us—even though Sweden is the center of the universe."

Sharon launches into a gorgeous radio laughter. "Right? Oh isn't that so sweet of you to think of little us from all the way across the ocean. Now, I'll let you get down and dirty. Why don't you play us a song? You have a couple of records out already, I hear from Pop in Luminessence, all of which are, and I quote, 'flippin' radical.' Which one are you going to share with us?"

Bo's laughter is bedroom-low. "Hmm, is it after ten p.m. yet?" he asks, turning to wink at me. My body reacts instantly, and I find myself pressing my thighs together under the flimsy skirt I'm wearing.

"Why, I believe it is, Mr. Lindgren." Sharon chuckles conspiratorially. "And for the benefit of all of you wonderful listeners, that means there's no need for censorship to our music. Bo?"

"Well, thank you, God, because this tune is so new it's not available on CD, and we don't have a bland version of it yet. I wanted to play it because…" He swipes another glance my way. When he continues, his voice is so loaded with sexual innuendo, Zoe titters like a schoolgirl at Emil's side. "Well, because we like playing it."

"Okey-dokey! Friends," Sharon says into the microphone. "I think you'd enjoy the view I have now. These musicians are not only talented but some fine-looking young men. It's Bo Lindgren on guitar, Troy Armstrong on drums, Elias Mikaelsson on bass, and Emil Vinter on lead vocals. Singing what again? Are you going to tell us the name of this song?" she teases.

"Fuck you." The quicksilver-smooth lilt of Bo's words makes me suck in a breath. It's obvious that he's not swearing at the radio host.

"Oh my," Sharon lilts back, and their little interaction causes the slightest stir of something at the bottom of my belly. "And that, listeners, was not Bo cussing me out. I believe it is the title of the song. Am I correct?"

"You sure are," he says.

"Aaaallllrighty then!" she trills. "I'll let you do this thing. And we'll get to hear the latest, very latest song from Clown Irruption!"

BO

WE'RE KINGS. On top of the world!

Between Emil's and my energy, we've pumped the band up so high the only one sitting is Troy.

The bass line. *Thud-thud-thud. Thud-thud-thud.* The whoosh of Troy's brushes against the skins of the drums before he flings them at the wall and snatches the sticks.

Emil is bare-chested, already sweaty and horny as hell, *mm-hmm*-ing out his tribute to Zoe. My riff layers over, adding to his foreplay.

In my peripheral vision, I see Nadia as Emil whispers his first "Fuck you. I want to fuck you." Eyes wide with surprise, her hands clench in her lap, tugging nervously at her skirt. She's so damn sweet, I'd pull that skirt up and fuck her this minute.

I let my voice grate low, accompanying Emil's and husking out what I want to do to her. The drums insist as Troy increases our speed, whipping, whipping them until they obey. The volume skyrockets at Emil's, "Come for me, why don't you—come again, again, again. I love you when you come!"

Zoe squirms and leans on Nadia, who's flushing a deep red. Shit, she's breathtaking. I make my strings squeal the way I want to make Nadia do. I rock against my guitar, losing myself to the moans of pleasure she tempers when I'm inside her. I move with her. I build her up. I drive her crazy—oh yeah, I do, yes—

And one day I want to make her sing *abandon*!

Ah I see it now, how she wriggles under me—welcoming, so welcoming—and taking me deep inside her. Troy reads my mind. He drums faster, harder, and Elias' bass does a frantic cycle, coming back and meeting us all. All too soon, it's over. I'm not done. I need more, but that final scream of ecstasy explodes out. Emil sobs out his relief, and it's so heartfelt, he might have ejaculated against Pop's mic stand.

The applause erupts. I raise my head and find Pop's giant grin in the window first. He flexes a bicep for me, displaying what he thinks of the new song before he tips his head in through the doorway, next to an equally grinning Troll, and shouts, "Viral, man. This is going viral!"

I'm not sure what he's talking about. The radio show? Troll waves his iPhone at me, and my slow, sexed-out brain catches on.

"Oh yeah, baby. Finally," Troll nods out. "I told you. This song is gold. I'm gonna edit this thing, and we'll… Emil. Emil! Are you listening?"

Emil has his back to us. He has climbed onto Zoe's lap and is giving her the dance of the ages, grinding his crotch against her stomach. Disturbingly, Troll returns to filming.

Zoe is hot and glassy-eyed, but she's snickering too. She has heard the song before. She came prepared. Nadia? Not so much.

I slide my gaze to Nadia's seat. It's empty. The room is small so I locate her easily, and she's moving fast, en route to the door. She's not going anywhere though. I lunge and grab her arm before she splits.

"And thanks again to Clown Irruption. Whew, that was *hot*!" Sharon says. "It's been a pleasure—and I want my signed copy of *Fuck You* ASAP, Bo, so you better get on that and record."

With my hand clamped around Nadia's wrist, I pull us back enough to tilt the radio host's mic toward me. "Definitely, Sharon. The first copy will be for you. And listeners: they say we'll be going viral. If you find a panting, half-naked Emil on YouTube, that'll be the one. Thanks for having us!"

Sharon's musical laughter follows us out the door. "Welcome, boys."

"Let go!" Nadia yells, and I'm surprised, because who knew she could raise her voice?

"You're mad, darling?"

Girls get upset over inexplicable things. I realize the song is graphic, while Nadia is everything *but*. Still, that would be a strange reason for a fit. Right?

"What did you expect, Bo?" she shouts, fuming. Yeah, she's fuming, and my heart feels weird. It's going soft in a bloated sort of way I've got no experience with. I want to suck her face and swallow a lump in my throat at the same time. It's insane.

I try to stroke her cheek, move stray strands of hair from her face. I'd like to shift them off her stunning cleavage too, but in this mood she might bust my balls. Literally.

Funny how my heart jumps at being yelled at by a girl again. I haven't been this close to anyone since Ingela. Even though Nadia is pissed, it feels great.

I steer her into a corner by the water fountain. Elias makes a quiet catcall and whispers, "Bo's been bad. Trouble in Paradise," as he passes.

Zoe passes too, with my lover-boy friend who's not in the shithouse, and says, "Find me when you're finished handing him his ass. I'll be packing up gear with Emil."

"What did I do?" I stare into beautiful, brown eyes that are even darker with anger.

"Oh I don't know—how about airing our business to everyone else?"

"Our business?" That. Is brave of her to say.

"Sooo… Wait, wait, wait," I begin. She shifts as if to run off, but I block her way and keep her steady with a push of my hips. "We have business, you're saying. Correct? And… you believe the song was written by me?"

"Um, Zoe told me."

"And you believed her. Doesn't this song sound more up Emil's alley?"

She squirms, but she's still too mad to be embarrassed. "Yeah, but it isn't. Zoe wouldn't make stuff like that up!"

"So... Zoe knows her shit?" I caress her face with one hand, running my thumb over her lower lip. She blinks slowly, the anger in her eyes receding. She's affected. *We're* affected. And damn, there's nothing like a little power game.

"Yeah. She'd have been super-happy if he wrote it for her."

"Okay." My voice comes out husky. "I admit I wrote it, dirty lyrics and all. But who's to say it's about you?" That delicious blush steals back up her throat. I've got her pressed so deep into the corner, she's stuck.

"I—I don't know. I... assumed."

I fold our fingers. Lift her hands over her head and press them against the wall behind her. Then I run my nose up the side of hers. "It could have been about another girl," I whisper with my lips pressed to her skin. She shivers. "Did we fuck like in the song?" I ask.

She tries to pull away. Of course it's to no avail, so she crumples her lids shut in an effort to protect herself. "No," she breathes. "Not like that."

"So you're wrong then?" I kiss her lips, and she accepts, opening.

"Mm-hmm," she manages.

"No."

She opens her eyes, meeting mine shyly. "What? I'm not wrong?"

"No. You're correct. The song is about you, about how you make me feel, what I dream of doing to you. I want to fuck you like that, devour you, and make you scream. Oh yeah. *Fuck You* is about us, darling."

Nadia's confusion. The flush rising in her cheeks. The stress and desire warring in her features. Everything about her makes me high. Every. Damn. Thing.

"Bo," she whimpers. "Why are you like this? I'm married. I can't... You need to..."

Anger flares in me. Over *a girl*. It's unprecedented and strange, but hey, Nadia came out here, and now she throws her husband in my face again!

And so? *What's it to you, Bo?*

Suddenly, exhaustion hits me like bricks. Here I am, trapping a beautiful girl I have no claim to against a wall in a dirty radio station corridor. I'm allowing whatever emotion to rule me, all sorts of non-premeditated stuff. Nothing good can come of this. Nadia is just a song, not above an exquisite new brand of strings for my guitar. Just—

I need to let her go.

"Thanks for supporting me," I start, closing my eyes. Then, before I drop her, I follow my instinct because it's strong and I'm tired. I sink down and bury my face against her throat in a way I don't recall having done with anyone before. "I really wanted you here."

PART 3
Bartering

Fighting hard
Because with determination
Comes success

Chapter Thirteen

VIRAL

BO

We go viral all right. Holy Mother of God, we go viral. What the hell was Troll thinking? We're not prepared for this! My number's out there, and my cell doesn't stop ringing. Emil's is the same way.

The video. *Shit, that video.*

When I confront Troll, he says, "Dude it was all you guys. All I did was film, and then I turned the file in to my bud, Hector, who's a pro. I *told* you you'd go viral, and now you're all pussy about it?"

What do you say to that? Troll's Norwegian, but he has spent most of his adult life in the States and has the show-biz mentality down to a T. While Clown Irruption? We're a small college band from a Swedish city no one has even heard of. We needed to ease into things, grow as a band before things went ape, but that idea just went down the drain with YouTube.

Yeah, I don't want to crash and burn because we can't handle fame. Troll wants the best for us. There's no doubt he works for us because he believes in our music, but—

Holy. Fucking. Shit?

Like a child, I miss home. I miss Ingela. But most of all, I miss New Girl. That's what Elias has taken to calling Nadia. Whenever he's sneaking off with his Nigerian princess and sending me smug looks over his shoulder, he whispers, "You gonna head over to New Girl's soon?"

"I wish you'd let me see it first," I tell Troll.

"The video? Hey, I'll take it down if you want me to," Troll offers, sounding metallic on the phone.

"No, it's too late now. Where are you?" I ask though it matters zip.

"Restroom. Sorry."

"Jesus, Troll. Why do you even pick up from the throne? Call me when you're done."

"Sure, man. A last squeeze-out, and I'm—"

"Bye, dude. Just, bye."

I haven't seen Nadia since she left the radio station three days ago. I miss her—and spend time pondering why. Beautiful women grow on trees in L.A.; what else has she done to burrow under my skin? I mean, she's married, melancholic, and hard to tease out of her shell.

Nadia saw me already in our first meeting in that crummy dressing room. She gets me through my music, which is so rare.

It's weird how people treat me separately from my songs. They want to ask questions in interviews, learn more about me, but never do they relate back to my lyrics, or to how I play the songs. To be honest though, it's better that way.

Nadia ran away from me *because* of a song. Because of the lyrics, the way I played it, and the way I "aired our business." A small twinge, part contentment, part disappointment, implodes in my chest at that.

My thoughts keep looping back to her marriage. I'm the last person to judge people's actions and the first to admit my own flaws. I used to run my life so badly. And someone else's—Ingela's. Yeah, unconsciously, I ran hers too.

That's what's happening to Nadia, I think to myself. She's unable to get out from under the husband's thumb. Maybe she's scared? Then again, he doesn't stop her from leaving the house. It's confusing. All I know is he's too lucky for his own lameness.

I grab the guitar at my feet. It's a brand new, high end Fender that was hand-delivered to me by a company rep in a barefaced response to our video having gone viral. I stride through the den with it en route to my bedroom.

"Bo. You good, man?" Emil asks from the couch. He presses two hamburgers together into one flattened mess, competitive-eater-style, and glances up at me. "Troy's on his way. We're playing World of Warcraft, I think, or— What's his latest game obsession again?"

I have no idea. I go along with whatever Troy whips out on the tour bus and don't worry about the details.

"That," I help. "But no, I'm not good. The whole viral thing is out of hand, and we need to do something."

"Turn off your phone," Emil says, eyes on the TV screen.

"What?"

"Kill your cell. And if they keep calling and you can't turn it back on, do what I've done." He winks slowly, the way he does on stage, and adds a tongue-click. "Get a secret number."

"You did that? When?" Sometimes, Emil actually has a point.

"I picked this baby up exactly…" He looks at his watch. "Thirty minutes ago. And you might get the number—if you promise not to complain the next time Zoe orgasms all over my bed."

"Jesus. Why the hell would I worry about your bed?" I ask.

"Not the bed, idiot. You know what I mean: *ah cooks—I can't take it anymore*," he mimics, and it's so real, it makes me wonder if he's faking Zoe's voice every night.

The next leg of the tour starts tomorrow. For the most part, it'll be an East Coast run. And already clubs are promoting our visits with "Luminessence and the band with the *Fuck You* video."

NADIA

I'M GOING BACK TO COLLEGE. My break has lasted long enough. I can't let my dream of becoming a veterinarian slip away because of Jude. A long time has passed since I finished my GED exams and started… sort of started… dabbling in a few classes at the local community college.

Jude's parents have set aside funds so I can begin

whenever I'm ready. They'll help me get into whatever school I want, they say, and they don't want me to worry about the money. I can't accept their offer.

Usually, I can't think of these things without wanting to hurl, but today's a good day. I'm still realistic enough to know I'm not ready. To sit still in class all day long would drive me crazy. I adore Scott and my regulars over at the diner, and I need my job for my sanity. Which is why I'm browsing online colleges.

I've got my tea lights flickering. Jude's with me. I stare at him and whisper, "I'll do it. I'll pick up school again if you…" I stand abruptly and head to the kitchen. It's early on my day off, and I wish it wasn't.

I feel him behind me as I shove items around in the fridge searching for…? I grab a yogurt. Pull it open and start eating without shutting the fridge door.

"I'll go back to school. Get us on the right track if I get my husband back," I promise him. "I'm too young for this. I can't handle it, baby. Don't you see?"

I swing around, but he's already gone.

"Okay, how about this?" I shout as I stomp into the living room. "I know I shouldn't have dropped out entirely, that I should have listened to you and stuck to the plan from the get-go: I should have rushed through college as a full-time student instead of wanting to split the responsibility and help support us."

I continue, lowering my voice because I don't want the neighbors to be on our door. "Let's do this: we go to sleep tonight. When we wake up, we'll have gone back in time to when Scott offered me work at the diner. This time, I'll turn it down. I'll turn it down, baby! Then do you promise me that my in-your-face, sweet husband who does everything right, will be back? And once we're done with our education and settled in great jobs, we'll have those three babies—two daughters and one son, because—"

I start sobbing. Of course I start sobbing. "—because we wouldn't be so stupid as to think we could raise more than one rebellious boy like you."

Today began as a good day, but here I go again. I wonder what Zoe's up to. I know Clown Irruption is leaving town, and she's probably upset. What if I snapped out of my own issues for once to go comfort a friend?

That's what I need to do.

While I pull an old T-shirt over my head, I'm still mulling over Jude and my options. "Okay, the time machine hasn't been invented yet. But tomorrow can still be a new day full of opportunities for us. Right?"

In shorts and gladiators, I grab my purse by the door and deposit my cell inside it. I cross the threshold before I swing to look inside. A brief trickle of contentment hits me at how I'm good at this stuff—at decorating. I make our home a home. It looks pretty.

I let my eyes swipe over the small, colored pots with flowers in them. Linger on the smooth roundness of the bigger, ornamental pot at the center. My gaze catches flickering lights between the plants on the table, and I take the three steps back in. I blow out the candles because Jude won't appreciate them the way I do.

"Tomorrow, Jude, we're starting a new life. If you promise that I'll be waking up with the one I married kissing me, loving me—maybe even *making* love to me,

I'll walk right on over to Scott's tomorrow, I'll quit my job, and I'll finish college so fast your head will spin. Then I'll do what you wanted all along: I'll be your sugar mama while you study to become my grease monkey."

OH JUDE. A lanky teenager with long hair and confusion in his eyes.

When he began attending sermons at the Heavenly Harbor, my world shrunk further. No longer could I visit the neighbor girls. Once Jude stayed behind to help me tidy up after church coffee, I was no longer allowed to attend that activity. I remember his stare on me when we left early the next Sunday, Mother with a firm hand on my shoulder and ushering me out.

We didn't know of Jude's tenacity at the time. His shrewdness and his knack for getting what he wanted. My family would learn soon. Me, I had no experience with sneaking around behind my grandparents' backs. At most, I'd learned to keep my biggest sins to myself. That changed after Jude caught me and kissed me behind the church.

"You're so pretty," he said as if that was reason enough, and I let him kiss me again because I had no one else. The next Sunday, he slipped me a note saying, "I like you a lot." And I? I thought he was handsome.

Shortly after their move to Payne Point, he appeared in my classroom, all grins and with a book bag slung over his shoulder. But a few days of minuscule lunch breaks was all we got before Mother handed in her resignation.

Thus begun my years as a homeschooled child of extremist Christians. Long dresses. Buttons so high they rubbed tight against my throat. I'd never owned a cell phone, so there was no remaining in contact with the outside world.

In hindsight I can see it: Mother changed me into someone that should not be approached, and with one exception, it worked.

Jude remained at our school for a few weeks with Ms. Sanchez, a stand-in for Mother. On the first Sunday after my domestic imprisonment, it was liberating to attend church, to get out of the house for more than walking my dog.

I remember Jude's eyes on me in church: searching, curious when he saw my new, old-fashioned clothes. I remember the shame flying up my face and covering it with scarlet. During a psalm, I needed to escape. Mother shifted anxiously in her seat when I slipped off to the ladies' room.

That's when Jude followed me and whispered against my ear for the first time. "What happened? You never returned to school? I'm stuck there now," he said, playful and serious at once. "No one tells me anything here. People are weird. Not you," he added even though it wasn't true. I was weird too.

"Mother homeschools me now. She says it's better education for me."

"Bullshit," he hissed, voice low and eyes narrowed. "How can it be better if the teacher is the same?"

My logical, sweet Jude.

"She didn't like it when we talked before," he said.

I shrugged, not used to such conversations.

"She doesn't like that I like you. She's got to suck it up, because you're beautiful. Everyone thinks you're beautiful. Blaine too," he added. Blaine! The guy who delivered groceries to the church kitchen?

The door to the nave creaked, and the psalm poured out as Mother exited. Jude pushed past the corner and whispered from the other side: "Nadia. Write me a note with your address on it. Leave it right there, beneath the doormat to the restroom. I'll come see you tonight—at seven."

"We eat at seven," I said before I could think. "And I can't, ever. You're a boy."

He rolled his eyes. "Boys are people too. You know what the Bible says, 'You shall love boys like yourself.' Eight?"

"No. What? The Bible doesn't say that. It's 'You shall love thy neighbor like yourself.'"

Mother's footstep sped down the hallway.

"Pff, that's splitting hairs. Nine?" Jude said.

"No! I have to be at home and…"

"Ten. I'll be in your yard—do you have a yard?"

"Yes, but—"

"Okay, ten p.m. in your backyard. Don't forget the note or I'll have to search for you on the Internet. Which I will." Deep blue eyes fixed mine from past the corner until I slid my gaze to the floor in shame. Then he pecked my mouth lightly and ducked into the men's room.

That night, he was there, just like he'd promised. Fear and thrill mingled inside me when I noticed him too close to the kitchen window.

"Bedtime, Nadia," Father rumbled from the den where he read bible verses for Mother after dinner.

"I haven't walked Daisy yet," I said, and I'd made sure it wasn't a lie.

"Daisy will have to wait until the morning," Father decided. "It's too late. Young ladies should never walk alone after dark."

Mother looked up, searching my face for secrets, but I slumped to pick up my little dog and bury my face in her fur. "I can come with you," she said, causing anxiety to prick at my nape.

"Maybe you're right, Father," I mumbled. "Maybe it is late and I should take Daisy out back instead before I go to bed."

Father's eyes softened with my easy submission, and so did the tension in Mother's posture.

And that's where I rendezvoused with Jude for the first time. In the dark, in a far corner of our backyard, beyond bushes and beneath oak trees. He lessened my shyness with his fingers on my cheek. With crooked quotes from the Bible that made me titter low. Each time, I told him he shouldn't keep coming. Each time, he told me he'd be back tomorrow.

"'*For I know the plans I have for you*—said Jude—*plans to prosper you and not to harm you, plans to give you hope and a future*,'" he quoted on the fourth night. A mischievous glint in his eyes made my stomach flutter at his words, but I shook my head and smiled at him.

"That was the Lord, not you who said that."

Jude groaned and held my face still so he could kiss my lips. "Is there anything I can trick you with from the Bible?"

"Probably not," I answered, confident in one thing. "It is what I do after all, study the Bible."

My Jude was skilled at sneaking around, having done so for years in San Francisco. He knew when to pull me out of the open and in under a tree, when my smile was too bright or I opened my mouth to speak where I was visible from our house.

Once, Mother leaned over the kitchen sink, staring out into the night. Jude noticed and handed me a branch to throw for my dog. When I did and Daisy refused to play along, he told me to shrug and shake my head to Mother. Her worry eased, a rare smile emerging before she disappeared from the window.

Jude's hands pulled me back into the dark. "I'm quitting the Heavenly Harbor to start at the public school." Sweet and lonely like me, he added, "If you kiss me again, it means you want me to keep visiting."

I did. I already needed him like air.

Jude kept his word. He returned, night after night. Splashes of color and kisses in cold winter nights. He'd hold me, tell me about his school. I'd live my teenage life through his stories. Shrewd and cautious, he'd allow us ten minutes together. "Until you introduce me as your boyfriend to the old bat, we can't let her discover us, can we?" he'd ask rhetorically.

I was never ready to see him leave. But the anticipation of knowing he'd be there like clockwork every night saved me even before *he* really did.

CHAPTER Fourteen

GOODBYE

NADIA

"There you are," Zoe says as if she's read the text I sent her on my way over. She usually doesn't. "About time. They're leaving from Emil and them's house in freaking half an hour! The tour bus is pulling up. You want to see the tour bus, right?"

I thought they'd left. Now something is happening in my chest. Double beats, and then a long pause as if my heart's trying to sink to the bottom of my stomach before resuming its rhythm.

"No. I just wanted to keep you company in case you were upset."

"Upset? Why would I be upset? I'm going on tour with them!"

"What?" My mouth falls open on the question, not really producing the "t." I've heard of no such plans. "You've known Emil for, what—a week?"

She starts giggling. "Nah, just messing with ya, babe." Then she tips her head up high. "But! Emil said we're invited to any of their concerts wherever the hell we want to go. Like Japan."

"They're going to…?"

"No! Ah you're silly today. Gullible little thing."

For the record, she's shorter than me.

"But, you know, UCLA. Stanford, etcetera. All of those places. And we can go backstage at the arenas. Emil says this is essentially a small club and campus tour, but they have a few arenas mixed in too. Basically, wherever we want to go, they want us there."

"Not Bo," I say.

"Right, not Bo because he's not obsessing over you," she mocks.

I don't need a replay of her opinions on this. I'm not sure why I opened that can of worms. She's been on repeat for days.

"I'll see you after, Zoe. You go check out the tour bus and kiss Emil goodbye. I'll wait here and make you a root beer float," I say.

"No, you're coming. Bo asks about you every time. How mean would that be to not see him off, Nadia? Super-mean!"

"Just," I sigh, tired again. Zoe is so opinionated. So stubborn. She reminds me a little bit of Jude. "This one you're not winning. I'm not going."

NADIA

"Isn't it crazy huge?" Zoe exclaims as she parks behind a silver bus.

"Same size as any old bus," I say, but she just puffs air in disagreement and hops out of the car.

"Guess what they have in the hanger behind it."

I don't know that I care. I really wish I wasn't here. This is just going to be awkward, and despite what she says, I have not been invited to say goodbye. "Their instruments?"

"Exactly, Emil told me everything last night. I totes know the layout of the bus on the inside, even."

"So why are we here then?" I mutter, too low for her to hear.

"Zee," Emil croons while opening the door. He cups her neck and draws her in for a kiss that lasts too long for me standing right behind them. Geez. I feel so out of place. How is it that she always wins? I look at my watch. It'll be busy at the diner soon. Scott would welcome an extra hand.

But then Emil opens his eyes, sees me, and exclaims, "Holy balls—*the muse* is back. Bo!" he bellows into the apartment. "Hurry up before Nadia sprints off. She's here but not for long, looks like."

So now I don't feel ten times more uncomfortable. Experience tells me the color of my face is a bright neon red. "I have work," I say, but then Bo's there too, eyes burning at me. Emil pulls Zoe out of the way, inside, and I'm face to face with my wet dream.

"You're here," Bo murmurs, brows raised in wonder. "I thought I'd bummed you out for life and I'd never see you again."

Crap, he's so magnetic. I don't understand how Zoe could just waggle her fingers in greeting before she took off with Emil to his room; Bo's presence sucks me in like the first night in that dressing room.

"You didn't… No, that wasn't it," I manage.

He doesn't hug me like he's done almost every time we've met. I miss it. He'll be gone soon, out of sight, all the way out of here.

"How long is the tour?" I ask.

"Three weeks."

"*Three weeks?*" I don't mean to sound desolate.

A flicker of surprise returns to his eyes. We're inches apart, a low threshold the only thing separating us.

I feel my layer of shyness crack. Suddenly, I need to spend these last minutes well and etch his features into my mind for long, lonely nights.

"You're going to miss me, huh?" Bo's voice reaches the lower register, right where his backup vocals are on his latest song. Right where he was when he whispered for me to—

Nadia, you're a freak!

I sneak an eyeful from under my lashes. I'm ravenous for his features. High, pale cheekbones; a perfect, medium-sized nose; and those frostbitten, grey eyes. His mouth, the only thing on his face with a splash of strong color. It's so red, so kissable, with defined lips forming a double, upper arc and stubble dusting down to it from the nose. The upper bow ends abruptly at the corners, meeting a lower lip that's fuller, plumper, and made to pull in between one's teeth.

Do I remember how it feels to pull on his lip? No. I haven't tried it. And Lord have mercy, right now I hate that I haven't.

"Maybe a little," I reply to his question and lift my hands to cool my cheeks.

"You're so very sweet," he husks. "It's only for three weeks. I'll be home soon." And finally his hand is there, replacing mine against my cheek. "I'm not done getting to the bottom of you, Nadia."

My body reacts with a hot stab to my abdomen. It travels downward, it's delicious, and it makes me want to squeeze my thighs together. But then my flight instinct sets in, screaming for me to spin and run like mad home to Jude.

I exhale quickly for courage. Before I do what I never thought I'd do. Bo wouldn't understand how unheard of it is when I tip my head back in search of his lips.

His arm goes around me and tightens, and I do what I dream of. I pull that fleshy lower lip into my mouth and savor it. Every fiber in me is getting ready for him, remembering, thinking this is it—we're doing it again.

Bo moans. He freaking *moans* into my mouth, and I can't stand how good it makes me feel. Our kiss becomes wet, slippery sweet, as his tongue parts my lips and finds *my* tongue to swirl with. Why, why does kissing him feel like this?

"Let's go inside," Bo whispers and draws me in, shuts

the door behind me before I can nod.

"You're leaving…"

"Shhh, not for long. You'll fly out and visit."

"I can't. Work—"

The words, the light disagreement cutting out between kisses. He falls to the couch and drags me with him, hands in my hair and around my waist, kissing, sucking.

"Some shows are closer… drive. Train. We'll make it happen."

His thigh is between my legs, pressing against me, and even with the way he's making me climb, I can't believe myself when I say, "Okay."

I jump high when someone bangs hard on the door. "Bo! Emil?"

"Dude!" Bo says. His body trembles a little beneath me. I let my hand slide up his thigh until I locate the outline of him, every slope and ridge hard and ready. "Ahh shit, Nadia," he murmurs. He thrusts once into my hand, making me inhale sharply with what could have been. Then he grabs my head and sucks a last dizzying kiss to my mouth.

"Open. It's road-trip time!" Elias shouts.

I curl up in the corner of the couch, knees high to my chest while Bo lets Elias in. Iridescently white in the doorway, he stares first at Bo—whose hand rests discretely over his zipper—then at me, and shakes his head.

"Wow. Unbelievable. He's been whining about you for days—"

"I don't whine." Bo moves behind the breakfast bar and leans his hips against it.

"—and now she's here. You guys. I congratulate you on

the timing of your little *reunion*." He waggles his brows. "Were you about to reschedule our departure? Send me a text ahead of time, man, like, 'Got held up. Leaving tomorrow.'"

"Zip it, moron." Bo grabs a glass and pours juice from the fridge. The juice will go old while they're gone. Idly I wonder what else they have in there. Probably milk... I hope he eats healthy.

"Frustrated much?" Elias quips. "I think you just had fun on the couch. Just not *enough* fun."

"Do you *ever* fucking shut up?" Bo barks.

"Geez, so touchy." Elias lifts his hand in the air, showing his palms in surrender. "Troll's outside, and Troy was pulling up when I came."

We make it to the curb with no one getting into brawls. Zoe's eyes are wet, which surprises me. She doesn't tend to *need* her guys.

We get the full tour of the bus, which is a big camper. They're going to be sleeping in one miniature room with floor-to-ceiling bunk beds and curtains instead of walls between them. For three weeks?

"You better be good friends, or you'd be bashing each other's brains out," Zoe describes what I'm thinking in less explicit visuals.

"We still do," Troy says. "Or they do." He points at the three Swedes. None of them denies the allegation.

Troll fusses with the coffeemaker in the kitchen and snaps something to the driver about it, then he turns to us and says, "Ready to roll? Are the girls coming?"

"I wish!" Zoe says, smiling big. "But no, we're getting off the bus. We'll come visit for sure though. Right,

Nadia?" she asks because she knows how I hate being put on the spot.

"We'll see…" I study a scratch in the rubber flooring.

"Ooh she's considering it," Elias goes. "Your charm might've finally worked on someone, Bo. And bring an extra friend, all right? Cute like you?"

"Nadia, a moment?" Bo asks politely and tips his head toward the lounge in the back of the bus.

Nervous, I follow him. I hope this isn't about us.

"Five minutes, Bo!" Troll calls, almost drowning out Emil's explanation about how Elias should just "grab" a groupie. As Bo slides the door shut behind us, I hear Elias' reply, "Same difference. Zoe and Nadia are groupies. Figured they'd have groupie friends, and it'd be handy if they all came out together."

"Sit?" Bo says, the lilt of his pitch indicating that it's a question, not a command. The bench is a square sectional occupying the entire back wall of the bus, and we wedge in behind a coffee table that's welded to the floor.

I obey even though I'm worried he'll crack my defenses again like he did at his apartment. Thankfully, he doesn't attack me with soft, firm, addictive lips. Neither does he lay his body over mine, commanding me with a warmth I can't resist.

Spikes of jet-black hair skip against his eyelashes as he fixes on me, and I don't think before I reach up to slide one of them behind his ear.

"Nadia," he starts, voice low. "We haven't known each other for very long, but I don't want to leave you behind. There's so much I want to talk with you about. And this tour, it's going to be damn hectic. The whole video-going-viral thing has booked us solid with radio interviews and guest appearances between shows that weren't even on the horizon before."

"But you don't like all the attention," I blurt out, impulsive in ways I only am with him.

"True, but my music is my life. Right now that means it's my chaos too." He shakes his head. "I know. I'm not making sense."

"No, I get it: like when you don't have to talk or act or make someone excited. You can just bury yourself in your songs?"

He nods. "And I'll be wishing you sat there listening to me, pouring out that sweet energy of yours. Plus, you don't chatter on and on when I play."

"You like the strong, silent type, huh?" I ask, smiling.

He rolls his eyes lazily and smirks back. "I like *you*."

Bo hasn't touched me since he shut the door behind us in the back lounge. Now, he traces the outline of my fingers against the table, and I shudder a little.

"See if you can come out next weekend," he says, stopping in the deep crevice between my ring finger and my middle finger. He lifts his gaze slowly and watches me. "We'll be in Vegas, working the Hard Rock venue. You can drive there with Zoe. Or take a bus—or I can transfer frequent flyer miles to you if you want."

My first thought is that thanks to Jude's parents, I have funds. I could fly to Vegas if I so decided. How twisted.

I would never.

"Give me your cell number," he says, a demand this time. I do. He instantly calls me and holds my gaze while I pick up.

"Hello?" I say stupidly.

"Hey… it's me," he husks out the way he spoke the other night, and it's way too intimate, way too much, and I get up and stare out the window.

I don't hear him stand. He's simply behind me, a hand on my waist and his chin on my shoulder. "Sorry. I didn't mean to scare you off. But you need to understand that the more skittish, the more secretive you are, the more I need to get under your skin."

"But I've told you… You know…"

"And yet you come back."

I have nothing to say to that. He's right. Why *do* I come back? Why can't I seem to stay away? This trip of theirs will be good.

Seven days I've known him. It's nothing. I can go back to before. Work. Home to Jude. Slowly, surely get back on track again.

Zoe and I stand side by side, backs against her car while the bus rocks into movement. She leans on me while I brace myself against the hood of her Mini for support. I register Emil's playful make-out with the front lounge window and Zoe's equally playful whining next to me, but the one I *see* is Bo poised behind Emil. He holds his phone against his ear, looks straight at me, and mouths, *Hey, it's me.*

And suddenly I think that death by ovary implosion wouldn't be the worst.

"He's so awesome! I love him!" Zoe exclaims.

We're one week in. I wouldn't say she gushes over every guy she's with, but… yeah. Probably not yet. "Of course you do."

"Next weekend," she decides. "Vegas, baby!"

"Have fun," I say, vowing to take on double shifts to not be involved.

"Let's go to my place and watch the video again." She claps her hands excitedly.

"I'm heading over to see if Scott needs me." And oh my God, I know I'm boring, and I can't believe my friend is my friend. She's stuck with me through thick and thin. I love her. "Never mind—I'll stop by your house and then go straight to work from there."

"Coolio. *I* actually do work today, remember?" I don't, which isn't a surprise for either of us. "We'll go together," she finishes.

At her place, Zoe's excited when she fires up her computer, excited enough to hold up a small bottle of Kahlua. "Want a drink? I'll make you a white Russian."

"Just turn on your machine," I say.

She does. Not only that, but she hooks it up to the TV like a pro, finds the video on YouTube, and sprawls Clown Irruption's handsome faces out all over her roommate's big flat-screen.

Zoe doesn't know it's my first time watching the video. How could I watch it at home? I recognize Bo's dyed-black bangs instantly, the first thing appearing. Then he tips his head up and stares straight into the camera, his eyes so smoldering I gasp for air.

"Damn, he's hot. Look at his *face*, Nadia! That face is for you—you know that, right?"

"Shut up," I mumble.

The video clips straight to Emil, who's in love with his microphone, all but making out with it. Eyes half closed and sweat dripping from his hair, he's hard, naked muscle with his T-shirt half-draped over one shoulder. Those little moans he makes. I recognize them from having been next door to them while…

Okay, shush.

I feel hot. I feel dirty. I stand, needing an escape—water in the kitchen—but Zoe grasps my hand. "Wait, it gets better," she says. I want to tell her that's not the problem.

Troy's there, hammering hard, looking like—yeah, I can imagine him too now, in my dirty mind. And then Elias. Wow, it's like they're in an orgy, all of them in a simultaneous build-up. Then it cuts to Zoe and me. Zoe's ecstatic, laughing, rocking in her chair, all blonde waves and moving in a way that's hauntingly similar to Emil's, while I?

Oh. Crap.

I've got a hand clamped over my mouth. My clothing is more daring than Zoe's. Part of my breasts are showing, I'm tugging at my short skirt, but I don't look like I want to cover myself. I look like I'm dying to… help myself. My knees tip inward, only the toes of Zoe's Loboutins meeting the floor. From the posture, I could have been taken for demure instead of wanton, I guess, only—

I've got Bo's eyes.

Eyes burning with lust and need and want and yearning.

"Damn, Nadia?" Zoe says. "Didn't notice you the first time I saw it. I know who *you're* looking at."

I don't answer because I'm glued to the damn video now, sucked in while Emil tells us how much he wants to

"Fuck you, fuck you until you come, come, come."

The angle zooms out, showing the whole band, how they rock their bodies in sync, shamelessly feeling the music, the need for a woman, dreaming, getting it all out. Just—

Jesus!

The video doesn't stop with Emil's scream. No, the camera follows him as he leaps to Zoe, straddles her, and gives her a lap dance. Then it fades into black as he buries his tongue in her mouth.

"You're crazy," I croak out. "Are you okay with that being spread all over the place and watched by… so many people?"

Zoe stares up while I shakily get to my feet. "You're kidding, right? He freaking *digs* me in that video—I'm so stoked! I swear, I'm like a mini-star now. I've got tons of friend requests on Facebook, mostly from girls who want to be me. Dude, and even a few guys. Not sure if they want to *be* me or *do* me though," she giggles out.

"You should screen them. People are crazy," I say.

"And you should check your own Facebook. Betcha you've got some requests too. Maybe from some porn pimp, because, omigod, Nadia. You were—"

"Don't! Ah please. I feel horrible." I turn away, swallowing the guilt in my throat.

"You have no reason to feel horrible. It's natural and beautiful to be into a guy the way you are with Bo." She continues, teasing me: "And I know you'll secretly be watching the video at home now."

She means well. She really does. But Zoe doesn't understand. How could she? She has never been in my situation.

"No way am I playing *that* under Jude's roof."

"*Your* roof."

"Either way. He can never see it."

"And Nadia, he *won't*!"

And here we are, with Zoe plunging us right into our biggest disagreement all over again. Sometimes we're from different planets, she and I.

Yeah. Here we go.

CHAPTER Fifteen

LAS VEGAS

BO

We're six days into the tour, and it's more than we could have dreamed. We've popped by radio stations, visited suddenly formed Clown Irruption fan groups. We took a detour for an impromptu gig in a rich, village-sized town that likes to flex muscle and compete with Vegas.

Now, we're in Sin City. It's been chop-chop since we arrived. We've deposited our shit in the complimentary hotel rooms. Sound-checked. Now, we're on our first two-hour breather to grab food and relax before the concert.

I stare at my phone and slide my thumb over the smooth glass. Nadia has answered two of my texts since we left, but only to tell me she isn't coming to Vegas. My reply was that she just poured gasoline on my fire.

I'm calm. Still collected. But I'm heating slowly from the inside out.

Zoe never stopped grinning from *front-of-house* during all of sound-check. The girl made it seem easy to speed into town and lunge herself at Emil. They're displaying way too much PDA for my taste, reducing me to what I was when I first came to the States two years ago: lonely.

I'm lonely at the center of a pulsing cluster of happy drunks, intense gamblers, and hot girls in short-short outfits and perfect war paint. When I'm like this, I miss my country, my parents, and my siblings, but most of all, I miss my best friend—the ex my cold heart never stopped demolishing.

I look around in the bar where I'm seated. Small, cobalt blue lamps tinge the darkness with a luxurious, detached feel. I'm anonymous here. No fan girl recognizes me. But Emil and Zoe do.

"Hey, man! Ready to rock?" Emil asks in his version of polite. That nugget of missing someone breathes beneath my sternum.

"Sure."

"Sorry about Nadia," Zoe says, slumping down on the stool next to me. "Don't give up on her, okay? I haven't seen her like this in a long, long time."

I flick my attention to her and feel my brows draw together.

"I mean, the way she is with you," she specifies without my asking. "When she's around you, she can't take her eyes off of you, and... Nadia is very composed. To be honest, besides her husband, I've never seen her look at anyone the way she looks at you. I think that's why she didn't come along this weekend."

Desire lasers through me and hits my crotch. Because

apparently my ears are connected to my dick.

"Dude, it's none of my business," Emil starts, making things his business before I can reply, "but you can do better, Bo."

Zoe lets out an offended huff. "What the *fuck* are you talking about? Nadia's the sweetest, nicest, coolest girl in the world. If she likes someone, she's there for you forever." She blinks quickly at her own words, and we might both be thinking about Nadia's marriage. "Anyway, she's amazing, and I totally get why you're in love with her."

"Hey now," Emil says, warning her, not wanting his girl to start a fight with me. Wouldn't be the first time one of them did. "Bo isn't in love with anyone, all right? He just digs having sex with her."

"Omigod, how rude! You did not just say that, Emil. She's so much more than sex."

"No, yeah, but I'm just sayin'. And your friend is using my friend. Does her husband get off on sharing or something?"

"Screw you, Emil—you don't know them!"

"Guys," I interrupt. "We are *not* discussing me."

Emil sticks a toothpick in between his front teeth and wiggles it hard enough to draw blood. "Yeah, but you do love sleeping with her. I mean, clearly. She's got you whipped."

This is so much more than I can take right now. I'm fuming.

"That's it," I say, clenching my teeth. "I'm outta here."

It's been a while since I called Ingela. The intensity of this tour, the close quarters with the band, Emil having Zoe here, while I'm barely getting two-word texts from a married woman—it all makes me want to hear Ingela's voice.

"Inga?" I breathe as soon as she picks up.

"Bo! Are you okay?" There are no nervous sighs or choked sobs from her. Back in the day, she'd curse me out first, *then* ask if I was okay, so it's a good sign that she goes straight to being worried about me.

Yeah. Ingela's life is good. She doesn't miss me in the sad way she once did. Sometimes I just need to be reminded that even if I'm lonely, my best friend is happy.

"Yeah, I'm okay. You've heard, right? Have you seen the video?"

"What video? Of Clown Irruption?"

"Yeah," I laugh, hoarse already. We've got more than two weeks left of the tour, and Troll has been on my case over saving my voice and using it right on the backup vocals. "We went viral."

"Dude, no way?" She's so excited she's squealing. I feel my lip quirk happily at the sound; Ingela always was loud. "Does that mean you'll be a rich rock star soon? Cam—baby!" She screams so loudly I go momentarily deaf in one ear.

"What?" he shouts back, matching her level. Then there are weird suckling noises and giggles for a few seconds before Ingela screams, "Oh quit it, you cocksucker.

Bo's on the phone, and he's got neeews!"

"Wrong cussword again, babe," he explains. "Try something simple yet efficient, like dork or— Wait, that's Bo? Bo!" he yells to me next. "Inga, speakerphone." Then comes, "'Sup, man? You a rock star finally?"

They're so in sync I can't stop the void stinging in my chest.

"Not exactly. But we're on tour. You taking good care of my friend?" I ask like I always do since we buried our hatchets.

"Always, man. And *she* takes care of *me*."

"I do not. This gay here doesn't need to be taken care of—not since I sold his squirrel suit. He finally stopped BASE-jumping from cliffs. I told you, right?"

"You did," I say. "Excellent." I suppress a laugh at our Swedish mother tongue still breaking her English; she has lived here longer than me.

"Guy, not gay," Cameron patiently reminds her.

"Anyway, we'll be in Deepsilver for a gig in eight days," I say.

Ingela cheers, much more excited about my coming to her little town this time than when we dated. "Where're you playing?"

"The Deepsilver campus. After the viral video, brats like you dig us."

"Whoa," she laughs. "Look at you, all indie, underground college band. But don't worry—we'll both be there to heckle you. Hell, we'll bring Leon and Arria for quadruple effect."

"Who?"

"Our friends. They own Smother, the bar we work at."

I vaguely remember now. Beautiful Indian-looking woman and a part Japanese guy. "Okay, sounds good. I'll make sure you get tickets."

I feel better after we hang up. Ingela's shrill, sunny voice, and her boyfriend being close by and loving her caused something to drop from my chest.

Nadia's situation had me freaked out. I have no impact on her fucked-up home life. She said he wasn't violent, but her answer, "It's complicated," when I asked if he was an asshole was a giant, red flag. Just knowing you can't influence a situation can piss a guy off.

So yeah, at least Inga is good since I handed her over to Cameron. She has written me off now, as a boyfriend, and it's the way it should be.

I need to find out more about Nadia. As I go on stage, I decide to play Twenty Questions with Zoe before she leaves.

I'm bad news for most women, but for Nadia? Hell, if that jerk she's married to—Jude was it?—plans to keep her chained to him for the rest of her life, I'll volunteer as the voice of reason. I'm not going to promise her what I can't give—love and an actual relationship. I'll be up front about my limitations.

Those five years with Ingela weren't for nothing though. I know what I'm capable of, and I know most pitfalls about myself. If a woman likes me for instance, she ends up liking me a lot. If I give an inch, they become obsessed. I remember Ingela yelling at me about charisma, intensity, and stoking a girl's greed for a man. Whatever the last part meant—Jealousy? Because they do get jealous.

We pour a smooth, loud-as-hell wall of sound out at

the audience. Troll grins from the sound booth and gives me the thumbs-up when everyone goes ape shit on Emil's shout of faux climax after the final song.

We're charged with two encores, the audience stomping against the floor, screaming Emil's name, then shouting mine faster and faster until we jog back on for a last song.

Afterward, Troy and I listen to Luminessence before we meet up with Emil and the others at the hotel club. Even for me, there's no going to sleep after the rush of a frantic audience. Thank God there's no backstage chummying tonight. My head is too full.

The band has found a quietish corner, and strangely Zoe and Emil aren't dry humping. I point at them, lifting my hands in surprise to Elias, who shrugs. He downs his beers while ogling some beautiful African American dancing queens. Damn, are they dancing.

"You got plans for the night, I see," I say.

"Dude, those are my sisters—nothing but honorable intentions, please," Troy jokes, causing Elias to snort.

"Check that one out." He points at the shorter girl, curvy and fierce on the dance floor as she launches into top-speed krumping. "Ah I could fuck her to Mars."

"Poetic." I nod.

"Let me rephrase that for you," Troy says. "*She* would fuck *your* brains out and shoot you off to some planet to never be seen again—perhaps Venus."

"Wow, I'm impressed, Troy. I'd give you an A in all sorts of college courses about—" Before I can continue, my cell buzzes in my pocket. The light flares from the slit, and I pick it up, finding Nadia's number.

Frowning, I push *Accept Call* and check my watch as I walk out of the club. It's two a.m. "Nadia?"

"Hey…" Her voice is tiny and sleep-deprived. And how do I even know that?

"Are you okay?"

She doesn't sound like she's been crying.

"Yeah, I was just wondering…"

I wait, leaving her to finish the sentence. Walk toward the elevators because I want her alone even if it's just on the phone. She doesn't finish though.

"Tell me, Nadia," I murmur into the receiver. "Please. I want to hear what you were wondering about at two in the morning."

She lets out an embarrassed titter. "Oh Lord. I'm an idiot. I couldn't sleep and started thinking… that I wished I were with you guys in Vegas. It's late. I probably woke you up. Ugh, please ignore that I called, and I'll hang up."

"Shhh, you're babbling. And no worries—I'm still awake."

The connection scratches and dies in the damn elevator on the way up to my room, but I call her back as soon as I get out on the eleventh floor. "Nadia, I hope I didn't disturb… anyone? I should have just texted you to call me back," I whisper.

"No, it's okay. Jude isn't complaining."

And that sucks bad. If I were him, I'd be awake and dragging her back to bed. Finding sweet spots to trigger on her body and make her meow instead of be on the phone with another man.

"Your ex," Nadia says. "What's her name?"

"Ingela. You want to know about Ingela?"

A shy laugh trickles through the speaker. "If you don't mind? I understand if you don't want to talk about her. I was just curious."

I smile because there was a time when Ingela's name in a direct question would have pissed me off. Not anymore. Shit, it's so much better to be alone than to drag someone down with you. "You want to hear the whole story?"

"Please?"

Goodness, I love the sound of that. I'd make her beg for other things if she were here.

"Get comfy because it's a long one."

And so I tell her how I'm two years older than Ingela. About always having known her. How we went to the same elementary school, middle school, high school in a tiny place in Sweden. Getting a puppy-crush on her. Beginning to date around the same time as I started my band. I'd sneak in through her window on forbidden sleepovers. Later, I began college in nearby Gothenburg. She'd travel to be with me for the weekend, and I'd visit our hometown so we could be together.

Nadia chuckles. "Been there with the forbidden sleepovers."

"Not with me," I hum out, and her breath hitches on the phone.

"Sort of forbidden," she whispers back. "It wasn't right."

"Felt fucking right to *me*," I retort, harsher than I mean to, and she goes quiet. I don't speak up until she does.

"So… how did you guys end things? Why?" she asks.

She's curious. Maybe she doesn't know how to end her relationship. She must be talking about these things with Zoe, but I want to get in under her skin. If I share my shitty story, maybe she'll share hers.

"I never loved Ingela." My voice sounds flinty in the tiled bathroom of my hotel room. I stare at my own reflection, the icy grey of my irises further broadcasting my lack of emotion.

I'd expect her to be offended on Ingela's behalf about now, but Nadia replies, "Hm. I think you love her a lot."

"In a different way, yes," I say. "I've always loved her like I love my good friends, my sisters, my dog. Sure, she turned me on—I'm a man. But she actually moved to the States to get away from me. I lasted two years before I followed her. I had a bright moment and chose the opposite coast. Sadly, it was still too close, so I just went right ahead and messed up her life again!"

I can't help laughing a little. "She'd come visit me here. I'd go see her in Deepsilver where she lives. I almost ruined an actual relationship that was *good* for her, the first she'd had in the five years we'd been on and off. Her boyfriend almost killed himself—"

"What?"

"Yeah. He's an adrenaline addict. Used to throw himself off cliffs BASE-jumping. One time, he did it to escape the situation Ingela put him in over me. He got sloppy and stopped calculating the danger."

"Wow, I'm sorry, Bo. You've been through so much."

I'm speechless. How does she see *me* as the victim in this?

It's like she knows when she says, "It's hard to watch someone suffer and not be able to do anything about it."

"No, Nadia. I was an A-class douchebag. I should

have done something sooner, but I remained comfortable, keeping things the way they were. Whenever she came, needing me, I enjoyed her. You don't know me, Nadia. I'm a dick. I knew she'd feel worse, not better after every time we were together. Even when she started dating Cameron, she'd come when I called, and it took me a good while to stop and *think*."

"Did she finally wise up?" she asks, again taking the blame off me.

"Not exactly. The two of them had so much distrust between them, so many misunderstandings, I had to help untangle their knots. I sort of…" It's been a while since I've talked about this. Come to think of it, I might not have discussed it with anyone besides Ingela and Cameron.

"What?" she prods.

"I kinda pushed them a little. Especially Ingela. She needed a full-on reminder that we both had to move on."

"And it worked?"

"Yeah. Has been for over a year now. The two of them are so lovey-dovey it's not even funny. Cameron spent the first few months mad as hell at me, but he's mellowed out. Gets that I only want the best for Ingela, which—at least for now—is him. It definitely never was me."

She's silent after I finish my sad excuse for a love story, and I kick my shoes off and let myself fall on the bed while I wait for her response. Wait for her to finally judge me, tell me what a prick I am.

"Wow. That's a nice thing you did there for them."

"Geez." I drop the hold I have on a pillow and scratch my forehead. Everyone knows I don't do nice. Ingela had a tendency of seeing amazing things in me that didn't exist, but even she never called me *nice.*

"Yeah, unselfish. She's your best friend, right? And did you give her up because of another girl?"

"No, I've been in Flingville since we broke up," I say, rubbing an eye with the heel of my hand. The exhaustion from the night is getting to me. The show, the club, the trip here. Not to mention the misconception—the delusion—Nadia has about my less-than-saintly past. "But don't for a second believe that I did it because I'm a good person."

"Why did you do it then?" she asks so fast I'm momentarily stunned. When I don't reply, her voice grows firmer: "Why did you help them sort their stuff out? You helped them find each other, didn't you? And why did you leave her be after that? You could have run straight back in there again and messed things up if you wanted to, right?"

I feel myself shrug against the pillows, and I say the first thing that comes to mind. "It had to be done. I couldn't live with myself any longer, knowing I was making someone I loved suffer day after day, year after year."

"Exactly. Unselfish. And you just said 'love.' The love you have for her is bigger than you think."

We talk for another hour. I can hardly keep my eyes open by the time we say goodnight. When I fall asleep, it's with a quiet in my chest. A peace. A guilt that's become smaller than it used to be. I'll never forget how I made Ingela suffer for the better part of five years. Still, Nadia sees me in a different light, and it's fresh wood on a broken guitar neck. Glue to a cracked ego.

Delicate features flash through my mind, lips moving

while she speaks. I wish I were the upright, noble man she believes me to be. And I wish upon her a better life than the one she must be leading.

Chapter Sixteen

CITIES

NADIA

I WORK A LOT. I try not to call Bo a lot. And then I still do. He's careful about returning my calls when he doesn't pick up, always texting me first. We're sneaking around. Every now and then he asks about Jude, and of course I dodge his questions.

They've made it to the East Coast now, after crossing the country. Too many "pit stops" as he calls it made the trajectory slower, and they've been on the move every day except for the weekend in Vegas.

I have a double portion missing in my heart. One for Jude—I raise my gaze and meet his at the thought.

And one for Bo.

Last night Bo asked me if I could send him a picture of myself. I said "no." What would be the point? He answered, "It's okay. I've got you on video." When he started pondering the possibility of isolating specific frames on the video and keeping a screenshot of me as the photo he wants, I gave in and told him I'd send him one.

Tonight they'll be in a big arena in Pittsburgh.

I need that pic, hot stuff, he just texted. ***Or it'll be screenshot-time.***

Me. Looking like I'm about to jump Bo's bones—spread all over his phone screen whenever I ping him. No. Just no.

What do you need it for? I add a whiny-face to my text.

So I have something to jack off to.

Oh my God. He did *not* write that. My face is hot with guilt and an odd sort of pleasure. I want to rub my brain free of the visual he's given me.

A while back, Jude wanted to immortalize everything we did with actual photos, better types of photos than the one Bo is talking about. My heart hammers as I walk to our closet and pull out a small box.

"Baby," I say out loud. "I'm going to take an iPhone snapshot of one of these. It's… the least of two evils. What Bo's proposing is way worse than him having a photo of me that I approve of."

I don't expect a reply. I don't get one.

Of course I don't.

I grab the stack of photos and fan it out on the kitchen table. These glossy splatters of color sum up our most intense years together. I know I'm going to get lost in the pictures. Remember beautiful moments. Heartbreaking moments. It's going to take me a while to go through them, even if the goal is simply to find one single photo that's appropriate.

And I'm going to bawl again over what Jude has allowed us to lose.

It's been a while since I pulled these out. I hope that I'm stronger now. My glance instantly goes to the bottle of wine I bought yesterday. If I can't stomach memory lane, I'll drown my sorrows right here, in the safety of our home.

I start out with a happy photo. It's of me still wearing the long, brown dress with half sleeves Mother wanted me in. But my hair isn't in a tight bun on the back of my head. It's free, blowing in the wind, and a cautious smile, like I can't quite believe what's happening to me, softens my features.

Yes, my hair is blowing. It's messy, wild, loose. Because Jude took that picture with the windows down in his car while we drove out of Payne Point, while we drove north, while the car was jam-packed with our belongings.

"Is this real?" I asked.

"Sure is, baby girl," he replied, nodding from behind the steering wheel. Not a trace of doubt marred his face as he bobbed his head to the music—rock music I'd rarely heard in my sheltered existence.

I remember the breeze, the smell of sage as we climbed Southern California in his small car: to me, this picture symbolizes the beginning of the rest of my life. I'd never again be controlled by my grandparents.

We had talked about it for years. I was nineteen, Jude just graduated from high school, while I had nothing to show for myself.

"We fled, huh?" I asked.

"We're *eloping*," Jude specified. "Just one stop on the

way to Vegas first. We need to do something."

In the next picture, I'm standing outside the Alhambra Apartments. My arms are spread, my mouth slack with shock, and my eyes so wide they seem to cover half my face. I'm forming a "What?" and I remember screaming it out, laughing, and Jude's toothy grin as he scooped me up and swirled me fast, fast.

"For you, baby, because I've loved you forever. Because I *will* love you forever. 'For now I have chosen and consecrated this house that my name—Jude—may be there forever. My eyes and my heart will be there for all time.' Because you're my heart, and my eyes will be watching you, baby. Forevah! You can trust the holy Jude!"

"Oh goofball! But how did you do this? How could you afford it?" I giggled the words out as he twisted the key in the door to our very own apartment in St. Aimo, Los Angeles.

"Sorry, it's not big," he said, his voice proud instead of apologetic. "It's my first time here too. Guess we'll have to see how it is, right? If it's a pile of shit, then there goes a ton of my mom's savings for me because I paid up front."

"And sight unseen?" My steps took me gingerly through the small den, the adjoining kitchenette only separated from the den by a counter. Cracks in the paint—surely only cosmetic. Dripping faucets.

"Naw. The realtor had videos up on the internet and tons of photos."

"You never showed them to me," I whispered, smiling big, negating the almost-complaint.

Jude pulled me into a tight hug, burying his face in

my neck and inhaling hard. "No. I wanted it to be a surprise."

"Oh goodness, it is. Our own place? Just you and I, no one else around to decide what we can do?"

"You got it." Jude's chest filled with air and dropped out fast with relief. "You and I. We've moved to L.A." Suddenly, he looked up. "We need to hurry though. Vegas next to find a drive-in church that can marry us. And we need wedding bands." He frowned. "I forgot about wedding bands!"

"Those are expensive…" I trailed off, knowing I had no money at all. Mother believed Father should be in charge of our finances, down to the smallest amounts.

Jude laughed softly. "Nadia, they are as good as free compared to this place."

"You bought us a house," I repeated again, incredulous.

"I bought a home for my girlfriend. And the next time we step foot here, this home will be for my wife."

The next picture is freedom. We'd driven all night, dumped our stuff on the floor of our apartment. With the sun rising in shades of pink and yellow, we rushed out of Los Angeles, en route for Las Vegas.

In the photo, I'm in the desert, trying not to lean against a prickly Joshua tree. My smile is so wide—I do look free, with just the smallest glint of insecurity at the corner of my eye. We'd been to the bank, where Jude took out as much of the savings he had access to as he dared. Then we went to a jeweler right as they opened their doors. While Jude took this snapshot, my mind was on the two rings in his pocket. They weren't in a fancy box because they charged extra for it. Beautifully swaddled in a thin silk cloth the jeweler gave us for free, they rested against Jude's thigh.

"A few hours, and we're there," he whispered just as he took the picture. "Once you're wearing this ring, you'll be mine forever. No old prick from the Heavenly Harbor can ever approach you again about the holy matrimony he wants you in. You'll be holy with *me*."

"Don't mention him," I'd said, because it was over. Never again. Never ever.

"Only me. Me, me," my Jude continued, dropping the camera and collecting me in his arms. "We'll talk about you and me—no one else. 'I will sing aloud of your steadfast love in the morning. I'll be your fortress and a refuge in the day of your distress.'"

I giggled. "You know how to woo a girl with warped biblical quotes."

"Years of experience." He smiled against my mouth. "You should try it sometime—it's been quite effective on my fiancée."

BO

Towns blur by. Small ones. Medium-sized ones. Big cities too. We're mostly with Luminessence, stirring up campuses, but on nights off, Clown Irruption also plays clubs too small for Luminessence. Which means nights off from gigs are far between.

Emil has spent his per diems on flying Zoe out twice, reminding me of how I'd rather have Nadia with me than the occasional groupie in a hotel room; since having a tour bus cuts into our touring budget, we only sleep in hotels when we play at the hotels' own venues and they comp us the rooms.

Tonight is a bus night.

"They'll be here soon," I tell Betsy or Betty, dragging her over me onto the bunk bed. She gasps, still in disbelief that her insistence during the backstage meet-n-greet paid off and she's going to be fucked by her "hero," aka me. I draw the curtain, giving us as much privacy as possible.

Knowing my fellow band members, they're still mingling, boozing up, perhaps moving on to a bar. There should be plenty of time to empty my balls and send Betsy slash Betty on her merry way. Then I'll get an early night, hopefully with minimal creaking from Emil's bunk above mine. He's got Zoe here again, and he's loud. Her hot little squeals are what keep the rest of the band from complaining.

"God, you're so sexy," Betsy/Betty pants. "I can't believe you chose me. I'm, like, nobody! My friend Trina won't believe it when I tell her. Can I take a picture?"

"Of what?" I ask, biting her lip and nudging her head into the scrawny, little pillow. "Me screwing your brains out?"

She titters. "I don't know—us? Hold on." She starts fumbling with her iPhone while I hike her skirt up, find a thong that's so skimpy it's completely buried between her buns. I dig deep and pull it off.

"Damn, you're fast," she moans, breath hitching. I'm getting points in the underwear department too? That's a new one.

"Thanks," I mutter and start on her blouse thingy. A few buttons in and she's left wearing nothing but a pink bra. Good look for her, actually. Maybe I should leave it on. She snaps a picture of my face as I push her boob far enough out of her bra to latch on with my mouth. A strange little *iiih* surges from her throat, but she doesn't stop snapping pictures. Whatever.

"Ah you're so freaking beautiful!" she moans as I pop two fingers into her pussy. Groupie-girl undulates on them, which is nice. Either way, I'm still hard from our last song on stage, Nadia's song, and don't need much in terms of chemistry right now.

"I've followed you on Facebook for so long, like months, and you're so… ah, on stage you're even more… I can't wait for you to make love to me!"

Jesus. And I wish she weren't a talker. How to shut her up?

I grip her chin and push the back of her head into the mattress. "So flippin' lucky—I can't believe it…" she keeps moaning, though the mobility of her mouth is partly obstructed.

"Shhh," I say and cover her mouth. Lash into it with my tongue, and she eagerly responds, kissing me back. Even her moans have that incredulous I-can't-believe-I'm-having-sex-with-a-rock-star tinge, and she's seriously starting to piss me off. I hope I can hang on long enough to come.

When I let go to fetch a condom, she hikes up on her elbows, panting and taking more pictures. Playfully, I hold the packet up, watch the flash go off with each new stage of revealing the rubber.

"Enough," I say once I'm ready, and I shove her hand—

holding the phone—under her body before I pull my pants down enough to wrap myself. She wheezes something about me being beautiful down there too, and I feel like slapping her.

"My mind is also beautiful," I hiss as I lower myself over her.

"Yeah, I bet—omigod," she whimpers, tilting her hips up. "You're soooo talented and sexy."

Dammit. Here goes my inspiration.

I hurry up and shove in before my cock gets the memo of us not being excited anymore. I rock quickly, while Bet—she's officially just Bet now—tells me how exceptionally great I feel inside of her. My eyes are closed so I don't have to see her face—nose excitedly tipped backwards, and short, yet somehow thick lips wide open while she takes me. Yeah, she's cute—she had a doll-like quality to her I hadn't tried before. It's why I figured why not?

"Soooo good at making love. Rock-star lovemaking. Ahh I had no idea," she whimpers, and I cover her mouth with my hand again.

"Bet, I'm just fucking you," I tell her as the doors to the bus rock open and Emil and Zoe's voices reach us. There's giggling. Something crashing to the floor and a muffled *whoopsie* courtesy of Emil.

"Ready to make out in my bunk? *Mi casa es su casa*," Emil says in a terrible Mexican accent. "I'm going to make you come like an avalanche."

"Yeah, but don't scratch me up with your nails again."

"Bah, that never happened, Zoay."

"Really now? Because these are my girly parts, and I

know. Just cut your nails, pretty-boy."

Overwhelmed Groupie Girl garbles something between my fingers. I *shhh* her and speed up. I really don't want to be double-dating with Emil and Zoe a few planks above us and plan to get to a quick and efficient climax.

Bet blinks, eyes wide with I-can't-believe euphoria more than sexual ecstasy, and again I realize why I feel like shit after these encounters. It turns me on to see the girl lose it from the pleasure I inflict on her. I want to be the source of that pleasure, make her beam at me for how I make her feel, not for how I look, who I am, or what I just did on stage.

With Ingela, I had that. It was natural from our first time together. We just clicked. We started out inexperienced but in sync. Together, we got to a point where we knew each and every twist, touch, turn of a hip—nudge of my dick inside of her. Everything I did to her was *for* her, and her responses made me so hard I'd splash all over her.

I had it with Nadia. There was a connection. She wasn't there to fuck the musician, the artist, the up-and-coming rock star.

I saw when she *saw*. When she looked past the exterior, my job, my looks. When she discovered *me* beneath everything else.

Nadia's hesitation. Her sensual response and how she tried to subdue it drove me wild. With her unconscious guidance, I returned to my sexual instincts, to what I love the most: finding what ignites my lover before even *she* knows. Stoking her fire until she's oblivious to anything else. In the perfect moment, I touch, lick, caress, pinch, press, until I—

Penetrate.

I'm losing my focus, thinking about another woman. It works though, because I've gone rock hard again. I'm back to the last night with Nadia in Los Angeles. Her skin is beneath my fingers, not Bet's. Her scent in my nostrils, not the mixture of tobacco and booze and sharp perfume under me tonight.

I ejaculate deep inside the groupie while she snaps a picture of my face and sobs, "You're even gorgeous when you come—how do you *do* that?" and then she makes some sort of noise I'm unfamiliar with, causing me to think I might have accidentally made her come too.

"Is that you, Bo?" Emil asks stupidly.

"Who do you think? It's my bunk, right?"

"Sorry, man. Didn't know you had a chick here."

"What the *hell*?" his girl shouts. "Nadia—"

"Zoay," Emil cuts her off. "If you think *my* friend is going to wait for *your* friend to get a divorce to get laid, you're out of your mind. You're being a hypocrite."

There's silence. Then she mumbles, "Whatever, Emil. I…"

"All good, Bo?" Emil interrupts, voice playful.

"If you're wondering if we're done, then yes," I reply dryly, and Bet giggles like she's won a medal.

"She made me come," I specify, mad. At myself, at the stupid girl, and at Emil.

"Who?" Emil retorts, laughing. He's not asking who's in my bed. He's asking who inspired me, and he already knows the answer. In my thoughts, I still answer.

Nadia.

CHAPTER Seventeen
TRAVELS

NADIA

"Seriously? You're doing it?" Zoe asks, playing up her surprise way too much. I stuff a second piece of my Belgian waffle into my mouth and suck the syrup off my thumb and forefinger.

"Yeah. I figured it's time. With Jude, the way things— Well, I just haven't been in shape to continue with school. I'm going to take three courses this first semester, and then we'll see."

"Ah Nadia. That's great. And about freaking time. You'd be stuck at the diner for the rest of your life like me if not, which was neither of you guys' plan," she reminds me. "When do classes start? And is it Cypress College again?"

"Yep, not many community colleges around these parts. And plus it's fine; I liked the place well enough the last time I started. One more year, probably spread over two, at least, and I'll transfer somewhere else."

"For the vet version of pre-med," she says, nodding and feeling clever. "Which reminds me: I haven't bugged you about getting a dog or a cat in a while. You love them, remember? I'll help you pick something out. Something cute that you can dye pink."

I laugh. "I won't be using dye on anything, Zoe, unless it's you needing my help." My phone buzzes out a text from Bo. It's ten a.m. on a Sunday, two weeks after Clown Irruption started their tour. They're on the East Coast, which means it's one p.m. there. Call me pathetic for instantly doing the math.

Nadia, are you awake?
Yes, breakfast with Zoe.
Oh good! I hope you enjoy. You girls need to hit Deepsilver.

"Bo's texting you again, huh?" Zoe asks.

"Mmm. Maybe." I press my lips together to not smile.

"You like it." She's so careful in how she puts it, I look up and find light irises twinkling with happiness for me. That makes it even harder not to smile, so I roll my eyes at her and go back to my phone.

I'm supposed to write, *No, I can't.* Instead I type out, ***When is it?*** and he instantly responds, ***Can I call you?***

I'm hesitant, fingers stilling on the phone. When I bite my lip, Zoe asks, "What's he saying?"

I really shouldn't tell her. Even if her schedule didn't allow her to come along, she'd still do everything to put me on a plane, train, bus—whatever—that will take me there.

Emil and Bo seem to have the sort of man-friendship

where they share stuff though, and Emil would surely tell Zoe. Which means I'm better off telling her up front.

"Bo wants me to visit when they play in Deepsilver."

"That's the place where his ex goes to college, right?"

I nod, and something doesn't sit right in my stomach all of a sudden. I'm not used to eating very much, so two big chunks of the Belgian waffle must be why. I'd really like to be at Bo's side in Deepsilver though.

Goodness. This isn't me being possessive, is it?

I type out **K**, and he calls right away.

"Hey, Nadia," he sighs out, his voice hoarse. I dig an elbow in against my belly and half-hug myself to subdue how my insides clench for him. "I wanted to tell you that the tour has been prolonged by a week. I wasn't sure if Zoe knew either. They tagged on New York and Washington. Luminessence is going home, but we aren't just yet."

A lead weight drops deep in my abdomen. On a daily basis, I work to repress how much I look forward to him coming back. We'd wait for a windy day and I'd take him to the beach and show him how to fly that kite.

I swing at the waist, away from Zoe, because I don't want her to read my expression. I'm sure it's naked right now. "How long…? When will you be back then?" My voice is small, and wow, I sound like a needy wife.

I am a wife. Just… not Bo's.

"In twelve days."

Twelve days is a long time. I feel like crying. This is his job, his life, his business in all senses of the word. Not my business. And yet I want to say, *What am I going to do in the meantime?*

It's ridiculous. What I'll do is what I've always done. Mind my *own* business. Spend my time with Jude, light my candles, have breakfast with Zoe. Work. I'll prepare for school starting in fall. Yes, I'll buy the books.

All of my thoughts don't change the fact that I can't talk right now because there are tears stuck in my throat.

"Nadia, are you there?" he asks softly.

"Are you okay?" Zoe asks, leaning over the table and touching my shoulder.

"Yep," I clip out, and neither believes me. Zoe pours me more coffee, guessing that I need it. I swallow a mouthful, letting it burn me.

"It's why I wanted you to come out," Bo whispers. "I'd like you to come, be with me for a few days. Can you get away? We have extra bunk beds on the bus. You don't have to commit to doing something you don't feel right about. I just want you here. I..."

He lets out a sweet little chuckle I'd drink from his lips if I were there—I know I would—before he finishes, "Yeah. Screw it: I miss you."

I don't think. I just repeat what he said even though Zoe's watching me intently. "You miss me?"

"Yeah, I miss you. There. Doesn't mean I'll be putting any pressure on you if you meet up with me in Deepsilver."

I don't have a good answer, so I don't reply. Just wrap my arm around my belly to keep from imploding with feelings and hope and sensations this man keeps rousing in me.

"Nadia, we talk almost every day. You know more about me by now than a lot of long-time buddies. We've discussed shit I don't even like to think about. How does it surprise you that I miss you?"

"You don't have to swear," I say, and a small smirk returns to my mouth.

"Really? That's what you're getting out of this convo?" he asks. "That I swear too much?"

"I miss you too."

He's the one who goes silent now. I've left him mum, and it feels really freaking good. I don't look at Zoe, who's busy choking a squeal and stomping her feet like fast, little drumsticks under the table.

"Jesus," he finally mutters. "Okay, well, that decides it. You're coming out. The sooner the better."

"When is Deepsilver?" My heart. It's beating so fast it's like I'm suspended off a wire in a crash helmet, about to speed down a mountainside.

"This Friday."

In two days?

"It's Friday," I whisper to Zoe, who mouths, *I know!*

"I can't, Bo. I'm working this weekend."

"I'll take your shifts!" Zoe leans over the table, eyes glittering. "You got Friday off, right? I've got the weekend off, but I'll work it for you. Then you have Monday off and Tuesday until eight p.m. Am I right?"

She says it so loudly, Bo lets out a pleased snicker. "So, after travel time, you could, in theory, be with me for three days?"

I have so many thoughts right now. I can't be away from Jude for that long. But I can't *not* go. Lord, I want to go. Crap, I don't know what to do. What if I went to their show in Deepsilver and then instantly returned? Just one night. It would be okay…

"I—need to speak to my boss. Think about it. I'll let you know."

When I hang up, Zoe launches into a one-person applause, then gets up to hug me. "Omigod, Nadia! You're going to see Bo!"

NADIA

"No! Why would you even consider taking Jude?" Zoe shouts.

It's Thursday night, we're at Foxy Lattes, and my heart is racing like I'm about to have a heart attack. I want to back out of my travel plans so much it hurts. The flight is booked. All is set. I'll be there—I'll be there in twenty-four hours! I'm going to Deepsilver, then I'm traveling with Clown Irruption to New York and home from there on Tuesday.

What in the world was I thinking?

Zoe. She took me to the travel agency yesterday. After breakfast with two strong mimosas each. We completed the transaction on-site; she didn't let up until she'd watched me pay up and get it all set. Even so, I'm the one who did it. It was me, all me.

"I can't," I choke out. "I've never left Jude for this long. It'll be good to take him. I'll just— And plus," I hiccup the start to my next sentence, "I like Bo so much—"

"So much you think it's time he meets Jude?" she screams at me. "You're *nuts*, Nadia! You've got to get a grip, okay? You need to tell Bo everything, or he'll think you're a freak show on wheels!"

"Please don't yell. I *am* getting a grip. I'm going crazy." I hear my own contradiction, but it's true; I am getting better. Just—

"Zoe, I can't go." I sob into my hands, losing it in front of all of these people. I hate when that happens.

"I'm sorry, Nadia. Sorry, sorry, sorry. I just want the best for you," she murmurs against my hair. "I shouldn't have yelled. I just get so impatient sometimes. I know. I can't put myself in your shoes and understand what you're going through with Jude. With the horrible stuff you went through before you moved here and after.

"But believe me when I say that I try every day, and what I know is that Bo is good for you. You come out of your shell with him. You blush when he texts you. You're thinking of school again. He gives you something no one else seems to manage—Jude definitely can't—and don't you think it's time to dig into a bit of happiness without guilt?"

I turn my head to the side and find her face through strands of my hair. "I don't know how."

NADIA

"I wish you'd told me. All those years and I never knew you had diabetes, silly boy," I admonish my husband in a light voice. I'm chattering anxiously while I finish my last-minute packing of a small, pink suitcase Zoe lent me since I don't own one.

It's sunrise on Friday, gorgeous hues of peach shimmering in through the curtains of our alcove. I'm in the process of obeying Zoe because I know she's right. I want to become a normal person, a girl who does stuff that feels good, and I want to do it without remorse. If only it weren't so difficult.

"What? Like you didn't have enough to worry about with your parents, that old rich man vying for your parents' attention—about *you*," Jude said when I first asked him about the diabetes two years ago.

"Don't make this about me," I'd whispered back, kissing the shell of his ear.

In the taxi to the airport, I have plenty of time to freak out over leaving him behind. I think about our first road trip, our escape via Los Angeles to Las Vegas.

I recall wondering what people in Payne Point said about Jude and me bolting off. No one in the Heavenly Harbor congregation could have predicted it.

"What a sly boy," they probably said. "He excels at duplicity. It's the mother and father."

A few hours into the Mojave Desert, Jude's eyelids began to droop. He shook his head, long strands of honey falling over his eyes, and I cupped his shoulder with my hand. "Are you okay?"

"Yeah, stop bugging me," he muttered, irritable. I remember how it surprised me since it wasn't a side I had seen of him before.

The car swerved. Jude corrected it easily, his reaction quick at my squeak. Alarmed, I watched him jolt in his seat, once, twice, each time as if starting awake.

"You're tired," I soothed. "Let's pull off the road and take a nap. We don't need a motel room. We can sleep in the car for an hour and move on more refreshed."

If only I'd had a driver's license already. We could have taken turns driving. I'd do it as soon as we returned to L.A., I thought to myself.

"No, Nadia. We need to get to Las Vegas. What if your grandparents track us down before we're married? What do you think will happen? You think they'll respect that you're an adult? Or you think they'll drag you right back to atone for sins and get married to someone other than me?"

Even though he was right, his crude declaration knifed me. He was usually so patient with me while he counteracted Mother and our church's opinions. Jude's preferred technique was to make me smile. To twist bible verses and proverbs they used against me into something funny and beautiful.

But his hands trembled now. He blinked quickly, quickly, the car swerving again, and I grabbed his arm and screamed out his name.

We jutted off at the side of the road in the middle of the desert. He bit his lip, sweating in the icy air conditioning.

"What is wrong with you? This isn't just being tired," I said, fear surging comet-fast in me and producing adrenaline.

"I… sorry. I have diabetes. I guess I need something to eat."

"What do you want?" I scanned the surroundings. Really, we'd been on the go, and we hadn't brought any food.

"In my backpack. Got stuff in there. Blue bag."

Old Mary from our congregation flashed through my mind. I remembered her falling to the ground, people thinking she was in religious exaltation until a nurse got up and ran to her, ripped her purse open, and gave her a shot. She returned to herself again afterward.

Diabetes. My boyfriend has diabetes.

I pulled out an insulin pen with a small Yu-Gi-Oh sticker wrapped around the lid.

His eyes flickered to me, and dazed, he shook his head. "Not that one. Give me the bag with the syringes. Glucagon injections. It's to help get my blood sugar up." But with quaking hands, he couldn't do it himself. "Follow… instructions," he slurred, giving up.

I read and re-read. Panic couldn't take over because the health of my love was in my hands. Somehow, I managed to draw liquid out of the tiny bottle and into the syringe. "What do I do?"

"Nothing. Give it to me."

I watched him lift his shirt and expose his sinewy waist. Then he re-decided, shaking his head. "No. This isn't insulin," he reminded himself. "Arm, Nadia…"

His head dropped against the headrest, and the tremors starting in his thighs made me die with worry. He groaned as I emptied the syringe somewhere in his upper arm—I had no idea; all I could compare it to were the vaccinations I got in Payne Point. Jude was so exhausted I didn't understand how he could remain conscious.

We stayed in the car for a while afterward. He stumbled in and out of sleep for a few minutes at a time. Whenever he woke up, he'd be my Jude again. Patient, comforting, explaining how everything would be okay. "I'm just tired," he said.

"Jude," I pleaded once he was well enough to take us the last two hundred yards to a gas station. "Don't wait so long the next time."

Surrounded by reddish sand and cacti, I focused on the tiny building, wobbled to my feet, and straightened. In the mini-market, a sleepy old man slouched behind an old-fashioned cash register. "We need to always bring food. Right? If I knew, I'd have made sure we picked something up."

"Yeah, I always do, but—I've been busy today. I wanted to get my girlfriend to Vegas!"

"I know, but still. Alive, right?" I only partly joked.

"It's okay. No matter what, I always carry glucose tablets."

"Do you always take them when you need them though?" I smiled at him; clearly, he didn't. Jude winked, eyes twinkling.

"My pretty fiancée made me forget."

"I don't think wives would let that go. Now that I know, I'll be hounding you."

Jude was still exhausted, a little shaky, but the color of his skin was normalizing. He lowered the backrest of his seat and drew a long, relieved breath. "Feels good now. That shit can sneak up on you, it's weird. If I'm busy with something else, I forget why I'm uncomfortable."

"And then what happens to your body? I mean, I saw, but I don't really understand." I smoothed all the hair away from his face so I could see his tired features.

"Just... I don't naturally produce enough insulin.

Basically, my pancreas doesn't work, so I have to take shots to kick-start it." He tipped his nose back against the headrest, looking down at me and straightening imaginary glasses. "Or as my doctor says: insulin is what makes our bodies able to exploit glucose—which we take in through food."

"And there's insulin in the Yu-Gi-Oh pen?" I asked, causing a breathy chuckle to seep from him.

"Yeah. And I need to eat afterward, because it's dangerous to have too much insulin and too little glucose—or blood sugar."

"What happens if you do?"

He rolled his eyes, head limp against the seat. "Nadia, nothing ever happens, besides this. I get exhausted and shaky and irritable. Then I eat. Then I'm fine."

"Good, yes," I said. "But what if you didn't have any food?"

"Everyone dies without food."

We drove on in silence. We shared two packets of peanuts and a sandwich, but my baby was getting short with me, angry about my digging for information.

"I'm sorry, Jude," I said as the city of Las Vegas appeared in front of us. "All I want is to be there for you, to know what to look for if something like this ever happens again. Can you tell me why you didn't take the glucose tablets before in time?"

"Pff, I could have still taken them. Straight into the vein was just faster."

"Why didn't you?" I don't insist where I'm not wanted, but this was Jude's health and I needed to understand.

He didn't look at me when he finally relented. Instead

he raked a tired hand through his hair and stared at the yellow line in front of him. "I told you. Because I start feeling icky. Next thing I know, I'm feeling worse. Depending on what I'm doing, I don't always put two and two together before I get upset and exhausted, and then I just want people to back off and let me rest."

Suddenly, he sent me one sharp glance before his attention returned to the road. "The insulin shock—the overload of it working on too little glucose—makes my body shut down. My brain isn't working coherently, doing what's logical, and I could launch into convulsions and faint. Then there's coma. After that, death. Da-dum!"

I sucked in a sharp breath, and he shrugged. "But seriously, that doesn't happen. Not since the dark ages. Nowadays, it's just an urban legend or something doctors love to scare diabetics with. Please don't create scenarios in your head. We're about to get married!"

I couldn't buy into his subject change yet. "What's the worst you've experienced?"

"Meh. I fainted once and had convulsions, but that was a long time ago, while we still lived in San Francisco. We'd been trekking with family friends, we ran out of food, and miscalculated the route a smidgen. My dad ran the last mile to the car with me over his shoulder." He laughed. "That was the most uncomfortable ride of my life."

The past still glimmers in my mind as I pay the cab driver and pull my suitcase onto the curb. The urge to send a message to Bo, tell him I'm not coming after all, is so strong my finger trembles against the phone screen.

But a boy that looks about nineteen slows down next

to me. He has honeyed locks that are little bit too long and a suitcase in one hand. Still, he offers to take mine.

I nod wordlessly even though mine has wheels and is easy to roll inside. Because in an airport like LAX, where people shove past and mind their own business, it must be destiny when a boy who looks like my past breaks the norm and shortens my road to Bo.

Chapter Eighteen
FLIGHTS

BO

I haven't been in Deepsilver since Ingela's meltdown, not since I helped her straighten things out with Cameron. The two of them visited in L.A. during Christmas break, but over the last year, that's all I've seen of them.

I sit in the front lounge of the bus with the TV blasting a Van Halen documentary on the way into town. Funny to be in Deepsilver, not to comfort Ingela or to find solace in her, but for a gig that pays actual money.

Clown Irruption has played the area before, but back then we rented a cheap van and the rest of the money went straight to gear rental and bills in general. We're nowhere near rich now either, but a year ago we were prototype starving musicians.

My phone buzzes, and I swear it's louder than usual. Which makes sense because it's Inga. I pick up quickly so

Troy, who's slumbering in the captain's chair next to me, can keep doing his thing until the bus parks.

"Bo!" she shouts. I hold the phone out from my ear until she finishes the question. "Are you here yet?"

"Ja. We're pulling up to some sort of museum? Says 'University of Deepsilver' on it. Guess we're in the right place."

"Cameron!" Her hand must accidentally be covering the phone because it's muffled. She muffles nothing on purpose. "He's here, baby!" Something clangs hard against the speaker before she's back on, yelling excitedly to me. "We can be there in, like, fifteen! Or wait... I'm showering first. And I need to decide what to wear. But we can be there in—soon, super-soon!"

It's four hours until showtime. We better be all set before Ingela comes, because the girl knows how to make an entrance and keep it that way. I'm a hundred percent sure it's a terrible idea to have these two hanging out while Troll's going crazy prepping the stage, setting up dressing rooms, and politely fighting with Luminessence's tour manager over details.

Already she has managed to wake Troy up. He's staring at me dazedly, golden eyes flitting from my phone to my face in question.

Ingela, I enunciate, and his mouth forms a quick "o." He's the only one in the band who hasn't met my ex. The rest has seen her at her best—*and* her worst. Troy has heard stories though. The less Emil has going on and the drunker he is, the more he'll rip into old adventures involving Ingela.

"We need to get ready first, but I'll put you on the

guest list as soon as we're situated."

"You sleeping over at our place, right?" she scream-asks. "The couch is gross, but you don't care, and I got thick, new Swedish duvets from my mom! You can have two!"

"No, I'm renting a hotel room tonight," I admit. Troy gives me the courtesy of looking away, knowing my hopeful plans with Nadia.

"Why? It's cheaper to sleep here. Cam makes poached eggs for breaky, and they taste like *real* boiled eggs. The *real* way!"

"Nice. Well, I'm having a visitor."

"What do you mean, a visitor? Someone from home? Not your sister, right? Oh my God, is it your sister? Cameron, you'll get to meet—"

"No one from home, Ingela." I can't help smiling at her ferocious enthusiasm. She's the Ingela I used to know, from our first year together. That lightness in my chest shines again. Damn, it's nice to know she's happy. "It's someone from Los Angeles."

For a moment, Ingela loses her footing. She has no retort. During the time we were on and off, we were both aware of each other having lives outside of our strange agreement but didn't delve into the other's hook-ups. Yeah. I suddenly realize she hasn't heard me confess to something like this before.

"Bo?" Her voice is so low it could be taken for a normal person's. "Are you freaking *dating* someone?"

And that's when it dawns on me that I should have kept my big yapper shut. I regret my sharing like a motherfucker. I can see so much go up in flames right now it's not even funny. Ingela talking with Nadia. Nadia's eyes going wide with incredulity at whatever cow dung Ingela litters out, like tips on stuff Nadia should try on me—oh Jesus.

"Ingela." I grab the cell with both hands and lean over my knees, cupping the device as if it's her face I'm restraining. "You have got to listen to me. No. I'm not dating this girl. Here's the deal:

"Her name is Nadia. I like her very much. She's special. She tries her best to stay away from me, while I try my best to get her to spend *any* amount of time with me. Get it? So do me a favor tonight: obviously, you'll meet her. Just keep your mouth shut. Don't make up stories—"

"Oh fuck you," she sings, the queen of random cursing as usual. "I never make up stories."

"Okay, fine, how about: don't warp the truth to make it sound interesting. Don't tell her I like her. Don't—"

"Really? *That's* the level you're at with her? You're a rat if you think she doesn't already know you like her. And, Baby Christmas, this can't be happening: Bo is worked up over a girl!"

I groan into my hands while Troy clears his throat to disguise how hard he's laughing. Speakerphones are a waste on Ingela. She's her own *loud*speaker. Pun intended.

"Why are we talking in English?" I ask, frazzled. "You make more sense in Swedish."

"Because Cameron is here, you douchewaffle! How else can he understand?"

Douchewaffle?

"How does he understand anything around you?" I mutter.

"Or 'douche*bag*,'" Cameron suggests sweetly. "See you

tonight, Bo," he adds.

"Good deal," I reply, though all I see is the night going up in flames, forest-fire style. Now, my only hope is that Cameron keeps Inga busy.

BO

According to Nadia's flight schedule, she should have been here by now. I text her but get no reply. I'm hoping she's delayed because the alternative is going to mess me up. It'd mean another harsh after-show workout and maybe some random chick from the meet-n-greet.

Troll grumbles about my per diems going straight into the hotel room and how it's up to me what I use it on. I nod once, because exactly: per diems are for us to do what we want with, a small daily advance on our income before we've finished the tour. And back the fuck off, Troll. I'm not in the mood.

Sound-check is over, and we're picking off of hospitality trays set out in our dressing room while the guys, or more like, Emil, downs beers.

"You heard from Zoe?" I mutter.

"Oh!" He widens his eyes. "You mean my chick? Who's working *your* chick's shifts so she can come out and see you? No. She's busy."

"She's not my chick."

"You act like she is."

"Shut up." I get up, grab the guitar, and exit the room. I hate hanging with everyone else before a show anyway.

We're playing the university's theater stage tonight—they offer performing arts as a major here. The backstage area is deep with layers and layers of thick curtains that divide it into roomy pockets. I find a dark corner in the back and sit down with my acoustic guitar over crossed legs.

It's quiet, and I feel the stress ease as soon as my fingers begin working the strings. I hum out a melody, a new one that came to me last night. It mixes nicely with this chord I've been experimenting with. I stop abruptly and add two raps with my knuckles against the wood before moving on.

I play another riff inspired by Nadia. I don't have lyrics to it yet. It's a platonic emotion, but I couldn't verbalize it without sounding ridiculous if someone asked. There's just the soundtrack to her skin for now and the way it felt beneath my fingers.

Stroking the notes out of my instrument, I ease myself into concert mode. It's soothing and opens me up to the audience.

This will be a ballad. Definitely a ballad. About the way she lies, arm covering a mixture of elation and embarrassment on her face after an orgasm. The paler, fragile skin on the inside of her arm, so exposed to me on top of the sheet.

"Bo!" Troll's gruff voice reaches me from beyond the exit sign. "That you?"

"Yeah. It's early still," I tell him.

He doesn't answer, but light footsteps move in my direction. I look up as a silhouette I don't recognize approaches. I keep playing, wishing I could keep my peace longer.

"Hey," Nadia murmurs, breathless like she ran all the way from the airport.

I set the guitar down, jump to my feet, and laser in on her. "Shit, Nadia. I didn't think you were coming."

She lets out air that could be a chuckle. "I almost didn't."

"Did he try to stop you?"

"No, not Jude..."

The plan was to not pressure her if she came out to see me. I'd play nice. *She'd* have to take the first step if she wanted more than friendly.

Screw that.

My arms are around her before I can think because damn it to hell and back. Her ribs are soft ridges under my fingers. Bird-like shoulder blades, neck delicate with small nubs leading into the fine hairs at the top of her nape. Nadia's mane is thick and silky in my fist when I pull her head back.

"Ah I've missed you," I murmur. Run my nose up the side of hers until our mouths are spaced only by warm air. I shouldn't. I don't want to scare her, but—

Her scent.

Her skin.

Her lips.

I crash my mouth to hers and kiss her harder than I ever kiss. All this time we've been apart. I don't even know her, and still I've missed her so much!

"I don't know what you do to me. I think about you day and night." My voice cracks, but I want to say more—talk, talk, talk to her.

"Bo," she starts, her voice rejecting something—me? What I feel? What *she* feels? But her arms squeeze around me with slender, strong hands that don't want to let go any more than I do. "Last flight was delayed."

"I wish you'd texted me."

"Sorry…"

She sits down with me after, when I finally release her from my embrace. She listens to me prepare, and we have a full hour to ourselves, there, on the floor. Nadia's dark eyes glint with unwavering belief in me, charging me up, making me stronger and more focused, and it's magic the way my notes spill out rich where they were stale before.

"You're my muse," I whisper, rewarded with her wordless smile.

"Fifteen minutes!" Troll bellows from the exit. "You need anything from the dressing room?"

"The other guitar, a water, and…" I bring Nadia's hand to my lips. "What would you like? A beer? Wine?"

"A bottle of water would be nice," she says, and I repeat it to Troll.

I lace our fingers and pull her hand behind my neck so she has to lean in. She does, and with her cheek on my shoulder, I tell her the title of the ballad she's heard me plunk out. "*She Came* is the name of this song," I whisper, kissing her temple. "And it's not dirty. Just: you came. Because I was worried you wouldn't."

NADIA

I'm behind Bo on stage in a concert hall that looks more like a theater. The band blares music out over velvet seats, gold walls, and enormous crystal-adorned candelabras that must be vibrating from the volume. It's weird and beautiful the way the boys desecrate this reminder of ancient glory.

Emil even sheds his shirt half way through the concert, perspiration glistening under red, blue, and green stage lights.

The orchestra pit holds no musicians tonight. It's jam-packed with girls dancing and screaming along to their songs. I don't remember people being so frantic at Clown Irruption's concerts in L.A. Is this what "going viral" means for a band?

All the way in the front, two couples tap the rhythm and bob their heads calmly. The couple to the left are both dark-haired and gorgeous; he, of some sort of Asian descent, and she seemingly Indian. The other girl, a skinny blonde with a short bob, sings the lyrics perfectly, and despite being cozy in the crook of her tall, equally blond boyfriend's arm, her eyes remain on Bo.

I'm surprised when I realize the boyfriend also focuses on Bo most of the time. He laughs heartily with his girl when Bo loses his guitar pick and fumbles for another in his pocket. At one point, the four of them shout-talk with each other over the music, and my heart jolts as I realize exactly who these people are.

The blonde, right there, is Ingela. Bo's ex, the one who made him think he was incapable of loving anyone. From a distance, she looks innocent, sweet, and the epitome of Scandinavian-model-gorgeous.

Wow. And suddenly, it's hard to believe he couldn't love her. I know I'm not being rational. Looks mean nothing and chemistry is everything. But what a cruel twist of fate when one person loves dismally and the other never did?

I stare at her for too long. She feels it, and suddenly her gaze slides to me. I freeze, too stunned to retract my attention, and I register the moment when she understands I'm here for Bo. Her eyes darken, the slightest tilt of her chin showing her recognition. I flush, caught, and look away until the song ends.

Bo's position has shifted, blocking her view of me. I realize I'll probably meet them afterward, but I need to digest this. She's so beautiful, so incredibly different from me. What does Bo see in me? It's strange to know so much about her, about their relationship and the intensity of her heartbreak over my—over Bo.

Lost in fruitless musings, I don't realize until too late that my stare remains on Bo's back. The bass drops violently in the song, and Bo drops too, revealing Ingela and Cameron's stares. They cut past him and straight at me.

I hold my breath. Force myself to remain still so I can absorb Ingela's disapproval. I steel myself for rage or a polite freeze-out, but instead her lips spread in a smile as gorgeous as all of her. She elbows her boyfriend, and in sync, they both lift a hand and wave.

I flush.

It's okay. They can't see my coloring in this light. Tentatively, I smile back. Lift my hand in response. Bo twists, registering my half-greeting, and floats a look down to Ingela and Cameron before his face lights up in a pleased smile.

By the time Clown Irruption launches into *Fuck You*, I need to not look at the couples in front of the stage. I'm ashamed, worried about how much they know. The song airs Bo's feelings, but it's a play-by-play too, of something that occurred between us in his imagination. What does the audience get out of this? Do they think all of it happened? Due to the video, most think Zoe is the "muse," I remind myself. Unless someone tells them otherwise.

I'm drawn to their expressions like a dimwitted moth. Ingela's boyfriend wears a small smirk. He withdraws his glance as soon as it meets mine and nuzzles against Ingela's ear. She though, stares right at me. Eyes wide, she makes no effort to hide how stunned she is.

My cheeks are aflame. I know what she went through with him. All those years she put into their relationship, while I—I've done nothing that could justify the desire he bares in this song. I feel like apologizing to her for what came to me so easily.

Once the curtains go down, I'm enveloped in Bo's endorphin rush. "There you are, my lucky charm!" He rubs his face into my throat, leaving me moist with his sweat. I let out a small squeal that makes him laugh.

"Do you hear them out there?" he asks. "Do you?"

They're stomping their feet against the wood, the echo rumbling through the space and demanding an encore.

"Yeah, that was all me," I joke, brave and influenced by his high.

"Yes, you were so gorgeous! You inspired me, standing there all sweet and supportive." Bo is outgoing and expressive like Emil, not his usual controlled self. He's nuzzling, smooching me, and I feel this crazy lightness grow and fill my chest. I feel bubbly… fizzy…

Happy?

God!

"'Kay, get back out there, girls," Troll shouts. "Ready?"

"Ja!" Emil replies in Swedish while Elias goes, "Yup-yup-yup!"

When the curtains pull apart, everyone runs back in, only Bo doesn't let go of me. Awkwardly, I bop after him, trying to hide behind his body. It's not easy because he's rock-star skinny.

He grabs the microphone, half-tilts the guitar over a hip so there's room to bring me closer. With me furtively struggling at his side, he yells into the microphone, "You want to hear another song?"

"Yeah!" the audience roars. "*Never Ever!*" The scattered calls start in the back of the arena but spread quickly toward the front until they grow into a unison shout that floods in over the stage.

I remember that song. It's sad and beautiful, a love song. It's about not being able to give what it takes, and if it's Bo's, he probably wrote it about Ingela. Now, he presses me into his side and kisses the top of my head.

"No sad-as-shit songs tonight!" Emil screams out over the audience. Troy takes his cue and starts drilling out horror-movie-fast beats on the drums.

Half the crowd cheers back at him, while a smaller group boos.

"Tonight! It's all about celebration. Because we're in fucking *Deepsilver*, people! And because my man Bo, here, has gotten his mojo back. He has stopped writing sad-as-shit songs!"

Elias' bass adds a strange rhythm to Troy's beats, jumping up and down in a melody I don't recognize as rock. It still complements the drums, and for a moment, I'm entranced by his porcelain-white fingers, which rip at those strings with such strength I'd break mine if I tried.

"Ha-ha!" Emil laughs to the crowd. "On drums, Troy Armstrong!" The band turns and mock-bows deep to Troy as he starts on a funk beat he speeds up until it morphs into something completely different. Punk-jazz... on speed? All I know is, Emil is cracking up.

"On bass, Elias Mikaelsson!"

Elias bobs his head, winking at me as he booms out a fast rumble on his instrument.

"On guitar—Bo Lindgren!" This is my chance to escape, I think, tensing in preparation, but Bo twangs a single string and raises it straight over his head with one hand. The thing howls, creating an intense feedback from the walls and almost drowning out Bo's *woohooh* into the microphone. His arm is a vise around my waist, and I want to die and laugh out loud at once.

The audience screams back, the applause thunderous as the noise fades. With one hand clutching the microphone on the stand, Emil points straight at me, arm outstretched. "On muse duty: Nadia Vidal. Guys! Tell her 'THANK YOU!'"

"Thank you!" Troy chuckle-shouts into his mic, and Elias follows suit. It's ridiculous, and I'm traffic-light red and squirming to break free. The audience seems to notice my embarrassment and hollers and claps.

Bo plays along, dips me toward the floor, and invades my mouth with a kiss. The move raises a flood of catcalls and whistling. It's too private in a public show, but I enjoy it—forgive me, I enjoy it.

I retreat into the merciful darkness backstage as Troy introduces Emil, and Clown Irruption moves on with their encore. Troll meets me there. Good-naturedly, he pats my shoulder and offers me a beer. I take it. I need something stronger than water.

"The boys are frisky tonight, huh?" he asks.

"Yeah," I say, breathless. "You could say that."

"It's nice to see them like this." He nods toward the stage. "Bo especially can be droopy sometimes, playing the whole dark, angsty thing up to an unhealthy level. Seems you're doing something to the boy."

The too-familiar brick of guilt coalesces again, its weight settling in against the floor of my abdomen. It's a double shot, remorse over having left Jude, and pain over having given a part of myself to Bo.

I am not free to give anything away.

CHAPTER Nineteen

RIOT

NADIA

THE AFTER-SHOW MEET-N-GREET GOES AWRY. The audience with backstage access trickles in calmly enough, but the count must be off because at least sixty strangers are suddenly pressed together in a small area wanting to take pictures and touch the band.

Girls push to get close to Bo or Emil. They get frustrated, and scuffling ensues. A drunk girl slaps another in the face, which fires up a strange-looking older man with a beer. I catch Troll muttering, "Backup security. Now," to venue staff.

Bo shields me with his body, a hand clamped around my waist behind him while he chats with fans. I have no problem decoding the tension in his voice. A few new guards take position at the door, efficiently blocking further entrance, and I notice Ingela by the wild hand gestures beyond them. She points at us, livid.

"Ingela is here," I murmur to Bo.

"Troll, can you get them?" he asks. The tour manager lumbers off with a nod. Ingela's annoyance dissipates as soon as they let her in, and she has no problem wheedling her way through the crowd, flashing smiles and *sorrys* at the huffs of disapproval. Cameron follows her, a hand on her shoulder and shooting off amiable winks at girls who have a hard time budging.

I stare—really stare at these people. Behind Ingela and Cameron with their gestures and sunny bursts of energy, walks the dark-haired couple. The woman has long, jet-black hair and golden skin that contrasts starkly with her eyes. When they meet mine, they're the closest I've ever seen to purple.

She's the opposite of Ingela, even shorter than me, curvy in the right places and gorgeous in an exotic way. Arriane, Bo said, is Ingela's best friend.

But the one who draws you in, in a way that's startlingly similar to Bo, is her husband, Leon. Funny how one's brain associates. *Ninja. Karate*, I think.

Tall and slender, Leon boasts the erect posture of an old-timey warrior. The slight tip of his chin and the pale eyes that completely ignore the frenzy surrounding us make him seem like he's surveying humanity from above.

Calmly, the two stride forward with no need to push their way through. People step aside, and many nod in recognition. I guess if you own the hottest club in a small college town, people know you?

"Bo!" Ingela squeals and throws herself around Bo's throat. "You dickshit! You could've let us in right away! How the hell does she get to be backstage and I don't?"

Dickshit?

"Hey, man," Cameron says, grinning and slapping Bo's shoulder.

"Dude, I'm sorry—we had no idea it'd be like this," Bo says, kissing Ingela's cheek and swinging me in front of him. "Guys, this is Nadia, a friend from L.A."

"The *muse*!" Ingela screams, causing the closest fan-girl to jump. "You can call me Inga. I'm so happy for the dork you've got there—he's a total ass most of the time, but I'm glad it gets you off. Hey, at least he rocks in bed, right?"

And no. She did not just say that.

Groupies suck in air excitedly around us, while I'm busy blushing harder than I ever have.

"Nice to meet you," I croak out and send Cameron a side-glance. The poor man must be mortified. Who says that about one's ex—to someone he's currently with—in front of her boyfriend?

My thoughts are interrupted by a guffaw. It comes from Cameron, and it's so hearty he throws his head back. "Ah," he manages and pulls Ingela in. "Not sure it applies to the occasion, but it's *dipshit*, babe."

"Pff, you Americans. Always so picky with words," she replies, rolling her eyes. "Right, Bo? Does Nadia pick on you too?"

Bo smiles at my side, inhales to answer, but before he can, I find myself burst out, "No, he's perfect."

What?

Yeah, he's incredible, but geez, Nadia.

"Ah!" Ingela retorts. "See, baby? People *like* how Swedes talk in the civilized parts of America."

"You're so, so perfectly crazy," Cameron pillow-talk-mumbles against her ear.

Sometimes things are just too intimate, too much, when I feel exactly what's going on between people—and my face might never lose the shade of crimson that's burning me right now.

The jostle isn't big at first, but then a wave goes through the crowd, coinciding with Luminessence strolling off stage and into the room. The lead singer—Pop, I think—waves at Bo, who tips an imaginary hat in greeting, and that's all we know before everything goes haywire.

The fans seem confused at first. Then instincts take over and grow into a club-sized version of mass hysteria as they shove against each other, reaching for Elias and Troy who've remained at the fringe of our group. I notice a commotion over by the Luminessence gang too, but security is thicker around them, so they seem to remain untouched.

Troll wedges in between the fans and us, using his solid body to thump people out of the way while speaking rapidly into his phone.

He turns, stares right at Bo, and says, "Backstage—load-in entrance. Go!" He flicks a dubious gaze my way, as if suspecting it won't be easy with me in tow. I don't comment because what do I know?

As we steal backwards through the crowd, through pawing hands and security elbowing people out of the way, my heart thuds like I'm the one about to get mobbed. Leon and Arriane, the last two of our group, join us at the top of the stairs, and only a few of the guest-pass holders remain close enough to make an impact.

A tall, drunk man launches himself at Troy, who

notices too late. The man's beer bottle races against us, fast in his hand, "Cheers, *Clown Irruption*!" he bellows, misses Troy's bottle by more than a foot, and hits him in the head instead.

Troy's eyes roll back into his skull. Somehow, before he lands, a blur of black rushes past me and smashes into the guy who hits the floor before Troy does.

That blur was Leon. God, he's fast!

He's got the drunk guy face down on the floor, arm twisted over his back, and with a foot, Leon presses down against his thigh. Leon's face is marble-still, and what I read from his eyes is… unreserved dominance.

For a frantic second, I get a glimpse of Arriane. Her eyes are large behind him, but she's as calm as he is, fearless in this anarchy.

"Walk on," Leon murmurs, staring pointedly at the exit before he catches Arriane's gaze again.

"Are you coming?" she asks.

I'm scared, worried, anxious, my emotions all over the place. I envy the trust Arriane displays, a trust clearly born from experience with Leon. She isn't urging him to listen and flee with her. No, she's just inquiring about his plan.

Leon assesses the crowd behind us and straightens in a silent challenge to a few following us. A light shake of his head accompanied by crossed arms makes them slow their pace.

"Yeah, I'll be there in a few minutes. Move now," he says.

"Dude, we'll help. You need backup to keep them at bay," Elias cuts in.

For a moment, Leon drills a sharp stare into Elias. "They want *you*, so we're better off getting you out first. I'll be fine."

"He will," Arriane assures us quietly.

Between Cameron and Bo, they get Troy to his feet. A gash trickles at his temple, and his right eye is already tinting into a deep auburn. It's going to swell too—I can see it.

"Run, peeps," Cameron whispers playfully behind us. Is he not taking this seriously? Me, I'll probably have a small meltdown once I'm to safety, but this guy?

"Yay, my adrenaline junkie's awake," Ingela bursts out too loudly for someone trying to leave inconspicuously.

"Indoor voice," Arriane whispers. "Even Cameron is using it now. You can do this."

Then we're outside. Then we're all crammed into Leon and Arriane's truck. Then I start shaking and Bo pulls me onto his lap and tucks my face into his neck. Then we rush off to some place—a hotel, not the tour bus—and there's a lot of Ingela wanting to stay in our room and pet me and feed me whiskey I don't want, and a lot of Bo telling her he's got this.

They finally leave when Cameron flips her over his shoulder, waves with one hand, and runs to the elevator with his girlfriend complaining the whole way.

Once the door shuts behind them, it's just Bo and me in the semi-dark of the hotel room. I don't have my stuff. I left it all behind at the theater.

His gaze shimmers in front of me, a hand stroking the curve of my cheek. "I'm sorry we scared you," he murmurs. "It's not always like this."

"Good," I say, letting out a small, weird laugh that doesn't belong to me. "You would never be safe. Troy…?"

"The guys are taking him to the ER. They'll keep us posted, but Troll will be there as soon as he's finished having everyone's ass at the venue."

I smile weakly.

"Are you hungry?" His voice is so low, he stirs something warm inside me.

"No," I breathe.

"Tired?" He's doing that thing where his nose runs slowly up the side of mine until light kisses pucker against the corner of my mouth.

His scent is pine and sweat, cologne and a faint waft of shampoo. An undertone of *him*, delicious and drawing me in even when I'm struggling.

I'm far away from Los Angeles. Far away from Jude and our apartment, from our bed, the one I should change out. It fills the whole alcove, and we're not using it for all it's worth.

My mind rambles while my body is focused, awake, and igniting from this man, whose quiet insistence, phone calls, texts, made me vacillate enough to fly here.

"Your ex is nice," I say, and my voice trembles, not out of fear but from his effect on me. Bo knows the difference, because his hand is sure when it smoothes a path up my throat.

"Yeah, she's great," he replies, not thinking of his ex. He thinks of us, of being close to me; his arm goes around my body, and when his mouth takes mine, it's open and craving me right away. I don't hold back. Yes, there's a kernel of guilt somewhere in the back of my mind, but in this moment, him, us, is what I want.

"So long," he whispers, backing me to the bed. "Do you mind?"

I don't. I so don't mind. My heart is racing again, and from the desire I see in his eyes, heat builds where I am warmest. I shake my head. He must understand, because he lets out a relieved groan and moves in over me on the sheets.

"Can I see you?"

See me?

"Don't you already?"

"I need to see you all the way. The photo you sent," he says, kissing me, "was only of your face."

"O… kay." I hold my breath for an instant; the gentle trajectory of his hands makes me want to pant. I don't know what he'll do next. It's scary, delicious, what I need from him.

He starts with my sandals. Slips one off and rubs beneath the arc of my foot. I let out a whimper, my hips lifting on reflex from my splayed-out position on the mattress.

"You like that?" He smiles down at me, grey eyes twinkling.

"Maybe…"

Bo's hands move beneath a pant leg and up my calf, kneading in ways that makes me think he does it for the both of us. "Ah. I'm only at your leg, darling, and my boner is painful already." A small laugh reveals his disbelief.

"You do things to me," he sighs, raising my leg and letting warm lips brush along the inside of my knee.

"I do nothing." My voice is barely audible, but Bo still hears me. He angles up to meet my gaze through black bangs.

"You underestimate your power." He lets go of my leg to unbutton my jeans and pull downward. His breath heats my skin as he trails behind the receding fabric, nibbling and nudging me. "I know it's bullshit to mention him, but the devil knows how he treats you at home when you don't see how amazing you are."

"Don't— Let's not…"

"I know." He guides my knees together, strong hands helping me curve my butt off the mattress so he can remove my underwear. "Ah silk. Just— You can't wear it tonight. I'll appreciate it some other time."

Men aren't the only ones whose blood rushes to their lower region. I feel swollen—sweetly swollen—and it's as if he hears my thoughts, because his eyes find me there, and a groan surges from his throat.

Still dressed and on his knees above me, he slides his hands along the sides of my legs until his thumbs fan inward, reaching my inner thighs en route upward.

"So beautiful…" He trails off on a reverent pitch. "On the inside. On the outside. Right here."

I bow into his hands when he forms them around my mound. He presses down enough to separate my lips without touching where I need him the most.

I'm so bare, so exposed. I crave the look he gives me, the raw hunger as his gaze glides from my face to my crevice. I want to drink in his expression and hide under my arm at the same time.

That little nub between my thighs. When his thumb

finally strokes it, I jerk on the bed. I am *Guilt*, and yet I need his weight on me.

With an impish glance, he lowers his head, and for an agonizing moment, he sucks me into his mouth.

"Ahhh," I moan before I can stop myself. He shakes his head slowly against me.

"Still a shy girl?" Bo is mock-disappointed. "Although not as shy as before."

Yeah… I shouldn't be this comfortable. It isn't right. It doesn't make sense. Why are things— Why am *I* easy with him?

Long, strong fingers trace my ribs under my shirt and stop at my breasts. "Let's get this off, okay?"

His calm approach. The way he teases me into agreeing, inch by searing inch. I'm writhing, trying to keep myself from hyperventilating. He studies his own hands, how they form around my breasts, and gather them at the center of my chest.

He pinches lightly, and I plead, "Bo."

As if mesmerized, his eyes remain on my boobs. His fingers slide open, making room for my nipples and squeeze so they swell between us. "Darling. You're incredible."

It's not true. I know who I am: a midrange pretty girl with darker features and long hair. Boobs the right size for a man's hands, but there's nothing special about me. Even so, for a moment, the appreciation vibrating in Bo's words makes me almost believe him.

I reach up, stroke his cheek. I'm not a vixen, versed in the ways of lovemaking. Sure, Jude and I, we… but it wasn't like this.

My fingers stroke taut, lean arms beneath the sleeves of his shirt, and I peek up at him, hiding beneath my lashes. Hoping he'll understand when I fumble with the buttons.

"You want me to take my clothes off, Nadia?" he whispers.

I shut my eyes but make myself nod.

"Will you say it too?"

Oh. The part of me still under Mother's heel, under my old religion's thumb, doesn't want to. "Why?" I ask.

"Because it's beautiful for me to hear that you want me naked as much as I want you. Do you like my skin against yours?"

"Yes," I breathe, cheeks flaming.

"And?" He's a little bit stern, a little bit playful, and a whole lot of hot and sexy and demanding.

"I… want… you?"

"You want me. How?"

"Naked… on me." I sound brave.

"*In* you?" he asks so sweetly I clench my thighs to silence the ache.

I swallow. Then I reply, "Please."

CHAPTER TWENTY
WEDDING

BO

IN THE MORNING, we have breakfast alone at the hotel. Quietly, she rests in the crook of my arm after we finish eating, eyes dark, secretive, but still with me. We're ready when the bus pulls up outside. Ingela and Cameron arrive at the same time with their brazen good-byes, and as we jump on the bus, I realize I'm not happy about Ingela getting Nadia's cell number and address. I can picture her now, visiting in Los Angeles and messing shit up.

This girl. I look at Nadia as the bus pulls out of the hotel parking lot; she's got her fingers fluttering in subtle greeting, so different to the two outside. Cameron has Ingela high in the air, trying to wave with her body, and Ingela's playing it up, all but dancing in his arms. I once almost fell for Ingela's vibrant charm. Now, my chest constricts over someone poles apart.

Nadia and I are reclusive on the bus. We keep to ourselves on our way to whichever destination precedes New York. In my mind, I already fret over wanting a hotel room again, but I know I should remain frugal.

I need to touch her. The back lounge is a quiet bubble where I keep her hand between mine, open fingers to study her palm, and joke about love lines. I keep eagle eyes on her phone, which never rings, never buzzes with a text, her husband absent from our lives.

She takes out her wallet, insisting on giving money to Troll for truck-stop supplies, and when Troll leaves, I take it from her and open it wide.

A young man with a huge smile and happy eyes stares back at me. He's handsome, with longish, windblown hair framing his face. Mostly though, what I see is Nadia's presence in the photo.

"You took this picture, didn't you?" I ask in lieu of asking who it is.

"Yeah," she murmurs. Posture rigid, she wants the wallet back, but she doesn't reach for it.

"He loved you here." As soon as I say the words, there's a sting going off beneath my sternum. It's uncomfortable. It hurts. The realization upsets me.

She nods quickly, energetically. Looks down at her hands, which aren't in mine anymore because I'm holding the photo of her husband.

She doesn't talk about her marriage. Zoe doesn't either. I've tried.

"He still loves you?" I ask.

Her head bobs in affirmation, silky brown drooping over her face as she bows.

"Do you love *him*?" Something like hope throbs in my chest, in that place where a love muscle should sit. Mine is just a heart. An organ. A blood pump. The last time I asked her something similar, she told me she did love him.

"Yes, very, very much."

I'm upset. No. A black cloud rises in me, and it's anger—it's fucking anger. Because it's unbearable that she loves him, and because I don't understand why she's on this bus.

"If he's so great, why the hell are you here with me?" I bark, making her flinch. I don't want her to flinch, but I think about this too damn much to let it go. I close her wallet. Throw it on the table. I can't stand his face in that picture.

"Never mind, Nadia. I get it. I'm the triple fling, no big deal. Just sex, yes? Are you at least learning a thing or two you can bring home to Hubby so you can spice up the home life?"

"Bo, please." There's a quiver in her voice, warning me that she's about to break. I don't listen.

"If he loves you so much, why doesn't he check on you? If you were mine, I'd check on you all the fucking time. You'd never be with someone else. Not even for a minute." I regret my outburst when she turns away from me, shoulders like shivering bird wings beneath her shirt as she hides her face.

"I'd keep you happy. I'd keep you satisfied," I mumble.

I get up, lean on the windowsill opposite her, and stare out. Woods. Woods, woods racing by. Nothing to interrupt the fight I've started. I don't want to hurt her, and of all people, who am I to judge anyone?

Just, I want to *know* this girl. Have access to her mind. It's crazy—when I'm inside her, I fucking always want to be deeper.

Possessiveness. I've never wanted to own someone before. Now I do. I detest that she's going back to her husband in two days.

She's crying behind me.

Sad, beautiful, lovely, sexy.

Why doesn't she humor me and answer my questions? Why doesn't she explain why she does what she does?

"You've got the answers," I say, my voice after-concert rough with emotion. "You just don't want to share, do you?"

"It's complicated," she whispers so low I barely hear it.

"Is that your standard reply to everything? Because I've heard it before. So many phone calls, Nadia. And what about last night? This morning? *Now?* Don't I deserve that you at least crack your damn shield open?"

I rush my hands into my hair.

"I'm sorry, Bo."

What is she sorry about? I don't want to know.

"Listen. No: *I'm* sorry," I say, because I won't lose the days we have left. "You're right. You're thinking we're not even friends yet. You've known me for, what, three or four weeks? And why would you talk with me about something that pains you, even if it is him?"

I peer at her hands. They're over the closed wallet on the table. The bus does a turn, causing the sun to stream in over them, mocking me with the bright gleam from her wedding band.

And I lose my repentant moment. Shake my head and return my attention to the woods outside.

"I can tell you… some things," she says in a small voice.

Crumbs. She'll give me crumbs.

"Yeah? Like what?"

"Like… stories."

"You're going to tell me stories about him?" I tip my head back to stare at her. She's suffering. I'm not comfortable being the one who triggered that quivering lip or the tear she wipes with the back of her hand.

"Real stories. Things that happened. When we got married, for instance." The blush sneaks up her throat, another reminder of how distressed she is. My fault.

Jesus. I laugh inwardly because, hey—my life's on repeat. This is just a new way of breaking a girl's heart.

"Oh I'm so dumb. Of course you don't want to hear about our wedding," she backpedals, but I'm not letting her. If it's what she wants to talk about, it'll be a piece to add to the puzzle that is Nadia.

"No, not dumb," I reply. "To learn about your big day is better than not knowing shit about you."

"You know more than most," she whispers.

"I know nothing!" I cut her off because I'm a jackass. Then I regret it and eliminate the distance between us, sink down beside her.

Her throat works through a swallow, so I nudge her shoulder gently with mine in encouragement. "Nadia, I'm a dick, okay? An impatient dick. Know that it's because I like you. Very much."

The little twist of her mouth encourages me. I cover her hand with mine on the table. Lace our fingers. Drag it down to my lap. "So how did you get married?" My question is so light, so offhand-sounding that she makes an almost-laugh.

"We… had fled from Payne Point." Absently, she raises our joined hands and holds them to her mouth. A dry kiss lands on my knuckles. With the story she's telling, it surprises me, but then again, nothing about Nadia is straightforward.

"Why did you run away?" She better prepare for questions because I'll be doing my best to milk more than the easy stuff out of her story. With her I'm a curious bastard.

"Lots of reasons."

"Like what." I don't make it a question. It's a demand for her to talk even though she's already volunteering. I'm struggling with my patience, not ready to let this be on her terms.

She giggles quietly, another surprise. I'd be annoyed if someone cut me off like that. "My parents. You know about my parents and my church."

"Yes, but what changed? You guys were nineteen, you said, and your parents and the church had pretty much been the way they were since you were little, right?"

"It got progressively worse. Mother didn't handle my growing up. The older I got, the more restricted my life became. I didn't own a phone, and in the end I was only allowed to walk my dog in daylight and with Mother. Thank God for Jude's astuteness. If it weren't for him, I don't know who I would have been today."

"You would have still been you. The question is *where* you would have been."

"No, I know where I would have been. In Payne Point,

married to old Mr. Haasch, the main benefactor of our church. It was no secret that his tithe for the year I turned eighteen was the reason why we could add a building to our church. Mr. Haasch needed a wife. I was of eligible age, raised right, and I could give him children."

"Jesus, Nadia. How old was he?"

"My grandparents' age. He was a childless widower."

"And they were going to just marry you off to an old man against your will?"

"Oh yes. It's not uncommon in our church. Just that year, we went to a ceremony where the bride was a girl from the Heavenly Harbor's school, and her groom was… not young. Jude and I fled town on the night before my engagement."

NADIA

To think about my wedding always makes me smile. Despite the situation, telling Bo about it brightens my mood, and in my mind I'm there, right there in the thick of Las Vegas, setting foot in my first real city under dreamlike circumstances.

I've fled from my destiny.
I'm getting married!

The trauma of Jude's insulin shock faded as we drove into the wonder of Vegas. Car exhaust. Perfumed passersby on foot. The streets were a melting pot of hope and promises as Jude scooted our little car in between others in a back alley. Jude walked around the car and pulled me out. The dry heat of the desert burned my nostrils, but it was good, very good. They burned in a happy way.

"Baby, did you know that 'He who steals a wife steals what is good and receives favor from the Lord?'" The desert wind wrestled with Jude's white shirt, a clean, new one he had picked up for the ceremony. I hurried to button him up and suppressed the smile threatening to spread at yet another warped proverb.

"No," I said. "Neither of us will because it's 'find' not 'steal.' Stealing is a sin."

"Ah you're a hairsplitting wife-to-be. Maybe I should reconsider? A whole life with such hairsplittery could be tough for me."

I giggled when he lifted me off the ground and tried to shake me. Of course I was too heavy for that.

"Plus, you're mine. Stupid Mr. Old Man from the Heavenly Harbor would have ended up in Hell for the thievery of an already taken woman."

"He didn't know though," I defend Mr. Haasch. A too-wide grin finally spread and didn't fall the way it used to in Payne Point.

Freedom. It was magnificent. The only person staring me down did so with love, with acceptance sieving from the deep blue ocean he watched me with.

"We made it," he whispered then, setting me down so slowly the tips of my toes touched the ground first.

"Yes, we made it," I replied, holding his gaze too, standing here on a narrow sidewalk with people and scents and sounds bustling by and around.

"Do you have your dress?" he asked, never repressing his happiness.

"I do."

"Remember those words for later. When you're in the dress and in the church."

"I will. I do," I said. "Not 'I don't,' right?"

"No, I'll ask you something really nice, see, and you'll say, 'Yes, I very much do.' That's the only option."

Silly Jude.

I loved all sides of this boy, and I did—I did want to be with him forever. I'd always love him. Every obstacle we met on our way, we'd tackle together. Life would be easy together. We'd grow old together.

Together. We'd always be together.

We were in a tiny, white church with fake wooden siding broken up by stained glass windows like a real church. I changed in the girls' room. My dress was white, light, and shorter than anything I'd worn in a decade.

My legs felt bare, and I slinked back out, ashamed, until Jude's approving gaze rested on me. The guilt disappeared, replaced with a shivering rightness, the same type of right that lasted for the hours Jude used to spend in my house at home.

But it was daylight now, not the middle of the night, and no mother was there to destroy our bliss. The only ones capable of that were *we*, and we would never destroy it. No, we would build our love, always build and cherish.

The lightness imploded in my chest at the realization we wouldn't even be living in sin anymore. Jude… was about to become my husband!

We exchanged unsure glances when Beauty from that Disney film strode into the church room with ballerina elegance. Then the Beast also appeared and lumbered up to her.

Jude shook their outstretched hands, formalities and paperwork taken care of as if our hosts were in their day-to-day work clothes. And they were.

Minutes later, the Beast looked solemn and regal at the front of the tiny church. He lifted a goblet and garbled something in a deep, rumbly voice. Also in character, Beauty stage-danced up to him with tiny steps and kissed his cheek chastely before turning to us.

I reassured myself by fixing my eyes on the cross behind them. It *was* a cross. A real church. Right? Jude followed my gaze and nodded once. *Yes*, he mouthed. *We're before God.*

Our priest opened his mighty fist—the Beast was a giant—raising it to the man on the cross as he rumbled on behind his animal mask. I was not always sure what he said. I answered questions, nodded my consent, but my heart was not with the Beast, with the Beauty, or with the cross behind them. Big, red, and swollen, my heart thumped for the boy at my side. The one who looked at me so intently.

Jude turned his body to me and took my hand. When he began to speak, he spoke our history and our love in bible verses used wrong, so wrong, and I loved him more than ever—his humor, his quirky charm, his ever-presence in the darkest moments of my life as well as this highest peak.

"And I will betroth thee unto me for ever; yea, I will betroth thee unto me in righteousness, and in judgment, and in loving kindness, and in mercies."

"A quote for marrying Jesus?" Inside me, orthodoxy fought the gut feeling that God had a sense of humor.

Jude snickered. Took my hands and squeezed them. "Naw. Today, it's from me to you. Especially the loving kindness and mercies part." My pompous, word-wringing boy.

"I will even betroth thee unto me in faithfulness: and thou shalt know Jude, your husband!"

I laughed too. "No—thou shalt know *the Lord*."

He shook his head, disagreeing and lunging into, "Let us be glad and rejoice, and give honor to him: for the marriage of Jude Bancroft is come, and his woman, Nadia, hath made herself ready."

For five years, our love had remained a secret, and Jude's subtle allusion to the matrimonial bed made me blush. I told myself the only ones listening were two fairy-tale characters, but—the costumes contained humans.

"'A man of knowledge uses words with restraint,'" I quoted and continued, "'Even a fool is thought wise if he keeps silent, and discerning if he holds his tongue.'"

Jude let out an amused snort. My ears burned with embarrassment, but Beauty held a ring out to Jude, and he took it, mirth receding from his eyes as they met mine again.

Pretension and messy proverbs vanished. Jude raised the wedding band and blurted: "Will you marry me now?"

"Yes!" I said louder than I should. The Beast har-rumph-chuckled, causing my ears to simmer hotter. "I do, very much."

Awkwardly, Jude screwed the ring on me like it were a bottle top, and it was okay, it was us—and we were getting married!

"Do you want to marry me too?" I asked, knowing better words waited on a post-it note in my bag on the pews.

Beauty took my cue. Held out Jude's brand-new ring with dainty cartoon fingers.

"Hell yes!" he exclaimed in reply, and I hushed him because it was not, not a good way to start our new life.

For a second, he humored me, saying, "Yes, ma'am, I do," but then he grabbed my waist and dipped me to the floor as he kissed me, a blatant, public display of love. I was weak with happiness and mortification, the wildest mixture that made me feel alive; Jude challenged me, my upbringing, my core values, and I had hung on for the ride since day one.

"'Therefore, behold, I will allure her and bring her into the wilderness and speak comfortably to her,'" he whispered, only for my ears.

"Very comfortably?" I surprised myself by saying.

He nodded against my mouth. "Yes, for my wife, I will do *everything* comfortably."

I don't tell Bo about our wedding night. The big hotel room. The smoothest sheets I had ever lain in. The inexplicable sensation of not being in danger of Mother discovering us. How Jude wanted the light on to see me the entire time. How we compromised by draping his boxers over the night lamp, and even with my eyes closed, his look seared me in awed perusal.

I tell Bo about Jude returning his dad's call. The screaming on the phone, the incredulity, the curse words. How they cut off Jude's funds, placing his savings in a trust fund "where it belonged until he got his shit together."

I tell Bo about the pet store we visited the morning

after. That we did it for fun, that I don't remember the last time I'd been in one. The hamsters, the cats. The puppies. Then the tiny monkey someone brought in on a leash and allowed to select his own toys.

"Quite the wedding," Bo says. His eyes don't glitter like Jude's. They simmer like a dirty glacier under the sun, the way packed snow looks on documentaries from the South Pole. And even now, fresh from the memory of the loveliest day of my life, I can't stop staring.

CHAPTER Twenty-One

SILK

BO

Her moods flow in gentle waves. The coffee of her irises swims with sadness then lifts into whiskey gold with the twang of my guitar. Left to ourselves in the back lounge, our silence is sinuous, laced with stories from my hometown, Skala, and Nadia's anecdotes from growing up in a cult. But when we're quiet, my fingers itch and find my guitar. Toy with strings and enunciate emotions she tries to conceal.

Sometimes, my riffs turn to ballads while lyrics splash out in patches of color in my head. Sometimes, when Nadia curves a hip to get comfortable, my gaze swims to her waist and shifts to her chest. The game of my chords turns loaded, adding a steady, slow beat, the way I do to make her climb when we're together.

Without words, she still hears my hunger. Watches my fingers work metal strings with a need that becomes

X-rated. And she sits up. Joins her legs and lowers her chin to her knees, demure, secretive, hiding behind her hair in shyness and not understanding that she's sexier than ever.

All these females. So many women and vixens with a past, a present, and a future—a full life I never wanted to be a part of. But now, I crave to bury deep under the skin of a single girl who is not single.

It's been a while since I spoke last, so my voice rasps deep when I say, "You kill me."

"I don't want to kill you. Do you know the *person* you are? How talented you are? You deserve so much, Bo, you don't even know, and the last thing you need is dead weight like me."

Dead. Weight.

I drop the guitar and lunge for her. Form my fingers around her face and dig in so she's still against the backrest of the sectional. "You. I don't know where you get these ideas. You are not dead weight. Whoever thinks you weigh them down should leave you the hell alone because—"

I kiss her to cut myself off. What I'm about to say is ridiculous, can't be true, not how I work. My brain is playing a trick on me.

The last thing I want is to hurt another innocent. With Ingela, I promised to be her boyfriend, which includes acting like a boyfriend and feeling like one. I failed.

I lick Nadia's mouth and suck a lip into my own. Why is it plumper, softer, firmer—*more*—than any other lip I've indulged in?

I'm twenty-five. I've done it all. The chance of all of

me being on some weird chemistry trip that'll wear off in a minute is still huge compared to the alternative.

I thread my fingers into her hair. Tilt her head back for more, and she stutters a breath that turns my dick to granite.

"Don't," I murmur, though what I want is for her to be exactly who she is and do exactly what she's doing.

Duplicity. Lies. Such a female thing, but it's not her today—it's my mind and my nerve endings lying to the both of us. I need to keep my tongue while I wait for it to end.

Nadia tangles into my licks with the same heat, same feeling, that thumps steadily beneath my sternum.

"Beautiful girl," I manage. "I'll get us a hotel room in whatever the next town is," I promise.

"Don't squander your money," she whispers, and when the night comes and we've played our show, I crawl into her shallow bunk in the bus after everyone is asleep, clip the curtains closed, and I hold her tight.

She's reluctant, sweet, tempting, and her hesitancy makes my fire roar, makes me want to growl out loud. We can't sleep like this. She doesn't want me to leave. It's quiet hitches of her breath with each gentle touch, with the slip of two fingers into her night shorts, and the shift of my body so I have her on top of me.

I help her. Burrow her mouth in the nape of my neck while I knead her ass. The slight shake of her head says her brain is alert and wanting to decide, but her hips move into my hand and her legs slide apart, welcoming the way I spread moisture through her cleft.

Nadia doesn't pant. She's silent, so silent no one hears

her when my fingers slip inside of her and enjoy her quivering climax. "You're so beautiful," I whisper, stunned with who she is and pressing my cock against her belly, rubbing, wanting, but not taking what she's not comfortable with giving.

She feels me hard beneath her, my abdomen taut where I can't relax enough to be yielding. "Sweetie," she whispers so close to my ear, and then those boy shorts slither off her hips.

The alarm goes off in my brain, too weak with the overload of femininity above me, smooth skin and silky stomach sliding over my edges. She's high. She's low—everywhere around me, a small hand forming around me and leading me astray.

"Baby," I whisper, strangled, but it's so good—I haven't done this since Ingela. Why is she giving me this? We're not prepared. We weren't going to...

Slick warmth hugs me tight, squeezing me and making me groan. She stills then, that small hand lifting from where it is and pressing over my mouth.

"Shhh," she whispers, a cagey vixen, slaying me, rescinding me, eating me so beautifully from the inside out.

My hips rock up high, hitting a depth I've craved for twenty-four hours. That's how long it's been since I was last here, only this time, this time— Ah.

"Why?" My single syllable is a voiceless song at her ear. I feel it in my bones the same way I do my raging orgasm as I explode, deep, deep inside of her—

With no protection whatsoever.

I can't stop kissing her afterward. I don't want to move,

just remain like this with her, shrinking within her channel and bathing in the balm made by the two of us. At home. Finally I'm at—

Enough.

~~~

BO

IT TAKES US TWO DAYS TO REACH NEW YORK. Two quiet days full of whispered words, music, and touches. For the most part, even Emil leaves us alone, not commenting and only expecting my presence and decisions right before a concert.

Nadia's eyes have a gleam in them that's new. I'm egocentric, deciding it's about me though it might stem from touring with a rock band. Sitting on a golf cart on the way to a festival stage while the crowd went bananas over a glimpse of us made her grin last night.

Those deep eyes shine as we pull into New York, our driver bustling us through midtown. I watch the city with her as skyscrapers slowly rock by. Cabs lay on their horns for reasons only they understand. It's old for me and new for Nadia.

I lean back against the seat as the door slides open and Elias pokes his head in. "Guess what?" he asks, happy.

"Ah. I can't take the suspense. Please don't make me suffer," I murmur in a monotonous voice that causes Nadia to giggle. I've put my guitar down so I can enjoy her body leaning against my chest. Her ear is over my heart, and when Elias entered, she was busy counting my heartbeats, getting a different number per minute every time. Lazily, my fingers make circles below the hem of her skirt, feeling soft skin covering bone and tendon and lean muscle.

Nadia would make a good tour girlfriend. The idolization, the unnatural attention before and after shows is easier to take with her around. With her silent approval of the music I wash out over the audience. With the smile she sends me in moments when she knows the audience's attention means nothing and the struggle to make a living even less.

"Ebele's coming to the arena tonight."

"Who?"

"The awesome chick from Nigeria. Remember her, from L.A?"

"She lives in New York?" I ask.

Elias shrugs so high his shoulders brush his earlobe. "Dunno. But she's coming. Troll's setting her up with an all-access pass, and I'm following your lead, man, and getting a hotel room." He winks conspiratorially. "If Ebele comes early enough, I'll keep her onstage with Nadia. There'll be two ladies waiting for us," he says, proud. "When are you going home again, Nadia?"

And thanks for ripping into that, Elias. We're in Brooklyn already, we have only hours to sound-check and eat before the Melville Center opens its doors to Luminessence's—and now our—fans. The last thing I want is to think about Nadia's departure.

"I'm leaving at the crack of dawn tomorrow," she says softly, sitting up and adding an all too proper space between us. It's bullshit. I feel stubborn and childish, and the frustration over her going home *to* someone leaves a foul taste in my mouth.

"Right, just—why don't you get ready, Elias? Are you gonna get off the bus in tighty-whities?"

His eyes enlarge, deer-style. "What? These are shorts."

"Fucking *short* shorts. Boy-shorts for girls, dude. Jesus. Your package is showing."

"Is not!" Elias rolls his eyes at me, and Nadia nudges me in the ribs with two fingers.

"Bo… let it go."

I can't help shooting out a last observation. "And since it's the color of your skin, it's hard to tell that you're wearing anything at all."

"Damn you're pissy. S'not my fault that Nadia's going home to her husband tomorrow," the asshole says, and I shoot up from the couch, cross the small lounge in two seconds flat, and slam him against the wall.

"Shut. The fuck. Up. Or I swear I'll rip your arms off and you'll never play bass again."

The room is a frozen frame on a film. I don't hear Nadia behind me. Elias' light eyes are transfixed with shock. He makes no move to get loose. For one crazy second, I recall another time like this, only I was the one crushed against the wall… by Cameron. He'd done it in a craze of jealousy and frustration, and I hadn't been surprised. Ingela had driven him to the edge for a long time.

This is different because I've only just started seeing Nadia. No, scratch that. I've only just started sleeping with Nadia. Or hanging out with her. Yes, that's a better expression. I have no claim to her, while someone else does.

"Whoa, whoa," Troll says, prying my fingers off Elias. "Time to simmer down, here. Elias, keep your mouth shut," he adds in case Elias didn't get my message.

Elias plods out, throwing a side-glance over his shoulder. "Dude, he's losing it. And over some chick? Seriously."

"She's *not* 'some chick,'" I yell, but Troll is between us, a blockage heaved up to stop me from ripping Elias' arms off.

"Really? Because she looks like one to me."

As we walk off the bus, the whole band is affected. Emil cocks an imaginary gun at my head and makes a fizzled *pang* with puckered lips, and it's not annoying and stupid as shit at all. I tell him.

Troll wedges himself in between us again, and Nadia is small and quiet at my side, her hand engulfed in mine.

I know I need to let this go, get a grip and all that, but the reminder? I really did not need a reminder. She said she's never been away from her husband this long before. What if the douchebag starts fucking her again?

I'll follow her to the airport tomorrow morning, but before that, Clown Irruption is supposed to shake up the Melville Center, and afterward, the night Nadia and I are going to have at a four-star hotel downtown needs to be memorable as hell!

"I'm not doing the meet-n-greet tonight," I clip as we enter the Melville Center through a side entrance.

"The hell you aren't," Troll says calmly. The annoying thing is that when one of the band members flips his lid, Troll remains collected, the total opposite of how he is while organizing show details with venues and stagehands. Screw that.

"Actually, I'm not. I'm taking Nadia straight to the Bel Age, and then I won't be seeing any of you fuckers until after she has left on that fucking plane."

"Bo, please," she whispers, mortified, but I can't even look at her. I stare straight into Troy's back. He's keeping a low profile, striding forward, and today I despise him for it. Until he stops, turns slowly, and says, "Okay, Bo. Listen up. We're a band, but we're your friends too. If you need to go—go. We'll cover for you."

I'd ditch the after-show anyway, right when I want to, but damn if it doesn't feel good with an ounce of understanding.

CHAPTER Twenty-Two
TOUR

NADIA

THE NEXT HOURS GALLOP PAST. Besides making sure I'm with him wherever he goes, Bo doesn't pay much attention to me. I'm behind him, fingers laced with his as we run through the hallways of the Melville Center basement on our way to pick up spare cables, new guitar picks, peruse deli trays, and grab beer.

I haven't seen him drink on the trip, but as the afternoon turns dusky outside the small windows, he flips open more than a few Budweisers and knocks them back in large swallows. We find a room at the end of a corridor where the door handle gives and we can go in. His cell buzzes. It's Troll asking if everything is okay, if he's ready for the set, and I text back because Bo doesn't care to reply.

Yes, we're in Room A24. He's got his acoustic guitar. Nadia.

OK, I'll get him in 30, Troll answers.

"You want to hear what I think about you going home?" Bo asks, gaze hazy as he peers out from under his bangs.

"Okay," I say because I don't have a choice.

He doesn't tell me. He plays it. It's sad and quiet and growing louder and into more. The thuds of his knuckles are there again, vibrating hard against the wood. Soon, the melody is a short, intense loop that speeds up, speeds up, until it screams his inability to stop me.

I tear up. The song is flamenco passion and hard-rock fury, and when he finishes, his eyes turn cool as a snowy mountainside, concealing the intensity he just let me see.

"That's all," he murmurs. I throw myself at him. He saves his guitar, setting it down last minute before I jump him.

"I'm sorry. I'm sorry," I say. "One day I'll—"

"Don't forget me," he whispers, mouth against my neck.

"Never. No way," I whisper back.

"I can't stand to think about you being with him. Please… I'm selfish."

God, Bo is pleading with me. He's hurting, and it's my fault. Doesn't he see that *I* am the walking heartbreak?

I wish I could take Bo's pain away. Soon. Maybe soon, I can. But now…? If I did, I'm not sure I would survive. I have to give Bo something though. Something to ease his pain so he can do his job. There are thousands of people out there in the audience, most of them coming for Luminessence. This is another chance for Clown Irruption to make an impact.

"When are you back in Los Angeles?" I ask.

"In a week."

"That's not long. And I won't be with Jude that way. The way you and I are." It's the first promise I've ever given him.

Cautious hope lives in Bo's gaze when he draws back to study my expression. Then he squeezes me, like I am his and he is mine to keep. "Are you saying you won't sleep with your husband? That you'll be waiting for me in L.A.?"

"Yes." My voice is sure. I'm light with short-lived bliss over the relief I see in his eyes, until my admission has me staring down the barrel of a nineteen-month-old reality, one I spend most waking hours trying to forget. That Jude and I will never make love again is just the tip of the iceberg.

I flush my mind of thoughts. I'm starting to master it. Whenever I keep them clean and organized, facing another day isn't the worst thing in the world.

Bo's arms scissor my back as he folds me in, tightening around me like he doesn't want to let go. I'm straddling him, toes on the floor and hands raked into a hold at the back of his head. We're still in this position, with Bo's lips on my temple, when Troll opens the door.

"Ten minutes and we're on." The tour manager jerks his thumb behind him. "Let's rock, lovebirds."

The stage is huge with a wall of spots lined up behind the band. Video screens blast out colors and clips of their faces, their hands playing their instruments. Troy's drumsticks whirl in the air and land safely in his grip before he plunges back in. The audience starts out listening, soaking in the light show and the sound. When Emil sheds his shirt on the second song, grabs the front of his jeans and thrusts hard, the crowd cheers wildly and the scattered cries for Luminessence fade and die.

Bo turns to me, feet locked in place. He winks once, sexy as heck, and that flutter in my chest turns into a *bah-boom, bah-boom*, joining Troy's beat and loving it all.

Right now, this is it. It's me not being me, not living the life I've made for myself in L.A., and I'm allowing it to happen without guilt. In a few hours, I'll be leaving. Who knows what the future will bring then.

Moments to live for. Moments to soak in. Seize the day, they say. I am, I am! When Ebele, the girl Elias likes, takes her confident place next to me in song three, I shake her hand, smile wider than I have in ages, and sway my body to the song.

I laugh when Elias turns to us, half kneeling in the air with his bass on his thighs. It's his not-so-subtle *Hello!* to this new crush in his life. Right now, right now, all is good, and when Bo's voice echoes back from all corners of the arena, "Do you want to hear *Fuck You*?" I shout out my *Yes!* with the audience too.

Ebele whoops at my side, lifting her arms above her head and shaking her hips. She's shameless, beautiful, full of life and color—she's exactly what I feel inside tonight.

I cherish this instant. Cherish Bo when he steps off stage and lowers his guitar to hug me tight. His sweat covers me as he rubs against my body and sucks me into a kiss. "I want to leave—now. Let's go to the hotel. I need you," he pants, from the exertion, from lust, or from the audience roaring for more behind him.

"I think you have to do an encore," I say, breathless

from his uber-presence rupturing the last inch of my personal space.

"I. Don't. Care. I need every second left with you."

Troll's already heading over, a hand in the air and swiping at the stage. "Bo. Get your ass out there *now*. I'm not your babysitter, okay? You'll get to your precious hotel soon enough."

Bo does listen, rolling his eyes lightly, a small smirk lifting his lips. He grabs my hand, but I know what he wants and I'm not going there. I slip away, hide behind Troy who covers me, while Bo bounces to the side, playful, not giving up so easily.

"I've *had* it for the day. Please, make my life easy for once," Troll sighs, grabs the back of Bo's shirt like he's taller than him, and hauls him up front himself.

Playful Bo. God, playful Bo is beautiful. Feelings inside of me mix and demand to burst free and be honest. Of course I don't let them, but the softness they create within me, the gentle tug to say more, *do* more, is unequivocal.

Bo raises his arms in a *fine-you-win* gesture out there. Troll blows his cheeks full of air and lets it out fast, exhausted by the crazy boy. Me, I can't take my eyes off Bo when he starts strumming his instrument.

"Ladies!" Emil bellows, and two thirds of the audience squeals a loud *Whoooo!* in response. "Ladies!" he bellows again, louder.

"Yeeeeeees!" the audience cheers back.

"*LADIES!*" Emil's microphone retorts his voice and throws it back in a squealing feedback that lingers on for seconds after Emil stops. I swing to see Troll's reaction, expecting him to be upset. He isn't. His eyes are hard on the band, jaws tense in approval and waiting for Emil's next move.

"*YEEEEESSS!*" The crowd is so loud, it's a wall of sound coming back at me. Ebele laughs, and it's contagious and I laugh with her, hard, and I don't even hear my own voice over the noise surrounding us.

"You ready for a completely new song?" Emil yells.

What?

"*YEEEESSSSSS!*"

They start, and I instantly recognize it. It's what Bo played in that dark corner of the stage in Deepsilver when I arrived. The melody has evolved. It's more polished. There are still no vocals except for a few "she came" and "she's here," moaned out by Emil in his signature *I'm-making-love-to-your-ears* fashion.

My face is a cooked lobster. *Thank the Lord Bo doesn't write books*, I suddenly think; song lyrics are revealing enough.

Thankfully, the stage bathes us in red light, softening the impact of my reaction. Ebele leans in. "Is this song about you too?"

I turn, and I'm struck by the openness in her expression. Elias is attracted to the opposite of himself, I've noticed—culture, skin color—but in addition, there's a lack of judgment and of jadedness in Ebele's expression. Has Elias noticed that in her too?

I'm used to downplaying and hiding, but Ebele makes it easy to be honest. "Yeah. I came out to see him," I reply, smiling a little.

"Your boyfriend is a sweet man," she says close to my

ear so I can hear her. I need to tell her he's not my boyfriend. Some other time.

BO

She absorbs my vehemence, my fury—my *love*. Yes, right now that's what it is. I admit it as I crush our hands against the tiled walls of the shower and take her with my mouth and my cock.

Her gaze had my back on stage, her belief in all that I do ever-present. Through my guitar solos, the backup vocals to songs I've made for her, for Ingela, or for life; whatever I did up there, she was with me in approval and a gentle pride that sat in her eyes. I know because I turned often.

She's my muse, my beauty, my other person. The woman I want around on the toughest day, during nights like these where the show is over and I let the fans slobber on me. Even then she had my back, a slender arm around my waist from behind while rabid girls attacked with CDs and T-shirts, navels to sign and butt cracks with Clown Irruption tattoos. Not once did she waver. Not once did it scare her off.

I can't stand that she's leaving.

So I take her hard against the bathroom wall, and it's not the way I'd planned to be with her tonight. I'm upset with myself, but I can't handle these emotions. The looming loss of someone who's never been yours is a crazy, crazy thing.

Her depths are smooth. She braves my frustration, my violence—my *love*.

Love does not last, mine less than anyone's. It's fickle, a cat, a woman, not something I'll bank on or profess to.

I plead with her. Wow, yes, I plead.

"Please wait for me."

"Yes," she replies, and I hope she understands.

My movements become spasmodic. She lifts one knee, embracing me with her leg, and I heave the other up so it's her against the wall, ruled by me. I keep her from falling, and she trusts me. It's beautiful when she contracts around me in slow tremors too.

"Don't worry. It's just us here. No one can hear you," I murmur, and she rewards me with a whimper as everything becomes too much for her to bear.

"Darling, I—" I cut myself off in time. Yes, I love her but that's now. Tomorrow I'll return to *me*. Shit's complicated, and I don't want to think about it. Her life. My missing love muscle. Or what if my heart's just weird and skittish? Anyway.

I lower her to the floor and drink lukewarm water from her lips. We're under the shower, breathing hard, and I've slid out of her and wish I hadn't.

"It's wrong," I hum to her.

"What?" she puffs into my mouth.

"To be outside of you."

A small breath hitches from her. It's a cute laugh. Everything is cute with her.

"I'm obsessed," I say. Carry her wet from the shower and dump her on our bed. She laughs softly as I lick her boobs free of droplets, grab an old hand towel from the floor, and start drying her off.

"I'm obsessed with you. It hurts. I still want more every time."

"I'm sorry," she whispers, but her eyes shine. There's love in there, hidden. It's of the kind that rages beneath the sternum of my own chest, of the kind I don't allow out, except as an obsession.

Obsessions I can live with.

Obsession is music. Stage. Guitar. Melodies. Lyrics.

Adding another obsession is fine.

"You're my latest obsession," I tell her, kissing along her hairline, down past her ear and to her neck. I suck on her collarbone, and she's content, her body a subtle wave beneath me on the bed.

"The bed is wet now," she whispers, and I say "yes" because I couldn't care less. Now, we're done with the meet-n-greet she made me do, and it's just us, enjoying our last hours together.

"Let's not sleep tonight," I say, hiking her knee over my hips though I'm drained and not ready for another round. I still thrust against her, needing her to remember where I've been, where I want to be, where I'd like to be the only man who ever—

Is.

Fuck, okay. This is the high after an amazing show. All performers are like this. Some get drunk off their ass. Some get high. Others have sex until they're exhausted enough to sleep, while the most wholesome ones work out like Olympians to ease down from the endorphin rush of a great show.

Yes, that's it. I am that way right now. I'm obsessed

with her, and tonight I love her. She's amazing. Exactly what I—

But all of this aside, once she leaves, once I'm back in the groove, life will be back to normal. My rushes will come from writing songs and performing them. Maybe a quick lay in the bunk with a fan.

I breathe out fast, anchoring myself to reality.

Yes, that's what it will be. And yet I ask, "You want to see the moon?"

NADIA

We watch the full moon from the hotel roof. The lights from the city dim the stars surrounding it, but with Bo's arms around me and my head against his shoulder, I can't remember seeing a more beautiful moon.

His chest moves with slow intakes and outflows of air while we watch. In a hard stab deep inside me, where he just shook me to Heaven, it strikes me just how alive he is. Bo. Is a living, breathing man who is obsessed with me.

Tomorrow, I'll be gone. I can't stand the thought of leaving him. I don't want to go back to the life of before. He'll return, I tell myself, be on break from tour in a week. Beyond that week, beyond his break, I can't even imagine.

Thoughts keep shivering through my head. I'm the product of my upbringing, my past, my marriage. I'm ruined.

In bed, we fall asleep with our hands stilling on each

other's skin. Cocooned in the air-conditioned room, I'm on his arm, a leg twisted with his under the covers, soft sheets tangling with our limbs and keeping us warm.

"Darling," he whispers through the pitch-blackness. "I'm so sorry. We have to get up."

My eyes go wide, my heart hammering out the too-early adrenaline shock I get whenever I wake up at an ungodly hour.

Four. Four a.m. Yes, he's right. If I am to get on my plane in time, this is it.

I straddle him to get up, but his arms weigh me down, keeping me in his embrace for another sleep-warmed moment. I sigh, nudging in against his throat and savoring the rightness I feel.

"Shower?" he asks, waking up beneath me, allowing silky hardness to prod gently at my core. I'm weak. I'm needy. I widen my legs to feel him one more time because soon I'll be on a flight speeding far, far away from this man who has woken me from grey slumber.

"We should get up," he hisses, and I love the heat rasping in his voice, how he has already surrendered and lets himself in even as he speaks.

"Yes…" I say, but what does it matter if I don't get that shower? Once I'm in L.A., I can take as many showers as I want.

The length of our bodies align in the darkness, the comforter hugging us while Bo's arms hold me still on top of him. Then he thrusts slowly, coolly, until I envelop him so completely, just the way I want him.

"Why do you trust me like this?" he whispers. "You should be protected."

"Because you'd never do this to me if I were at risk."

"Not since my ex have I—"

"And I… not since my husband."

We're quiet, undulating with each other until my breath becomes irregular and he ignites his phone and shines it on my face. It's unromantic, ridiculous.

"What are you doing?" I ask, my question truncated, and he replies—

"Memorizing how your face looks while I love you."

I have no answer, and once the room returns to black, I already shiver in his arms, his presence overwhelming inside of me. I slow our rhythm, and he adjusts to my need, hard as bone and waiting until I am ready.

A breath as fast as a sob escapes me, and this beautiful person understands. It's a rush that he understands, and I've never felt closer to anyone.

"Now?" he whispers seconds before my climax ripples in, and I do sob then, when he knows things people don't know.

Pushing my spine down with one hand, he locks the other over my behind to secure himself deep inside of me. He moves in small, barely contained jerks that drive me insane.

"Bo!" I scream, and it's surreal, weird, wild because I never scream.

Bo whispers, "Yes… Darling…" before he comes apart too.

In the back of a dark cab, he brushes the hair off my face and stares into my eyes while we two-wheel it through back alleys and orange lights. I'm so full of him I don't have words to share.

"Will you wait for me?" he repeats once the airport appears ahead of us, and I nod because there is no doubt in my mind. I will, I will.

PART 4
Gloom

Dancing in the dark
Because the light would illuminate the truth

Chapter Twenty-Three
THE FALL

NADIA

The plane heaves me up high, but it can't keep my mood from dropping. It doesn't hold the power to alter my loss and my guilt. A new love corrupts my nerves.

I'm in love with two men, and I can do nothing about it. There is no salvation from the doom coming my way. I've escaped my past, my family, but no one can abscond from what's right and wrong.

My mind is a smogged-down cloud that allows me to doze off when we hit higher altitudes. This new love of mine beats like moth wings against the walls of my heart and refuses to vacate. But in sleep, in sleep, the love invading my dream is my forever:

"Jude," I shout, shaking him. The bed is rumpled and my sweetheart weak between the sheets, a glass of water the only thing on his nightstand. "Wake up, baby. Have you eaten today?"

Jude has Sundays off from his job at the gas station. He's the assistant janitor of the Alhambra Apartments too now, which leaves us with minimal utility bills. Today, on his day off, the plan had been to fix the gutters outside.

I don't know if he has done it, and I don't care, because I'm just home from my eight-hour shift at Scott's Diner, and here I am, finding this.

"Jude!"

He stirs. He's paler than our cream-colored sheets. "Nadia. I'm fine—just resting." He sounds trustworthy, but it's the fourth time in eight weeks that I've found him like this.

"Did you finish the gutters?" I say, and he smirks, eyes still closed. "I don't leave a job until it's done."

My pulse settles at his attitude, knowing he's right. "When did you eat last?"

"Women," he says. "I thought I'd finally moved out of *Mom's* domain. I'm fine, Nadia. You don't have to keep an eye on me. I'm good."

"Tell me," I insist. "When?"

I recognize the signs. He's feeble and opinionated. Wants to be left alone. When he's okay, Jude always wants me close. He greets me at the door when we work shifts that don't match. Sometimes, he lights the candles I love so much, the ones that smell like peaches and lemons. He waits for me with some sort of foody concoction neither of us enjoy much, but the main thing is, he makes it. Like I do for him when he's the one coming home late. Tonight, there's no food on the stove.

"I had breakfast with you."

"Jude. That was nine hours ago. And you've worked after?"

"Nadia." His voice is stern despite the slumped posture on the bed. "I. Just. Need. To rest."

My next question is a make or break. "Did you take an insulin shot any time after breakfast?"

He blows air out between lips that are unnaturally pale. "Of course. I never miss an insulin shot."

My point exactly.

I don't say anything else. I just hit up his supply of glucagon. I consider if I should take a chance on pills or go straight to the shots. He registers my rummaging in the nightstand and says, "Don't work yourself up, babe. The gutters just worked me over is all." He sounds like he knows what he's talking about—that he's in control of his bodily reactions, but I know better. Right now he isn't.

"Pills or syringe," I say though I know I'll have to decide.

"So insistent," he sighs. "You're wearing me out."

"Shot then," I say and pull the syringe full from the ampule it's wrapped with.

"A pill would work," he breathes, already weaker. Fear for him makes me tremble, and I need to give this shot to him before my hands start shaking.

He groans when I empty the syringe into his arm. I'm lucky—I've been lucky both times I've had to do this over the last three months. I've read up on how to inject it, but I'm not a nurse and will never be one. It's a miracle no air bubbles slip in with the injection. That would be dangerous, I think… God is good and with us even though we're bad apples disobeying our parents.

The miracle of glucagon might never stop surprising me. Minutes later, my husband's skin tone morphs from ghostly to his natural, golden hue. An apologetic smile stretches across his face, replacing the rigid denial painting it before. "Nadia. I'm sorry. I didn't mean to scare you."

"Your mother told me," I say again, just like I have before. "You're reckless with your medicine. That's why she didn't want you to leave Payne Point."

"Yeah. Well, it doesn't matter. I had to get you out of there, and she finally gets that," he says firmly.

"Sure, but it doesn't change that you need to keep an eye on yourself. You're an adult. You have to understand how dangerous it is for you not to eat. I won't always be here when you forget."

"Hey, I take the insulin shots."

"As you should, but even if you're in a hurry—have some sort of protein. Boil an egg," I beg.

"Yeah, yeah, bossy lady. Come here," he whispers.

I can't stay mad at him. I am stubborn when it comes to his health though. "Not until you eat. I'm making hot dogs, and I want you to eat at least three," I say.

He chuckles low in his throat, the way he does sometimes when I crave him in the way of wives. "Okay. I owe you three hot dogs. Then afterward," he starts, lifting to his elbows on the mattress and letting his gaze skim over my body. "Afterward, 'I will give her her vineyards from thence, and the valley of Achor for a door of hope: and she shall sing there—' I will make her sing."

Despite myself, I snicker. My Jude and his proverbs. "You're so silly. First you'll eat. And then you'll make me... *sing*?"

"At least sigh happily when I—"

"Ugh, stop."

"Why? You're my wife. I can tell my wife what I plan to do to her. I want to—"

I jerk awake at the abrupt scratching from the speakers above me. "*Ladies and gentlemen. As we start our descent, please make sure your seat backs and tray tables are in their full, upright position. Make sure your...*"

Jude, I'm almost home.

NADIA

"Because you're depressed!" Zoe yells. "That's why you want to sleep nonstop. I remember that from right after the ceremony too. You went into hibernation and didn't want to come back out again. It was me and... what's-her-face? We took turns sitting with you to make sure you always had a friend with you. We didn't even go home to sleep. We camped out on your couch, remember?"

"Of course," I say from within my sheets and comforters.

It's the second day home from Bo's tour, and I hate the way I feel. I go to work and do my thing there, because I'm a master at blocking stuff out. But all I want is to sink under my covers with Jude's pillow at my nose and work hard to forget the rest.

Like how right everything felt while I was with Bo. How happy I was. His response to me while I was there with him. The way he looked at me.

Like how I miss him.

I peek out from the covers, my stare landing on a photo of Jude and me on the nightstand. Zoe took it at the boardwalk, right after we came off the rollercoaster for the first time. I loved it. My first time on a rollercoaster ever. I'm wearing a wobbly smile courtesy of motion sickness. Jude's fingers dig into my hips, barely keeping me on my feet. And his face is alight with humor.

So amazing together.

Zoe flips the photo over. "Enough. Get up. You've avoided me for two days at work, and I'm not taking any more of your bullshit. I want to hear about the tour. Emil told me that Bo totally freaked out when Elias mentioned you going home—"

"That was mean," I mumble. "And don't mention *him* in our apartment."

"—but I want to hear it from my friend. You need to tell me what's going on. Why are you regressing right now, just being a nightmare all over again? We're not doing this, you know. That time is over." She folds the comforter neatly to the side and plops a stack of clothes next to me.

"We're going out. Maybe a movie. We'll have drinks and talk. That old-fashioned cocktail lounge on Craig's Street will do."

So the tears start seeping again, and it's different this time. I've tried to block out reality, but reality is in my face, gritting teeth and showing fangs. What would remain of me if I faced it? Wouldn't it be my demise?

She doesn't comment on the tears. Just hands me the pieces of clothing one by one and watches me get dressed.

In the living room I stop again. Sink to my knees in front of the coffee table and look into Jude's eyes. I blow out the candles he won't tend to while I'm gone. Rearrange the tiny cactus pots around the bigger one with white birds on it.

"Bye, Jude," Zoe says, lifting her hand in a wave at him. She pulls me to my feet and keeps me steady over the threshold. I turn and look again, and for a fraction of a second, I want to die so bad it's like a gunshot to my stomach. I can't do this. I can't move on from our love—the beauty of that one person that used to make me whole.

"He completes me," I say brokenly in the car.

"No," Zoe says, steadfast. "He *completed* you. He doesn't anymore. Now, someone else seems to complete you, and it's time you open to the present, sweetie. Take it in. Understand."

I have a blue martini in front of me when Bo calls. I don't hesitate. I pick up on the first ring. "Hey," he says, alive and intimate, so close on my ear. Zoe winks. Gives me the thumbs-up like I'm doing something huge by answering my phone.

I guess she's right. I haven't been good at picking up lately.

"Are you okay? Is everything okay?"

"Yeah. Thanks, I'm good," I answer mechanically.

"You don't sound good."

That brings the lump back to my throat, and I swallow, trying to get in charge of my voice. "Nadia, darling. Did I do something?"

You broke through.

"No, you did nothing bad. I had a great time on tour with you."

I laughed. Ah I laughed out there with him. The way he looked when he barged off the stage to grab me after the shows? Jittery fun-bubbles fizzed in my throat. Those shows, his energy on stage, God. God.

"How's… Jude?" He finally says my husband's name.

"What do you want me to say? 'Good?'" I quip because I can't answer that.

Bo is quiet, probably mulling over my retort. It wasn't nice of me. I'm adding to my stack of wrongdoings. Another little brick of badness.

"I'll be home around noon on Friday," he breathes into the phone, and something happens to my body. It remembers that sound. "Are you working then?"

"Yeah, I'm off at five," I say.

"Okay. Can you… get away afterward?" he asks carefully, not mentioning Jude a second time.

"I can."

Zoe whoops behind her hand and dances a little on her seat, clearly guessing the conversation.

"Give me your address, and I'll pick you up, say, at seven?"

My heart drops. Pick me up… as in from the apartment? He can't come to our apartment! No. Of course, that's not what he's suggesting.

"Hold on," I say and cover the phone with my hand. "Zoe, you haven't told him about Jude, right?" I stare deep into her eyes to keep her from lying.

She lifts her hands high, fingers spread. "No. I don't break promises. I'm totally against how you're handling this—you're making it way worse for yourself—but I love you and you're the one who needs to figure stuff out."

"He wants to come and pick me up at the apartment!" As the explanation falls from me, dread sinks to where heat pooled in me a moment ago.

"And? It's a natural thing. Just, you need to clean up in there. You can't have it the way it is or you'll freak him out."

"No. Our apartment stays the way it is."

"Then you need to *explain* before you let Bo in."

"He just can't come in."

"Girl. Enough already. Just. Tell. Him. Everything."

I stare at her for a long moment while Bo's voice buzzes from the speaker and into my hand. "Nadia. Are you there?"

"Yeah," I finally say, and I'm tired, so tired again. I don't know what to do.

"Hey, it's Zoe!" Zoe says loud and clear into the phone. It's gone from my hand, in hers now. I scramble to retrieve it, but she turns her back to me and rattles my address off into the phone. Then she strides toward the restrooms, and I lunge after her, desperate, only it's too late. Zoe, my awful friend, slams the door and locks it from the inside, while I stand outside with my hand over my mouth.

NADIA

BETWEEN BO'S PHONE CALL and Zoe's interception, they

broke me out of my hibernation. I tidy up at home. Peer at Jude's sock on the bathroom floor. It's been there for a while. I've been cleaning around it for a while. I let it sink in how he's not going to pick it up himself.

He *can't* pick it up himself.

It's time I stare reality in the eye. I pick the sock up—I do. Then I cry.

I sheathe myself in old dreams within the safety of our blankets. When Zoe calls, she surprises by saying that my "bawling" is a step in the right direction.

"Gotta face the music, girl. About time," she pep-talks, but the expression makes no sense and disparages the devastation in my mind. "Face the music, Nadia."

I spend the last days mulling over where Bo and I could meet. I wish we could agree on a different place than here, but if I start a discussion about it, Bo will probably dig deep and I don't want to fight. Above all, I don't want to hurt him any more than I already have.

I can come straight to the restaurant tomorrow, I type out.

No, don't. Your house is on the way.

I bite my lip, worried. ***Seven, you said?***

Yeah. Can't wait.

A flutter in my chest.

Illicit joy.

CHAPTER Twenty-Four
BREAK

BO

I'M OFF TOUR. I'm tired. It's been a long month on the road, and if it weren't for the adrenaline kicking in at the thought of seeing Nadia, I'd be dead on my couch right now, probably not even getting my ass to bed.

The tour bus pulls up later than expected, and I barely have time for a shower. I rush my hands through my wet hair and shake it in the mirror. I notice a little stubble on my chin—I'm not graced with a thick beard—and shave it off thinking of how it will feel to run my face along hers.

I grab a bottle of cologne even, feeling fancy. Some musky sort of thang we got from a sponsor in Miami. I don't want to overpower her with it, but girls tend to enjoy a little fragrance. Nadia, I'm guessing, is no different.

It's easy to find her apartment complex, a small, square

building shaped into a U around a desert garden. The sign reading *The Alhambra Apartments* is more imposing than the construction itself. I park and start on the flat stones leading up to an open arc. Beyond, the building proffers numbered front doors in a line, the way I'm used to from motels.

It's small and intimate. Cute. Appropriate because Nadia is all of those things. As I walk on, I wonder how she's solving the problem with her husband.

The brief guilt over pursuing her dissipates quickly; after all, Jude drags her down, just like I did with Ingela. I always knew Ingela deserved better than me. Does he get it too? If not, he's an idiot. He really shouldn't be surprised that someone else comes knocking, even if the dick isn't man enough to let her off the hook.

"Hey!" Nadia says, breathless, tiptoeing toward me on high heels. She's gorgeous, with long, sleek hair brushed into a shiny mass that falls over her breasts. She wears a simple dress, a green one, and my eyes go straight to her cleavage.

"Hey. I was about to knock," I explain as if it's my invention and not something everyone does at people's door.

She blushes, eyes wild. He must be inside then, and she doesn't want us in the same room. Can't fault her. Can't help the sting of disappointment.

She passes me quickly. She almost traipses in front of me down to the stone tiles, and I have this urge to stop her and embrace her hard.

I know it's a possessive thing, to want to do this in front of their apartment. I'm wretched and more obsessed by the day.

See, it didn't get better after she left. I kept thinking of her. And I still think I love her a little. That mush in my chest hasn't disappeared yet. I hold back until we're right outside the garden gate, but once we are in full view of whichever windows are hers, I tug her to me by the belt circling that little dress, and she stumbles into me.

"I've missed you," I try to say in a calm voice, but it comes out gritty as a growl.

I expect her to push me away. One thing is high school with her father glaring from the window. A whole other level is to have that person be her spouse.

She doesn't. Her body trembles a little, like she's as affected as I am, but her hands move around my neck and let me pull her in.

"Me too," she whispers.

"You've missed me too?" I ask, and then I fucking hug her so hard. A light hum escapes her mouth, and I suck it in, tasting the bubblegum flavor on her lips.

"Yes," she says, not moving us away from the windows of the Alhambra Apartments. It makes me daring, happy, and I risk it all for more closeness, lifting her knee so I'm cradled deep between her legs in the most intimate clutch.

"You are… so… special," I say. "I—am taking you out of here."

NADIA

The way Bo looks at me when he picks me up. There's no detached rockstardom to him. Nothing playful or smugly charismatic. There's just *him* looking at *me* from beneath silky, dyed-black hair. His mouth, sensual and slack with missing me, with his need to hold me tight. I see it. I recognize it. Because it's how I feel when I look at him.

He half lifts me on our tangled way to his car. It makes me smile, and he kisses my cheek so sweetly, apologizing for not being a, "strong-ass body builder."

"Come on, fling me over your shoulder, He-Man," I say, because suddenly I feel like joking, and he listens and play-tumbles under my weight so we both end up on the hood of his car.

I sober quickly, public displays of affection are something I have little experience with—everyone could be watching. Bo's smile is high, beautiful, and while he drives, his eyes are on me as much as on the road.

"I wonder what Emil and Zoe are up to," I say to disturb the blissful tension between us. I'm not wondering. They're in his apartment, and one of them is telling the other what they're doing wrong love-or-kissing-wise.

"Fighting," Bo says, grinning.

"What? Why?" We park in front of a small Italian restaurant, and Bo helps me out of the car.

"He picked up the phone during the meet-n-greet the other night, just when some girl was moaning into his ear. Apparently, she sounded like the real thing."

"Oh no. How silly of him."

"I know. He has been on the phone with Zoe nonstop since then, trying to convince her it was nothing. The only girl he wants to play doctor with—at least at the moment—is her."

"What about you?" I blurt out and bite my own tongue.

"Does it matter?" he asks, serious. Seated in the booth across from me with candles dancing between us, a distance creeps in that's bigger than the table.

"No," I hurry out, avoiding his eyes. "Of course not." But there's so much sinking in for me these days. These *nights*. It does matter.

Jude won't hold me in his arms again. He won't sleep with me. Won't tell me he loves me. What is left of my relationship with Jude is...

Even in my head, I can't say it. The important thing is—

"I think I'm sort of moving on," I begin. Let my hair cover my face as I stare at the table. "Never mind."

"Moving on from what?" Bo is suddenly the hyper-present star that makes people turn heads and get sucked into his space. His charisma reaches me through the curtain of my hair. He draws it with steady hands and leaves it over my shoulder before he cups my cheek with a palm. I breathe in courage, knowing it's time to tell him about Jude.

"Zoe hasn't told you?" It's hard to believe. She's a loyal friend, but she wants my relationship with Bo to develop and I could see her break rules for it.

"About what, Nadia?" he asks, and when my eyes for a fleeting second graze his, those winter-grey irises penetrate me. "Zoe reveals nothing about you. The last time I tried, she said flat out, and I quote, 'Take a fucking hike.'"

As a bottle of beer and a glass of red wine land on the table, Bo leans closer and nudges my chin up with the crook of his index finger. I have no choice but to meet his gaze. "Why? What should she have told me?"

The question is too direct. What would he do if I dodged it? I'm a coward, and I don't want to cry in public.

"Jude is heartless for leaving me," I burst out.

Bo's eyebrows shoot up. "He left you?"

"Yes. No! Ah crap. I don't know, Bo. I don't know how to explain this."

"It shouldn't be difficult. He either left you or he didn't. Is he divorcing you?"

"No, he's not divorcing me. What's with all the questions?" I say, not myself and with that damn lump bobbing in my throat again. I hate lumps. I need to talk about something else. Steer his attention away, but I'm blank, blank—because all that's left in my mind is the truth, and to let those three words hang in the air, expressed once and for all, I cannot do.

A calzone arrives, sliding in between us and staining the tablecloth with rust-colored grease. The steam wafting from it is cheese and ham and tomato sauce, an aroma that should comfort me, but I'm in a showdown, a face-off, that's too much to handle. "Careful, it's so hot it's dangerous!" the waitress chirps.

"Thanks," we both mumble. I'm the first to start cutting off pieces and eating absentmindedly. I need to find a harmless way to ease into my explanation to Bo.

"He... I only learned about Jude's problem after we fled Payne Point."

"What problem?" Bo's gaze can be so powerful. I feel it on me even when I'm not looking.

"Diabetes."

"Is that debilitating? Hampering?"

I shrug, wanting to cry again with the realization that's been setting in full force over the last few days. "Depends on the person. Jude and I had been secretly dating since we were thirteen. After the first few months, we met almost every day. We were only apart when his filthy rich Silicon Valley guru father took his family on lavish vacations. And even with all the time we spent together, Jude didn't tell me about his problem."

"Problem." Bo chews on my wording with his first bite of calzone. "It's considered a disease, right?"

"Yeah, but a manageable one. It becomes a problem when… the person isn't on the ball."

I risk a glance at him and find his eyes narrowed. I can tell his brain is going a hundred miles per hour trying to read past my words. So many half-told stories. Bo is used to me not explaining myself. To me dodging questions. Avoiding. Deflecting. I feel bad.

I crush my eyes closed for courage to continue. "Basically, his mom had been administering everything for him—the insulin and his meals. When he needed glucose tablets, she'd make sure he took them. If he needed injections instead of pills. Mrs. Bancroft literally kept him free of symptoms for years straight.

"I got my first scary glimpse into an insulin shock when he almost crashed the car on the way to Vegas."

"Jesus. When you eloped?"

"Yeah. He didn't admit to anything. Said he was just tired. It took him way too long to confess that he had diabetes and tell me where to find the shots he needed. He could have lost consciousness."

"I'm sorry. That sucks, Nadia." Bo strokes my hair with one hand, smoothens a lock and lets go. "Did he get better after the shot?"

"Yeah. That's the crazy part. The time it took for him to return to himself again, even joke about what happened, was just—nothing. I still think about that. So fast."

And then I can't stop the tears from dripping along my nose. I suck in a noisy breath and lift my napkin to wipe them off.

"I don't understand why anyone would want to neglect something like that."

"Yeah. I begged him to be mindful from then on, and he did well. Even so, over the next months, he still had a tendency of taking his insulin shot without eating right after. It's why he'd get sick."

A strange chuckle escapes me, because Jude. Impossible Jude. "I found him in different states of shaky, sleepy, bleary-eyed three or four times afterward. I don't get mad easily, but once I even yelled at him while we waited for the glucagon injection to work.

"His mother would drive up from Payne Point often too. She'd stay nearby in a hotel a few days at a time."

"Why? To nurse him?" Bo lifts the beer to his mouth and takes a sip.

"Yeah. One night, he got tired of it and told her off. I wish she hadn't used the opportunity to nag at him about college every time she came up too. If she hadn't—"

I can't finish that sentence. "He wasn't supposed to work at a gas station, see? In his mother's mind, he was destined for bigger things than some blue-collar job."

"And he wanted to stay there?"

"Only until I'd finished my education. I was supposed to support him afterward."

Bo twists his mouth, pondering, and I recall telling him that I started working at Scott's Diner a few months after we moved to the Alhambra Apartments. "Jude's salary was low, which is why I took the waitressing job at Scott's. Jude hated it but got my point. He was on the lookout for a better-paying job when…"

"When what?"

"Um. When… his mother stopped 'bugging' him." I jerk my head up, meeting Bo's gaze for the first time since we sat down. "Are you full? I'm done. I think I'm ready to leave."

Bo moves into his seat, spine hitting the backrest while he studies me. I can't fool him. Heck, there's nothing to fool anyone with. It's just too much to keep talking. Thing is, I can only recall this an ice-cream scoop at a time. I hope he understands.

"So that's it? These are the morsels you're handing me tonight?" Bo asks, voice measured. The controlled anger that simmers beneath is palpable.

I'm not used to sharing. My only friends in this city, besides Zoe, are my colleagues at Scott's. Zoe shut them up right away by telling them the only thing I'm not telling Bo. They know no details thanks to her, who always has my back.

"I don't know how to do this, Bo," I whisper, suppressing the urge to cry.

"Do what? Be honest? Give me enough of an insight to understand what's going on in your head? In your fucking heart?" He shakes his head slowly. Frustrated.

Disappointed. Hurt—again.

He longs for me, there, on the other side of the booth, and I can't give what he needs. It hits me harder than ever; I'm an impostor, here to ruin Bo's life like mine already is. Bo is an innocent, a bystander and a casualty. He shouldn't be in this situation.

The signs were there from the moment I met him. I shouldn't have allowed as much as a kiss between us. If you love something you don't deserve, let it go. If it comes back, it's still not yours. If it doesn't, it never was.

And so I stand. Lean over the table. I give him a small kiss on the lips, and say, "You're right. I don't have it in me to make you happy. I hope I haven't messed with your life too much." Then I walk out of the restaurant. Alone.

BO

I LET HER WALK TOWARD THE EXIT. I watch her shoulders sag, and she's small, beautiful, and I love every detail about her. Her sadness, her joy, the thoughts she doesn't share, her skin against mine, her heat and her light snores when she sleeps tangled with me.

I've only known her for five weeks. In those weeks, I've learned everything and nothing, and for each seed of new knowledge, each nugget of information about her life, even her marriage, I need more.

She thinks I'll let her leave. I drop a stack of my per diems on the table and get up just as she reaches the front door. The restaurant is quiet. Quiet enough for her to discern my voice when I say, "I'll be knocking on your door."

She twists quickly, long, dark locks swinging over her shoulder, and stares at me. Well-deep doe eyes storm with feelings, and my balls tighten on instinct; how hot is it to find a whirlwind of desire, anger, hope, and exasperation in the stare of a woman? It makes me want to break her. Turn her into lust, bring her to where the only one she wants is me.

"You can't be serious," she hisses as I approach her calmly.

"Oh I'm serious. You think you can run away? You're not going anywhere until we've finished our talk, and we've barely even started. This. Is going to take a while. We're going home."

"Home where?" she squeaks, and a part of me wants to say, "Your house because this involves your damn husband too."

I don't say it. I'm holding it together for one reason and one reason only:

The other day, a fleeting moment of *love* for her rocked in over me. That fleeting moment must be frozen in time. Because it's still happening.

I reach her. Crowd her against the mess of small bells jingling in the front-door window. I slide a hand up her hip until I grip the firm dip of her waist and say, "My place."

CHAPTER Twenty-Five
TALK

BO

"Just pull it to the side. It's crazy sexy that way." Emil's muffled voice seeps out from his bedroom, and I groan inwardly.

"Not very handy though, is it?" Zoe replies.

"That's not 'to the side.' *Past* the lips, Zoe. Like a curtain so I can still get in. Hold on."

"Geez! You owe me thirty dollars."

"You kiddin' me? That super-tiny scrap of fabric is…?"

"Yeah. *Was* thirty dollars. Now, thanks to you, it's zero dollars. No one would buy it now."

"You'd sell used underwear?"

"No! I'm just sayin'. And it's lingerie. And I still hate you."

I should have predicted this. To talk things out with Nadia here while Emil and Zoe bicker over makeup sex is the antithesis of a plan.

"You want to go somewhere else?" I whisper, securing her hand in mine so she doesn't run away. I don't have a good alternative at the ready. We could go to some romantic place, a park, the planetarium. But to be honest, I want her close to a bed. I can't just make her cry over what she has to tell me without easing her pain afterward.

"I'll get us a hotel room," I decide and grab for my phone.

"No! No… it's okay. This is good," Nadia says, eyes wary and not backing her up. I don't wait for her to reconsider. Instead I tow her with me past Emil's room and into mine. His bed already convulses against my wall, but this time I'm not having it. I barge my fist into the wall and yell, "Fix the *bed* situation or I'm coming in there myself!"

All goes dead silent. Then Emil mutters, "Yeah, yeah," before an eerie sort of screeching ensues.

I meet Nadia's quizzical glance and answer, "He's pulling the bed out to stop their touchy-feelies from interrupting us. Anyway"—I hook an arm around her waist and pull her down on the mattress with me—"what do you want to do first?"

She blinks slowly, eyes glassy. I'm not sure if she's sad or turned on, but right now, with her scent tickling my nose and her chest heaving beneath me, all I want is to feel her. Nadia's mouth offers pillowy, parted lips that accept my kisses and suck me into a moist welcome. Her tongue dances with mine, like she wasn't just storming out of a restaurant in an attempt to escape.

"You ran," I whisper between our kisses. "Don't ever run."

"I had to," she stutters, but her body's already pliable, a warm wave against mine. I ease a hand under the hem of her shirt and bring it upward. With a quick shove, I've wedged it under her bra and we're stuck together this way for a moment before I roll it upward and release her breasts under her T-shirt.

I get up on an elbow just to look. There's something magical about this—lush tits free and utterly touchable beneath a thin top. Nadia's breath moves in rapid sighs. I cup one breast, squeezing lightly, and shut my eyes at the sensation of her hardening nipple. "Have I told you that you're beautiful? That everything you do is beautiful?" I rasp out.

To please a woman—drive her insane with need for me—is the ultimate pleasure. She shakes her head at my question, and I find myself staring deep into her eyes in a way that's new to me.

Nadia doesn't scream or moan loudly. Doesn't tell me how I turn her on. This girl doesn't make a show of things. But her pupils dilate until they leave only the smallest trace of brown irises, and her chest doesn't stop shuddering out small breaths. When I pull her cleavage down with a finger, revealing smooth skin over bone that thickens into soft flesh below, I imagine the quick, quick heartbeats beneath.

"You are, you know. So beautiful. And all I want, all the time, is to be with you." As I help her remove her shirt, I continue talking, my tongue delivering what my soul has known for a while. "You were my quiet in the storm on tour. My rock. You believed in me."

"Bo, everyone does."

"Yes, but it's different. They want something from me. You watch me when I play, when I mock up a melody. I see it in your eyes—you trust my crazies to become a song.

"Even when I doubt, Nadia, you believe. You keep me company, and it's not for what I can do for you, for the favors I'll extend later. Not for a private interview or an autograph." I grimace. "Not for a scrapbook photo of when we have sex."

"Photos?" she repeats, chest bowing toward me as I kiss my way down to her navel. I sink my teeth into the small ridge circling it, licking, sucking, and the scent of her skin makes my blood boil. God, I have missed her.

Again, jealousy knifes me at the thought of this woman sleeping night after night in another man's bed. It's excruciating, intolerable because—she. Was made. For me. He makes her suffer, while *I* want to give her the world.

My desire for Nadia stirs up a haze, and it's difficult to remain coherent. "Did you keep your promise? Have you been only mine since you left the tour?"

"Yes… Yes, I keep my promises," she says, skyrocketing my energy, pouring gasoline on it, and I don't know how to slow down, how to be what she probably needs. I'm back on tour in our last hotel room, snarling my hunger out against her skin, pressing my fingers into her muscles and making her whimper.

"God, I love you," I moan, like it hurts, like *I* hurt, because I do.

Is this love? Is this how people walk around feeling? Because if it's this much, this big—how do they not burn up?

I eat my way down her stomach, draw a new kind of cry from her. She helps me with her pants—we're fast, and there she is, bare and beautiful, unafraid and… unashamed.

For an instant, I'm on my knees between her legs. She's glorious, eyes open and balmy, and it's how I must look staring back at her. The tiniest curve of her lips tells me she's happy. I skim her stomach with my thumb again before I dive down, tearing my shirt off on the way.

"I can't wait to feel all of you," I whisper. "Everything. Your heat, the slickness. Ah it's been a whole week." I croak the last part out as I kick my jeans to the floor. "I can't be away from you a whole week again."

My dick jerks as if it's her touching me when I grab it, and I probe her core with its head. Soft and killing me, she parts and takes me deep, every inch of me until I'm as warm, as enveloped as I can be.

I force myself to lie still, chest meeting chest and hearts racing. For her I can freeze the moment.

"Move," she pleads, but I press my mouth to hers, breathing slowly, my control fortified by her impatience.

"So eager," I whisper against her mouth and she moans, she moans, and it's the prettiest thing I've ever heard. Then I do move, small rolling efforts on top of her, pushing her into the mattress and forcing myself in far between her legs.

"So good," she stutters, pelvis high and begging for more. I let my arms circle her ribs. Tighten my hold so I can move her on top of me without losing our connection.

Carefully, I push against her shoulders, a test—does she trust me enough to ride me like this? My nuts draw up high in expectation. She's timid, but she's turned on now, very turned on.

She opens her eyes again, meeting my gaze and understanding without words. Unhurriedly, she obeys. Draws back up like a beautiful little jockey ready to sprint the last yards to her goal. She arches over me, nipples hard and pointy.

My hands go up, kneading her as she rides me. She's slow, like I knew she'd be if she controlled the pace. Her head falls back, throat curved, and if I'd been there—if I could reach her, I'd eat her there too.

She's a dancer, torso swaying on me in slow motion, owning the feel of me inside of her and pushing down against my crotch.

"So gorgeous," I pant. "So delicious. I love you. Still. Still I love you."

When she approaches her climax, I catch it from the quiver in a thigh. From the sudden strength in her grip as she bends into our kiss. I lock my arms around her. I want her trembling against all of me so I know it's *me* who gives her this.

When she does, she muffles a scream into my neck. I wish she hadn't. It is the sweetest sound when this woman comes.

I'm a selfish man. While she trusts me with her climax, I mark her with my kiss, a blue rose waiting to bloom on the delicate skin beneath her ear.

A flash of satisfaction runs through me.

What will the competition think now?

BO

SHE'S UPSET. So upset. Why is she upset? I don't understand. She's hot as a forge and sad as the ocean, interweaved in mysterious waves. Her face over me on the bed. I brought her to the moon, but here she is now, crashed.

"Are you thinking of him?" I ask, jealousy making my voice gravelly. "Is it too much to ask that you don't think about him when you're with me?"

"Bo, you can't even fathom," she says, getting dressed like I only bought her for a few hours. I'm still on the bed. I haven't even cleaned myself up yet. No, I'm on my back with a knee wide, showing her the goods she enjoyed so thoroughly minutes ago.

I can't win!

"What's happening right now," I say. I get on my feet and swallow the distance between us. I'm in her face when she straightens, her eyes glossy again—again she's ready to cry. "How is it that I make you cry?"

"You don't. You make me happy."

"Sure doesn't look like it!"

"Please…"

"And how the hell can I 'fathom' anything when you say nothing? Nothing! You're thinking about him. Why? Is it because you want to leave him?" I take her hand before she can bend back down to strap her shoe on. "Because if you do, I'd be the happiest fucking loser in the world. I'm begging for scraps, here, and it's what I get too—fifty-seven minutes of temporary bliss. Hey, is it that you can't help sleeping with me and regret it every time?"

I'm thinking with my heart, not my brain—I can't believe what I'm dealing with right now. My intestines grind with the need to own her because the love just doesn't budge! It's destroying me. I need her to make her mind up.

Fucking pick me!

"You've got to choose," I grit out, bold, so much bolder than I am.

Her gaze lifts from my hand that's white-knuckling hers.

"Choose what? I told you there is no leaving him." She's cruel. Too honest. Darker, much darker is her gaze, and it's not from passion. It's from grief, fear, anger, and all I can do is throw my arms around her and jerk her close. I bury my nose in her hair and inhale her fast, needing her so much I ache.

"Stay," I plead. "Just stay. Tell me more about you. Make me understand what's going on because I'm so fucking lost. I'm lost in you, and I hate this confusion, Nadia. Nothing should be this confusing."

Hesitant, she links her arms around my waist. We breathe together, hearts thundering between us, wall to wall.

"Do you like me?" I ask, pitiful. "A little?" She can't say no, or I am crushed. Nadia, my beautiful girl who strings me through Hell to Heaven and drops me back off downstairs once she's done. She lifts her face from my chest, secret-keeper eyes penetrating mine in one, big,

full, right-on, truthful stare and says—
"I'm in love with you too."

NADIA

Until tonight, I didn't realize the extent of what I'm doing to Bo. I saw it in the words he threw at me, in the frustration of his embrace, and even now, after I've agreed to stay the night, the strain lingers in fine lines around his eyes.

I don't want to make anyone unhappy.

My own misery is understandable, they say. It's how it goes; every person's trajectory through my evils is different. Even if my sadness lasted a lifetime, it would be natural. It doesn't mean I should drag Bo down with me.

Bo loved me again, after I agreed to stay. And I closed my eyes and forgot about shame, about guilt, about everything ugly. With him, it's easy to do. With him, I find a calmness to be at home in.

"I'm glad you're here," he murmurs nighttime-hushed. With my head on his arm and his nose in my hair, I'm good. For once, the scabs from the past don't bleed.

"You made me." I smile, and he feels it, pulling away enough to study my face. That small frown on his forehead reappears.

"This has gone on for long enough. You need to tell me what's happening, darling. Don't keep me in the dark."

I rub my eyes with my fingers. It's a short reprieve from his intensity. We were good. I thought we were on a break from my confessions. "But I'm barely starting to get a handle on it. How can I tell everyone until I can endure it myself?"

"'It?'" His voice is soft as velvet and strong as steel. "I'm not 'everyone.'"

I tug the corner of the sheet over my mouth, hiding, but he loosens my grip and draws it away. "Look at me."

Bo's eyes brim with concern and love. It makes me braver. It makes me want to try again. As if he sees, he says, "Talk to me."

And I do.

"I became Jude's emergency nurse after his mother's visits turned less frequent. Despite his reassurances, I started worrying that he wouldn't eat while I was at work. We'd fight over it. Then we fought over whether I should stop working and study full time."

I close my eyes and relive what I tell him.

"Nadia, I'm a grown-up! I'm your husband—you've got to stop with the worrying. I'm supposed to take care of *you*, not the other way around, dammit. I didn't all but kidnap you from your house for you to hound me!" he shouted.

"You're acting like a kid," I said. "How many glucagon injections have you been forced to take lately? I can tell, you know, how many are left. It's not difficult. Thank the Lord your parents didn't cut your health insurance the way they did your savings. And plus," I'd added, "the one who should go to school and finish up is *you*. If you did, both of our lives would be easier. Your mom said it straight out: if you start school, they'll pay for it and living expenses too so you don't have to work at the gas station."

"Bull. Shit! They know I'm not budging on this; it's my wife first."

We fought over what was best for each other, and nothing could alter his mind. "Here's the order, Jude: insulin shot. Food. Insulin shot. Food. Rinse and repeat. And here's what's *not* on your short list: a glucagon injection because you wait too flipping long to eat. You take more injections than pills!"

"Nuh-uh," he scoffed, rubbing his face hard. "I take the pills way more often."

"Wait." I hadn't even checked his supply of glucose tablets. "You put yourself in danger even more often than the missing syringes suggest?"

"Shut up!" His fist slammed into the drywall between the sleeping alcove and the den. "At least I'm not double-grabbing *insulin* shots!"

I sit up in bed and force myself to meet Bo's gaze. My cheeks burn with what I'm reliving, the blood speeding through my veins, because these, my worst memories, I tuck away so deep they're hard to find.

"But then he did once," I say, watching Bo's dark brows sink.

"Did what?"

"He— Ah. The two types of shots look different, but he kept them in the same kit. It was a small thing, so easy to fix, but we… just didn't. Once, he mistook an insulin shot for a glucagon shot."

"And he got sick?"

"Very. He was unconscious already when I came back from work. Thankfully, the empty syringe lied next to him, so it wasn't difficult to understand what had happened. I injected him with glucagon and called 911."

Bo doesn't try to pull me close. He sits with me, keeping my hands quiet in his and willing me to continue.

"He woke up in the ambulance, but they still hospitalized him for twenty-four hours. He needed a long conversation with the doctor, they said. Jude was good after that. Very good. Stayed on top of his meds."

That's when I burst into tears. The big, ugly kind of tears that don't stop flooding. In the midst of it, I think that I don't understand what Bo sees in me. My baggage—

Bo hushes my thoughts tenderly. "Shhhh, that's good, Nadia, darling. It's good." He pulls me back in, and when he weaves his arm around me, his nearness is all that I want.

"I know," I sob out. "I know."

He tips my head back and holds my face, kissing my tears away and abrading me with soft stubble, a short-lived pain I welcome, one I can easily take. "Are you afraid he's doing it again while you're gone? That he'll forget to eat and take the wrong medicine—is that why you're crying?"

"No." I shake my head anxiously. Bo holds me, still holds me. The truth abrades in rougher ways than stubble, and I'm in danger of bursting open.

What will happen if I do?

"No, I'm not afraid of that," I say, a truth I can acknowledge. I'll never again find Jude in that state. "I… It's enough for now. Later, Bo. I'm tired."

Before me, beautiful features tense, understanding giving way to hurt before his eyes go cold as lakes freezing with the onset of a Patagonian winter. Again, I haven't given him what he hoped for. Again, I keep the most important part of myself to myself.

Bo lets me fall asleep in his arms. On his bed. In his apartment. With no promise of a conclusion. With his only knowledge of me being my struggles.

NADIA

When the dawn scatters its first beads of daylight across the room, I rise and watch him while I slip into my clothes. He looks so young. He looks like someone you should never hurt. Like someone who shouldn't be subjected to the onslaught of someone else's pain.

I walk quietly to his bathroom and stare at the girl in the mirror. She has black eyes and the ability to stain her grief onto others.

When will he hate me? It is only a matter of time.

The faucet creaks as I open it, allowing a few droplets to leak out. I steal them soundlessly and wet my eyes to wake up. This new man in my life. What I feel for him is not puppy love or savior-of-the-world love. It's different from what I feel for Jude in so many ways. Incomparable yet equally wonderful.

I push my palms down on the sink and fix my stare into the mirror. I don't just see the sad girl. I see the selfish one too, the one Bo must see when he's angry and can't take my cruelty anymore. What a good man he is for still spending time with me, for letting me sleep next to him and consoling me while I stew in my too-private misgivings.

I hate my inability to bare it all. Soon. Soon, I will do it. Once I see Bo again—maybe later today?—I will tell him. If the rest of my story scares him off, then I will at least have been brave.

What will he think when he wakes up to an empty bed? That I've returned to soak up the last remnant of the night in Jude's arms? He'll think I'm a loose girl. A slut. A floozy. A tramp, a hustler, a—a—whore?

He can't think that. If he still retains a sliver of belief in me, I need him to keep it until I am strong enough to share. So I pull my lipstick out of my purse. I press it against the mirror, and I write the only thing I can say.

CHAPTER Twenty-Six
RAGE

BO

My dreams are a fusion of soft hands and loving gazes, images of happy guys that swell and turn homicidal when their stares glue on me. I punch them smack in the face. Somehow I wield an awesome ninja sword that I jab into Jude's forehead and rotate until a red hole appears above his expression of murderous bliss.

I startle awake, cursing the man out for being an asshole, a fake, for stringing along women who deserve to be happy. Then I remember I'm *with* her, that I can make her happy right now. I turn and find nothing next to me under the sheets.

When reality bashes me in the face, I don't take long to act. Hell no, I stand before I can think straight. With a towel around my waist, I race to the den, the kitchen, and loop to the bathroom. She's not there either—she's nowhere, but she has left a message I don't understand.

Please don't judge me.
I am not *what you see.*
I am the opposite.

I don't care what that means. I'm out of here. I'm hopping into old, black jeans and the whatever-shirt I tossed on the floor last night. I hit the front door running, the handle denting the outside wall and the door smacking closed on its own.

I survey the driveway and find Emil's truck by the mailbox. It blocks mine now? Whatever. I return to the apartment, push his bedroom door open, and shake his jeans until the keys land in my palm.

It's seven fifteen in the morning and *my* girl better not be sleeping with her asshole husband. If she's there, I'm dragging her the fuck out with me, because we're getting to the bottom of shit. *This is it!*

On the way over, I think of the snippets she's told me. Everything she hasn't. I'm mad. Mad, that she's still with him even though she came out to be with me on tour, gifting me all of Heaven with no side of Hell. What was she thinking?

The Alhambra Apartments' parking lot holds five cars. I see none I can picture as Nadia's, but there's a big one, a road-rage Hummer waiting to be smashed. I've never been the caveman type, but I store that damn steel-colored machine into the back of my brain for afterward. If it's her man's, I'm bashing it to smithereens. Because vengeance. Because of the jerk finding my girl before I did.

I'm here, stalking through the archway giving to the building itself. Iridescent grass, coral-colored stucco, and fifteen-watt corridor lights take me to her entrance.

And there it is, with a goddamn heart on the door, and I'm raging, thinking of that heart being mine and hanging on some other guy's door. It's got a crack in it. Fitting too, the way he makes people suffer.

I bang on the door, hard.

My thoughts reel. The idiot doesn't make love to her. He didn't call or text her during the four days she was on tour with me.

When Nadia and I were together the first time, she was starving. I've seen every inch of her skin—studied it, loved it, devoured it. Her husband might not cause her bodily harm, but I know better than anyone that you can trap your lover with your mind. He isn't trapping my girl anymore!

There's no response from the other side. I bang on the door again.

My phone buzzes in my pocket, and it's absurd at this hour. I grab it impatiently, wanting to turn it off, but on reflex I check the smiling face on the screen. Ingela. My heart slams in my chest. I'm not in the mood for her probing, but my index finger twitches, and I press "Answer" anyway.

"What?" I snap.

"It's me, Inga," she says, sleepy.

"And?"

She's calling out of nowhere. When I first arrived, she had a sixth sense. She'd be on the line whenever I felt alone and miserable in L.A., when I missed Sweden so much I wanted to bang my head against the wall. But since things sorted themselves out between Cameron and her, she hasn't been calling much. I hear more from Cameron than from Ingela.

"I dreamed about you. It was sort of a nightmare," she murmurs. "You were super-confused and sad and crazy mad over something, so I wanted to make sure you were okay. Are you asleep?"

"No. Clearly, I'm awake. I'm okay."

"Well, you sound *really* awake. Isn't this early for you?" she asks.

"It's not that early—" My voice breaks as I say it.

"Bo. What's going on?"

Something is blocking my throat, so I don't answer.

"How is that girl I met?" she continues like she knows it's my problem, and I wish she didn't. "What's her name again?"

"Nadia." My jaw tenses as I lean my head against the doorjamb. I don't want Inga to worry. I try to suppress the fury, the frustration, but it's hard. "Shit."

"What?" Alarmed, she turns her volume up to Ingela-level.

"Shhh," I rasp. "Don't do that. Is Cameron still asleep?"

"Shhh," she retorts. "Yeah, he's an ass, sleeping through everything. Hold on—I'll go to the living room if it makes you feel better. One sec."

Seconds later, she demands, "What's happening!" in that no-nonsense, no-question tone of hers. She always was so bossy. I never understood that side of her.

"Nadia is fine. I think." My heart boulders heartbeats down a mountainside and straight into a loud-as-hell ravine.

"BS."

"*Why!* Do you always insist on English, Inga?" It adds to my stress level that we don't speak Swedish when we've known each other forever.

"Because if Cameron wakes up, he needs to hear we're talking about someone else, not me, his girlfriend."

Ah yeah. This is about my crap, not his and Ingela's, and there's no reason to stir up their dreamy-lovey existence back there in Deepsilver. Cameron has been through enough.

"Spill!" she yells, Ingela-loud. "You said, 'Shit' about Nadia, and yet you said she was quote-unquote good? Well that's not *good* enough for me. Sorry. This is me you're talking to, and you better spill everything."

True, all of it. If there's anyone I can trust in this world, it's Ingela. "Things are messed up with Nadia," I say.

"How?" She doesn't last long before adding, "Where is she? Is she with you?"

"Nadia is about a hundred meters away from me. Inside her and her *husband's* apartment. My guess is she's in their bed, sleeping in his arms. After leaving *my* fucking bed"—I check my watch—"about an hour and a half ago."

Ingela is never speechless.

Now, she is.

After the initial *Whoa!*, there is no sound on the other side. I count to ten while I wait for Inga to scoop out the ugly truth, paint it clear and bright for me, the way no one does better, leaving no doubt as to what a douchebag I am.

"You're outside her door?" she asks.

"Yeah."

Ingela is genuine to the core, and she'll latch on to what she finds most important. I wait for her to say, "You're pursuing a married woman, you scumbag!" or "That girl, Nadia, is *blah-blah-ing* you despite *blah-blah*!" or "How can you be such a cock?"

"That's crazy!" she bellows. "I had no idea you had it in you—Bo, you've always been the, uh, Ice King! I never thought you'd, like, totally go ape-shit over a broad. What happened to you?"

"I dig her," I finally grate out, sounding childish and silly. Even if Inga is happy with Cameron, I can't make myself tell her I'm in love with a woman I've known for five weeks. Hell, I was with Ingela for five *years* and never managed to feel this way.

"And her husband *keeps* her? Doesn't he get how you two feel about each other? She was damn obvious on the tour, all sugar-loving you like a motherfucker."

What?

"Please, Inga. You're not helping. I'm pissed, and I want to break down this door. Dude's a lowlife—" I stop myself before I tell her he doesn't even have sex with her. "But she's said straight out that she'll never leave him."

"Seriously? He's got something on her, Bo! He's keeping her prisoner. She could be a rich heiress or something, and he wants her money. Oh! What if he's slowly poisoning her?"

"You're killing me!" I yell, and it's way too loud in the hallway. I brace myself against the door, trying to remain cool. This is so damn crazy. I've never felt this way before. Here I am, pining for a woman outside her door. She's got a life in there, with some husband.

But when she's with me, she's all mine!

I hang up. Inga doesn't want me to. I power off my phone because I can't have her call back. I wish I'd brought my guitar. The guitar reasons with me while it strums out my shit, makes the notes cry and squeal and die so I don't have to. And it's at home, not where I need it to be, and all I can do is obsess, rage over how this girl is meant for *me*.

I bang on the door. People get up in adjacent apartments.

"Nadia!" I scream. And scream again.

CHAPTER Twenty-Seven
PLEASE

NADIA

Of course I wasn't asleep. How could I be? I've lit my candles, watered my miniature flower pots, and I've been running in and out from our alcove, tidying up, telling Jude I want to change out the bed and—

Not knowing what to do.

I don't know. I don't know.

Bo bangs on the door so loud I think he's about to break it down. He can't come in. I need to think, figure things out…

What I land on will impact my existence to a degree people wouldn't understand. *Bo* wouldn't understand.

"Go home," I creak, and it's not how one makes people leave. While Bo rattles the door and insists I open, I say, "No, please leave," and my mind pressures me, insists, mixing in another time.

It's me calling home. Jude not answering.

Me working at the diner and Zoe narrowing her eyes at me, aware of my problem with Jude. "All good?"

"Can't get a hold of him." That's me, upset. It's been busy—the Hollywood Boulevard midsummer crowd has kept us on our toes. Even so, I always call whether he's at work or not. How I wish he called *me*. But when he's sick and irrational…?

"As handsome as your hubby is, there's only so much of my patience he'd get," she scoffs, but when she realizes I keep redialing, redialing, without an answer, she squints deeper, her grimace becoming suspicion.

"What's he up to, Nadia? I'll cover for you if you want to run home and check."

"Thanks," I manage, and something in my expression makes her pause. She pivots fully and stares hard.

"Do you want me to come with you?"

"No— It's okay. He does this…"

"I know. All the time. Great if he didn't," she adds.

"Nadia. If you don't open this door, I'm breaking it down." That's Bo outside, bringing me back and skyrocketing my heart. Hysteria rattles, a wary snake beneath my surface.

"Bo, please. I'll see you tonight." My voice shakes.

His is muffled by the door when he replies, "No! You're opening now. Jude?" My hands shoot up to cover my mouth. I look behind me and stare straight into Jude's deep blue eyes.

I don't want to be there, but I'm pulled back to that night. Running from Scott's Diner, passing by Jude's gas station.

"He got off at six, right?"

"No, early leave today. Five," the bubble-gum-chewing teenaged girl says, pressing fingers idly into the keys of the cash register.

I run home, turn the key in the front door—it's L.A.—we always keep it locked.

"Last chance to save your door!" Bo's words pierce through, the wood shaking from his attacks. *"I'm coming in!"*

I'm back again, back in the past.

"Jude?" I shout, worried that I'll find what I fear. It's not what I need, not what either of us needs. Jude promised to always be here, to support me, to be my love, my guide, and my light in the darkness.

But our house is quiet. The fridge door is open. I rush a quick look over its entrails but can't see anything missing. I wish I did. The TV is on, blaring colors and overly excited contestants. I stalk through the den, into the bedroom, and—

Crack.

Our front door slams open, and then Bo's there, staring at me, eyes too wide for seven in the morning, hair tousled, fists locked. "Where is he?" he grits out. "I'm having a talk with that douchebag."

"No!" I shout, dying, needing this nightmare to stop, but Bo's eyes already roam the room. He sees it. Every detail he takes in, while I cover my mouth and *charge* back to that moment when Jude—

—He's in bed.

I'm relieved, but then he's too still, his skin whiter than marble? He has assumed the smooth, cold, colorless surface of the angels at the Recoleta Cemetery.

I jump my love, shake him, but those deep blue eyes don't open. They don't close either! His eyelashes, long and even, don't even flutter from their half-mast position. My Jude, he's quiet, so unnaturally quiet beneath the covers, the tip of his nose burying into the pillow like he never was but a fleeting dream that came true before it left.

Dreams don't need air because they vanish when you wake up.

Dreams don't need sugar, don't need food, don't need *me*.

There's an ampule next to him. A syringe in his hand. I wail because he tried. He tried, he tried, and with shaky hands and bleary eyes, he grabbed the wrong one, while I was at work and didn't know. He convulsed here, alone, while I waited tables. He—

"Why did you do this to me?" I scream, and it's over, all over. I don't want it to be over—I can't allow it to be over, and yet it's irrefutable. *Unless I deny it, unless my mind stops it from happening!*

I sink on top of the table as Bo walks toward me. I'm dizzy. My throat rasps with oxygen I inhale too quickly. He isn't shouting for Jude to come out anymore, for him to man up and have that talk.

Bo's eyes are wary, understanding fighting confusion at the back of frosty irises. Chest heaving with anger that's depleting, his hands wilt at his sides as he approaches me. He doesn't speak at first, but eyes the darkest grey I have ever witnessed don't let go of me, and I cover my mouth.

"Darling?" he whispers. Careful. Incredulous.

I'm a wild animal, and he is cornering me.

"Is this Jude?" Bo's stare floats to my first love, my only husband. I follow his gaze. See what he sees. The portrait of a boy, blond, tousled hair over a dusty forehead, lively eyes glinting and full of humor. Pointy canines showing in a wide grin.

I nod.

"Is… that also Jude?" Bo asks, his voice hoarse with final realization. And it is. What he sees is also my love. Brave, so brave in the midst of my grief, Bo hunches down in front of the table I sit on. Cautiously, he moves the tea lights to a side. Next, go my miniature flowerpots, and there he is. There.

Bo—

Is holding Jude.

I sob because it's too much.

Bo holds Jude with both hands, raising him before me, and his eyes are lustrous like mine. Between Bo's fingers, white porcelain birds interrupt the serenity of light blue ceramic. I never could let him go. For a year and a half, I should have allowed those doves to fly off and take Jude to a better place.

Bo sets Jude's urn down as carefully as he lifted it. He picks up my husband's portrait. Fastens his gaze on him. When the next words fall from Bo's mouth, the two of them are having that talk after all.

It's short. It's sweet. It's—

Good.

"Jude," he murmurs to my cheerful, blissed-out husband with the windblown hair and the desert-dusty forehead. The one whose eyes gleam mischief and youthful arrogance.

"It seems you needed to move on. Please—"

I look up. Watch Bo's Adam's apple bob with emotion and determination before he continues, "Can I take care of her from here?"

PART 5
Acceptance

Letting go of fear
Facing the future
Because, darling, just fucking own it

CHAPTER Twenty-Eight
EXIT

BO

"Are you sure?" I ask her for the fifth time though it's obvious that she is.

She's curled up on my lap in a corner booth of a non-distinct restaurant neither of us frequent. Light walls and tourists surround us, the waiters efficient yet personable as they set a root beer float in front of her and a coke in front of me.

"Yeah. I want them to meet you. And I need you here if I'm going to give him up."

A fifty-something couple enters. He's lanky with dark eyes and the woman petite with a gaze that could have been animated. It's the same color as Jude's in the photo. The man instantly zooms in on Nadia and says something to his wife. She grabs his arm and pulls herself closer as they approach us.

Nadia gets on her feet first, and I stand, hands on my

back, until they're done greeting each other with warm hugs.

"This is Bo," Nadia says, a small smile lifting her lips.

The woman grasps my hand with both of hers, squeezing. "Bo. We're so glad to meet you. We didn't know what to do for Nadia. She… wasn't getting any better."

She cries when she sees what's on the seat behind me. The urn remains inside Nadia's bag, but the flap has slid to the side showing a hint of white birds.

It's strange to sit here and chat with the parents of your girlfriend's husband. He's here with us—in memory through the stories they share, and physically, in a small, sky blue container.

Over the last couple of weeks, Jude has become tangible in my mind. He wasn't the devil I'd made him out to be. In life, he didn't make my girl suffer. No, Jude was a stubborn, caring troublemaker who broke rules and ran off with the prize. He wanted to be a good husband, but he was too young to look after himself enough to be one.

Nadia curves into my side again, and the approval in Mr. Bancroft's expression is unambiguous.

"You're ready then?" he asks Nadia. "As I told you, we're holding a small ceremony for Jude when we join your half of his ashes with those already in the mausoleum. It would make us happy if you came up to San Francisco for it."

Nadia and I discussed what would be best for her before we came today. My thought was that she should see Jude off in person, but she feels she has said goodbye for long enough.

She lifts her gaze and meets her father-in-law's. "I

think it's better with this reunion, right here. I can see him off with you now. Who better to trust with his remains than his mother and father?"

Mrs. Bancroft's mouth trembles. She purses it to stop the movement, but a tear still slides from the corner of her eye. I nudge Nadia in against me, making sure she knows I'm here. She sends me the briefest glance for courage. I nod, giving it to her and guessing what she's about to say next.

"Bo, he's been pushing me, over the last few months. Ever since I met him, actually." My girl lets out a breathy laugh before she continues. "You knew I couldn't let go of Jude. But it was worse than that. I took denial to a new level, spending all of my energy on living like I never lost him. I couldn't take my chances; it felt like I'd lose my mind if I opened to the grief.

"But no matter what I did, the heartache was just excruciating." She swallows. I kiss her forehead, but I don't help her explain. She needs this struggle. It's the only way out on the other side where I want her.

"I could dodge the truth and live in oblivion with everyone else. Even my best friend let me get away with it most of the time. But Bo? He—"

Her eyes gloss over again, and I grab a napkin and dab it right beneath her nose, making her laugh with embarrassment. "Bo didn't take my crap," she continues. "He insisted, to the point of breaking down my front door for answers. Once I saw Bo see Jude… that's when—God, I saw it too. I saw what I'd become, the fantasy world I was living in."

"Oh honey," Jude's mother sobs out, lifting her hand,

wanting to stop Nadia from suffering. But Nadia isn't in pain. She's living. Crying, allowing stuff out the way she should have done for so long.

"I'm okay," Nadia manages. "Yes, once Bo learned the truth about Jude, there was no going back to before. It was like he crumbled the walls to the world I'd created and forced me to see the truth too. Since then he's been boot-camping me through the process of grief."

Mrs. Bancroft hides behind her hands. Above them, her eyes shimmer with tears, but her gaze broadcasts relief over sadness. "Thank you," she murmurs to me. "Thank you."

Nadia kisses the arm I've got around her. "Jude will always be there when I need to visit him, so I won't come up to San Francisco for the ceremony. The funeral service in 'the Garden' was enough for me." Nadia's pitch breaks on the last sentence. She clears her throat before she continues, "Plus, Bo and I have to prepare for Argentina."

Mrs. Bancroft's eyes widen, delight mixing with her sorrow. "You're going home, Nadia? Visiting?"

Nadia smiles that beautiful smile I love so much, the one saying she has hope, that she's looking forward to something.

"Yeah. Bo's band has been invited to Buenos Aires, to play Luna Park, an old concert hall that means a lot to people there. It's not a big arena or anything, but I remember aunts and uncles of mine talking about it when I was little, and I always wanted to go."

Mrs. Bancroft locks her hands together, earnest. "That's amazing. I'm so happy for you. You will be back in time for school, right?"

All her attention is on my girl, making her seem more like a mother than a mother-in-law. "You *are* picking up your studies again, right? Ever since Jude… left, it's been my biggest regret that we didn't help you two financially when you wanted to do it your way."

Her husband rubs her shoulder. "Hush, it's okay."

"You know what I mean, honey," she says, unable to keep her voice from shaking anymore. "All Jude wanted was to watch Nadia finish her studies first. He wanted to support her through school before he moved on with his own education."

"I know, Ruth. I know."

"Nadia, you're our only child now, and things won't be easy for us until you accept what's yours."

"It's not mine." Nadia bites her lip, unsurprised by Mrs. Bancroft's insistence, and I get the feeling I'm privy to an exchange they've had time and time again. "If I'd been there when he overdosed on insulin, he would have been alive today. There's no way I can accept his trust fund."

"Oh Nadia. Your guilt. It's pointless. My son was young, but he was an adult when he moved away from home. I struggle to accept it too—I'm his mother—but you have to understand that Jude had lived with his disease for a long time. He knew what to do to manage it. He just didn't do it."

"But I should have been there! You can't just say 'he didn't make it, too bad,'" Nadia bursts out and instantly covers her mouth.

"You were at work, sweetie," Mrs. Bancroft answers, voice low. "And that's not what I'm saying. See… I called Jude that day."

Nadia sucks in air sharply at my side while Mr. Bancroft says, "Honey, you don't have to do this."

"No, it's overdue."

I stroke Nadia's cheek as she steadies herself with a hand on my thigh.

"I think mothers have a sixth sense when it comes to our children. I was in a charity meeting when I had the sensation that Jude wasn't okay. I called him. He didn't answer—which of course was nothing new. My son wasn't a phone person, but he used to reply with a text message to keep me off his back. This time he didn't."

She tucks her lips between her teeth, nostrils flaring with emotion. I'm an intruder to her reveal, but I'm here for my girl. I'm here, supporting Nadia and doing what feels right.

"I was in Payne Point, hours from the two of you in Los Angeles. I'd called you so many times, Nadia, and this time—this time… I didn't."

Mrs. Bancroft's eyes fill with moisture again. "I called 911 instead," she says, shifting off her husband's arm. "While they dispatched to your apartment, I got ready to drive to St. Aimo. You were in Silicon Valley that week," she reminds Mr. Bancroft, who nods.

"But, see, a paramedic from the ambulance called me back. And he assured me that my son was fine. Jude hadn't let them into the apartment, he said, but he sounded coherent, even impatient with both them and me.

"He'd told them he was playing some online game, something about warlocks. That he needed to go or he'd lose some prize or points. The paramedics even warned him that they would send a bill for the dispatch, which my Jude had been okay with; in so many words, they admitted he'd mentioned making his mother pay."

"Oh God. That is so Jude, isn't it?" Nadia sniffles. "The video games. Sending bills your way… Exactly how he was when he was one hundred percent lucid too."

"I know." His mother's voice warbles with emotion. "I believed them. And if you still think you did something wrong, Nadia, imagine how I felt. Despite my gut feeling, my instincts, I trusted the judgment of people who did not know my son, and I *didn't* drive to L.A. *Didn't* arrive. *Didn't* grab your spare key under the front-door flowerpot. And I *didn't save my son!*"

Nadia flies from my arms and into Mrs. Bancroft's. She hugs her tight, tight, pleading with her, "Ruthie, you didn't know. How *could* you know that this time was different? Right now, I swear to you, he must be up there, looking down at us from Heaven and saying, '*I* created that mess.'"

The two women, one older, one younger, hold on to each other, consoling and easing guilts, soothing pain and losing blame. I meet Mr. Bancroft's stare over their heads. In the older man's gaze I find ever-cloudy skies. I see stagnant grief and resignation.

How they have suffered. I hope by God they find an exit from their hell. All I know is that I'm going to ensure *my* girl's happiness.

"Help us rectify one thing," Mrs. Bancroft finally says. "Help us fulfill Jude's biggest wish. Daughter: please go to college. Become a veterinarian. For yourself and for all of us, give up the waitressing and move on.

"Take a good look at yourself, Nadia," she continues.

"The book of your life has spread open on a shiny new page. You're traveling—you'll see your family again with Bo at your side. Please, Nadia, it would mean the world to us if you let us be a part of this; allow our small contribution. It's just money."

"Ruth, I'll take it from here," Mr. Bancroft murmurs. "Nadia, these funds will not be touched unless you accept them. As our daughter-in-law, you're not just in Jude's will. You're in ours as well. It's only a matter of time before they are yours. You might as well accept them now while you need them for college. Make Jude happy. Make us happy. You've atoned for sins you never committed for too long."

While they insist, Nadia shrinks back into my embrace. Like a small child, she hides her face against my throat and drives air out slowly through her nose. It fills me with a tenderness that's too big for my chest. I love this girl so hard I want to walk with her through Hell so I can bring her to Heaven when she's done.

"We sued the hospital over it, Nadia," Mr. Bancroft says, his trump card. "They paid up without as much as a hearing because all evidence, the recordings of Ruth's 911 call and the paramedics' conversation with Jude, pointed at how they had misjudged the situation.

"Even though Ruth explained Jude's history of refusing treatment, they trusted his words over hers. They should have broken down the door when he didn't open, and their lapse in judgment left Jude to die.

"The money has now been released to *your* trust fund. Nothing, Nadia, no money could be more yours than this."

Chapter Twenty-Nine

TWO MONTHS LATER

NADIA

We're escorted from the airport by the director of the venue. We're late, and we're exhausted from layovers in Brazil and Chile, one of which was unexpected. The director, Salvador Battoni, gesticulates, mingling Italian-laden Spanish with English as he rushes us to Luna Park, New-York-taxi style and on two wheels most of the time.

"No, no, no. No time for hotel!" the director insists as if the band has suggested such a thing. Troll surveys all of us from the front passenger seat, ending it with a playful wink at me. "No. No check-in first. Luna Park it is, Mr. Battoni."

"Salvatore!" our guide corrects him. "Salvatore, like *la mia nonna* called me!" Bo sends me a curious look, and I whisper, "His grandma called him 'Salvatore.' Italian version of the Spanish name 'Salvador.'"

"People from Buenos Aires like to chatter, huh?" Bo says, and I nod, smiling. *Mi gente*, I think, because they are.

It's dark outside. I don't get the full view, but I smell my city and my country. Memories and love for this place glide through me, and as Salvador fans a hand behind Emil, hurrying him in the back door to the concert hall and muttering stuff even I don't understand, that small smile I've worn since we passed through customs spreads into a full-blown grin.

"Is my girl happy?" Bo asks, heaving me off the floor in a playful, one-armed hug with the hand that doesn't hold his guitar. A little something—a joyous little something—bobs in my throat at his question.

"Maybe." I purse my smile low. He sees though and winks at me. Sucks a kiss to my lips before staff swarms us. Their serious faces boast glittering blue eyes, cat-green eyes, and amber eyes concocted in the crazy melting pot of races that is Buenos Aires.

Fast and efficient, the stagehands unload the truck, and I think that they could be my next-door neighbors in La Boca all grown up. That joyous something bobbing in my throat grows and fizzes and makes me let out a giggle.

A different déjà vu hits me in the dressing room. There he is, my baby. Bo with dark bangs spiking over a fine-boned, pale face as he hunches in over his guitar, tapping on strings, finding peace in his music before he goes on stage to be wooed as a symbol of rock, sex, whatever.

I'm where he wants me, in this dressing room so he can lean on my faith in him. His faraway gaze remains on me while he plays. He's here for me too—the whole band is—by accepting this single South American gig for *me*.

It wasn't easy to commit to coming here: the anxiety of having to retell my story to my mother's family; the overwhelming love I'd feel at the hearth of my family; the sadness over the years I had missed in their midst. I wasn't sure I could do it.

But while I have Bo's back when he walks out there on stage, he'll have mine when we go to my *Tía* Rosa's tonight.

This moment is so big I could cry.

"So much going on in my head right now." My tone is unsteady.

"All good stuff, right?" Bo's irises shimmer already, knowing. This man. How could I be so lucky? How is one person afforded two deep loves in one lifetime? What did I do to deserve this?

He leans in, hair that's not black anymore but taking back its original ash-blond shade tickling my face. In an attempt to hide how moved I am, I scrunch up my nose, acting like the feather-soft caresses of his hair bother me.

"You're about to cry. Good-cry," he teases, silky voice vibrating against my skin. "My little Nadia can't take all the pleasures I bring her."

"My little Bo is full of himself," I tease back.

"Hmm, I'll be happy to share. I'll fill *you* up too."

I'm dimwitted and overwhelmed and don't understand until his hands start roaming. Feeling, trailing down my ribs, my thighs, and working to hike my skirt up.

"Baby," he moans, playful and so delicious. "I can't believe you didn't want to play mile-high-club with me. Thanks to you, I'll be too uncomfortable to go on stage.

Unless you give me—"

The door flies open the way it always does in dressing rooms during Clown Irruption concerts. First in comes Emil. He's long-distance-fighting with Zoe on the phone, brows drawn and trying to explain that he has been in the air or in airports all this time. Next, comes Troll, rumbling out, "Ready? We're going straight from sound-check to doors."

Emil scoffs, covering his ear against the tour manager. "Zee. I *told* you I wanted you to come along, and no, I'm not going to sleep with all of Nadia's cousins."

Bo snickers.

"What?" Emil presses the phone against his ear. "Of course I didn't manage on the first try—I was chasing a moving target. You have to stay *still*. You can't wiggle your butt when I'm trying to get in, Zoay."

"TMI?" Bo suggests. I nod, feeling a blush spreading at their typical indiscretion.

"Okay, next time I'll just buy some rope and shit," Emil says, "and just bondage you all up. That way you can't wiggle away. Yeah, I'll do that."

"Geez," Elias mutters. "Everyone, get a room. Romance so thick in here I'm about to puke."

Emil stuffs a finger in his ear. "No, it won't help if *you* tie *me* down. And no, I'm pretty sure you tried to break my wiener. That'd ruin all the fun, now, wouldn't it? Really? You don't think so?"

"This *was* our room," Bo replies to Elias. "Why didn't you stay next door?"

"Because Emil was in there fighting with Zoe."

"But now he's here."

"Yeah, there's no peace anywhere."

Troll pops a piece of cheese in his mouth and hands Elias a bottle of water. "Here. Now, head in the game. Grab your instruments and get out there. Sound. Check."

NADIA

WHITE AND BLUE SPOTLIGHTS flash over the audience in sync with Elias' bass and Troy's drums. Slow yet insistent, the beat thunders out, and the crowd's attention locks on the guys as the first song picks up speed and the volume steadily increases.

Troll has me by the shoulder. Nods at me through the wall of music, telling me to follow. Uniformed policemen focus on Troll's explanation first, then on my face. One of them squints, bobs his head, and aids me the few steps down from the stage to the floor.

The standing area in front of the stage is chock-full of people younger than me. They're bouncing to the rhythm, dancing, hands in the air and ready for more. We move along the wall. I send a nervous glance in Troll's direction and find him surveying me from the steps and giving me a thumbs-up before he returns to his post backstage.

Down here, half forgotten scents reach me full force. Perfumes. Detergents and fabric softeners of my childhood. Whiffs of cheerful memories. The scents mingle with my excitement while the police make way for me to row three. The youngest of them turns, badge glinting from his jacket as he waves for me to pass the girls on the first chairs.

I obey. I pass them, nerves and happiness sparring as I watch six young men and women rise in their seats, mouthing something. Smiling. Eyes glistening with unshed tears. A hand stretches out, clamps around my arm. It's not in a handshake, no—it's to draw me in against a neck. Wet smooches move over both my cheeks, soundless against the loud music, and return for a repeat on my left.

I'm breathless, processing the enormity of this. I gasp while they pass me among each other for more kisses, more sobs, saying *amor*, saying, *te echamos de menos—tanto, tanto!*, saying *años y años sin verte, Nadia*, saying, *no lo puedo creer*—

And I do speak *Castellano* still, I assure them. I do speak Spanish. I can talk with my cousins. Hug them. Love them back with the same fervor they show me because I'm like them. I'm from here too. We are blood and family, all so much thicker than water, and in this moment I can't believe I have survived all these years without them.

"Sit between us," Mariana shouts over the music, pushing Diego to the side. "Do you recognize the twins, Adriana and Andrés? They look the same, no?" she laughs. They don't look the same. They were babies when I left.

"No, but I recognize your eyes," I say in Spanish to them. "They were yellow back then too."

All six of my cousins slap shoulders and laugh as they repeat among themselves what I said. Adriana leans in, screaming to the others and assuring that they back her up before she tells me, "You have to stay at our house.

Grandma can't wait to hold you in her arms again, and she lives with *Mamá* now. She said to tell you, *te amo mucho.*"

And I'm overcome with the love. With the shouting of words in my mother tongue over music created by the new love of my life. As I think it, Diego's gaze goes to the stage, a chin-pump indicating the band that's seamlessly shifting into the next song.

"Who's your husband?" he asks.

He doesn't know—I haven't revealed much to them in the few weeks since I found Mariana on Facebook. My heart doesn't hurt at Diego's question. It doesn't ruin the moment. So I smile back at him and say, "He's not my husband, but my boyfriend is the one on guitar."

BO

Backstage Luna Park is a riot in the literal sense of the word. I'm drenched with sweat after three encores, two of them containing *Fuck You*. We generally don't do encores of a song from the set list, but the vehemence of our Argentinian fans is persuasive. Our host and venue director, Salvador/Salvatore, even appeared backstage, nodding furiously while explaining to Troll that we'd have anarchy on our hands if we didn't heed their wishes.

"Mariana!" A girl with long, smooth, black hair and violet eyes introduces herself, smiling big. Without invitation, she proceeds to triple-kiss my face before she steps back into my girlfriend's side, hugging her close. "I'm her *best* cousin!" she explains, a small hand gesture underlining the validity of her statement.

Mariana swings and yells something in Spanish to a group behind her, pivots back to me, and translates, "I told them that you are beautiful. So beautiful a man. But skinny like rock star. Is my other cousins. There." Her hand flutters behind her in the general direction of the others.

"Warm, yes?" observes a teenaged boy with amber cat eyes. He points and continues. "You're… hmm. What is called?"

I wipe my brow and smile. "Sweaty?"

"Yes, I would say 'sweaty,'" replies the female replica of Cat-Eyes Cousin behind him. "And *I*. Am Adriana." She lifts her chin, proud, before she lunges past her brother and straight at my neck for her own version of a triple French cheek-smooch. I try to dodge the boy when he follows suit, but I am too slow.

"Andrés," he says. "I am Andrés. And you are Bo. My cousin's boyfriend. And you will sleep at my *Tía* Rosa's house tonight because is not possible to sleep in hotel."

I send Nadia a puzzled look. She bites her smile and shrugs. "I think we have no choice but to spend the night at my family's. They want the entire band there too, but at least us."

"At least you," says a tall guy Nadia's age. He's close enough to push through lightning fast for another full-on set of loud kisses. "Diego," he says. "Not Maradona! Just Diego Garcia. I'm also very, very good in the football."

"Soccer," another cousin specifies in case I thought they played American football in Argentina. The new cousin lifts a hand, pinching her fingers together like she's grabbing a small fruit. "Soccer!" she repeats.

"Ah yes. *Sí-sí-sí*. Soccer."

The fans flood into the small reception area backstage. In the beginning, everyone is polite, sweet, swooning over autographs above belly buttons and on CDs. But when the crowd thickens and shoves to get to us, I loosen Mariana's hold on Nadia and tuck my girl under my arm; there's no way I'll allow frenzied fans close enough to put her in danger.

In a repeat from a show in the US, the scuffle starts at the door. Only the pushing is more violent. Fans shout to get in, and it's not venue staff guarding the door—it's police with guns and batons on their hips. A stagehand translates when I ask what's going on. "Someone has reproduced backstage passes and sold them on the black market. There are at least a hundred of them out there, waiting to come in. The fans thought they bought real passes, and they're very upset."

"Troll!" I yell over Nadia's head. He's onto the situation and already speaking with the venue director. At my call, he makes his way over to us, bushy brows drawn with concern. It flashes through me how lucky we are to have him; he'll do anything to keep us comfortable.

"Bo, we've got a situation on our hands," he begins.

"Yeah, I heard."

"Okay, we'll have an escape van ready at the emergency exit in five."

"No, let's make Buenos Aires happy," I say and feel Nadia's gaze on me. "Here's what we'll do. Is everyone out of the main venue yet?"

"Well, except for the hundred or so with fake backstage passes."

"All right. Let's move this party back out."

Troll gets it and instantly runs with my idea. "Okay. I'll keep you guys on stage. The fans can come up and meet you one by one—doesn't matter that the stagehands are working around you—and we'll bring the leftover drinks out so they have something to hold onto while they wait their turn."

"Perfect," I say. Salvador arrives in time to catch Troll's logistical input.

"*Perfecto!*" he chimes in.

"Ah you are sooo lucky!" a blonde teenager with black eyes exclaims to Nadia, beaming. "He wrote that song about youuuu?"

Nadia has that pink tint to her cheeks, the one I love to make crawl down her chest. She fidgets, unsure of where to keep her hands, so I take one of them and pull it to my mouth for a kiss. "*Sí,*" I say in Spanish, making the girl giggle. "She's my inspiration for everything."

"No-no-no, not the sad song?" the girl asks, jutting out a pouty-lip.

"True, not the sad song."

"I hope you never, never write sad songs about her!"

"I won't let him," my shy girl pipes up, adding in her mother tongue, *"Nunca,"* and I think I know what it means.

"I will tell you what love is in Spanish," the small

blonde declares. *"Te amo."*

"Te amo?" I say to be sure I pronounce it correctly.

"Sí!" She claps her hands together and holds them there expectantly. Her gaze flicks from me to Nadia and then back to me.

I turn to my sweetheart and say, *"Te amo,"* and somehow that's bigger for her than all the times I've said it in English and Swedish. Nadia's eyes well with liquid emotion, and her cheeks take on a darker shade of pink.

"Siempre?" Nadia whispers, and I look to the girl for help. She squees and claps her hands in small flutters, dragonfly-style.

"She ask you if always! Will you *always* love her?" Then she holds her breath on Nadia's behalf.

"Sí," I say. *"Siempre. Te amo siempre."*

"Siempre te amaré," the girl specifies, but she nods so she must be okay with my version too. Nadia nudges a bashful kiss to my shoulder, but I lift her chin so the second kiss lands on my mouth. Exactly where I like it.

CHAPTER Thirty
SIX MONTHS LATER

BO

M
Y LOVE, she nibbles on two fingernails, a rapid blink of dark eyes revealing how worried she is. Hired help shoves furniture into a moving truck, while two others upend her couch and push it through the doorway.

"Darling," I say, pulling her in under my arm. "It was time."

"I know, but still..." She covers her mouth with the hand that doesn't rest around my waist. I kiss the top of her head, nudging her closer, the need to protect her enveloping me in now-familiar ways. "I've lived here for so long." She pauses, swallowing her emotion. "So much history."

"We're making new history." I turn her enough to kiss her temple. "New memories." I kiss her again. "*Our* memories. He'd approve."

She laughs softly at that, a relieved laugh that tells me I am right. "Yeah, he would. He wouldn't want me to live the way I did."

"No, because apparently he wasn't a bad guy," I add. We've played this game for a while now. Me bumping up against the comfort zone of her grief, and Nadia tolerating it a little better with each jolt.

"You're so weird," she says. She tilts her head back and gazes at me, irises moist. "No one says the stuff you do. You're supposed to, like, not talk about it that much. Definitely not almost make me cry all the time." She smiles though, knowing my head-on approach is working.

"Right, because shutting up about it worked for you before." I fake a stern expression to keep Nadia's attention; I want to keep her from registering the huge cardboard box noting *Jude's photo gear + clothes* being half carried, half dragged out of the apartment.

"Anyway," I continue, "you're not burning any bridges. If you get sick of me, you can make up rules your new tenants have broken, evict them, and move back in."

The giggle she emits is as beautiful as water lapping over stones in Swedish mountain brooks.

"Meanie," she says. "I'd never do that. And you can't throw me out either. Have you thought about that? We're moving in together, Bo. It's a lot different than just staying at each other's house," she warns me, her voice boasting belief in our future.

"All the time," I say.

I release her. Link our pinkies and start walking toward my car. As we pull out of the parking lot, I ask, "You know what your name means, right?"

"Yeah. Hope," she says and smiles, guessing where I'm going with this.

"Hope." I stroke a stray lock of hair away from her face. "Hope wasn't there when we first met. Now, it's written all over my darling. Every day, it peeks out at me, and I think—"

"Let me guess. You think you've got something to do with it?"

The last traffic light before our new apartment flashes red. I stop, drop my head back against the seat, and put on a show of being indifferent, aloof, and "rock-star cool" as she calls me.

"You're silly, Bo. I see right through you, you know," she hums before she leans in and plants a kiss on my lips. "Unfortunately, you showed your true colors that very first night in the dressing room. Since then none of your stone faces trick me."

"Really now?" I feel myself smirk. Her confidence is sexy as hell. "So little Nadia thinks she's got me all figured out?"

"I do," she murmurs, suddenly close to my ear. Faintly, I register the traffic light sliding from red to green, but I remain under her spell until cars start honking behind me.

I jack the Saab into gear so fast, she lets out a squeal. "That's the sound I plan to elicit from you in about, hmm—thirty minutes," I say.

"Yeah? Because you'll be speeding? Watch out for the L.A.P.D. First night in our new home and my boyfriend is locked up for being a traffic criminal," she jokes.

"Not exactly what I had in mind." I husk the words out and let my stare smolder at her. And from the pink marks appearing on her cheeks, I'd say she gets what I have in mind.

CHAPTER Thirty-One

LOVE

BO

I WANT HER ABANDON. I *crave* her abandon. Sweet and molding to me, she's softness and warmth, slick moisture and all perfection. This girl has given me love and made me love. She has squeezed and wrung my inexperienced heart on a rollercoaster ride to this moment.

And now, here we are. She's mine, all the way mine.

Our place is a mess of boxes, furniture, guitar gear, clothes, and pillows. The new bed is not set up, but the brand new king-sized mattress I surprised her with is at the dead center of the living room. We'll be renting storage space for the things we don't need anymore, where reminders too painful to keep in sight will be brought to rest.

For now, all we've unpacked is Nadia's candles. Not her old tea lights but the new stash of big, scented ones from some home décor store. They paint our home with glowing orbs of green and orange.

Skin alive in the shifting glow, she's beneath me, eyes hooded and expectant at my touch. "All mine," I whisper, and I revel in the smile she responds with.

"Yes, all yours," she answers. I sigh with contentment

as I let my lips travel down her stomach. I lick fragrant folds and make her jut up against me. Tonight she's not shy when she lets her legs drop open. Tonight she doesn't press her lips together holding back the moan in her throat.

With one hand under her ass, I lift her into me. With the other, I press against her abdomen while I lap and hasten her pleasure.

"No," she whimpers, wanting to take her time. I don't allow it. I want her to come fast and hard. Then she'll be slow and delicious with me afterward.

"Let go, darling. Be lovely," I rasp out. I'm hard and needing her soon.

Her eyes open slowly, and I find no shame in them. They're void of guilt, of worry. Tonight there are no anxious concerns.

In the pocket of my jeans, on the floor, next to her crumpled-up dress, there's a ring that would sparkle if the sun hit it. But I'm not rushing things. Nadia just removed Jude's band. I won't present her with my ring on the first night in our own home.

It's there though. It makes me happy that it is. I'll carry it with me—for months—for years—however long it takes to read in her eyes that she needs our bond to gleam in gold and diamonds as much as I do.

Love exists. Love is patient. For some, love lurks, waiting for that single woman who can ignite a man's love muscle. And when that beautiful person enters his dressing room, love strikes hard.

The End

Want More?

Meet the characters from Walking Heartbreak in other books, Some you can find in their own books. Others, will have side stories in the main action.

The stories full of humor, love, hard choices, unexpected twists, heartbreak, and breathtaking happily-ever-afters. To read more about:

Zoe, Emil, as well as **Bo and Nadia** and the rest of the band: **In the Absence of You** (A book in the Rock Gods Collection)

Bo, Nadia, Emil, Zoe, Troy, Elias in **Indiscretions of a God**, where they… "interact" with the owner of an adult entertainment studio (A book in the Porn Star Boyfriends Collection)

Bo, Nadia, Emil, Zoe, Troy, Elias in **Sylvie + Shandor** (Rocker Shenanigans I)

Troy, and the rest of the band: Title TBA (A book in the Rock Gods Collection, with expected release Fall 2018)

IN THE Absence OF YOU

CHAPTER One

LOVE FIRE

AISHE

I come from a family that burns with love. You wouldn't understand unless you were one of us. I'm not just talking my father and my mother—I'm talking every one of my ancestors. It's in our genetic build to spend all of our energy on love.

Once we come of age, it strikes and blazes with a fire that eats you alive. This love is a plague that boils in my race and in my culture, and I wouldn't know a different way unless I'd broken free and seen strangers love with milder flames.

Tonight, my eyes go from the merchandise on my table to the blond-headed burst of life hopping off the stage. His gaze shimmers with amusement, a cocky lip twitching as he slaps high-fives to guys and pinches girl-cheeks on his way over.

"Aishe! You got those super-tight, hot little tees with the broken heart thingy on the front? The ones the chicks dig?" he asks once he's in front of me, Emil, the vocalist of Clown Irruption, one of the hottest alt-rock indie-bands out there. I've been their merch girl for a few months now. Each night, I zoom in on Emil with less and less difficulty.

"Yeah. Troll picked them up this morning," I say referring to their tour manager.

"This is so cool—finally we see actual merch money," Emil laughs out. Then he sets a hand to the table and squints at me. "You've done much better than your cousin. I mean, Shandor, man." He shakes his head playfully. "He couldn't draw dudes to the stand worth shit."

My face loosens in a smile. I send a subtle glance at Shandor, who's busy wrapping things up on stage, coiling cables and breaking down drums. To sell T-shirts wasn't what he burned for. Shandor was born with the plague of our people too, but he hasn't found his beloved yet. My people, we need something to obsess over, so if it's not a man's love for a woman or vice versa, it's something else, and Shandor, he loves his music. Once the band promoted him from merch guy to monitors on stage, he recommended me to fill his spot, and *voilà*, here I am.

Shandor raises his head and stills on us, focus intent from under dark locks. He's got a sixth sense for when guys chitchat with me. Like me, he left our traveling community years back, but the need to protect any girl of our people is so deep-rooted I doubt he ever questions it. Shandor would do everything in his power to stop any man, employer or not, from toying with his little cousin.

I straighten so that I'm tall for my height. Though I'm not overly curvy, I'm lean and strong. Supposedly, I'm also fiery, a bit fierce, a bit ferocious, traits that make me who I am, traits I don't need here in the outside world as opposed to amongst those I was born to.

I intimidate most men with the stance I take right now, but I can't intimidate Shandor. He glares, telling me without words what *not* to do, and next he pierces his stare into Emil's back. Oblivious, Emil juts his index finger at the case of lukewarm beers behind me, wiggles it back and forth quickly, lips pursed in anticipation. "Hand over one of those babies, will ya?"

I pop one open for him like I'm a bartender. "Here, for the tsar of Clown Irruption," I say.

He snorts around a swallow, the sound proud instead of mocking. "Hell yeah. Good show, huh? Did you see the crowd on Nadia's song? Did you hear the screams when I threw my shirt? I should've thrown it earlier. And this is a fucking *small* club. How hilarious if we'd miked the crowd up."

I nod. Tilt my hip a little as I lean on the table with the heels of my hands. He catches the movement, gaze flickering down my waist. I won't lie. I love it when he looks at me like this. But his attention floats right back up again and fixes on the wall behind me.

He bobs his head toward the price tag on the black

T-shirts, the favorite of Clown Irruption's male fans. "Why do we keep it at fifteen? We sell out of them all the time, and Luminessence takes, like, twenty-two for theirs."

I'm disappointed when he changes from interested to casual in seconds flat. For a moment, he looked at me the way he does his nightly rush of groupies. Then—*bam!*—it was over.

"Twenty even," I correct.

"Since when do you care about tees, man?" That's Elias, the bass player. Tall and wiry, he's milky white with eyes so light it's eerie. Elias has that undead beautiful thing going for him, which turns half of the audience into banshees when he does a solo. "Oh never mind. Since Aishe started working for us," he answers his own question, slaps his friend's back, and whizzes me a grin. "You got more of those warm beers?"

I hand him one, but I don't open it. That special service is for my favorite blond spurt of joy who's still half naked and sweaty from his exertions on stage.

"Backstage meet-n-greet in ten. You ready?" Troll bellows, nodding a few guards over so the band can chat and have their beers without being run down by my customers.

Troll's got a voice on him. Sometimes the band actually listens to him too. "Although forget the backstage part. This meet-n-greet will be yonder." He juts his chin at an opening in the wall behind me.

"What, too many people to fit backstage?" Bo asks. He's the bandleader and plays lead guitar. With his mysterious sex appeal and almost androgynous beauty, besides Emil, he's a huge part of what attracts the female audience. Despite their publicist's direct orders, Bo is outspoken about how very much in a relationship he is.

My attention floats to his side, and I automatically smile. Nadia smiles back, accepting her man's grip around her hand. With her long, dark hair and darker eyes, she could be one of my people, I often think, and there's a depth to the love between those two that's familiar. It's how my parents are with each other. How Shandor's parents are, our grandparents, and all of the others who beat the plague of my clan.

Troll blows his cheeks out and releases a burst of air. "The floor's rotting backstage. They're afraid of being sued if people start stomping around and breaking legs and what-have-you. So yeah, it'll be yonder. It's bigger though, so we're good." He stretches a chunky finger toward the Cokes sitting on top of a box of our least-bought T-shirts, some XX whites with gold writing. I'm not sure who chose them, but the same box has been with us the entire tour.

I hand Troll a soda. "Anything else, guys? Whiskey on the rocks? Sex on the Beach?"

"Sure, babe, bring on the sex on the beach," Emil halfway purrs. "And hey, if there's no beach in this town—is there, Troll? Where are we again?—I'll make us one."

Nadia rolls her eyes over Emil, the poster child for sexy, flirty, extroverted lead singer, but I bite my lip, enjoying his haphazard games. It's Shandor's fault that Emil rarely flirts with me.

As the guys drift by, Troy strolling into the room last, my mind returns to where it often does—to my plan for beating my genetically induced love tribulation.

I'm twenty-three, and my people get lovesick at a much earlier stage in life. The girls especially are knocked down quickly; I've been there when girls of fifteen and sixteen have committed suicide over unreciprocated love. The men take longer, but by Shandor's age, twenty-six, they're either married to the love of their lives or they've gone mad.

Besnik is our oldest-living plagued one. He's eighty-two, and no one understands how he has survived. His love for Jofranka, the ardent wife of another for fifty-eight years before she passed away, is so strong it beats death. Besnik never had eyes for another woman, and as beautiful and tragic as that sounds, it's been damn inconvenient for the quality of his life.

I left our community at seventeen and traveled the world alone for a few months before Shandor caught up with me. Since then, most of the time, we travel together—his preference. When he's not overly controlling, I like it too. I do love my cousin.

I've been in most countries in Europe, most states in the United States, and I've dipped into South America and Asia as well. It's why I'm still sane.

I'm fleeing, which has worked out great. As long as I don't run into my soul mate, I'll be fine. If I do though, I know for a fact that it's checkmate.

I'm not a virgin, but I don't sleep with men who can take over your mind or your heart and cause you to think and worry. What I do is safe and nice, and I only do it on my last night in a town so I won't get tempted into repeat entertainment.

But after nights like this, when I've watched Emil rock his body to the music and unleash his stage persona, I feel myself respond. My reaction is small, but I know what it could be: a bad omen for my heart and my welfare. It could be the start of my fall as a sane human being. What would I do if I plunged into the abyss of the Romani love plague, if I went mad out here without my community? Several of us are locked up in mental institutions across the world, surviving off of pills and water.

I think Shandor is right in one thing: only a Romani man can match the fire in a Gypsy woman's heart. It's why he protects me so fiercely from male attention.

I sell a last broken-heart T-shirt to a girl who's too big for our largest size. She wants it even after I hold it up and show her it won't fit. Then I look at what she's wearing and realize "tight as sausage skin" is her style. I give it to her for twelve instead of fifteen because I've already packed my change.

Stagehands break the table down for me, so I trail into the meet-n-greet area. I hold a lukewarm beer of my own and nurse it as I watch the guys interact with backstage-pass winners.

"Yeah, that's fine. Just let in the last group over there by the hot dog stand," Troll says to security.

"Weird how they sell hot dogs," Elias says.

"That didn't weird you out before the gig," Emil quips. "Five hot dogs, dude, in two buns. You have any idea how bizarre that is to watch you eat? It's like you're *swallowing*. Not to mention all the mayo, you know what I mean?"

I'm half-listening as they banter, my beer can clicking in my hand as I squeeze it.

I used to think I had two options to beat my people's plague: find gasoline for my love fire in a Romani man, or wander from place to place until I die, fleeing from a soul mate I've never met. Such a life may sound bad to many, but my restless blood craves traveling anyway. It's not much of a sacrifice.

"Jesus, you're gross. And I totally ate them separately."

"If by 'separate' you mean half of one bun with three hot dogs in it, and half of the other with only two hot dogs, then yes."

"Guys! Guys, guys." Troll is exasperated, which isn't new. "Focus. You've got fans to please." He has no qualms saying this right in front of said fans. Bo sets a laser-grey stare into Emil, who opens his hands wide in a *What-did-I-do?* and seamlessly launches into a groupie-melting smile to the closest girls.

I've mulled over a third possibility lately for beating my family's plague. What if I found someone I was attracted to that wasn't my soul mate, someone whose highest love only simmered at a medium to low flame? As long as we had common interests and the road in our veins, could we not have a good, simple life with an unpretentious affection that didn't kill with its intensity?

Emil throws his head back laughing, white teeth gleaming with the hint of a sharp edge to the canines. It's how I've come to see him: easygoing, fun, with just the smallest suggestion of an edge. Emil is never upset, never mad. He doesn't get stressed out like some of the others. No, he's a hot, confident, cocky rock star with a penchant for carnal needs. Which with my genes I'd have no problem matching.

Emil travels for a living, and even though he doesn't act on it, there's definite chemistry between us. If I developed a mild strain of the love fire for Emil, if I extracted him from the groupies and he reciprocated with his snow people's better, healthier version of love, we could be a good match.

Children, my thoughts rush on. *Eventually, we could have children.* They'd have golden skin and brass-colored hair, the way the most beautiful children do amongst my people. It's shameful when they're born this beautiful, but we don't speak about it; the mother has lain with someone fair-haired, someone not from our community, and it's not the baby's fault.

I think my uterus skips. It's how I realize it's been a while since I've slept with a man. It's the hotness onstage influencing me every night then watching Emil, sometimes Troy and Elias too, advance on a girl or allow a girl to flirt with them until they whisk them off somewhere. I'm not jealous—they are my friends and my employers. But it makes me miss giving in to desire.

As I think it, Shandor sidles up beside me. He watches the guys interact with the fans, and chuckles when a tall, redheaded girl bounces in front of Emil and kisses him straight on the mouth. Emil widens his eyes in affected surprise, then grabs her neck to pull her closer and deepen the kiss.

"So…" Shandor finally begins the third degree. "What did Emil say over at the merch table? He looked awfully chummy."

"Oh stop. He just asked about T-shirt prices and wanted to change them."

"Yeah, well, it looked like more to me. He's cool, Shee, as a musician and a buddy, but you're pretty, and you know how he is with women. Don't. Trust. Him. And don't forget your roots. Outsiders never get us, and if anything happens to you, the two of us drop everything and scram."

"Enough—please. Nothing's going to happen. Plus you're not the boss of me." The words hiss from my mouth in the beginning, but then they fizzle at the end. It's hard to be mad at someone, domineering or not, when you know all they want is your best. Deep down, Shandor is a wonderful person. I love him, and he loves me like I'm his twin.

Undaunted, yellow eyes fix mine, his quiet vehemence growing. "Emil's a loose cannon, Shee. I see how you look at him. You want him as a man. If you make the smallest advance, he'll be all over you. He may not be of us, but he takes every opportunity that comes his way, and you're not squandering your treasures on him."

Someone bumps into me. I look up to apologize, but it's the tall redhead passing with Emil. All smiles, she's got an arm wormed around his waist, and he's chuckling at something she says.

"Emil. Emil!" Troll's bushy brows have sunk so far down, his face clouds over from it. "'Scuse me. 'Scuse me." He shoulders his way after Emil and catches the couple at the door. "Hey man, give it a half hour. There's a line." He jerks his head toward the back of the room where sad-faced teenagers watch Emil retreat.

The man of the hour blows a kiss their way, one of his signature grins lighting up his expression. "Giv'em the signed posters, all right? Gotta go. I've got a bad case of blue balls." He winks at the girl, who has the decency to blush. "Or if they wanna wait around, I'll be back in fifteen."

Fifteen?

I feel more than see Shandor shake his head next to me. I elbow him in the stomach, because the last thing I want is for our employers to notice his lack of respect.

"Every time lately," Troll mutters and lumbers back to the rest of the band.

"Does that mean Emil wasn't always like this?" I ask my cousin.

"Emil has always been Emil… but he had a girl before."

"Like Bo?"

"Definitely not," he says, sucking his lips in between his teeth, suppressing a smirk. "Emil and Zoe were nothing like Bo and Nadia."

Acknowledgments

No novel has been like Walking Heartbreak for me. It assaulted my mind in the car one day, then fogged up my walk on the beach. For weeks, it made my legs jump with impatience under my day job work desk, to the point of having my good friend and co-worker say, "Please, can you *stop*?!"

It took six months before my other books were done and I could finally write the first words. I'm an author, but to describe the relief I felt when that first chapter had been written is impossible.

As with all my novels, there have been villages involved. Villages consisting of the same loyal people with skills and talents that mean the universe to my final product.

First, a huge kiss to my husband, Michael, who's a patient man. He's also in the music industry and tours for a living himself. Thanks to him and what I've seen out there, there are some pretty damn realistic scenes in this book.

I'm also grateful for my daughter, Alexandra, who reads and loves all of my books. And I'm over the moon about my son, Nicolas, *not* reading them; he's still scrubbing his eyes after accidentally opening Stargazer on the wrong page.

I can never thank my author besties enough. We're in this together, loving, fighting, and loving this journey some more. Dead honest feedback is how we roll, because how else can we keep getting better?

Lynn Vroman, again you cracked your whip of awesome at a manuscript of mine. Your input, your enthusiasm, your steady expertise made me trust that I could polish it into the novel it now is.

Angela McPherson, you grabbed Walking Heartbreak and turned around the medical know-how I so needed in mere days, helping me hit my deadline. Your sweet attention kept me from panic attacks in moments of need.

D Nichole King, you always locate inconsistencies and typical issues I am known for by you. Insert winky-face here. You're my honest, honest girl, and the fact that you put this book baby on your favorite shelf means stars and moons and distant suns to me.

Cheryl McIntyre: your feedback, your love for my stories, the way you see things in sentences no one else sees. How you read depth of characters and extract symbolism I can play with. Your emails make me smile and tear up, and your tiniest corrections shoot me off to tweak my draft. I say it nonstop, but hell—this is *my* book so I can say it again: you have no idea how much your feedback and friendship mean to me.

Laura Thalassa, again you've done it, helped me polish and find those last details, the ones that I'd hate to find later on published paper. But most of all your swooning comments made my day this time. Thank you, thank you!

Dawn McIntyre, do you realize it's been seven books? I'm so grateful that you enjoy my novels so much that you've helped me every. Single. Time. Your response means ions to me. Your genuine, clear input, telling me what you want, what you love and don't, is exactly what

I need to nudge my stories up a last step before release.

My beta readers, Renee McMillan, Rachel Spurlock, and April Martin—there is nothing like you reading my baby and affording me your impulsive responses as you read. I'm humbled that you dropped your to-be-read stacks to squeeze in Walking Heartbreak.

I've never mentioned my loyal blogs in my acknowledgments, the ones who are pivotal when it comes to spreading the word about my cover reveals, releases, and sales. There are too many to pull out single names, but you know who you are, you beautiful, beautiful girls and boys who *are there* for me, making my books visible in the overgrown jungle that is the indie market. Just—I cannot thank you enough, and I want you to know you're on my list. Not on my black list or my white list. No. On my golden list.

And then, above everything, there is *you,* sweet reader. Writing equals breathing for me, so I would write without you, but boy, what a difference it makes to have you along for the ride.

You. Are my star.

Thank you for reading.

About Sunniva Dee

Sunniva Dee is a reader, a lover of everything beautifully written no matter the genre. As an author, she pens flawed characters and seeks the flip side where the soul hides. Once there, she wants to be pulled out of her comfort zone by stories taking on a life of their own.

Sunniva has written paranormal and young adult. She's committed contemporary romance verging on erotica, and she's dabbled in supernatural mystery. But her heart is rooted in new adult of the true kind: young adult all grown up, with conflicts and passions that are familiar to college-aged readers and readers who remember those days like they happened last night.

Contact Info

NEWSLETTER

My subscribers are the first in the know of a new release or a crazy offer:
http://bit.ly/Sunnivasnewsletter

SUNNIVA'S ANGELS FACEBOOK GROUP

Do you want to become an Angel?
www.facebook.com/groups/SunnivasAngels/

WHERE TO FIND ME

Website: **www.sunnivadee.com**
Goodreads: **http://bit.ly/SunnivaGR**
Facebook: **http://bit.ly/SunnivaFB**
Twitter: **http://bit.ly/SunnivaTW**
Pinterest: **http://bit.ly/SunnivaP**
Instagram: **http://bit.ly/SunnivaInst**
Spotify: **http://bit.ly/SunnivasSpotify**

Other Books By Sunniva Dee

NEW ADULT/CONTEMPORARY

COLLEGE ROMANCE
Beautiful Freedom

Leon's Way

Adrenaline

ROCK STARS
Walking Heartbreak

In The Absence Of You

Rocker Shenanigans

MMA FIGHTERS:
Dodging Trains

The Fighter And The Baroness

PORN STAR BOYFRIENDS
The Truth about Porn Star Boyfriends

Twin Savage

Indiscretions of a God

Regretfully Yours (April 2018)

YOUNG ADULT
Path Of Thieves

PARANORMAL
Shattering Halos

Stargazer

Cat Love

Find these titles and more at:
http://bitly.com/SunnivasAmazon

Made in the USA
Coppell, TX
27 January 2022